THE STALKER

Anchalee Viva

Praphansarn provider ip

literalpublishing

LIBRARY OF CONGRESS CATALOGING-IN-PUBLICATION DATA
Names: Viva, Anchalee, 25 January 2025—author.
Title: The Stalker : a novel / Anchalee Viva.
Description: First edition. | Houston, Texas: Praphansarn IP Provider &
Literal Publishing, 2025.
| Summary: "A chilling psychological thriller set in 1940s Bangkok.
A man haunted by his past becomes fixated on uncovering the truth about
his mother's disappearance. As he navigates the fog-shrouded city,
his descent into obsession reveals terrifying secrets that threaten
to consume him. But is he searching for the truth—or running from it?"
— Provided by publisher.
Identifiers:
LCCN 2024044978 | ISBN 978-1-942307-64-8 (hardcover)
Subjects:
LCSH: Stalkers—Fiction. | Obsession—Fiction. | Psychological trauma—
Fiction. | Bangkok (Thailand)—Fiction. | Mystery and detective stories. |
Psychological fiction.
Classification:
LCC PZ4.V58S7 | DDC 895.913—dc23
LC record available at (insert URL if applicable)
10 9 8 7 6 5 4 3 2 1
First Edition

TABLE OF CONTENTS

Prologue

The Midnight of December 8, 1941

Tonight, the heart of Bangkok
was unusually damp and chilly.
The fog floating over the river since dusk
had begun to creep onto land,
swallowing dim streets and dark alleys along the river quay.
All sounds muted into eerie silence;
All colors blurred into gray hues.
Even the amber lights on street lamps
glowed ghostly in its dull, dark, damp blanket.
The fog—an indistinct form of an enormous creature
with its immense open mouth,
grew more capable of swallowing every existence
from rows of homes and buildings,
to clumps after clumps of trees,
to lines of motor cars and trolleys,
to every soul lost in its foggy path.
The visibility above and beyond became so poor
even infinite and unreachable stars,
high, high the Heaven above,
seemed to vanish into its massive mouth,
one after another, till none seemed left in the skies.
So surreal it could occur only in a realm of dreams
where the Stalker reigned for infinity.

To night, I watched the fog's uncompromising invasion, half in apprehension and half in awe.

What a morbid beauty—the sublime creation of Darkness. For a whole week, the fog had appeared at nightfall. On the first night of its primordial birth, most people barely noticed the wispy and almost transparent thin layers that began to linger and hover on the surface of deep, cool water in the river. But as each night passed, it kept on growing and growing. And tonight, its gray mass appeared so dense it looked alive and even animated.

It seemed hard for everyone to ignore its threatening presence. This phenomenon rarely happened in Bangkok in the past decades since the climate stayed hot, humid, and sultry day and night nearly all year round.

It could be explained by the simple fact that this period was in the midst of winter, with a temperature naturally dropping at certain degrees at night. And this year, it became unusually cold, especially after sundown. The water at night turned cooler, yet the air retained heat from the sunny day, creating unprecedented creepy fogs.

But many people, particularly the old ones, had never considered the simple fact of the fog manifestation as I did. The sea of fog spreading everywhere as far as their eyes could trace had scared them out of their wits.

At nightfall, when the veil of fog boldly appeared, they stayed behind their locked door, never thinking of stepping outside into the cold embrace of fog. They lay prostrate before the Buddha altar, praying amidst the curling smoke from burning incense, asking for His boundless mercy to save all of them from the Maleficent One who always followed the fogs.

They were superstitious people ready to embrace their belief of a dark and sinister side of all existences still unknown to them. The fact of cause and effect would never be applied in their mental domain. To them, all uncanny and unknown phenomena would be promptly pronounced evil, and there would be no need to prove otherwise.

They believed the unprecedented fogs en masse were the

ominous sign of an impending calamity: an epidemic plague of a colossal scale or some unimaginable Apocalypse, wiping half of humanity from the face of the earth.

Doom Day, in short.

That was the day I set my mind to commit suicide. There would be no more prolonging.

And also, this particular day happened to be my twenty-fifth birthday.

The reason I chose to end my life was that if I broke down twenty-five years of my life into days, it meant I had so far lived my life for ninety-one hundred twenty-five days. Or, for a more vivid picture, that was thirteen million and one hundred forty thousand in minutes that I had already carried my life through.

Have you ever asked yourself if you ever felt true happiness just for one or two minutes a day? I wondered what your most honest answer would be.

I bet the answer would cause you to lose faith in life forever.

As in my case, if I tried to pull all minute moments of rejoicing from my long nine thousand one hundred twenty-five days and then combined those scattering moments of joy to see the outcome, of course, the total moments of happiness that I had all my life would still hardly amount to one single day, which meant after taking out that single happy day, I still had nine thousand one hundred and twenty-four days full of misery left with me.

If someone had lived for twenty-five long years and had the combined moments of happiness out of those twenty-five years as short as barely one single day, there should be no point in going on.

A moment of joy was as scarce as a tiny drop of cool water one was searching on a vast expanse of empty wasteland. A barely visible speck of particle against the infinite universe. It always made me wonder if ninety percent of our entire lifetime had to be spent entirely on pain, hurt, grief, despair, distress, loss, agony, shame, and, of course, incurable hatred, hatred, and hatred, with no room in life left to fulfill a dream that worth our breathing, if so, what was a purpose of our existence? It remained the most profound mystery no one had ever comprehended, let alone making sense of it.

All we were able to acknowledge and be aware so far were only the fact that our from-cradle-to-grave miseries had been gnawing our existence, day in and day out, down to the core of our life, crippling our mind, numbing our heart, clouding our creativity, weakening our spirit and even corrupting our soul—like a hungry carnivore predator devouring its prey, cracking its bone and sucking its marrow until the last drop of life perished.

All I wanted, while drinking my life away with liquors and with no one bothering me, was to brood over most parts of my life, the parts I desperately wanted to wipe out from the face of my whole existence.

You probably wonder if I detested them that much, why I still bothered brooding over the worst parts of my life and feeding and fattening their presence. Why didn't I make them perish for good by forgetting them all, like living in oblivion? My answer was logical, and yet was also complicated. My agonizing pasts, like cancerous cells, had been taking up most of the space in my life. If I had destroyed them all, I would have destroyed ninety-nine percent of my existence. If so, with only one percent piece of me left, I would have barely existed. My whole being would have shrunk to near zero. And barely could I have any evidence, out of the nearly invisible piece of me, to prove my existence on earth. I needed to save that hopeless existence to justify the suicide.

I wanted someone to stand in my shoes, just for a moment, to feel the weight of these nine thousand a hundred twenty-five days and understand why I couldn't bear to add another. Perhaps then, they'd understand how despair can slowly, silently consume everything, until there's nothing left but a shadow of a life.

* * * * *

Part One: The Prey

Part 1: Chapter 1

A Speck of Life on Infinity

T he mystery of my mother started right at the dawn of my existence, and this was the core of my story from the beginning to the end.

I was born on December 8, 1916, the year of the Dragon. For as long as I can remember, my father was my whole world. He had never talked about my mother. However, when I was six, I began to wonder about her and was so persistent to know. Soon, I told him that every boy in our neighborhood had at least one mother and even knew his or her mother's name. One of those boys even bragged that he had three mothers (and five fathers) and asked me how many mothers I had now.

I lied to him that I had ten.

After that day, I begged my father to find just one single mother for me instead of a wood truck toy for my coming birthday (which Lek, his close friend, would make for me). At first, he did not answer. He only gave me a dark, strange look that made me afraid I might say something deadly wrong. I began to cry because I had never seen him with that look.

"There, there, don't cry, Baby Boy."

When I was that age, he always called me by that funny name, *Baby Boy*, rather than *Pran*, my real name.

"Everyone has only one father and one mother. No more or less. I tell you, that boy made up a story. It's probably because he doesn't have parents, poor kid. That's why he has no idea about the right number, "

Suddenly, he picked me up in his arms, his eyes flickering.

"All right, I'm going to show you your mama now. Aren't you happy?"

"Papa, Really? Where? Where is she?" I shrieked.

He didn't say anything more. Instead, he carried me outdoors onto the veranda, pointed his finger to one huge cloud floating in the late afternoon sky, and told me tenderly.

"Your mama is *up there* now."

I swiftly turned my face upward and squinted hard at the above clouds. My heart began to beat fast.

"We can't see her because she lives amid the clouds, but she can peer down and see us. Look! Look! There she is. Her face's emerging from that cloud now. Look! She's over there!"

The blinding sun now was too intense. I had to close my eyes briefly and slowly reopen them.

"Where? Why don't I see her?"

With a surge of excitement, I screamed and started to jump up and down.

"Oh, no! Now she's gone. You just missed her,"

I began to sob. Quickly, a sob turned into a wail.

"No, don't cry, Baby Boy, don't cry…" he hushed me. "She just can't let us see her longer than a split second because she no longer lives among us. Her home now is in heaven. Well, at least I could glimpse her waving hand and smiling sweetly at us. So, don't be so sad, Baby Boy. Just remember your mama is always up there. Now, you know she always sits on one of the soft, fluffy clouds watching over you. Always."

"Papa, you saw her, right? What does she look like?"

"She has a shining rainbow aura around her face," said my father, his face coated with a smile that seemed a little too bright. "So, always do good things to make her proud of you. Promise me, little one?"

I nodded vigorously. Then, another question just popped up.

"Is she happy, Papa? Is she lonely up there?"

"Never be happier. She's always with a thousand like her as birds flying to wherever they dream of for eternity up there," he nodded. "Yes, for eternity."

"What is my mama's name, Papa?" I finally asked him timidly.

"Her name..." he paused, frowning, and then cheerfully said. "Her name is Siri."

I gasped. "Is that Mama's name?"

He nodded and smiled.

Now I knew her name as everyone had known their mother's. What a lovely, lovely name. *Siri*.

My father told me that before this house was built, the constructors had dug out a large amount of soil from the ground to fill up the lowland on which the house now stood, protecting against the seasonal flood during the monsoon. As a result, they left an elongated large hole in the backyard area, which eventually became a pond.

In the dry season, between January and April, the water in the pond dried out. First, the brimming water slowly turned into soft, cool mud. Then, the soft mud hardened into parched, solid cakes of dried mud. All lives and beauties perished, buried deeply beneath the dry crust, but miracles suddenly occurred as soon as the rain returned. More miracles followed each day as more rain poured down in great abundance.

When the rain came to visit the earth, it blessed our pond, turning it into my father's favorite site. On some wet day, he brought me to watch the pond through the thin sheet of soft, light rain. Fresh raindrops rolled down our wet clothes in crystal beads, soaking us from head to toe. I stuck out my tongue to taste the rain, which rendered a thin, sweet aftertaste. He said the blurred pond seen through the white rain sheet reminded him of Claude Monet's impressionist dreamlike paintings, a blooming avant-garde French artist at that period. My father loved paintings and art, although he never practiced them.

In the pond, I saw a picturesque display of lovely and shiny water lilies blossoms, soft pink and pure white, blooming above their glossy green oval pads and spreading their beauty everywhere. Sunshine, in the late afternoon, bathed and brightened the sea of water lilies until all looked like illuminating lanterns against the pale blue sky. Soon, shadows at twilight came to soften and darken them until they were mere silhouettes against the deep purple horizon.

Bees, bumblebees, and gauzy-winged dragonflies busily visited the pond, droning, humming, and buzzing all day. Frogs croaked cheerfully as they jumped into the cool water, hiding under lily pads and creating endless ripples, one after another, as they swam to and fro. With one loud splash, we would glimpse the water bubbling around a lily pad as fish emerged to gobble up some water bugs while skimming the thin surface of the water.

It was a spot always full of sights, sounds, and movements of life. Yet its atmosphere was so serene, so tranquil that one could—my father assured me—hear a sound so mysterious yet so magical that one could not hear elsewhere; it was the sound of silence. Then he murmured verses in a poem, which I found later that he had written himself.

Not through all five doors of thy Senses
But a window of thy Soul
That thou could see a blaze of Darkness
And hear the thunder of Silence

"When I was young, I dreamed of living by a big, big pond filled with water lilies. So, when I moved to live on this property, I planted them in this pond and waited until they turned into the sea of water lilies as we see them today."

He closed his eyes and sighed. That was the only time I ever heard him talk about his childhood.

I sighed with satisfaction at every answer my father gave me.

Sometimes at night, before I let the sleep take me completely, I had sleepily murmured to him,

"Papa… When am I going to see Mama?"

"If you are good, when you leave this world, you will stay with her in heaven forever."

He confirmed me as he stroked my hair gently on our shared bed.

"And you too, Papa? Will you go with me up there, too?"

"Of course. Now, close your eyes and sleep."

"You mean three of us will be together up there."

"Yes, my Baby Boy, three of us, " he said with a vigorous nod.

With a long sigh of relief and contentment, I promptly did as he said.

However, the rain also showed a dark and terrible side.

When the monsoon came, dark and menacing storm clouds perpetually overwhelmed the whole sky, followed by flashes of lightning and the furious roaring sound of thunder.

First, as the sunny sky suddenly darkened, the atmosphere turned unusually sultry and oppressive. Not a single leaf on any twig rustling, a piece of laundry on the clothesline fluttering, nor a swing on the tree swaying as they usually did, so still and lifeless like one whole dead painting. As if all were not enough, it was so steaming and suffocating hot that I was bathing in my own sweat. I felt as though a force of some primal elements was crushing down on the bungalow and squeezing me into a pulp with its utter stillness, so hard that I was about to explode from its tremendous pressure.

Suddenly, there came the deceptive, cool, refreshing breeze

that swiftly turned to a chilly gust of wind swirling and blowing small things like dead leaves and scrap papers on the ground on its path. Thunder started to rumble in the distance, and the roar of the storm escalated.

I was safe and sound under my roof while looking out the window, watching rows of trees lining up the perimeter of our small bungalow sway against the gusting of the wind. However, I could not help looking up at the sky, my eyes scanning around with a concern for somebody up there.

At that moment, I watched with dread as the sky split open. It screamed the loudest painful moan, echoing its rage and agony over and over before exploding and pouring down dense white sheets to sweep the face of the earth. Millions of raindrops were lashing the ground, slamming the closed window with such a ferocious force, and hitting the roof with their deafening noises.

And across the front yard, my homemade swing hanging down from a sturdy mango tree limb, was now shaking and swaying so hard in heavy rains like a helpless tiny piece of toy tossed back and forth by a gigantic invisible hand. Its dense leaves and smaller limbs rattled against the stormy wind as if its trunk would be uprooted and swept upside-down in an instant by the monsoon storm. Suddenly, another thunderbolt struck the earth. *Boom!* The light was so blinding. And the sound. Oh, the sound! I heard a ringing in my ears as if my eardrums were splitting open.

At that point, I rushed to my father as he got down on his hands and knees, busily mopping the rain-splashing floor in one of the kitchen corners. He looked up and saw the sheer alarm on my face.

"Papa, Papa, the lightning's going to strike her now. Do something to help her."

"Her? Who is she?" he frowned.

"It's Mama!"

I screamed at him almost hysterically. Heaven was exploding. The skies were turning upside-down. There was no way she could find someplace to hide up there.

"There, there, there, Baby Boy."

He put the mop away and drew me into his arms as I was still shaken from fear.

"Mama's going to die, Papa, please…"

"No, no, and no. Have you heard of a fish dying of drowning? No. Right? That's the same with your mama. How could she die since she is already immortal?"

Though I did not quite understand his answer, I nodded with great relief. The translation was that she was all right.

"All *Devidas* are always thrilled when it rains. Why! They are having fun in the open air without bothering to take a shower. How convenient!"

A *Devida* that he mentioned, meant a fairy in paradise.

My face brightened up. I liked his second answer a lot better. He knew how I hated to go to the bathroom to clean myself.

Every answer always satisfied my hunger to learn about my mother. He kept on feeding me the single image of a loving and caring mother who was now living in heaven and still faithfully waiting for us to join her up there. I was never tired of listening to this part of the story over and over.

These were beautiful white lies meant to shroud me from ugly, dark truths.

When I became a grown man, I even felt sorry for my father's lies. However, this made me feel deeper affection toward him. I realized that he had painstakingly invented those lies not only to protect me alone but also to himself from some unbearable truth.

He had been living in his own lies, like a pupa huddling inside its cocoon in serene oblivion.

Those lies fed his desperate need to feel good. Simply put, he needed to feel good about everyone he met, in every occurrence he had taken some part with, and on every *why* he must answer—such as a why at my mother's absence from our life.

If I told him that the slimy creature I hated most was the earthworm—a glimpse of its wriggling on the soil made me cringe—he would gently pick it up, letting it wriggle freely and vigorously on his palm, and watch me screaming and shutting my eyes with dread nearby. (At least he did not force me to touch it.) And then he began to lecture me in a solemn voice.

"Don't you know what will happen without this little critter?"

I shook my head, and I didn't care a bit as long as there would no longer be a swarm of slimy red-brown earthworms crawling onto our cement-paved backyard and taking it for their temporary refuge from the monsoon flood. And, of course, my father acted as their rescuer; if he came across that calamity, he always rushed in alarm to pick them up from the cement floor one by one and put them back safely into the soil.

"There would have been no life on earth—only bare rocks and craters, and dust just like the moon," he replied grimly, and that startled me a little bit.

"Its contribution to the world was far greater than all living things combined. Why? For millions and millions of years, they've been busy making every single grain of soil on earth for us. Besides, this little poor critter never ever harms a soul."

Then again, he gingerly put it back to the soil where it had belonged for millions of years.

Another time, while we were having lunch at a noodle stall by the street sidewalk, a leper approached some other customers at a table nearby and asked for a few coins. His repulsive, grotesquely deformed face instantly turned down my appetite. The hungry disease that afflicted him had chewed up a chunk of his body, with half of his nose and the tips of his fingers now gone. All the men and women at that table looked at him with alarm and disgust. They even moved away to the farther corner. My father did the incredible, earnestly beckoning him to come to our table.

Everyone in that shop, including the vendor, gasped and frowned heavily on him. However, he seemed unaware or even naive of it. A couple at the table by our side who had just walked in and seated themselves on the stool suddenly jumped up and walked out as they covered their noses from the awful stench permeating the leper's partly rotten body.

"Papa, don't let him come here," I whimpered. "Look, people are glaring at us now."

He frowned at me as he smiled up at the leper now standing humbly at my father's side, folding his hands palm to palm as a gesture of begging. He seemed so cautious not to let any part of his body make contact with anyone nearby. His foul smell was overwhelming now as if he were hanging a chunk of rotten meat around his neck.

"May prosperity and longevity be with you as the rewards of your kindness, sir," he started reciting his well-prepared blessing with a trembling and raspy voice, his eyes meekly down casting.

My father gave him a handful of coins from his pocket. He put them into his clean white handkerchief, making a secured knot, and dropped it into the leper's palm, making him almost in tears from his unexpected luck. My father even thanked the leper for the blessing he had given him.

"Papa, his face really scares me. Aren't you afraid of him?" I still trembled from fear and disgust even after that leper was gone.

He looked me in the eyes and said, "If you see someone you hate or someone so awful or deformed or so wrinkled and shrunken with old age...then try this tactic. Picture him way, way back when he was just a tiny weenie innocent baby in his mother's arms. He might even have dimples on his little chubby, soft cheeks. Everyone was a cute baby once: you, me, or that leper. And believe me, it works. It's my secret to help me not to hate anyone..."

He paused, then winked at me.

"...And to stop me from hitting someone's face who's

pissing me off."

But when he made one man very happy, he could make another unhappy equally. The vendor rushed to our table, yelling furiously at my father. His eyeballs nearly protruded from sockets. The vein on his temple throbbed. I believed if he had had a gun or a club with him, he would have undoubtedly used it against my father.

"Look! Look! You are driving my other customers out of my stall. Every day, I fight tooth and nail, trying to make my business hang there. Now, you're ruining it, you stupid son of a bitch!"

I gasped at such an unexpected attack, but my father had just given him an apologetic smile in return and promptly paid him for our food before walking out.

Yes, I believed my father did not see a mean and miserable owner of this shop in front of him but a disarming baby, perhaps with the cutest dimples that once he had been.

This overwhelmingly optimistic nature of my father had made him a strange or even—forgive me—a weird person, one of a kind among the ordinary ones. I was unsure whether to call it a curse or a blessing. For all his short life, he'd lived in a state of denial of all the dark sides under the sun. It, in turn, assured him of going about his life more happily within his cocooned world full of self-made illusions. Should we judge the worthiness of a thing by its genuineness or its usability? Had my father had a chance to answer, it would have definitely been this.

"Give me one good reason. Why do you live with what's sinking your heart over what can lift your spirit, only because the former is real and the latter not? Why does painful reality have greater value than healing hopes and dreams?"

I believe no one could come up with a better version of reason than my father.

* * * * *

Part 1: Chapter 2

Dark Side of the Tide

*M*y father was my best memory, one percent of happiness out of ninety-nine percent of the miseries I endured. If I had ever learned love, I would have known how to love people from him. We only had each other against the whole world. He alone brought me up. And as an inexperienced young man of twenty-one then, he had done a great job raising me.

Who I am today was not his fault or responsibility. On the contrary, I could have been worse without my cherished but short childhood episode I shared with him.

He said I was born in a small bungalow house in the Old Capital. Its front faced a canal that ran sluggishly and smoothly in an ebbing and flowing tide. That canal connected to the main river, the Chao Phraya, which divided the banks of the Old Capital and Bangkok. Small rowing boats were our lifeline, the essential vehicles for crossing to the other side to do any business.

Beyond our backyard were our neighbor's orchards and groves—mangoes, tangerines, plantains, coconuts, betel nut palms, and so on. Far beyond lay fast fields of green vegetables belonging to the Chinese community.

Our small wooden frame bungalow had a baked clay tile shingles roof and a narrow wood veranda running around its four sides. It always lay under the cool shade of interlacing branches of the tall, canopied mango tree. Papa said it was a new tree grown from the old stump whose trunk had fallen during a storm when I was born. The bungalow was built ten feet or so above the ground for flood protection, leaving the spacious, cool space between the ground and floorboards of the house for me to play and run through and for my father to read a book and listen to his brand-new radio set broadcasting news at mid noon and to doze off after that on his hemlock tied between the two strong stilts of the house, each made of a stout log. He had an old gramophone for playing authentic Siamese music and Beethoven's Pastoral, his favorite Western classical piece. Yet, nobody else in our neighborhood had even heard of this Pastoral.

My father could not afford the costly installation of electricity and running water, a system recently introduced in Bangkok; he had to choose one. Finally, he decided on electricity due to his love of reading. No wonder that around the house, there was a row of large red ochre earthen jars stored with cool rainwater collected from the gutters lining the roof edge. It was our primary source of drinking supply.

Water fetched from the canal during the high tide at night, especially on full moon night, was considered good and clear enough for bathing and washing clothes. During the ebbing tide at noon, especially during the dry season, the water became muddy as it sometimes receded nearly to the bottom. I could go down and even wade in knee-deep, quaky mud until I reached the other side of the bank. All canal traffic inevitably halted; all trips were canceled until another high tide came to rescue them as soon as the evening approached.

Bangkok and the Old Capital Thonburi of that period were

well-known to foreigners as Venice of the East for its hundreds of canals meandering and sprawling like a network of interconnecting wires across its vast and low flatland. During a boat trip along one of these numerous canals, one could locate a sprawl of wooden and thatched-roof house after house along the winding and lush green bank since it rendered the richest soil for cultivated land and the most convenient area for living and traveling.

However, at nightfall, one could glimpse only the dark silhouettes of those dwellings and shadowy clumps of trees. Above was the huge ink sky glittering with millions of stars; below, millions of insects were chirping in darkness, drowning all noises on earth, if there were any at all, in the dead hour of the night.

Yet, in dense bushes along the two winding banks, one could witness a fantastic phenomenon that could take one's breath away. It was a spectacular display of glowing and twinkling fireflies reminiscent of thousands of golden lights on a Western Christmas tree lit up against the night's pitch darkness.

But rivers and canals had their ominous, dark side.

I vaguely recalled one afternoon when I was barely four years old. I was playing alone on the veranda. Suddenly, I heard shouts from a plank bridge that jutted across the canal's edge into the water under where our small row boat was tied. From the alarm of their voices, I knew something terrible must have happened at the bridge.

"Stay where you are. Don't go over there."

My father told me sharply as he jumped the flight of the bungalow steps, and off he went to the bridge in front of our bungalow.

I stood up, stretching my head out, trying to look out. Then, I focused on my father from a distance. He was helping these men carry something from under the bridge onto the bank. My curiosity grew until I could no longer resist. I tiptoed toward the bridge, bending myself low so he would not notice my approach.

Then I stopped short, unprepared for the awful stench that suddenly hit me as if someone had used a solid club to hit me with a hard blow. I choked and held my breath tightly, crouching and hiding behind the dense brambles. What I saw made me immediately recoil and come close to vomiting.

On the edge of the canal bank lay the naked body of a child about my age.

I could not guess whether it was a boy or a girl because the body was severely decomposed and bloated beyond recognition. One of the child's eyeballs protruded from its socket like the bulging eye of a goldfish, and the swollen tongue hung out from small rotten lips. The flesh on its cheek exposed part of a white skull, probably by fish nipping and gnawing. What appeared on the missing patch of flesh was part of the white skull. And Oh! The stench, the intolerable stench that pervaded everywhere.

"There *she* went on a prowl again," I heard one of our neighbors say as he shuddered. "I always warn the children."

Superstitions had been predominating the local people. They all believed there was a dead female roaming our neighborhood at night. Some swore they had seen her appear in a white bundle. A rumor spread that that dead woman had been looking for something or someone she had lost. Never would she rest in peace until she could find that one she wanted.

As a child, these stories terrified me. But my father ardently denied it. He declared it's one of the most nonsense things they put into a child's head.

I fled home from that gruesome scene as fast as I could. Fear gripped me until I couldn't sleep well that night.

In the wee hours, the sound of footsteps suddenly broke up the silence of the night. Someone was stomping along the veranda with a loud *thud-thud-thud*. With half fear and half curiosity, I got up from bed, tip-toed toward the bar window opposite my bed, and gazed out.

What I caught was a figure in silhouette. The moon illuminated that figure's long hair, showing it must be a woman, not the drowned child I was dreadfully expecting. A thick white blanket bundled around her body made her slightly stagger while she tried to move.

Though her face was obscured in shadow, her eyes were somehow gleaming in eerie moonlight, like the eyes of a cat in the dark. As if knowing I was watching her through the bar window from my bedroom, she suddenly turned and moved toward me. I wanted desperately to run, but mounting fear kept me paralyzed. A terror of fear was at its peak when I saw her open a dark hole that had once been her mouth.

Pran, it's your turn now…

I realized that I was screaming when my father abruptly shook me awake.

"I saw someone out there, Papa. A woman." I pointed to the window. "She was all covered with a blanket, and she…" I stumbled, "She…tried to get in," I shuddered as I managed to continue. "Then she said…she really said…*it's your turn, Pran. She…knows my name, Papa.*" Then I burst into tears.

Because the room was dark, I could only hear his soothing voice and feel his warm, reassuring hand clutching mine.

"Look, I did see you still in your bed when I rushed in. It means you didn't get up from bed or walk to the window and see whatever you thought you had seen. You just had a bad dream. Now, go back to sleep, Baby Boy. You know I will never let anything in the world come in to harm you. It would be best if you didn't have this nonsense nightmare again. So tomorrow, you will go to sleep in my room. Better?"

Yet, he didn't go back to sleep. He turned on the lamp, went straight, and shouted as if expecting his voice to carry far into the dark beyond.

"Get out! No more boogeyman, once and for all!"

Then, he shut the window panes with an unnecessary force. *Bang!*

Later that day, I eavesdropped on the adults' conversation. One of them whispered that Pim, our neighbor's little girl, was missing after she had strayed into a pretty isolated area along the bank and played alone. A few days later, the current brought her body down that canal, and it finally got stuck beneath our wood bridge.

The news horrified me and kept me crying for several days. Pim was my playmate. Her parents worked in the orchard near our house, and we knew this family well. Papa said her mother had helped him look after me once in a while when I was a baby and fell sick all year round. Pim and I usually played hide-and-seek and tree climbing together in the afternoon. That day, she asked me to play outside with her as usual, pointing to an old tamarind tree by the barbed fence.

"That woman yonder… Look! She's hiding behind that tree. She wants me to take you to play hide and seek near the canal."

"Oh!" My eyes followed her finger over there, squinting to look for whoever she talked about, to no avail, "Do we know her?"

"Nope," she shook her head before smiling as if she was holding some secret. "But she said she has toys and stuff for us. Come on! Let's go." Pim urged me in her jolly voice.

But that day, I had a mild fever, so I told her that Papa wanted me to stay indoors.

The last thing I saw of her was her romping merrily without me toward that tree and then out of sight.

I was too scared to tell Papa or anyone what'd happened between Pim and me that afternoon. I felt so guilty about her death that I took some part in it. Soon after, my father taught me to swim with coconut shells as buoys, knowing the danger canals posed to children. He tied a pair of big coconuts around my chest so that I could bob up and down safely in the cool brown water until I could get the hang of it. The fatal rate of drowning among small children was as high as natural death, such as succumbing to typhoid and pneumonia. Therefore, swimming was inevitably a necessity as walking.

Before sunset, when the water was still at high tide, my father and I would stride together, side by side, to that long plank bridge to take our daily bath. As we plunged into the water, diving, and swimming in its cool embrace, we always waited for peddler boats or fishing boats floating past us so that my father would beckon them to stop and buy their catch of the day.

That evening, he would happily cook fresh charcoal grilled fish. The thick smoke spread all over as the delicious smell permeated the air in the small kitchen. We ate our dinner quietly yet contently under the dim lamplight as he listened attentively to the broadcast from his radio set. It connected him to the wide world far beyond our cocoon of a small bungalow.

At an early age, he decided to stay home to care for me since he trusted no one to do this task. He still had some money left in the bank. The source of that money was unknown, as he revealed little about his past. But most of the land back then, still dense with trees and bushes, was affordable. And with the monthly interest from his savings account, he had enough to get by, though not quite comfortably; it gave him some peace of mind for having me by his side nights and days.

He told me in good humor that it was such a miracle both of us survived the most torturing two-month period of my infancy. I was a screaming machine operated twenty-four hours without a turn-off switch.

During my early infancy, he woke up every couple of hours at night to feed my hungry mouth with bottled milk, as good quality powdered milk as his meager money could afford during that decade. (All powdered milk was imported from Western countries during that period.) Throughout the night, he had to cradle me patiently in his arms, pacing in a circle around his small room with his eyes half closed because I had never stopped shrieking and screaming from my colic pain, which uncannily attacked me every night when the clock exactly struck midnight. Fortunately, that indigestive symptom eventually faded away when I was three months old.

I remembered that on my seventh birthday, he surprised me by bringing me to the edge of the backyard toward an old, tall tamarind tree by the fence of our house, a favorite place for us, Pim and me, to sneak out and climb up its sturdy trunk to pick its sweet and tart brownish meat in the pods. My father was not happy whenever he found me playing around that tree. He would call me back to play elsewhere, saying he'd found snakes in that dense, overgrown area.. But that day, he stopped under the shade of that tree. And out of the blue, he bluntly said.

"Look. Do you see that spot under that tree? That's where you were buried."

"What…?" I asked blankly, not getting what he meant at all. He patted my head fondly and amusedly smiled.

"It means you were born twice."

"Born twice?" I repeated, perplexed even more. "Is it the same as a chick? Before it is actually born, it must be born first inside an egg, right?"

"Smart boy!" he beamed.

After that, a gruesome yet fascinating story unfolded.

Since birth, I had been a frail, sickened baby. At his first glance on the day of my arrival into the world, I looked just like a tiny newborn hairless mouse with raw red skin as wrinkled and shrunk as the ninety-year-old man's. Upon my arrival, the midwife grimly announced I was stillborn since I neither moved nor breathed. My face was so swollen and blue as if someone had tried to choke me to death.

As an old custom, when a newborn died at birth, they would put its body into a clay pot and bury it right away under some large and shady tree. The faster, the better, for the soul, they believed, would reincarnate into the same family without unnecessary halt. My father had covered that pot with the lid and buried it under that old tamarind tree near our house with my unmoved body underneath a shallow grave that he'd dug with a shovel.

A short moment later, he thought he heard a feeble cry, so weak he did not at first pay much attention because he thought the voice he was hearing might be from some stray cat hunting for lizards among the bushes nearby. He was about to leave that spot when all the work was done.

Then he gasped.

He suddenly clutched his shovel and threw all his strength into digging out the buried pot a few feet underground. He panted and panted with extreme fear mixed with exhaustion as he threw the lid open. Inside that clay pot, he saw me opening my mouth, wailing and gasping for air while my tiny hands and feet were flailing feebly, clinging to life, fighting Death.

So, he salvaged me. He took me out, bundled me in his loincloth, cradled me in his arms, and wept.

He told me I was born a fighter. That meant I was destined to live a fighter and would never die a loser.

"Although you are always my Baby Boy, you must have this auspicious name that I gave you because *Pran* means *breath of life*,"

He then crushed me into his chest and whispered his blessing to me.

"Many returns of the day, Pran. Wherever you are, may your life be your best gift ever."

My father was a born storyteller. He loved exaggerating his stories to hold attention, especially tall tales. But pulling me out alive from my grave in time must have a grain of truth in it.

He also told me that the first time he bathed me in a tub, he nervously held me around his arm as if my body was made of a fragile eggshell so easily to be broken just in one single drop. Every early morning, he painstakingly washed and scrubbed my soiled diapers, hung them neatly on the clothesline, and let them crisp and dry in the hot sun side by side with his clothes. He always proudly watched his laundry billowing cheerfully in a soft breeze as if it was one of his most outstanding achievements while a flock of sparrows was hopping and chatting amiably under the laundry's shade.

Through my first year, he eye-witnessed my progress from my first creep to my first crawl to my first stand up and finally to my first step, which I wobbled toward him and fell in his arms. And one day, while I was sitting quite in a good mood on a training pot doing my bowel movement, he told me he suddenly heard me utter my very first intelligible sound—*pa... pa... pa... papa... papa*—while I was grinning from ear to ear at him, forcing him to blink back his joyful tears.

As in the old saying to my father, the sun rose and set on me.

Whatever a mother should take care of her child, my father did them all for me except sing a lullaby to coax me to sleep. It was beyond his capability because he had a terrible, off-key voice. But I was not an easy sleeper, so the national anthem, the only song he could sing, was often used to make me fall asleep.

I grew up among the sea of books, some stacking up neatly on the bookshelves and some scattered at every corner of every room in our small house—under a bed, dining table, chair, and carpet. Once, I found a book, the one my father had been frantically searching for a whole week. It sprawled deep inside the kitchen cupboard with a couple of day-old left-over foods. Who had absentmindedly left it there if not he? If my father was somewhere and not to be seen in the house, he could be tracked easily by the books he left behind right after he had finished, like a deer in the woods that could be trailed from its droppings by a bloodhound.

So, I learned how to crawl and walk with all the sprawl of books beneath my feet. When I started teething, my favorite thing to gnaw on vigorously was any book I could find within my grasp. I ravenously shoved it into my drooling mouth, maddening him more than anything I had ever done to him. I always looked up at him so disarmingly that it swiftly melted his anger away.

I had never seen even one piece of luxurious furniture or decoration in his room. My father said we had no money for such things, but there was no space for them either. A full-sized bed, a chest of drawers for keeping our clothes, and a desk were squeezed in, and that's all. If these things were not absolutely necessary, I believed he would, without a second thought, throw them out for more space. All the four corners of the world and its seven seas were somehow shrunken and crammed into his room—from foreign literature and volumes of poetry by prominent authors such as William Blake, Walt Whitman, Charles Dickens, Leo Tolstoy, Fyodor Dostoyevsky, Miguel de Cervantes, Rabindranath Tagore, and last but not least his favorite of all Herman Melville and his Moby Dick. However, those alone never satisfied his craving and enthusiasm for knowledge. He included history books, religion books, Buddhism and Christianity likewise, philosophy books, both Eastern and Western, science knowledge, and finally, tons of his law textbooks stacked neatly and separately on one dedicated colossal shelf.

Those thick and solemn law textbooks told me about some of his untold life. They forced him to reluctantly admit that he had dropped from the prestigious Royal Law School in his second year and had struggled ever since, trying to find odd jobs here and there to take care of me. In short, he was my walking encyclopedia, whose brain had an uncanny ability to consume all kinds of pure knowledge without exhaustion.

Consequently, there probably was no room left in his mind for learning human nature. Its mystery and complexity seemed beyond his awareness and comprehension.

If I had to describe him in a nutshell, I'd say my father was a naïve child in a man's body, with the mind of a savant, the heart of a saint, and the soul of a rebel.

There were two topics my father tried as much as he could to avoid.

One was about my mother. Another was his own family.

No matter how frantically I searched, I could not find a single picture of my mother in the house. I had played a detective, looking for any hard evidence to prove her existence and every time, it seemed like I was back to square one. Her identity was anonymous to me except for one thing: she was in heaven. That was all I knew about her from him—no more and no less.

Yet, in the case of my grandparents, it was even dimmer. My father must have his parents somehow, somewhere. He couldn't be dropped from the sky onto the earth like a shooting star. Yet not a word ever slipped from his mouth when I curiously asked about their whereabouts. I told him that I often saw a Grandpa or a Grandma come to pick up my classmates at school. When my father had brought me to a place like a preschool for little children nearby, I saw those grandparents' faces shine as their little grandchildren jumped with joy, greeting them. One of my classmates bragged that Grandpa was even better than Papa because Grandpa always indulged him with candies, toys, and hugs.

Immediately in the middle of the conversation, he pretended to look for one of his books and abruptly walked out on me, leaving me there on that spot, puzzled and hurt.

But one afternoon, while my father was taking a nap in his hemlock, I was doing my daily chore—dusting his mahogany desk and books lining up on the shelves in our bedroom. His desk was always cluttered with half-open books. (He never had enough patience to finish one book before starting another.) The top drawer in his desk was always locked, but today, I found it left ajar.

He must forget to lock it back, probably in a hurry. My heart was drumming rapidly as I slowly pulled open the drawer, trying not to make any squeaky noise. I knew I wasn't supposed under any circumstance to peek into his private possessions, but it was true that curiosity could kill a cat.

My father loved to tell me children's stories, both folklore and foreign tales. I remembered he had told me a story from ancient Greek mythology about the first female on earth named Pandora, who pried open God Zeus's forbidden box out of curiosity and released all kinds of evils ever known to men, like plagues, famine, misfortune, and so forth into this world. So fortunately for us humankind, my father said she closed the lid of that box in time. That's why Hope, the only thing Pandora was able to save inside that box, had remained with humanity up to today. He had told me he always wondered if that story had become the other way around, what would have happened to us now—living in a heaven-like, perfect world but without hope and dream since there was no room left to hope, perhaps? To him, it could be as good as living in hell.

I anxiously squeezed my eyes, bracing for what I would find.

The instant I opened my eyes, what I found inside disappointed me. Instead of some treasures as I expected in a pirate's story, as my eyes swept thoroughly, I found only one worn, black, covered thick journal book and one old, manila paper envelope at the bottom of the drawer.

In sulky silence, I flipped through all the journal leaves, still searching with flickering hope for more exciting items. But all the pages were only filled with my father's scribbles, which I could not read since, at that time, I had just started school.

Half the letters scribbled in black ink on that journal book became blotched and blurred from rain soaking. Rain must have leaked from the roof and seeped inside, damaging what he had written until the first half of his journal was barely readable. I curiously flipped through the second half and found those pages, though worn out, still intact and in relatively good condition. But if I could understand their content, it would surely bore me to death.

Then, my attention shifted to that brown envelope. My hands were trembling from excitement as I began to remove its contents individually.

What came into view this time was a real surprise. They were three worn-looking, old photographs in fading sepia color taken in the past.

The first one was the picture of a middle-aged lady in her elaborate and old-fashioned dress seated in her grandeur on a couch, with a strikingly handsome boy around four or five years old on her lap, wearing a sailor uniform and a sailor hat. The boy looked straight into the camera with his soft, dreamy eyes, his bright smile revealing two cute, deep dimples. An English cocker spaniel dog was crouching by their side. Even the boy my age knew that no one at that time could afford such an imported pet except that they must be well off.

My eyes glued on that boy almost breathlessly; no doubt he must be Papa—his smile, eyes, and characteristic dreamy expression. There was no doubt that the elegant-looking lady had to be his mother from the way she was holding him in her arms in an excessively protective manner. *I had a grandmother!* I knew I had one, although I had never expected my grandmother to look so superior and ladylike. Even though she seemed in her middle age, I had never seen any woman anywhere, especially in my neighborhood, having even half of the grandeur and beauty she possessed.

But I had no idea who the man in the second picture was— the middle-aged Caucasian gentleman in an imposing European suit perching on the arm of a big armchair with his walking cane clutched in one of his hands. Yet he must be significant enough for my father to keep his picture with him for all those years.

What turned out to be the most intriguing was the last picture, a portrait of a young Siamese girl in her mid-teens, dressed in the European fashion of a refined lacy blouse and long skirt. One of her hands was holding an open-laced parasol. This photograph was taken outdoors, somewhere in a flower garden. Yet the landscape background was far from familiar to my eyes. I assumed it must be taken in some foreign place far away, perhaps in one of the European countries where the rain mystically turned into ice upon falling on earth in winter.

It was too bad that the girl's features were quite homely: a square, plain face, a broad, large nose, flat cheeks, and small eyes, hardly impressing or attracting anyone at first glance. Yet, her subtle beauty lay in her smile that seemed to shine and radiate strangely out of the photograph, immediately captivating even a small boy like me. What a striking smile on such an undistinguished face. And although the girl's actual smile, which she had opened in front of the camera, might last merely a few seconds before it naturally faded and lost its existence in time, that smile had been captured and perfectly preserved in that photograph to be marveled and cherished by anyone of a present-day who found this long-hidden picture and had a chance to steal a glance at the timeless smile of hers.

In a flash of lightning, something struck my mind. The impact of that sudden thought made my heart skip a beat.

She must be my mother.

I was breathless and thunder-struck. She fit the description my father had given of my mother—a kindhearted fairy in heaven.

Without that unique smile, her face was far from pretty. Perhaps I'd inherited her plain looks, which explained why I wasn't as strikingly handsome as my father.

As my eyes transfixed her warm yet plain face, as if spellbound, I felt inexplicable tenderness toward her. My eyes lingered on her face and welled up with tears. At that most heavenly moment, I was oblivious to every existence in the world, especially the fact that the person in that photograph was an absolute stranger to me.

On the back of that photo, I found a line of foreign script, which I assumed was English, written in my father's distinctive hand.

I jumped, put those mysterious pictures back, and closed the drawer as I immediately heard my father's footsteps approaching. I suddenly realized that I had violated his privacy. I'd just trespassed right into the heart of his bygones, which completely excluded me. However, when he rushed into the room—as if the room was being on fire—straight to his desk with his nervous and suspicious look to lock that drawer, he only sighted me at another corner busily dusting his bookshelf, my back on him as if unaware of his presence.

As soon as he saw me turning to face him, he sighed with relief as if surprised at his sudden ambush. Then I flashed him a saintly smile, making myself smell like a rose. And thank heavens, it worked. I only prayed my father would never hear my heart-beats, which were thundering behind that open-my-heart smile.

I had asked myself a million times since that incident why I didn't go straight to him and ask him if that was a picture of my mother. But instead, I had never told him I had discovered his 'keepsake' inside that drawer. I always decided against it at the last minute because I couldn't stand to witness his dread if I forced him at bay. It was as plain as day that he didn't show me those pictures because he didn't want to, for whatever reason.

Perhaps all earthly reasons known to my father, who had steadfastly revered logic and reason as his God, were useless to save him in the face of some specific crises. Therefore, the only tact to deal with what had been haunting him was to seek refuge in such a way that had nothing to do with reason. Therefore, locking up his family pictures in a dungeon-like drawer for good was chosen as his means to solve his problem.

I never found another chance to glimpse those three pictures. Since that day, that drawer had been perpetually locked up. Each time I came to clean up the room after that day, it became my secret habit to check that drawer, hoping for one more chance of Papa's carelessness. But never again had he left it unlocked.

By then, I learned that he could not confront what deeply troubled him. Somehow, he could close his eyes from it but he could not force himself to believe that those troubles, whatever they might be, had never happened to him.

Everybody can reject reality as long as he lives, but no one can deny its existence.

* * * * *

Part 1: Chapter 3

Sail across the Seven Seas with the Wrong Hand

I *always remembered one episode of my life when I first started school at six.*

It was a private preschool for small children before entering the elementary class. The school was run by a fifty-year-old matriarch, a well-off widow whom everyone called *Kru Riam* (Teacher Riam). A section of her house was converted into a classroom with a capacity of twenty children, where she taught and ruled alone. My father left me in that place among all the unfamiliar faces for half a day before he came back to bring me home.

In this way, he would have more time to find a temporary job, from a part-time store clerk to a hired laborer and a fruit picker in nearby orchards. Any job was indiscriminately good to him as long as it was an honest and decent job. With his fluency in English, he could quickly get a more prestigious and well-paid job, such as a translator for the government or a school teacher. However, he told me those works required time and all commitments. He'd rather wait until I could be more independent, care for myself, and stay home alone during his absence.

The first day in school for a new student traditionally fell on Thursday, considered the most sacred and auspicious day of the week for obtaining wisdom. As a tradition, I carried with me a bowl made of woven banana leaves containing a large cluster of red Ixora flowers, a handful of grass blades, and a small bunch of purple eggplant blossoms—all grown and found in abundance on the ground around our backyard—together with a few incense sticks and candles, all for honoring and paying respect to my teacher.

A cluster of red Ixora flowers with their tiny needle-like shapes symbolized sharpness and brilliance; hardy Bermuda grass blades grown everywhere in abundance, flood or drought, stood for resilience and a profusion of knowledge; and bow-down eggplant blossoms signified obedience and humbleness. These were the three traditional virtues that a student should bear.

In the early morning, as long blades of grasses on the ground still moist and fresh with glistening morning dews, we trudged our way across our backyard, through a dense tangerine, plantain, and mango glove and finally gingerly and precariously tiptoeing on a slippery extended palm tree trunk cut and used for crossing a narrow ditch. Once in a while, sunlight peeked in, filtered through dense foliage, and dappled our faces. As we trudged into the deeper shade, the fresh scent of moss-covered, damp, soft earth from last night's drizzles permeated the air.

Suddenly, I caught sight of something that almost took away my breath. Above our heads, a circle of multicolored butterflies, golden yellow, lime green, copper red, and indigo blue, danced with their fluttering wings as if they were on a parade dressed in fancy embroidery costumes. As the lead singers, magpies sang sweet songs among tree branches, and a chorus of cicadas and other insects were noisily chirping among dense underbrush and thick brambles.

"Listen to this symphony orchestra of life, listen..." he

whispered in awe. "Today, the world is rendering its brightest side to you. Listen to the sound of the earth pulsing with life to celebrate you, son. It's the best promising sign for a new chapter of your life."

My father was exuberant in his lift-up spirits. He, not me, acted more like a boisterous schoolboy on his first day. He even whistled some old tunes, a rare habit for him, while holding one of my hands, guiding me ahead, whereas I felt nervous about facing an uncertain new world awaiting my arrival. On our way, he sensed my increasing nervousness. Therefore, to encourage me, he loudly recited a poem, his favorite, from a Siamese literature textbook when he was young. His voice was strong and clear as these verses flowed from his lips.

Knowledge is a priceless cargo from a faraway land
Thus, prepare to set yourself as one dignified barque,
Your hands as the sails facing a blow of wind
Your feet, two anchors holding the barque–
Your fingers, the ship's masts
While ominous tempest lurks
Take your perseverance as an inexhaustible workforce
To traverse against all odds
While your eloquence, a navigator,
Your congeniality, your supply provision;
Your sense, a propeller on its rout
Your insight, a field glass guarding your vessel
From reefs and rocks
Throughout the long voyage across the seven seas
Lassitude will emerge like a school of sharks–
To wreck the ship
It must be slayed by a cannon–
Fired from your adamant heart
Then, through all hindrances–
With your most ardent effort
Will you at last reach the haven of your destined port

After fifteen minutes, a walk trip to school was done. We emerged onto the clearing where my school stood. I held my breath and clutched his hand as firmly as possible.

Behind the row of pink oleander and bright red hibiscus shrubs stood a two-storied house with four sides of veranda running around it, somewhat like ours except that it was much larger. The capacious space between the house and the cement-paved ground below was converted into a classroom, yes, a classroom with no walls except for the thick bamboo blinds that could be rolled down from the ceiling for all four sides when it rained or was too sunny. There were no chairs except for a single one belonging to the teacher. Instead, a large mat was thoroughly paved to cover the ground so all students could sit. There were four rows of foldable low desks for students and a large blackboard in front of the class.

As we approached the classroom, curious eyes from sixteen boys and three girls turned to us. Those open stares churned my stomach and weakened my legs. My father squeezed my clammy hand gently to signal his encouragement. It was the first time I encountered a new world and new faces—so many simultaneously.

My father nudged me toward the lady teacher at her desk. Her gaze fell steadily on us, mostly on my father. I had to kneel in front of her as I presented her with my bowl of offerings. She accepted it with a half-smile and her traditional blessing in return. Her acceptance of my offerings officially pronounced my status as her new student and assured me I would belong to this domain where she had been a sovereign from that moment.

It was the first and last smile she had ever given me while I was attending her school.

After that brief ritual, my father had left. Kru Riam pointed to one unoccupied desk in the middle row, gesturing for me to settle myself over there, which I did promptly. All the desks were so low everyone had to sit on the floor paved with a large mat. After that, she taught the class how to write the Thai alphabet. She stood big and tall in front of the class, with a piece of chalk in her hand, neatly and carefully writing all the forty-four letters onto that large blackboard. The lesson has now officially started.

Then, she asked all her new students to trace those letters onto their slate tablets, traditionally made for young children to practice writing. This way, we did not waste notebook paper because we could erase what we had just written down from the slate and start again. The whole class followed her command. Everyone bent his head and kept himself busy with a slate pencil and tablet. A few moments later, she began to strut past every row of desks to check each of her students' work.

I froze as she brusquely stopped at my desk and peered at my still-blank slate tablet. I felt my blood turn cold as she frowned at me. My palm, as it firmly grabbed a slate pencil, was now damp with cold sweat.

"You don't listen to me, young man. I've just told the class to copy some letters on the blackboard onto the slate. Now do it!"

"Yes, Ma'am," I lowered my voice to a whisper.

I took a deep breath and then slowly let it out. How stiff my five fingers had become as if I had long neglected them to rust in the rain. Why was my small hand so weighty, as if it had already turned into a slab of stone? It was so heavy that I could not control my whole hand as I forced it to drag a line and bend a curve to form the first letter of the Thai alphabet, which seemed quite easy to command just by the look. Finally, I drew my breath again. That letter came out at last. But it seemed out of proportion, too illegible to make any sense: something as close as a scribble of a two-year-old on the wall.

"Now what?" she thundered. "What's wrong with you, young man? You can't make out a straight line or a curve to form a letter, right? Or do you want to give me a hard time?"

"No, Ma'am," whispered I again, too scared to say more to aggravate her temper.

"Let's see whether you can improve by tomorrow," she declared.

As I dazedly blinked and looked around, desperate to see hope, I found all eyes ranging from mildly curious to nonchalant to intense get-what-you-deserve stares.

There was no friendly smile on their face, only a cold sneer.

When the class was dismissed in the early afternoon, I spotted my father waiting in the front yard. His brightest smile greeted me, and I immediately jumped into his arms as soon as I had glimpsed his sight. He grabbed my hands so tightly that he spun me around and around in a circle, as he usually did to me, just for my having fun.

"How is your first day at school? Lots of fun? How many friends can you make so far? Let me guess. Nine? Ten? Or the whole class? Hey," he winked at me as he went on, lowering his voice into a mischievous whisper. "Any cute girls?"

He cheerfully bombarded me with question after question as I managed to smile at him.

"Are you all right, Pran?" he stopped. His smile faded as he sensed something not quite right stamped on my face. "You aren't happy in school, are you?" He looked me in the eyes.

"Yes, yes, Papa, I'm fine," I nodded vigorously, averting his scrutinized stare. I know how happy and relieved he was to see me start school. I did not have the heart to ruin any of his dreams that he was intent on making it come true for my future.

"I…I just feel sad…because I miss you."

What I replied to him was not a lie since this was one reason for my misery at school. However, I intended to omit another reason, a more serious one: the hostile atmosphere of the whole class.

"Miss me! Come on, you aren't a baby any longer," he groaned and chuckled good-naturedly as we walked home. "Soon, you will be a young man with your own family to take care of. I will become a grumpy old man. And one day…I won't be around any longer."

I burst into tears. I could not bear the thought that one day, he would be gone and not with me anymore. It was more than the sun and the moon, and all the stars in the sky stopped shining altogether.

As a few more days passed by, I hardly showed any progress, infuriating Kru Riam more. Everyone in the class could write many letters without glancing at the blackboard, but I still struggled. She must think that I was either a troubled boy enjoying challenging her or had a big hole in my brain beyond her help. What? A six-year-old grown-up boy with the writing ability equal to a two-year-old toddler. However, she decided to cling to her first thought: I was a bad boy.

Kru Riam was a matriarch who took care of large areas of orchards. She was one of a handful of women who could read and write. People in our neighborhood sent their small children to her school because she had a good reputation as a strict teacher who ruled her students with chalk in one hand and a stick in the other. Chalks were for writing, and sticks were for punishing.

Throughout a decade, these two guaranteed her students' success. Years after years, her students finished her school with good handwriting and some scars on their butts as a bonus until I came to ruin her pride for the high respect she had earned in forcing all her students, even the dullest ones, to know how to write. What if one of her students had told his parents about her incompetence in teaching one single boy to write?

If one parent had known the whole neighborhood would too, she thought so, and overnight, all her good reputation would be in question.

Therefore, to save herself from all the blame, she must let the whole class see with their own eyes that I had a problem with my dumbness, which was beyond her ability to help.

So, one hot afternoon, as her patience ran thin and thin, she asked me to stand up in front of the class. I was handed a piece of white chalk to draw on the blackboard to show the class how progressive my alphabet was. Still, I struggled with my weak, baby-like muscles. My hand seemed lost in the vast blackness in front of me.

"Not the slightest sign of progress!" she contemptuously declared. My repeated failure finally pushed her over the edge. "Why! This boy reminds me of…"

Suddenly, she paused and turned quickly to the class. Apparently, something was crossing her mind.

"…Of what? Can anyone give me your best answer of what he reminds me of?"

A few hands were raised simultaneously, but Kru Riam picked one earnest boy sitting in the third row. He was the oldest boy in the class, with his stout body and small, restless eyes darting repeatedly and never staying still. His name was Poon.

"I know, Ma'am; he reminds us of…" that boy answered promptly and then paused because of an interruption of his uncontrolled giggle. "Sorry, Ma'am, he reminds us of…a buffalo!"

A torrent of laughter followed. Their bodies were squirming from their laughing fit.

"Ah! We can't find a better answer. Thank you, Poon.

To spice up the scene, my teacher's hand fumbled inside her desk drawer and eagerly pulled out a picture. She lifted the picture and showed it to the whole class, causing noises of laughter to reach a crescendo. It was a pencil-sketched drawing of a water buffalo immersing its body in a muddy pond, only its dump-looking face and a pair of long curved horns surfacing.

"Put down the chalk and come over here."

She beckoned to me. I dragged the weight of my limbs toward her, step by step, as if on my way to the execution gallows. The closer I approached her, the clearer she was on the verge of drooling. She wiped her red, saliva-ridden lips with her red-blotted handkerchief.

Before I realized what was happening to me, she had strung

that picture with a thread and hung it around my neck. She burst into a shriek of laughter so hard I believed she would have a fit. The horrible sound of her laughter terrified me to the point that I nearly wet my pants.

To the Siamese, some animals represented something due to their appearance and behavior. Elephants signified sacred and greatness; peacocks signified grace and beauty; horses velocity; feline stealth; canine loyalty; crows slyness; monkeys agility and mischief; vipers villainy; and cattle, especially water buffalos, stood for downright dumbness.

Then, she asked all my classmates why she had put me up front. Everyone shouted and pointed at me in synchrony.

"It's because he's so dumb, Ma'am."

"Does anyone want to be like him, class?"

"No, Ma'am, we don't," they all chanted like a chorus supervised by their conductor, their arms folded, their eyes explicitly mocking me.

The scene ended with her satisfied smirk, followed by the second round of wild chortles from all my classmates. Hot tears streaked quietly down my face, but I hung my head just in time to hide them. I was too afraid to cry openly and risk more taunting.

Her plan was carried out successfully, so after that scene, no one would ever blame her for my incompetence in writing.

That night, I cried my heart out as my father was snoring steadily beside me. I had never experienced such a humiliation up to this level before. However, I decided Papa would be the last person to know. I would ruin all his hope in me if he found out what a dumb boy he had. I lost almost all my appetite. At night, I tossed and turned, weighed down by guilt and shame. Worst of all, I avoided being with my father as much as possible for fear that I would not be able to hide from him my agony.

But he did notice it. Nothing about me could escape his keen eyes. One afternoon after school, he caught me alone on the veranda, my head bending to my knee, quietly weeping.

"All right, this is a man-to-man talk. What's troubling you

lately? Can we share?" he was straight to the point. "Now, take me for your trusted friend, not your authoritative parent."

Only one glimpse of his encouraging smile made me downpour all my hidden agony on him like a torrent of water gushing down a broken dam. I tried with a choked cry to utter words between my sobs.

"Papa, I can't make out any letter in the class. My fingers are so stiff I can't force them to move with a pencil. And Kun Kru...she...she put me in front of the class and...and forced me to hang...hang a drawing of...of a water buffalo while all my classmates laughed and called me dumbo—"

Before I finished, he grabbed both my hands and inspected them thoroughly. Then he asked me to wiggle all my fingers, which I did with no problem. It seemed he couldn't find anything wrong with either hand.

There was a dead silence.

He stared at me as I sat with my head hung to avoid his stare. Neither reproach nor console slipped from his lips. Only the whole silence drowned the entire room. So silent that if someone accidentally dropped a needle onto the floor, it would startle me as if hearing the gunfire.

It was the most dreadful moment, far more terrifying than the humiliation and intimidation I had experienced in the classroom. I would have endured that kind of bully every single day from my class rather than being seated in front of my father with absolute silence. I could not afford to lose his trust and the fondness that he had been giving me.

Papa, please say something to me. I welcome a spanking more than your silence.

He now seemed absorbed in his thoughts, shifting his absentminded gaze from that sheet of paper to me back and forth. Finally, it was he who broke the terrible silence. He told me he needed to be alone to figure things out. Meanwhile, he allowed me to step outside and have fun with my recent favorite plaything, a slingshot.

Lek, his friend, had made me a slingshot a couple of months ago. He sharpened a guava wood stick, considered the most qualified for carving a slingshot. He then made it into a y shape and tied rubber elastic between two arms to propel small pellets of solid dried clay. But Papa said it would belong to me only on one condition: he would never allow me to shoot all animals: sparrows, squirrels, lizards, small reptiles, or whatever that breathed. I promised him promptly.

The living things I found around my house daily, except slimy earthworms, fascinated me. Those which I loved to spend hours watching curiously were mourning doves cooing sadly on the roof, crickets chirping in harmony at dusk, or a swarm of tiny tadpoles with their little tails swimming to and fro in the shallow rain pool after the rainfall, or dragonflies with their iridescent and gauzy wings hovering and ferreting in pairs around the lily pads in our pond.

Consequently, slingshot shooting targets were reduced to bark on tree trunks, an empty can and bottle on the ground, or any small, unmoving objects dangled on a rope.

Surprisingly, after a short practice, I could hit a target with accuracy. Even my father teased me that I could have a promising career as a hitman when I grew up.

Usually, he let me play alone in the front yard. But today, I found him stepping out and standing at the corner of the veranda under the deep shade of magenta bougainvillea, which covered the lattice trellis over his head. He was gazing down at me while I was toying with my slingshot.

His arms leaned against the railing while his squinting eyes focused on every movement of mine, hard and long as if he had nothing else to pay attention to. It was hard to tell what was on his mind. I sheepishly glanced in his direction and slowly breathed a sigh of relief. At least I did not detect any hint of anger on his face. Indeed, it was rare to see him on edge or ill-tempered with anyone, let alone in genuine anger.

He shouted at me across the yard.

"Can you aim to hit a can over there?" He pointed his finger to an empty can lying on the ground by the barbed wire fence that lined the perimeter of our property.

"It's too far for me, Papa," I protested hesitantly, afraid to upset him.

"Just try it once," he coaxed me. "You won't lose anything by trying. But if you don't try, you might lose a chance to know your potential."

So, I tried it. I hold the slingshot firmly in one hand, stretching its rubber elastic with another. With a steady and deadly aim, I narrowed one of my eyes, let a clay bullet go off, and held my breath.

Bang!

The can bounced off and spun like a top in the middle of the air before dropping to the ground. It kept rolling a few feet forward before completely stopping. I ran to pick it up, and it was a shallow dent caused by the bullet right on the can. The feeling of triumph radiated all over me. Now, I saw my father clapping his hands with excitement on the deck as if he had performed all the shooting himself.

"The fun is over," he announced. "Now, it's time to get back to work. You come right up to me."

Now what? He brought me to our desk at one corner of our packed bedroom with his larger-than-life bookshelf looming against the wall. With heaps of books squeezed in, the bookshelf alone took up the whole length and height of one side of the walls. The left-over books, which were hopeless for cramming in, were stacked on the floors by their category. There was barely enough space to move freely because those books cluttered the whole room. On the opposite wall stood our bed, which I had to inch and zigzag my way to sleep under a canopy of white mosquito net protected from an army of nocturnal blood-thirsty mosquitoes.

He told me to sit before him as he handed me one blank sheet of paper and a pencil. His face now turned serious, and my heart started pounding. I began to shift uncomfortably in my chair. It was not hard to guess what would be happening.

"Now, write any letter that you can memorize, and let me look at it," said he solemnly.

"Papa...Papa...please," I stuttered.

The brief glorious triumph I had tasted a short moment ago immediately evaporated. Shame and an intense feeling of self-worthlessness loomed over me again. I had no choice except to let him witness what I feared the most. I was downright insulting him. The man who valued books over wealth, prosperity, and all other earthly possessions had a son who struggled to write one simple letter.

I forced my rust-eaten hand to grab a pencil. Gritting my teeth, I drew one letter on the sheet as slowly and meticulously as possible to delay time to hand it to him.

There it was. No miracle occurred. What appeared plainly on that sheet was a grotesque and distorted letter *Ko Kai*, out of shape and control. My eyes brimmed with stinging tears as my father picked it up and peered down.

The biggest surprise of all was seeing his smile return. I blinked a couple of times, yet my eyes were not mistaken.

"Now try to use your other hand instead," he said heartily. "The one you always use for holding your slingshot. Try that one."

"Papa...the whole class writes with the right hand," I gasped, too stunned to find more to say. "Kun Kru ordered everyone to use their right hand to hold a pencil."

"It never hurts to try. You know I don't like to give orders like a commander. I'm asking you to try this just for your own sake, please."

We were generally brought up to look at our teacher as a towering, venerable figure. A teacher's words were treated as being absolute. I wondered how he dared to challenge a teacher's authority over her students. However, to please my father, I started to draw the same letter, switching a pencil to my left hand. The fear was now overwhelming. I was too afraid to peer down that sheet, and even though I did, I probably saw nothing. The tears were blurring my vision.

"Look! Look!"

I heard him shouting, so I blinked to clear my cloudy vision. I heard him cry again in exuberance. His voice was bursting with pride.

"This is the letter *Ko Kai*. No doubt about it."

I blinked my eyes again in disbelief. A miracle did happen this time, but I did not know how. The letter's line suddenly came out sharp and straight, its curve smooth and gentle. It was as good and clear as a six-year-old could make it out.

My face flushed with a thrill of triumph. I tried another letter, at first, with reluctance. Once again, the curve came out curvy, and the line was straight. I tried another and another, each time with increasing confidence while my father was beaming at me.

Have you ever seen a nearly dead fish lying stiff and gasping for air on the dry ground? An instant later, it was picked up by a merciful hand and thrown into the water. In one splash, it vanished from one's sight. Down there, under deep water, it was alive. It swam and swam tirelessly and freely in every direction that its tail and fins could propel, exploring the soft, cool world that was once again its home.

Freedom at last.

When our exaltation from discovery died down a little, he put me onto his lap as if I were still a little child. His voice turned grave again.

"You are left-handed. But it's absolutely no problem. The only problem is you do have an ignorant teacher,"

I gasped, but he still used his matter-of-fact tone.

"Well, probably it isn't her entire fault either if she presumes the only way to write is with the right hand because she has seen that all the time. But let me explain more. According to the latest medical research I have had a chance to read, the right side of our brain takes control of the left part of the body and vice versa. To make it shorter, the left brain is basically more powerful than the right brain in controlling our anatomy. That explains how the right part of the body of most people, including their right hand, can function better, such as in writing and handling things. But in your case, for reasons still unclear to us, it's all reversing. Your right brain instead becomes dominant, making your left-handed work more handily for you. You are born not only different but also unique, son."

"Are there other left-handed people besides me?" I asked skeptically.

"Of course," he gave me a reassuring smile. "But not so many, only a handful of your kind. And since people always believe in the *more* over the *less,* the right-handed believe they are *right* whereas you are *wrong.*"

"So, it means at least I'm not different from everyone in class, right Papa?" I almost smiled with relief. Who wanted to be an outstanding and easy target to pick on?

"Yes and no," my father sighed. "The lefty and the righty have nearly everything in common. The only difference is the mind of a lefty seems more creative, while the mind of a righty is more practical and logical. Well, both can coexist in harmony. However, the world needs both of them to maintain its existence. So, both can't live without one another, just like Zen's Yin-Yang that coexists to balance one another," he completely forgot I had never heard of such words like *Yin-Yang.*

"Tomorrow, I will talk with your teacher when I walk you to school. So, she will be more open-minded about your being lefty. Feel better now, Pran?"

I said yes to him, but I know I did not.

"How about you, Papa? Are you lefty like me?" I asked with hope. I had never noticed which hand he normally used.

"Oh! Unfortunately, I'm not," he shook his head sadly and laughed good-naturedly. "I am just an insignificant right-handed person among millions and millions." Suddenly, it seemed something was crossing his mind. "Oh, I forgot. Lek is left-handed, too. And he's a wizard of all handicrafts." He was talking about the only friend he had.

That night, Kru Riam came to visit me, not in reality, but in the dream. It was an ordinary dream at the beginning, the one that rendered your everyday life. I was seated with the rest of the children in the class; a slate tablet was in our hand, waiting for the approach from our teacher. Then, the nightmare started with a thundering footstep followed by a shriek of laughter so piercing it rattled the ceiling. Everyone looked at one another, and immediately I heard someone shout—*run everybody, run for your life*.

In a flash, the class was deserted. All the children left me behind, alone and terrified beyond words.

Where's everybody? Don't leave me alone, please. Is anyone still here?

I heard my hollow voice echoing back and forth, mocking me. Then I gasped. I felt someone was breathing heavily behind my back. And I heard something dripping, dripping to the cement floor. *Plink! Plink! Plink!* I swiftly turned around and winced.

There, right behind me, Kru Riam was standing with her legs spread, her blood-red saliva from chewing betel nuts dripping down the floor. *Plink! Plink! Plink*! Every time she put one step forward, I recoiled another step backward. In one of her hands, she carried a heavy bamboo-woven basket. I could not peer down what was inside because a lid covered that basket. Then, she handed it to me as she opened her hearty smile.

I have something for you and hope you'll love it. Be a good boy and open it, dear. A little boy like you is always curious, aren't you?

She coaxed and urged me to take that mysterious basket from her, but she was probably unaware that her blood-red saliva kept on drooling from her gaping mouth and dripping to the floor. *Plink! Plink! Plink*! And that creepy *Plink! Plink! Plink* sounds forced me to take more steps farther from her.

Before I was fully aware, all my classmates had come back. I heard their quiet footsteps closer and closer. Now, they were standing in a circle, Kru Riam and I facing each other at the center. There was no way to flee, no way to run. I was in their trap and their grip.

Open it. Don't you want to see a good present from our teacher? Open it. Open it now.

They all growled and snarled in unison while taking a few more steps to threaten me.

I knew I had no choice but to reluctantly open the basket's lid.

When I saw the inside, my hands brushed that basket away in shock. It thumped on the ground, forcing dozens of severed hands to fly out before they lay scattered on the floor.

All were left hands, clean cut to the wrist.

Some were still soaked with blood. Some looked mummified and dried with gore. But one of those hands looked so fresh I saw its blood-riddled fingers still move feebly. Sheer horror gripped my throat and sent icy shivers over my skin. I felt like I was going to faint.

Whoever writes with his wrong hand will meet their fate this way.

As she thundered, her finger pointed to that horrid hand, which was still alive. It started crawling clumsily along the floor, its fingers scrambling blindly to find a way to escape. When she saw the hand was moving away, she swiftly lifted one of her feet and stomped it with all her force. The hand trembled and came to a stop, but its fingers still struggled beneath her shoe, wriggling and wriggling to set the hand free.

I chopped that damned hand myself just minutes ago. Ooh, its fingers are still moving. See that? Now, your turn is coming!

A big, razor-sharp butcher knife appeared out of nowhere. Now, it was in her grip firmly.

I stood paralyzed in the same spot only a few feet away

from her, too terrified to move, let alone to think right. As the butcher knife flashed over my head, I tightly closed my eyes. In a split second, I heard the funny sound of a sharp thing penetrating the air. *Chop! Chop! Chop!* I opened my eyes again, baffled, only to see a jet of blood gushing down my left arm, causing a blood-curdling scene with blood splashing all over the floor and spattering my clothes. Still baffled and numb, I heard my classmates laughing and shouting.

Look! Look! Look what's on the floor now, you dumb ass.

So, I did what they urged me; I peered down and looked. What I saw with my own eyes was my left hand—the wrong hand that sailed—lying stiff and lifeless by my feet like a chunk of dead meat.

Abruptly, my hand jumped up my throat and, with all its attempts, tried to choke me to death.

I opened my mouth and let go of a scream so loud that I felt someone shaking my body hard, pulling me out of the whirlpool of my gruesome nightmare. My eyes were wide open as I suddenly saw my father's face peering at me, his eyes showing concern.

"Are you all right?" asked my father as he stroked my hair, trying to comfort me. "You must have a nightmare. It's only two o'clock in the morning. Let me scratch your back so you can go back to sleep."

I was fully awake now and still sweating profusely. It was still so lucid, so real, the sight of my severed left hand. But I said nothing to him. I closed my eyes again and pretended to fall asleep. Soon enough, I heard his steady snores. I felt terrible about disturbing my father, who had already collapsed from his day-work exhaustion.

Although he did not tell me in detail about his discussion with Kru Riam, I sensed that it should have worked better or, in other words, failed.

Most people in his contemporary were illiterate. If some males were fortunate enough to enter school, taught mainly by monks at a temple, their education range was limited to mere spelling, reading, and basic mathematics like addition and subtraction. Science, politics, foreign languages, and so forth were not introduced outside a small royalty and prestigious elite circle. Most females have yet to have a chance to own a pen to practice their writing, let alone lay their eyes on any book. Only pots, pans, threads, and needles were counted as tickets to their domestic achievement.

A career given to a few literate women was limited to teaching small children at the entry level. Yet it made them carry their pride up their shoulders like warriors carrying their weapons. On their warpath, they always craved some bloodshed of any souls who challenged them.

No wonder why my intellectual yet naïve father severely bruised my teacher's ego and sense of superior authority. He might give her some of his well-intentioned lectures on the scientific fact of the influence of a right brain over a left hand, which she probably could not make heads or tails of what he was talking about. Who the hell he was? A Nobody. A nobody who spoke with his big and fancy words meant to hit her at the heart of her self-esteem.

Poor Papa was never aware of her grudge, which fiercely erupted after that day.

The Cold War then started.

She let me sit undisturbed, using my left hand freely and easily to copy words on the blackboard. It was hard to deny that my handwriting was outstanding compared to most of the class. I had no clue whether my left-hand ability surprised or even shocked her. As far as I was concerned, she ignored my handwriting and my presence in the class.

She neither scolded me, asked me questions, nor urged me to participate in any activity with the rest of the class. In certain circumstances, she could no longer avoid my presence. She would speak to me with her icy cold voice and scornful look.

Soon enough, her hostility against me spread across the classroom like a plaque. One by one, the children in my class began to imitate her. No one talked to me.

Everyone, including me, brought their lunch from home. While they clustered together at the far corner, eating and chatting boisterously, I had lunch in my lunch box that Papa had prepared for me at the opposite corner, all alone, and wondered what I had done wrong to deserve this kind of punishment.

I figured they now must hate me for one more reason. I used to be their laughingstock, their ugly duckling. They had enjoyed targeting me for my writing incompetence for quite a while, and one day, I knocked them out hard. I suddenly emerged as a white swan, as if in a fairy tale Papa used to tell me. Not only was I able to write, but I also performed better and faster than most of them, especially the boy Poon who used to pride himself on his writing and spelling progress. Yes, all from that forbidden hand of mine.

So, they ganged up and started attacking me with their new game. As long as I was still in the class, they only smirked, sneered, and hissed at me when they walked past where I was seated. But when the class dismissed, and I tried to sneak out as quietly and unnoticed as possible, they ambushed me with shrieks of laughter as they started chanting.

> *Left hand for wiping shit*
> *Right hand for writing verse*
> *Who writes with a left-hand*
> *May his ass rot from our curse*

Over time, they found a new name for me: *Mr. Shit-Hand*.

One day, after the class was dismissed and as I walked home alone because my father said I was big enough, three boys in my class stalked me. They sneakily followed me and then ambushed me midway on my way home. I was totally off guard when two of them suddenly hurled themselves at me, forcing me to stumble and sprawl on the ground, face down. I felt blood slowly streaking down from my nose, dripping to the ground.

As I struggled to my feet, still shocked and baffled, one of them raised his foot and stomped hard on the back of my hand: *Stomp, stomp, stomp.* A sharp pain shot up my whole arm as if someone was stabbing that part with a sharp knife. Then, I was forced into the kneeling position like a convict who was awaiting his execution for a serious crime he had committed.

The third boy, Poon, the biggest and stoutest one, who had stood folding his arms and acted as an on-looker since the beginning, started to unfold a small wrap made from a strip of banana leaf in his hand. I'd never forgotten that he was the one in the class who had raised his hand and introduced the name 'water buffalo' to the teacher for calling me. As he opened the wrap in an exaggeratedly slow ritual act, the stench of feces suddenly hit my nostrils. While the other boys held me firmly, he jabbed a thin wood stick into a small lump of feces inside the wrap, drew it out, and smeared the feces still glued to the stick thoroughly on my left hand.

"Your shit hand is now finding its match," the boy Poon hissed at me. "That thing inside the banana wrap was freshly dropped from my ass and as shitty as your left hand," he turned to his gang. "Now, let him smell his hand; how disgusting, so he will never work on that hand again, ever."

The other boys, obviously his followers, seized my left arm as their ringleader commanded. Terror froze my body as I saw them pull my smeared hand closer and closer to my face. All I could do was squeeze my eyes shut from that nauseous sight. Suddenly, he raised his hand to make a sign.

"Hold it. I'll give him one more chance," he turned to talk to me for a bargain. "Prostrate yourself and lick my feet and beg. Maybe I'll change my mind and leave you alone if you beg hard enough. Now beg!" He raised his voice to a scream.

I managed to wrestle with all my force to set myself free from their fierce hug, but their hands were now on my throat, gripping and squeezing until I almost choked.

"Aha! This bastard is so damned stubborn. So, we'll have him taste my shit for extra punishment. Now, let's do it," he shrieked.

With wild, gleeful chortles, the two boys bent my smeared hand until it finally touched my face. The palm of my hand was now rubbing against my face repeatedly. That stench punched me so ferociously that I almost gagged. As they forced open my mouth and watched their chief approaching me with the stick coated with feces, ready to jab it into my mouth, a lump of nausea shot up my throat so forcefully that I had to let out my uncontrollable vomit. Whatever had left inside my stomach now exploded with all its force. With screams of disgust, all the boys shrank back, hastily dropping me to the ground.

Before I could scramble to my feet, they all had fled the scene and disappeared. They were aware that the tide was turning. After this, I could easily take revenge by tainting them with my repugnant hand. They left me alone to squat on the ground and went on emptying my stomach until nothing was left but the bitter-sour taste of bile in my mouth.

At one corner of my eyes, I saw a slight movement in the banana wrap those boys had left on the ground before they fled. It was lying open with Poon's feces inside. Terror seized me the instant I began to see the things that made the wrap move was a knot of pale pink worms wriggling and crawling inside his feces. Of all the creatures in the world, worms were the most terrifying, especially when these disgusting creatures came right out of someone's bowel through his feces.

I staggered home and flung myself into the canal, cleaning my body thoroughly. I threw my torn shirt, smeared with his feces and my vomit, into the water and watched the sluggish movement of the current carry it away from my sight. If my father questioned me about the bruise on my face and the sprain on my left hand, I decided to tell him I had clumsily slipped and fallen on my way home. It wasn't a lie, just a half-truth.

Since that day, I always carried my slingshot with me to school. No more whining. Like an abused dog at bay, dread and frustration could turn someone into a daredevil. I took great caution on my way to and from school. I walked every step so warily, my eyes alert, my ears perking, not a slight movement escaping my awareness. I could sense they always lurked somewhere nearby, behind a clump of trees or even on one of the tree branches, crouching and waiting like a claw of malicious panthers.

Once again, on my way home, as soon as I suspiciously heard a faint rustle behind a bush, a clay bullet flew from my slingshot. The bush squirmed once it hit a target, followed by a muffled cry. Then, some retreating footsteps. And finally, the dead silence. I stared at the slingshot controlled with my left hand in awe and disbelief. The sense of triumph was so overwhelming my whole body was shaken. At least I had let them know that I was not a chicken shit as they had assumed. I fought back and would fight hard. An eye for an eye if I had to. Papa once told me I had fought to the hilt for my breath in my grave the day I was born, so I survived as if a miracle had occurred. And so he named me *Pran*, meaning the breath of life.

The following day in school, I noticed a swollen bruise on the ringleader's forehead. It worked. At least a bump on his forehead kept him away from me for a while. A big bully like him would never tell other children what caused that big bump, and neither would I tell anyone.

I wanted to keep my brief victory secret to savor the sweet taste of vengeance alone, with no need to share it with the world and dilute its zest. For now, my retaliation had surprised him and made him shun. However, the tension stayed, and it kept me on my toes. Any time, any moment, they would gang up like a hungry hyena pack, ready to attack me once again.

As I became a grown man, whenever I recalled this traumatic episode, I realized that under some circumstances, children were always capable of committing cruelty beyond their presumed naive appearance. Once those primal instincts were triggered, they were not different from a pack of wild animals on their prowl. When they smelled the presence of any weaker child on their way, they ruthlessly jumped and pounced at him. School became their perfect hunting ground, and a weaker, less favored fell into their perfect victim. The only difference was animals hunted their prey for their sole survival, whereas children hunted for a far more sordid and darker purpose. Their purpose was to torture a weaker and defenseless child, physically, mentally, or both, so that they could see the pain and humiliation of their victim. The pain of others brought great pleasure and satisfaction to them. Children were adults in the making. No wonder why the world had to be what it always was since the first human being emerged.

Most of my classmates did it to taunt and bully me, but at least a few did it for fear of displeasing their teacher if they openly showed their sympathies to me.

A girl my age was seated in front of me. She sometimes sneaked some of her hidden candies to me after carefully craning her head to ensure no one had seen her. Her Chinese father owned a grocery store in the nearby market. Yue Liang—meaning 'The Moon'—was her Chinese name. For a girl, it took quite a brave heart to do that. Smuggling anything to eat in class, including food and candies, was strictly forbidden. If a student were caught red-handed, he or she would be spanked with a long and thick ruler, a girl on her palm, and a boy on his butt. We never had a chance to exchange words, but when no one saw us, Yue Liang would quickly turn her head to flash me a kind, sympathetic smile. She seemed to be my only ally in this small, hostile world. Every day, as our eyes met, we shared a secretive friendship with a hasty smile used as a code of camaraderie.

As little as it seemed, it became sunlight shining through a tiny crack in the icy cold, thick walls that were trapping me within. I felt warm and not alone anymore.

Whether or not I was too young, I told myself I fell in love with that big-hearted girl. Her rosy, round face with two long pigtails and deep dimples were on my mind most of the time.

But as far as I knew, any good thing only lasted briefly.

One morning, as the class was about to start, I sensed something had changed. Right before me, Yue Liang was seated so still, her posture stiff, her eyes fixed only on the blackboard, and all her attention focused on Kru Riam, who shot a sharp and infuriating glance at her occasionally. She apparently avoided my eye contact for the whole day, no matter how often I tried to signal her with gestures and my whisper.

The following day, she began to act in unison with the rest of the class. At first, with some embarrassment, she tried pretending she had never been aware of my presence in the class. By the end of the week, her transformation was complete. She could walk past me with her eyes so blank that it seemed my existence was not in her field of view.

I accepted that change with tears to shed from losing her for good. But in fact, I was not surprised. Yue Liang had no other choice. Poor girl, I couldn't blame her. Who dared to challenge a teacher whose word was law?

Another factor was added to this case. Using right hand for tasks like writing, was believed to bring auspiciousness to the owner. Therefore, the far inferior left hand was left entirely to handle dirt and impurities. Violation against this superstitious belief might result in bad luck and misfortune throughout one's life, they believed. Since using one's left hand on certain things was strictly forbidden or at least inappropriate for so many, once a left-handed child emerged in school, he would be coerced to convert to the right-handed by all means.

In severe cases, his left hand would be bound to his chair with a rope by a stern teacher, forcing him to use only his sacred one thoroughly. If he were caught using his left hand, the teacher would try to figure out the most effective way to punish him.

Pulling his fingers backward, bending them until tears from pain ran down his face was considered one suitable method. He must be possessed by a demon. He needs to be purified. The teacher would announce. Very few survived such a humiliation. Sooner or later, he would surrender. He would be reborn and emerge a right-handed child like the rest of humanity. The teacher's credentials accrued regardless of the inner damage she had permanently done to that child.

My father had rescued me from that kind of 'exorcism.' He had fought against that conviction, which was, in his view, based purely on superstition, only to pay a more costly price afterward. He won the battle over Kru Riam based on the scientific fact of the coordination between the brain and hands. I believed he must bring with him and show her some medical books printed in English, even though he knew she did not understand a word, only to prove this indisputable fact.

But it was me who'd lost the actual combat in my classroom. I became the Untouchable, no different from the one at the bottom of the Hindu caste system. By close contact, by sharing a meal and a roof, or more ridiculously, if an untouchable's feet stepped on the shadow of a higher caste person intentionally and accidentally likewise while they were walking past one another, the person of higher caste would be instantly contaminated and doomed by that untouchable's impurity. Consequently, the poor untouchable's life would be in grave danger in allegedly committing both a severe crime and an unredeemable sin.

I had sat at my desk, invisible and cut off from the small yet active world surrounding me, for almost a month as I waited for my father to enroll me in another school. Each day was nothing but the addition of unrelenting torment.

Then came the day when the gang of three found a new way to insult me, besides calling me a shit-eater. Now they recited a riddle every time they passed me.

Let's guess, who is he
Whose father is a wimp
Whose mother a whore
Himself a bastard to his core?
Let's guess, who is he?

My father wanted me to leave Kru Riam's place right after his failed attempt. He planned to enroll me in Bangkok's most prominent Catholic school, which he told me he had attended when he was young. However, I had to wait for approval from the administration staff, which took quite a while. Though he knew how frantic I felt with each passing day, he kept asking me to be patient, attend class, and hold on to that situation for my best benefit.

"Papa, now they start calling me Mr. Shit-Wiping Hand," I wailed. "I can't take it anymore, please Papa. Let me wait at home for a new school."

"If your hand is shitty, but your head is not. For me, that only counts."

"Why does everyone hate me? I wish..." I swallowed the sobbing, "I wish Mama could have come to bring me with her. Maybe no one will pick on me up there."

I suddenly broke into hysterical tears. And my breakdown startled me. At school, I tried to keep my composure in front of everyone. I walked tall and straight, plugging my vulnerability with my nonchalant and impassive face and lying to all of them as well as to myself that all the unfair and cruel treatment did not concern me in the slightest. Until that terrible feeling had come out and become the actual words, I had never been aware of how close I was to the hysterical outburst.

"I want Mama to bring me with her...Papa."

His face suddenly darkened. So, I stopped my whimper, too stunned to see his tears welling up his eyes. But before they ran down his face, he swiftly wiped them in time with the back of his hand. I had never seen his tears, not even once, so I threw myself into his arms in great alarm. We huddled and wept together, I loudly, he silently.

"Never say that again. Promise me," he crushed me onto his chest, his voice so strange it frightened me, "I won't let anyone take you from me, your mother or not."

After collecting himself, his voice became softened.

"Pran, don't hate anyone. You don't have to love everyone but don't hate any of them. You hear that?"

"But…they are so mean," I shivered, "they are all bad people out there, Papa. You have no clue how bad they—"

> *Whose father is a wimp*
> *Whose mother a whore,*
> *Himself a bastard to…*

I was glad he could not hear what was echoing so deafeningly inside my head.

I never expected to see him nodding, a defeated sign, he admitted, although grudgingly. He might still fear that accepting that fact would significantly impact and tear apart the eggshell wall defending his world.

"Yes, you are right," he managed a feeble smile, his face surprisingly saddened. "They are mean and vile… I know."

He lowered his voice to a whisper and seemed again absorbed in his thoughts. Our conversation suddenly lapsed into another long silence. He moved his gaze to a far distance through an open window, across the front yard, the tamarind tree by the fence, the canal, and far beyond, his eyes so bleak and his body slightly shuddering. I wondered who he was thinking of at that moment.

Oh! Who had ever harmed him? Terrifying him? Who had still deeply injured such a saintly person like him for so long? I wondered.

At least he admitted that bad people did exist.

After a long pause, he finally came back to me. This time,

he managed to hold his voice more steadily.

"Yes, there are bad and even evil people. But I want you to have gratitude for your life, that you were born a good human being instead of an evil one. Because a lot of them weren't. Instead of being outraged at them, you should feel guilty for having better chances than they do. Had anyone ever had his own choice before he entered this world, do you think he would have chosen to be a good or a bad one?"

"A good one, I think," I muttered darkly, yet my eyes clouded with doubt.

"That's why you're lucky. No one has a choice. They have to be what Fate has chosen for them. Perhaps Fate flipped the coin before each of us was born. If a head side turned up, you're lucky; if a tail, you're inevitably born evil." He chuckled at his imagery, but there was no amusement in his voice.

"Papa, what if you're wrong? What if bad people are instead the lucky ones?"

Now, I was thinking of Poon, the bad boy in the class who suddenly gave me that weird idea and an urge to slip it out. And at the corner of my mind, I couldn't help including one more, Kru Riam.

"Papa, bad people can do whatever they want, like hurting people, and they never feel bad about doing it. Aren't they lucky? But, oh my! I am not that lucky because though I really want to hurt someone, I feel bad to hurt him even though he deserves it. Just like indulging the bad to go on hurting people because he knows we won't hurt him back. Sometimes..." I gulped. "I wonder what's so good about being good."

It seemed what I said had stunned him. He kept staring at me, a strange expression crossing his face.

"Papa, is something wrong?" I was alarmed at his strange expression.

"Where did you get that idea from, the idea that bad people are lucky?"

"But aren't they lucky?" I whispered. I felt scared now at

his grim voice.

"Um…I know you try to explain to me that the good are born prisoners of their own mind while the bad are born free to roam everywhere and feel free to take everything from imprisoned people like us. Now, listen to me. Of all the creatures on Earth, only humans possess this unique quality. Can you guess what quality I'm talking about?"

"We are smarter, right?"

"No. I mean a quality that enables us to know right from wrong while all other creatures are guided only by their impulse to help them survive. Now, I'm talking about 'conscience'."

He went on with a more serious tone. He probably forgot that I understood less than half of what he was discussing with me, not to mention a grand word like 'conscience.' Poor Papa was desperate to share his insight into things with someone. But he needed someone his equal to discuss such a substantial topic with, not barely a seven-year-old boy like me. However, he had only me. So, I tried to please him by absorbing it at my best.

"I read that humans are the latest species that emerged onto earth. We are different from the other animals that appeared in this world earlier. It's because we are a single species that has developed a conscience, although animals' impulse still occupies parts of our brains. However, our consciences are just budding and need to mature more. But the main point is that the growth of the conscience differs for each individual. Many are still far behind others, making their minds somewhat close to the level of animals, which means they have little conscience or none. The worst is that those conscience-free men become dangerous to fellow humans like us. Because their primitive, animal-prone minds are covered by their human shells. There's no distinct sign to warn from their looks telling the difference between them and us. And this is why the good and the evil mix perpetually in this human race. The evil always takes, and the good always gives," he sighed. "Perhaps this is what we're meant for in the first place and will remain that way till the end of this human race. Or maybe this is a balance that is set for humans. Or maybe both good and evil have no values to begin with. Yes, you may be right, and I'm wrong… But what if you're wrong and I'm right."

He kept on, his face more and more saddened and despaired.

"No matter what, one thing is sure; everyone comes into this world with a mind and a body he never asked for in the first place…" he sighed deeply. "So, don't hate any of them. No one chooses who they become," mumbled him again as he closed his eyes to hide his tears. "Promise me you won't let these bad creatures set alighted your hate. Pran, they need our pity more than our hate. If I am not around one day, remember my words: hate doesn't destroy the hated as much as it destroys the hater. I know someone…whose soul was badly destroyed. No one did that to her. Only her own hatred destroyed her…" he was shuddering. "Someone who had once told me exactly what you just told me: conscience-free people are luckier because they are carefree to hurt anyone, while good people are perpetually paralyzed by their own conscience."

His voice was nearly inaudible now. He turned his head so I would not see his eyes. Yet I could feel his agony.

His sudden change started to intrigue me.

"Who is she you're talking about, Papa?"

He paused and then firmly shook his head.

"Oh! It doesn't matter. Just someone you don't know, and I'm glad you don't. But what matters the most is not begrudge anyone. Promise me. Now!"

After my firm promise made him more relaxed, my heart rebelliously shouted. *But they deserve my hate, Papa.* I vowed that no day would pass without my hate for anyone who deserved it.

At the end of that week, he withdrew me from Kru Riam's school after I'd finally decided to tell him that a group of bad boys in school called me a bastard. That word melted down his determination to see me staying in that place and learning to be more resilient and stronger. However, I skipped the worst part of what they had called Mama. I couldn't imagine its consequence if I ever let him know they called her whore.

"Papa, why does Kru Riam hate me? She encouraged the whole class to bully me. Why does my left hand bother her that much? Isn't it unusual?"

I saw a flash in his eyes. An instant later, it had gone, leaving his eyes relaxed and calm as ever. If he hadn't known why before, he must now have known the reason. But whatever he knew would never unfold to me. It seemed to be his way to solve any problem. He would shroud a mystery by adding a new one on top to cover it, heaping them up more and more until they grew into a staggering, unreachable height.

Was it possible that my father was really a wimp, a namby-pamby, as those bullies had made fun of him?

* * * * *

Part 1: Chapter 4

Skies Falling

I got accustomed to our way of life. I could recall never seeing a face from 'the outside' show up at our doorsteps, except for a few of our neighbors who came occasionally to play chess games with my father or to ask for a hand.

I didn't exaggerate to say we were living with almost no contact from the outside of our small world. Fortunately, my father had at least one company, Lek, who had regularly visited him since I could remember. My father never told me clearly about their relationship, yet I could tell how they were so fond of each other that they must have been good old buddies before I was born. Lek appeared to be the only fellow my father was close to and felt at ease to share most of his confidential and private matters with.

Not only was my father, but I was also looking forward to Lek's visits. When I knew from my father Lek was coming up that day, I would keep looking out from the veranda to be the first one to spot him.

If I saw a small sampan boat being rowed into view and

then pulled over at our plank bridge, I knew the instant later a man figure who stepped off that boat must be Lek. He usually hired someone in our area to give him a ride to our remote home, which took at least an hour along a narrow, winding canal that split off from the larger one.

When I spotted him, I sprinted up from the veranda, bustling with joy to greet him. Each time he showed up, he always brought me his 'custom-made' toy, which never failed to thrill and fascinate me.

To a small boy my age, those toys were the most miraculous things in the world—a top that kept on spinning until you had to make it stop or a miniature windmill made of dry palm leaves on a bamboo stick that created funny and rattled sounds while it was whirling cheerfully in the wind. And the most stunning of all, a small kite made from kite paper, cut in the shape of a butterfly and painted in riotous colors, fiery vermilion red, brilliant viridian green, and bright gold, glowing with rich radiance as it soared triumphantly across the sky.

Once Lek stepped into our threshold, he would glance around cautiously, looking for cracks in the wall to plug, broken steps to repair, or any earliest sign of damage that he could fix in time with his hammer and nails and all kinds of equipment in his box, which he always carried with him. Whenever my father had found a new hole in the roof while the sky was looking ominously overcast, all he could do was sigh mournfully and pray for our rescuer's appearance.

"Oh, I wish Lek could come today before we get soaked and start pneumonia. Oh, how I miss his magical hands. He has a way of fixing things while I never get the hang of carpentry work."

I did agree with Papa's lament. It was a puzzle how camaraderie between them ever occurred in the first place, let alone continued and even strengthened into the present day. For all I knew, they were completely different in so many ways, especially in their looks and characters. My father had a tall and slim body, with hands so soft and fingers so delicate they seemed unable to lift anything weighing more than a pen. I bet Lek could lift him with just one of his muscular arms and carry him on a shoulder as if my father were a small sack of cotton balls.

Lek, a couple of years older than my father, had a massive build and muscular body that contrasted to his benign face and candid smile, always ready to laugh at my father's stale joke. And since Lek was the person whom I was so fond of, only second to my father, I felt sorry not only for his unattractive, broad, flat face marked with pocks and pimple scars left from his adolescent years but also for one missing front tooth that was revealed whenever he laughed heartily. That might be the reason he remained unmarried.

On the contrary, even to the eyes of a small boy like me, my father was such a handsome male with naturally ravishing smiles and a refined, genteel-like demeanor. When he emerged from his secluded life on a rare occasion, such as joining an annual religious assembly in one of the local temples, all eyes from the group of girls always focused on him. He became the center of their attention as the most handsome male in that neighborhood.

They whispered. They marveled. They wondered. But no one seemed to know much about him. The bold and pretty ones approached him with flirty giggles and meaningful smiles to arouse his interest. Now and then, the most attractive girl in the neighborhood walked into our bungalow, paying a brief visit to Papa with goodies cooked for him, like grilled smoked fish or custard or rice cake, hoping to advance their relationship. But he always turned down their enthusiasm by remaining courteous and aloof, rarely paying particular attention to any of them.

So, they mocked him in return. They called him 'the ball-less ascetic' behind his back and just gave up on him. And yet, apart from his striking appearance, his strange remoteness, his complete detachment from all sorts of social life, and an air of impenetrable mystery that he usually carried with him never ceased to intrigue and enthrall girls.

Although they were only a couple of years apart in age, I always saw Lek shamelessly treating my father the same way a guardian pampered and doted on the child under his care. If my father started a cough in front of Lek or complained he was under the weather, the next day, Lek would show up with a whole bunch of herbal remedies, half begging and half coercing my father to take it promptly.

Yet, on the other hand, he oddly looked up to my father as if he were a priest or even a prince. Lek's tone when speaking to my father revealed respect as well as great affection. They seemed to lose themselves in untiring conversation for hours when they met. My father was always the performer, and Lek played an excellent audience.

I paid little interest in their conversation since all my attention at that moment was shifted to a brand-new toy Lek had made for me. I regarded their strong bonding with respect, but sometimes childish envy emerged. Papa did not belong to me alone. The affection he was supposed to give me whole had to be shared.

Lek usually stayed with us until late afternoon. Each time he left, my father would give him a boat ride, always bringing me along, and drop him off at a dense community at the mouth of the canal, which connected to the main river, Chao Phraya. From there, Lek would board a ferry heading to his Bangkok residence.

I had never been to Bangkok, located on the river's left side. Whenever we dropped Lek off, it was my only chance to glimpse the city from afar. But as far as my eyes could sweep across the broad Chao Phraya River, there were only countless floating houses on rafts calling a floating market clustered at the other side along the Bangkok busy quay. Beyond that point, it was unknown to me. However, life on the riverbed, with the slow movement of countless boats gliding up and down the sun-flickering ripples of water, fascinated me endlessly.

I'd come to see Lek off two weeks ago, seeing him ducking

his head under the ferry roof that was just about to carry him home. As I gazed at the panoramic view of the river, my father told me about the prestigious Roman Catholic school, which he would send me very soon. It was the all-boys private school run by the Catholic priest administration on the riverbank at Bangkok's side. But that school site was beyond the bend of the river. We were not able to pinpoint it from the spot we were standing.

Abruptly, he turned to me and asked.

"Are you ready for a field trip in Bangkok tomorrow, Pran?"

I was speechless for a moment because of the unexpected. Then I burst into an ecstatic cry: "Papa, do you really, really, truly mean it?"

"Of course, I'll bring you into the heart of Bangkok tomorrow for your excursion and adventure. Brace yourself for what you're going to see. I suggest you bring your spare eyeballs with you. You need more than one pair to observe and watch."

He put his comforting hands on my shoulder and smiled at me. Oh, how I adored him, my papa.

The night before the trip, my mind was so occupied with anticipation and thrill that I hardly closed my eyes and fell asleep. Finally came the sunny morning. We started the trip early by taking the ferry to the left bank of the river, where the hub of this country was situated.

My father looked sparkling in his new Chinese black silk trousers and white, crispy, long-sleeved, royal-patterned shirt. He carried the aura of someone extraordinary: a debonair genteel with even an air of aristocratic poise. Not a single young woman walking past us could resist the urge to steal a glance at him.

I had been overwhelmed with daze since the first step when we got off the ferry onto the busy pier, teeming and bustling with people from all walks of life and activities. But that was considerably insignificant compared to what was coming into my view.

As we started strolling on the street adjacent to the pier, I suddenly saw a gorgeous and modish-looking car running along the edge of our street. It was painted yellow and red, and its brown and white striped tarpaulin awning rolled down to shade the noon sun for boarding passengers. My jaw dropped at that sight.

"It's a trolley, Pran. And we're going to board it now for sightseeing," he told me, squeezing my hand in his exuberant mood.

I was so excited I couldn't keep my hands from being shaken.

He explained that the trolley was a newly invented vehicle run by electrical power fed by its overhead wire. A trolley pole connected the car with the above wire on the roof. One side of the street had a long, straight track built for the trolley.

We got into the trolley and were seated in the first-class compartment while a khaki-uniformed conductor stood up front operating the car. My father paid for our tickets for a ride to a ticket boy who was coming to collect our money. From time to time, the conductor stamped the floor to ring a bell underneath his feet to warn the passers-by, *Clank-Clank-Clank,* and the trolley picked up its speed. It was the most wonderful ride I had ever had.

The trolley route cut through the commercial district where modern European architecture buildings as high as four stories loomed alongside the bustling two-lane street. At the turn of the century, apart from the motor car, the electrical trolley, which some called a tram or a streetcar, was the most recent innovative vehicle introduced into the streets of Bangkok, in addition to the old-fashioned transports such as horse-drawn carriages and the rickshaws drawn primarily by immigrated 'China-men.'

We finally got off the trolley at the heart of downtown, lying within the old city wall. We happily strolled hand in hand along the sidewalk under the cool shade of mahogany trees lining the street.

"Brace yourself," my father said. "We are now entering…"

he paused and smiled as if I had become his accomplice, joining him into some mischievous adventure, "...the Road to Snobbery."

My father was right when he said I should bring spare eyes. That street where we had just entered and began strolling along lined up with a series of modern department stores at that period, mostly owned by German and English businessmen. I tried as best as I could to feast my eyes on numerous unfamiliar and lavish things behind display glossed windows alongside the street walk—from imported jewelry, clocks, and watches, silk fabric, crystal ware, fine porcelain, delicate bric-a-brac, western-styled men's and women's apparels to all kinds of exquisite furniture and appliance.

As we were about to walk past the grandest and most luxurious European department store, we had to stop and wait for a small group of women inside that exclusive store to stream out.

I saw two well-dressed ladies emerging into our view. One was older than the other. Yet they shared the same unmistakably calm and haughty bearing. A European gentleman, the store manager, held open the door. He bowed at these two ladies with excessive courtesy, waiting for the two of them to strut through the glass door. Another two inferior-looking women, presumably their maids, were trailing behind, trying respectfully to keep their appropriate pace close enough to their mistresses. One was carrying a heap of whatever merchandise the two ladies had shopped, another pushing a baby buggy with a cranky toddler boy sitting on it.

That little boy was struggling and howling at intervals at the top of his voice. He threw his brand-new big teddy bear doll in his arms to the floor and looked grimly satisfied to see his nanny scurrying to pick it up and promptly hand it back to him. Maybe that was the usual way for any rich child to enjoy manipulating people to move around his finger to get constant and unwavering attention.

The two ladies started their graceful gait toward a magnificent black motor car parked on the street under the shade of a mahogany tree in front of the store. They were followed by the maid with heavy packages in one hand, who quickened her pace to catch up with her mistresses. To protect both ladies from the glaring noon sun, she dropped the bags onto the ground and hurriedly opened a big white parasol so they could stay under its cool shade while they were waiting for someone in front of the store.

Another maid, the nanny of the little cranky boy, quickly adjusted the overhanging roof of the buggy for her little master before pushing the buggy into the open sun. Once a man inside that motor car, a chauffeur spotted them, he hastily got out of the car, ran to the other side, and hurriedly pulled open the car's door for the ladies to get inside as conveniently as he could do for them.

All the services for the two ladies by their attendants were done with flawless procedure and great care.

I looked on and kept staring at the group in awe and fascination. I knew watching people overtly was considered rude and poor manners. But this was the first time I had glimpsed at close range the rich—apparently the aristocrat class—and their superior air as they strutted past my father and me to their deluxe car. I marveled at the flowing grace of their movement. However, the two ladies seemed unaware of our presence or probably didn't care. They settled comfortably in the backseat of the car without glancing around, their eyes only straight to the direction ahead of them, their face nonchalant to the surroundings, and their look, the silent scorn toward the whole world.

The presence of these two ladies had intimidated me as much as it impressed and fascinated me. Their expensive perfume's rare and sweet scent still lingered in the air. I hastily inhaled that dreamlike scent before it was all gone.

"Where are we now, Papa?" I whispered.

"Oh, we're passing Batman and Company," he said after glancing at the store's front door. "Here, you can find whatever trendiest things recently imported from Europe."

Then he feigned a regretful sigh. "Well, if only we were millionaires..."

My father hardly paid attention to its extravagance, let alone the group of these elites in front of us. His eyes then switched to the direction of a nearby bookstore that sold foreign books and imported magazines. No, it's not because he felt humiliated and bitter compared to them. I knew he was uninterested in their superior presence.

Unlike me, I was now tremendously curious about what it was like to be immeasurably rich and how one would feel to spend one's whole lavish life in endless and carefree extravagance. On the contrary, all that my father and I could afford was to window-shop along those sprawling stores, which was nevertheless a feast of the eyes, dazzling enough for a mediocre boy whose most fanciful things he had ever laid eyes on were perhaps some hand-made wooden toy-cars Lek had given him.

Luckily, the magic of being young and uncorrupted still saved me. My eyes could still turn simple things around me into great wonders that almost had nothing to do with wealth or the lack of it. To be considered 'poor' hardly stirred bitterness as long as I had Papa and always felt the familiar warmth of his hand while holding mine.

Suddenly, one of the maids seated in the middle row of the car peeped out the window, and her eyes caught sight of us instantly. She turned abruptly to the older lady in the backseat and whispered to her mistress, causing that lady to turn her face immediately toward us.

I was so surprised to see the lady's abrupt change of expression. It jumped out on her face the instant her eyes swept across the direction of where we were standing and were ready to walk out from them.

I saw her gasping, her mouth opening as if about to let out

a choked cry. I did not know whether that sudden outburst sprang from her astonishment, fright, or raptures—or perhaps from a combination of all three. But she didn't utter a cry as I had expected. Her lips closed once again in self-possess, though they still uncontrollably quivered.

My father might have sensed that intense stare because he sharply turned his eyes toward her. As their eyes met, I felt my father's hand, loosely holding mine, suddenly turn clammy from cold sweat. His hand then clasped mine in a tightened grip.

The strangest expression I had ever seen started spreading to overshadow his face, so odd that I became near panic as I watched him. Their eye contact lasted perhaps only a split second, yet it seemed close to eternity in its extreme intensity, which was able to paralyze both of them temporarily.

Suddenly, the spell was broken. That lady abruptly turned her head inside the car, quickly resuming her poise and her usual impassive, stone-faced look. In the next instant, the car took off and was gone, leaving my eyes to follow that car in bewilderment until it turned left at the next crossroads and completely vanished from my field of view.

My father quickened his pace, half running from that spot as soon as the car was gone, bringing me in his tight grip. Apparently lost in thought, he kept walking and wearing that strange expression, seemingly oblivious to my presence, although his hand was still firmly on mine. We wandered down the sidewalk under the brazing sun without exchanging words until he seemed suddenly aware of my exhaustion from his aimless walk. The sunbaked sidewalk cement started to blister my feet through the soles of my shoes.

"Oh, my poor, poor little fellow," he cried softly as he knelt down and crushed me into him.

"Papa, what's…wrong?" I gathered all my courage and asked him in a half-whisper.

Perhaps the frantic look in my eyes brought him back to the present moment. His body began to relax, and his strange expression dissolved into the warm smile that I was so familiar with.

"Nothing, Pran," he spoke in a calmer and steadier voice. "Just some moment of embarrassment, not worth bringing up to ruin our day out together,"

"That haughty lady acted like…" I gulped. "Like she has known you, Papa. I believe you nearly gave her a heart attack when she turned her face and saw you."

"Oh, nonsense," he scoffed, rolling his eyes and shrugging. "She must mistake me for someone else she has known. That's all."

He rubbed my hair and said in his brighter tone.

"It always happens when you walk in a crowd. One time, a man screamed at my face and started to run. A minute later, he walked back and stared at me, still shaken and pale as a ghost. I asked him what was wrong. He then laughed nervously and told me that, at first glance, he thought I was his dead brother who returned from the grave to haunt him. Good grief!"

Of course, there he went again, spicing up the story to make it more like a joke. Yet, his answer of someone mistaking him almost convinced me. It was so plain that there couldn't be any tangible connection between an ordinary fellow like my father and those blue stockings in the luxurious motor car. Yet Papa's reaction to that lady who apparently lost her head at the sight of him still mystified me. But I saw no point in bringing it up while we had a good time together.

My father surprised me even more by nudging me into a delicatessen store nearby, where imported Western foods, dairy products, and cold cuts such as cheese, butter, fresh bread, bacon, cold-cooked ham, sausages, and turkey were sold. The sweet smell of freshly baked pastry and cookies agonizingly permeated my nostrils.

Inside, I tasted Western food for the first time. My father ordered our lunch, which consisted of cream of mushroom soup and ham-and-cheese sandwiches on sourdough. Our dessert was an immense scoop of rich and creamy vanilla ice cream served on the side with a blob of jelly as bright red as a ruby gem. There was a long counter at one corner of the store with a row of stools where we could perch on and savor every spoonful of such delicacy as though we were blue blood royals. I knew this stuff was far from cheap coconut milk ice, the imitation of ice cream sold by street peddlers.

The ice cream tingled my tongue with its delightful ice-coldness. I winced as it slowly melted in my mouth, giving me a pleasant chill.

"Ooh… Papa, I never taste anything so-o wonderfully cold. My tongue's as numb as a slab of stone now."

"You remind me of myself. I had never seen a lump of ice when I was about your age. I had heard water could become solid like a rock when extremely cold. The temperature has to be below zero degrees. But I still thought it was impossible. That's just a tall tale."

My father said abruptly and smiled. The ice cream might spark off some part of his childhood memory. I saw a flash of joy in his eyes.

"I remembered, as instantaneously as I put a small lump of ice into my mouth, I was so frightened I spat it out immediately. It felt like my tongue was on fire, the fire that burnt my throat with its unearthly cold."

"You didn't know the ice back then?" I believed he was joking because, to me, there was not a single thing in this world that he didn't know. But his voice carried a serious tone.

"Nope. But now, we even have ice factories right over here. No one thinks any more ice is as bizarre and otherworldly as it was decades ago. But when I was very young, ice had to be delivered from Singapore on a big ship. They had to be covered with sawdust to keep them from melting, and not all children had the privilege to taste, let alone to glimpse—"

I longed for more details of his childhood story. But as abruptly as he started, he stopped that subject and resumed eating his ice cream in silence, absorbed in his thought that was impenetrable to me.

"Only the rich were able to taste the ice back then. Right, Papa?"

My father nodded absentmindedly. Then he laughed and rubbed my head.

"And you are going to say I must be rich because I knew how the ice tasted. Am I right, smart boy?"

Now, I knew no matter what, I could not outsmart him.

Some minutes had passed, and slowly, my father said reflectively.

"How about taking a visit to Lek on our way back? It's good that you'll know where he's living. It's not far from here."

"Yes, Papa, let's go now," I complied with his suggestion without hesitation.

After our wonderful lunch, he hired a rickshaw to where Lek was living. It was the first time as well that I had a ride in a rickshaw pulled along by a middle-aged scrawny Chinese coolie.

By then, I had forgotten entirely the brief episode in front of that sumptuous store. We were heading to the Chinatown quarters. It was one of Bangkok's most bustling and populated areas, where the overseas Chinese immigrants had settled down and been doing their flourishing business for generations. But those new arrivals, like the rickshaw man giving us a ride, had to take any labor work to survive.

Finally, the rickshaw brought us into a narrow and rundown alley, bursting with Chinese coolies wobbling in and out of the nearby warehouses, with a heavy hemp sack loaded with rice grains carried on their shoulders, their bodies squirming from ache and exhaustion from the sack's enormous weight. Their naked back was soaked with sweat as the sun continuously grilled their scrawny body.

I was stunned by that pitiful sight. Before we came, they had walked in and out several times incessantly, balancing a heavy burden on their backs.

"Papa, why are very few born rich, but so many aren't?"

"Honestly, no one truly knows why," my father replied with his exaggerated sad expression.

"Even you?" I cried in disbelief since, to me, he always knew every existing thing.

"Yes, including me," he corrected. "So, the best we can do is to cling to the answer we want to believe. Most of us, the Buddhists, choose to believe in *Karma*. The consequences of what we did in the past will follow us to shape our present, like our shadow that never stops following us. Probably, that sounds logical enough compared to other beliefs."

"What are other beliefs?"

"The non-Buddhists believe it is God's will, and so be it. Men can't question or say no to whatever God has done for them. But a reason why God works this way or that way is beyond men's comprehension."

"But…how come God put those people to work all day in the killing sun? Can God make a mistake?"

"If you have only a single drop of water, how can you turn a desert into a sea? Show me."

He went on when I kept quiet. "This is called *Ajintai.*"

"What?" There he went again with some strange term.

"That term refers to something beyond our human capability of conceiving and understanding. The worst thing is that *Ajintai* things are surrounding us everywhere. Ironically, we were born into a world still so unknown to us and yet call it our home."

Still, the farther that rickshaw trudged down the alley, the more disheartened I felt.

It carried us past low, shabby, wood-boarded row houses lining the alley's length. A narrow ditch with filthy, dark water and floating garbage ran parallel to those shelters. As we approached nearer, the stench from the polluted water began to disturb my nostrils. I couldn't guess whether it bothered my father because his face reflected no repulse. I never had any idea this dark and dingy neighborhood was indeed the place where Lek had settled himself.

At the end of that blind alley, a small row house Lek had been renting came into view.

Two stray dogs crouched nearby began to bark fiercely at us after the rickshaw had pulled over and let us climb down. The dogs stopped their barks. They were now growling and snarling in their throat as soon as they sensed we were about to walk past them. I cried out, mortified, but my father pressed his finger on my lips and said in his calm voice.

"Pran, don't move or shout at them. In their eyes, we are trespassing on their territory. And they are right. Let them check on us to prove we come in peace, and they will let us go."

What did he think of those dogs? The patrol guards? However, I stood rigid and immobile as he told me. The dogs rushed to us as if they were about to charge. But since we stood still, they stopped short and sniffed feverishly at us.

"Good dogs. You good dogs," he kept staying unmoving, but he started talking to them in his friendly and casual tone. "How about giving us a warmhearted welcome?"

Finally, our innocence was approved. The dogs gave in and retreated to where they lay crouching earlier, completely ignoring our presence.

My father surprised the rickshaw coolie with a generous fare and even thanked him profusely for giving us a ride as if it was a free trip. Of course, in exchange for some meager money to earn his living, my father felt that the poor soul had to sweat blood to service his passengers as if he weren't a human but a working horse. I knew what he had seen a moment ago in those warehouses moved him more profoundly than it did to me.

Beneath my father's vulnerable and fragile appearance, he had nerves of steel to relieve those struggling with their misfortune, regardless of the limit of his capability. My father always overlooked that he was barely better off than those he believed needed his charity. Had he somehow owned one million in his pocket, I thought he would have feverishly spent them on those poor souls and become penniless just overnight as a result of his bleeding heart. No one could change him. He stayed true to what he was born into until his last day.

When he saw us, Lek emerged from the door like a dog with two tails. Of course, he didn't expect to see us showing up at his door right into the heart of the slum where he was living.

"Good heavens! You two here," he shouted excitedly. "I heard my dogs barking but never dreamt it would be you."

"Your dogs?" asked my father in his amused tone.

"Well, actually, they are stray dogs, but whenever I have some leftovers from my meal, I feed them. Otherwise, they'll go hungry for days on end. So, they claim I've owned them and watch the house for me. But they should have more sense that nobody comes, thief or not, in this place."

"They are good dogs, Lek. They guard you and your property. If Pran doesn't have the problem with his chronic asthma, I want him to have a dog, too."

We went inside his room, which was dark and cluttered, with mess and junk at every corner. This surprised me because he would put all his efforts into keeping it as tidy and clean as he could in our bungalow.

"Oh, let me check how much weight my Baby Boy has gained since last seen."

It became a ritual every time we met to check my growth. He would toss me onto his shoulder and shake me until I was breathless from laughing.

"Let me go! I can't breathe. Let me go, now," he expected me to resist by screaming out. So, I screamed my head off to please him.

"Oh, no! You're still a bag of bones. Why? When I shook you up, I heard only your bones cracking," Lek exclaimed. "If you promise me next time I see you, you will fatten yourself more, I'll show you right now something that will guarantee to take your breath away."

The word 'something' was music to my ears. "Yes, yes, I promise. I'll eat up a whole elephant to please you if you want."

"Now, squeeze your eyes shut and count to three. And don't ever think about cheating me!"

I was taken aback when I opened my eyes again and nearly jumped. What was dangling from his arm was unmistakably a snake—a sinister, grayish-brown, three-foot-long reptile.

Lek was grinning. It must be his pride to make me jump out of my skin.

"Tsk, tsk. Can't you tell a fake snake from a real one?"

He plopped that snake onto the floor, letting me carefully examine it with half suspicion and awe. At a closer look, I saw that it was actually made of small, lightweight pieces of wood smoothly shaped in a cylinder; each piece was joined together through a string three feet long. What amazed me was when I put that crafted snake onto the floor and shook it by its tail, the body of the snake wriggled and coiled as if it were alive.

Moreover, the glossy grayish paint on its wood body rendered a slime-like appearance, as seen on a real reptile's skin. Lek even brought more life into that thing by painting a detail of a small white circle-shape on the top of its head. My squeals made my father poke his head out of the kitchen door. He had gone inside to put some street food he had bought on the way for Lek.

"There you are again, spoiling my brat."

Did Lek spoil me? I wondered. Papa always ignored the fact that the one Lek always spoiled should rather be him.

"A monocled cobra!" my father stared at my new toy in mild surprise. "Look so-oo real! You have a golden touch in craft, Lek. But, no, we don't want *more*, real or fake. Don't you know my place's teeming with these creatures? Last week, I found one coiling at our doorstep during a heavily rainy night. I wish you could see the moment he lifted his head off the ground, flattened out his neck, and swayed as if in dancing, almost touching my fingertip and then hissing at me to exert his dominion over my own place. What a flowing grace of his movement! His hood was flaring, not different from the one we see in the crown of an ancient Egyptian pharaoh. And I saw an unmistakable white monocle mark, the cobra's signature!, on his gray head as plain as day. What a majestic and enigmatic creature! Anyway, even the most lethal reptilian, like a cobra, needs some comforting shelter when it's cold and wet out there."

"You should get rid of that beast right away. It almost bit you. It didn't deserve your mercy."

Of course, Lek couldn't help wincing. His concern was clouding his eyes. Though he got used to my father's exaggerated way of spicing up all his stories, he couldn't deny there was a grain of truth in it. Lek lived alone in this bustling and rundown area in Bangkok, renting a shabby row house and earning his living as a hired carpenter. Rats, roaches, and mosquitoes from the filthy ditch were the daily problems he had to deal with first-hand, but never snakes and vipers.

"Pran must be the one who needs to be warned, not me," protested Papa amusedly. "I'm sure he must open the door one day and invite those creatures to come in. Why! He desperately needs some snakes to drag geckos from our bungalow for their dinner,"

He then laughed heartily.

"Ewww…" I cried in disgust. "Gecko's skin gives me goosebumps. They have gross white speckles all over their knotted skin."

My skin crawled as I mentioned the hideous-looking domestic reptiles living under our roof, nestling on the house beams. They looked like lizards, only bigger and more hideous, threatening looking. I rarely saw those geckos during the daytime, for they always cozily hid at some dark corners. But at nightfall, they came out to hunt for moths and insects, crawling across the ceiling as comfortably as we humans walked on the floor, their bloodshot eyes goggling as big as saucers, their shrill cries echoing repetitively in the dead of night as I trembled on my bed, listening with dread to their sinister coarse voices. Children believed that if a gecko jumped on you, it would stick and cling to your skin for life unless you had to eat three bowls of duck poops and drink three big jars of water.

My father knew how terrified I was of their presence, yet he never thought of poisoning those ugly creatures as some people did. He said these poor things took up so little room in our house and even helped rid bugs and flies as if it were a way to pay our rent. His lecture would surely follow that; this world was neither our living room, the ocean, our tubs, nor the woods, our backyard. I needed to learn to live in harmony with others because each creature was born for its own purpose rather than to serve humans' whim.

"Don't be too worried, Lek," my father said. "Those poor snakes bite in self-defense. They bite because they're frightened of men, which I admit they have a good reason for. Those poor reptiles are capable of sensing human's malicious nature. They don't bite because they enjoy biting us. On the contrary, it's us who enjoy slaughtering them just for fun. You can't ignore this fact."

Like me, Lek seemed no longer surprised by my father's peculiar perspective. He just rolled his eyes in defeat and abruptly switched the course of conversation to something else.

"So, how's your little one going along?"

"I've already enrolled him in that Catholic school where I used to attend. He's waiting to attend next month," my father proudly announced the news to Lek, who turned to beam at me. Then he frowned.

"So, he has to make a trip via ferry. Are you sure he's able to?"

"In the first week, I plan to drop him at school and pick him up after. Oh, he's a big boy now. He can take good care of himself."

"Don't worry, Lek," I chimed in. "If the ferry turns over, I know how to swim. I can even help carry any old passenger across the river to safety."

I nodded vigorously to convince Lek, but what followed my bragging was a burst of laughter from both of them.

"As long as he has a good education for years to come, there won't be anything else to worry me about," said my father.

"That's excellent news for him and you as well. You will have more time for yourself, like finding a prestigious job and thinking of…" Lek paused and then continued cautiously, "…thinking of turning over a new leaf." He paused once again and lowered his voice. There was a beseeching tone in it. "I know you can find some perfect girl as quick as lightning if you only show more enthusiasm."

My father chuckled softly.

"Have you ever heard an old saying; a crippled carrying a humpback? Before telling me to find some girl, you'd better show me how to. Let's see. Try to find one for yourself first,"

He smiled at Lek, his eyes glowing warmly.

"I know. I know your concern. I'm fine, Lek, as long as I have my Baby Boy and you."

Lek swallowed a lump in his throat and quickly turned away from my father, but not before I saw him choking back his tears.

The pair must be the best sample of 'an odd couple.' Their looks are the opposite of night and day. But their comradeship and bonding were more vital than if they had been born blood brothers.

By the time we left Lek's place, it was late afternoon. The snake toy proved to be quite a burden to carry along all the way home since my father had to bring a few books he had earlier asked Lek to buy for him as well. Lek promised to bring it with him for his next visit. But my father, upon catching me lingering on the toy longingly, finally decided to put that snake toy in his bags and took it home.

We rode on another rickshaw and boarded the trolley back

to the same pier. While on the ferry, the western sky flushed deep pink, fiery red, and golden orange, gilding the river bed with the last ray of light before sunset. The ferry cut the slow current toward the other side of the river bank, where the towering spire of the Temple of Dawn stood in silent majesty, erected and conspicuous in silhouette against the backdrop of glowing twilight sky, so awe-inspiring to all eyes.

"Did you enjoy today, Pran?" While the ferry was carrying us in midstream, my father put his hand on my shoulder as we watched and marveled at the most beautiful sunset, the breeze from the river flowing softly past us.

"I will never forget today, Papa. Never! We're so, so, so happy together, right?"

"Yes, we are. We really are," that was all he said, but every word carried the perfect meaning. I leaned my head against his shoulder as he pulled me closer to him, and we watched the forlorn sunset together in silent rapture.

When we walked from our plank bridge toward the bungalow, it was already late at night. Since this was a moonless night, the clumps of trees and bushes looked like dark blots, the ground still soaked with last night's rain. In utter silence, bullfrogs croaking from shallow rain pools scattering around the bungalow echoed into my ears like rumbles of thunder, their perfect time to call for their mates.

All around us was pitch dark, but at least we were familiar with our walk home. My father had to take extra care to prevent himself from stumbling and tripping over the slippery ground because he had to balance the weight of his heavy bag, which he was carrying on his shoulder.

The high and jolly spirit during our day out still stayed with us. My father merrily whistled the tune of the national anthem, the only song he could whistle and sing, as he led the way, marching toward the bungalow while I followed him and sang along at the top of my voice.

Glorious Siam
Our golden motherland…

While we were moving up the plank steps to the veranda, my father's bag slipped from his shoulder and tumbled down onto the ground with a loud thump six or seven feet below us. I was about to climb the steps to help him pick it up from the ground below the bungalow. But he told me he would do it himself, and I would instead go straight up to the veranda and turn on the electric light for him instead.

The light from the light bulb flooded that small area and helped us better see the ambient surroundings. My father bent himself close to the ground, his hand reaching out and groping for that bag. Suddenly, he shouted at me.

"Look! I spotted your snake."

From where I stood on the veranda above him, my eyes followed his finger and saw that toy thing. Over there, it was dimmer. Although the light from the veranda barely reached that spot, I could see the toy he pointed at. It was thrown off the bag and flopped down on the ground a few yards from the stairs. My father dropped himself to the ground level. He squatted, his hand swiftly grabbing that toy. Suddenly, I heard him laugh softly. That laughter carried a tone of surprise.

"Hey, who has ever thought Lek could make his snake that real?"

"What, Papa?" I asked.

"Well, I can't believe his snake just bit me," my father said humorously. He then chuckled. "It's so funny. I grabbed it, and I felt it resist my hold and strike me right on my neck."

"How come? It's just—just impossible," he must be joking with me as he loved to when he was in his jolly mood. It was too absurd to think otherwise.

"Yes, I did feel a twinge, like a sharp needle pricking my neck. What—"

I jumped to the ground in a flash and found him bending on

his knees, his hand holding his neck, his face starting to contort as if in pain and confusion. As I rushed to him, he looked at me in bewilderment. His eyes showed me he didn't believe what he had told me either.

My gaze swept the spot where he was kneeling but found nothing.

"Where is that toy you said, Papa? I don't see it."

"It's just gone..." he said in his perplexed voice. "I know it sounds too bizarre. But I don't imagine things. The pain is real." He made a slight grimace as he rubbed his neck.

Not far from him, I spotted that bag which was now sprawling behind one of the house slits, close to the spot where Papa hung his hammock. I darted to grasp and shake it to force out whatever was still inside.

As my snake toy emerged from that bag in my hand and fell, it moved and wriggled, resulting from the force of impact as it hit the ground. Then it lay motionless, as dead as the piece of wood should be. My father's gaze froze on that thing for one long minute before his eyes slowly turned to me.

We exchanged glances in silent shock.

I'd never forgotten the expression slowly creeping into his face as he began to grasp what was happening. That expression would imprint in my memory till the day I died.

He realized that he had grabbed the wrong snake.

"The one that's just bitten me... I swear... In the dim light, it just looked...exactly like the snake toy in this bag."

Suddenly, he crushed me to his chest, his voice suddenly calm, so dead and calm it seemed not his own but of someone whom I'd never known in my life.

"You remember how to get to where Lek is living, right? Go to his house first thing tomorrow morning," his trembling fingers fumbled into his shirt pocket and fished out a small set of keys. "Put it in your pocket and give it to him. Tell him to use one of the keys to open the top drawer in our bedroom and look inside. He will know what to do after that."

Why was he ordering me to do this? I felt my blood freezing with acute fear.

"No, Papa, no…" I croaked. "I'm going immediately to get some help from our neighbors. You'll be safe in no time."

I started to dash out at that instant, but he stopped me.

"The bite is on my neck, too close to the heart. I know I'm not going to make it to the medical station. The trip takes too long. Just leave me here and stay with one of them tonight. You aren't safe to be alone in our house. You hear me?"

"I'll never be alone. I have you, Papa." I shouted back and disappeared into the dark.

When I returned to him about five minutes later with two of our nearest neighbors, my blood suddenly turned to ice at that startling sight.

I found my father sprawling face down on the spot where I had left him, his whole body going limp as if he were heavily drunk. When he heard our footsteps, he tried to lift his head, but I could tell it took tremendous effort to shift any part of his body. His breath was also coming out harsh and irregular. I rushed to support him in my arms.

Under the bright light from the lantern one of my neighbors had carried with him, I had never seen his face so swollen and feverishly redden. A streak of saliva started running down from a corner of his quivering mouth.

I threw myself on my father and began to wail hysterically. Then, I felt my neighbor's two strong hands pulling me away from him.

"Don't panic, son. You're making things worse. Move over and let me help him."

One of them raised his lamp and looked closer at my father's wound on his neck. He also tried to open his half-closing eyelids to check my father's condition.

"Holy Buddha, it's as plain as day he was bitten by a cobra. That paralyzing symptom!" One of my neighbors whispered in utter horror.

"Yes, he is," another confirmed and shuddered as if in a sudden cold. "Last year, my uncle was bitten by a deadly Pit Viper. Within an hour, he died in a pool of blood from his massive hemorrhage. Blood leaked from all openings on his body like hell. I prefer a cobra if there's a choice."

"Please help him, please... Don't let him lie there." I howled.

They told me they would bring him to a new medical station in Bangkok as fast as possible. At that particular place, my father would receive the injection of cobra venom antiserum, the new treatment for snake-bitten victims recently introduced by the local Red Cross. But it would take nearly an hour to get there by boat.

Besides, the bite wound was on his neck. If the bite were located on an arm, a leg, or a lower body part, it would be much better because they could more or less help slow down the venom from spreading into the central bloodstream by wrapping a piece of cloth above and below the bite wound. But in my father's case, the tight wrapping would instead strangle him to death.

"He could die in an hour or even less. So, we must be faster than hell."

So, two more men in the neighborhood were called immediately for emergency extra help. They hastily carried him into a big flat boat, his head snuggling on my lap while the rest joined together, rowing and rowing with all their strengths to race him to the destination. Under the furious sweep of the oars, the boat speeded through the seemingly infinite canal length with the speediest motion it could ever attain.

It was pitch dark everywhere except on some of the shrubs and bushes along the banks, which eerily shimmered with clusters of blinking lights from fireflies, adding an eerie, surreal atmosphere. There mustn't be a moment to lose. The boat moved at raging speed against the chilly night breeze. But because of the utterly tormenting hope, I felt as if I were being licked by the flame that was burning me alive.

"You keep slapping his face. Don't be afraid of hurting him. Do it real hard. Just do whatever to keep him awake and still stay with us. Do it! Do it!" one of them kept screaming at me.

This couldn't be real. I was sure now I must be in the midst of dreaming because all sorts of things that did not make sense occurred only in dreams, mocking the rule of reality with its complete absence of logic. That could explain why I found myself out of place in this boat, facing this unimaginable terror.

If I pinched myself hard enough, perhaps it could startle me awake. I would doubtlessly find myself lying instead on my bed as the day was breaking, my ears beginning to hear the clamor from a flock of cuckoo birds calling each other among tree branches outside the bedroom window and my eyes slowly opening to see actual reality—seeing my father still sleeping soundly and peacefully by my side and if I just stretched out my hand to tickle his hairy underarm, he would no doubt jerk his eyes open immediately followed by his startled crabby cry—*Ouch! Stop bugging me. Stop!* But when I gritted my teeth and braced myself to peer down, I heard my own voice immediately rising in a terrified scream.

"Help!! My father's choking!" I wailed frantically. "Can someone do something? He can't breathe now. He can't…"

"The venom makes his breathing passage so swollen it is blocking his breathing…and we're still halfway to that station," one of them said quietly with a grim look. Then he groaned and prayed in his shrill voice. "Oh, Yama Raj, Lord of Death, please spare him. He's pure and sinless; there's no reason to take him away. Please…let him live… Oh, Lord Mara, stop giving people suffering… "

At that most terrifying moment, I saw the worst written on all those faces. Their gaze froze on my father, who began to utter sounds from his throat that were almost unintelligible to everyone in that boat. He tried a few more times but was still with no success. His voice was at times cut with a pause of prolonged shuddering spasms. Yet, his effort to speak to me was so ardent. I battled a wave of horror, bent down, and strained my ears with all my effort to listen intently.

Something utmost important to him he needed to, had to, and must tell me.

"Promise...find...f...for...m...me...why...w..."

I was holding my breath until I just couldn't anymore.

"Why...we...suf...suffer...why... find it—"

He finally managed to force out his last broken words through convulsing lips. Yet, so much unsaid was left to be figured out and understood because that last wish was unfinished.

Oh, Papa...what do you need me to find for you? What is it? What in the world?

Then he lapsed into a coma. It felt like an eternity as I was helplessly watching my father dying on my lap.

* * * * *

Part 1: Chapter 5

Ashes and Fire

*A*nicca, Dukkha, Anatta,
   None ever lasts
   None brings thee true happiness
Since none is real
Nothing ever belongs to thee, not even thy breath
What thou borrow shall soon return to their origins
And that is Dhamma—
The true nature of all existence
To reach Nirvana
The ultimate serenity in one's state of mind
Thou let go of what thou desperately attach to
Liberate thyself from possessions, passions, and illusions
All created from what thou perceive
Through thy deceptive senses
Of sight, sound, smell, taste, touch, and thought
Coming from the eyes, ears, nose, tongue, body, and mind
One whose soul is enlightened
By freeing oneself from greed, aversion, and delusion
And embraces this ultimate truth

Shall suffer no longer
One who believes otherwise
Shall remain a blind
Living in infinite darkness and suffering, he shall
Yet, neither from the punishment of the Almighty
Nor of any supernatural wrath
But from his self-deception
Caused by his blindness to this truth
Tathata.

In a dreamlike state, voices droned in my ears. Movements passed my eyes in the form of waves and shadows, weightless and insubstantial, until I became aware of someone's hand nudging me and shaking me harder. All diffuse voices gradually became more distinctive, and all vague forms and shapes became more tangible.

In my full awareness, my ears began to pick up the chanting of Abhidhamma Sutta from a row of saffron-robed monks echoing in bleak harmony inside the temple's funeral hall. My blurred vision started to focus on my father's wood coffin, which was placed a few feet in front of my seat, surrounded by white, fragrant flower wreaths. A ribbon of smoke from incense curled slowly, as if mourning for him.

And yet, this present reality seemed to belong to someone else.

The person who had shaken me into awareness was Lek. He now silently seated himself on my left. Since the day of my father's death, which to me was still more a dream than reality, he had come to keep me company and rarely let me out of his sight.

He didn't try to console me with all kinds of sympathetic words with which I had been showered incessantly by others and hence hardly carried any significant meaning. He only kept me by his side during the funeral ceremony and made sure that I would not lapse deeper into a void of loss.

Seeing that exquisitely carved wood coffin, I found no words to describe this state of mind I hadn't known existed. But since it came to crush my whole being at this very moment, another terrifying thought followed. With such staggering loss, how could I endure each hollow hour for each day, which stretching infinitely before me?

The four men who tried to save my father's life were sitting in the far corner. My father's death was spread overnight to all my neighbors, and everyone promptly came to the funeral and crowded the hall. All of them offered help and money. Despite my father's remoteness, I felt a little better to witness how well-liked he was. One of the four even extended his help to go to Lek and bring him here as I had asked.

Amid the performance of profound prayers, there was some stirring movement at the hall's entrance.

I turned my head in that direction and watched someone leading a small group of strangers along the aisle toward the front. The group leader was a limping elderly man in his late seventies, wearing a woven peacock feathers hat and walking with the support of his walking cane, whose handle was made of solid gold. On his side stood an elegant middle-aged lady exquisitely dressed in black silk.

Everyone hushed one another at their presence, causing the large hall to fall into eerie silence for a moment. While that elderly dignified man and those following him were walking past them in superior and austere bearing toward the armchairs at the first row, most guests in the hall bowed their heads and folded their hands to them as a gesture of courtesy and high respect. And as instantly as the elderly man and the middle-aged lady were quietly settled in their seats, the whispers behind them started like a swarm of buzzing bees. And this time, there seemed to be nothing that could hush them. Obviously, this dignified, elderly man became the center of all attention.

As this group of strangers came into plain sight, I had never seen Lek look more nervous, almost panicking. But when he turned to see me watching him in wonder, his face became more controlled and composed. He asked me in a low whisper to go to that elderly man and prostrate myself at his feet as humbly as possible.

"Who is he?" I whispered back to him in a growing puzzle. "Why did he come to…" I gulped, forcing the outburst of tears, "To…Papa's funeral?"

He hushed me. "I'll tell you later. But now, please do what I said."

I sensed the desperation and urgency in his voice, so I did as he said. The old man's eyes fastened on me when I crouched on my elbows and knees at his feet, my eyes downcast to the floor. My legs were shaken terribly because of the hawk-like expression piercing from his deep sockets.

The elderly man looked frail and thin due to his old age and prolonged illness. Yet, that external appearance seemed unable to deceive who he indeed was, which was vibrating from his eyes. They were the most powerful eyes that could pierce the heart of the world. He beckoned me to come closer to him.

"Are you Ananda's child?"

His voice tore from his throat, followed by his uncontrolled coughing and wheezing. Intimidating as he appeared, he could not conceal the physical weakness gripping him now. The middle-aged lady rushed to support him, but he waved her away indignantly.

I stammered, feeling like a ground mouse wriggling in the pouncing claw of a sky hawk. I collected all my courage to reply to him. Yet my voice was no better than a whisper.

"Yes, sir…"

"Look up. Let me see your face closely," he commanded. And I did immediately as I was ordered.

I wanted to shut my eyes so desperately to avoid his stern glare while he was scrutinizing me, up and down, several times. Then, he began to look into my eyes with a steady gaze. I didn't think they were eyes now, but a sharp cleaver was feverishly working on me, splitting open layer upon layer of my body and cutting it into smaller and smaller parts with the efficient skill of a butcher. Yet I was too mortified even to flutter my eyelids or draw my breath while his eyes were working on me that way. It was a torturing moment that seemingly lasted for eternity.

Suddenly, I heard a soul-piercing shriek that startled me to such a degree that I couldn't help uttering a wincing cry.

"Get out! Get out of my sight, you bastard!"

I was taken aback by the old man's sudden fierce attack, which I had never expected to hear from him. I had no clue of the eruption of his rage. He was so old. Perhaps this was a sign of senility that abruptly caused his head to muddle up. As he screamed, his entire body shook with the force of his rage. Oh, his eyes; they could burn me alive with that pure pulsing hatred. Now, I looked into his eyes with dread mixed with fascination.

With feeble strength, he clutched his walking cane, leaned against his armchair, and raised it right over my head. I raised my arm over my head instantly to protect myself. But in utter shock, I saw his hand suddenly stop in midair, letting go of his walking cane. And before it crashed down my head, it slipped from his hand and thumped on the floor.

He gasped, slumped in his seat, and collapsed amid frightened screams from all the guests who were attending my father's funeral.

The chaos immediately interrupted the whole funeral ceremony. The old man's limp body was carried out in haste to lie down on a large carpet in front of my father's coffin. The lady who had accompanied him bent down her head, her ear on his chest. She suddenly burst into shuddering hysterical sobs as she crouched on the floor, hugging him fiercely. She whispered something into his ear before stretching out her trembling hand to close his still wide-open eyes. It was apparent that his breathing abruptly stopped from an acute heart attack while his eyes were still wide open, still gazing at me with all the hatred he possessed.

Lek was the one who pulled me out of that turbulent scene, for I was too shocked to move.

"Now, you go back and prostrate yourself at his feet one more time to give him a farewell,"

Lek paused and then decided to go on.

"He's the father of your papa. Please don't ask me more. Just do it. We'll have the rest of the time to discuss this later."

I was thunderstruck, way, way too stunned to pick out any essence in his speech. Slowly, my brain began to register. Then I cried out, still in a whirlpool of confusion, disbelief, and shock.

"You mean he's…" I shuddered, "…my grandfather?"

Lek looked at me gravely. Then, he slowly nodded to me.

"Just go to him," he repeated tonelessly.

Hundreds of questions began to swirl in my head, but Lek firmly shook his head and nudged me to go to him.

As I prostrated myself at the old man's feet, this time, I had the courage enough to steal a glimpse of his cruel, lifeless face. At the close-up, I could see my father's young face superimposed on that old wrinkled one. How amazing, indeed, that father and son were so resembled in their countenance and yet so different in their soul, like the eyes of a hawk and of a fawn taking turns to lay claim to the visage of the same person.

But once that early middle-aged lady caught sight of me, she stopped dead. Her eyes turned into something more frozen than lumps of ice itself. She seemed temporarily oblivious to her own grief as she raised her voice to call Lek, the tone in her voice authoritarian and disdainful with a mix of resentment. They both must be familiar with each other to some degree.

"Nai Lek, take that boy out, now. I said *now*! And don't ever let him come near the lord again."

Something in her look suddenly stirred my vague memory. Have I ever met her before? That sudden thought was so strong I scarcely paid attention to her harsh reaction. Her look was unmistakable. Like a flash of déjà-vu. But where? When? And how? Another wave flashed in my head, with my father's strangest expression on his face floating, followed by another and another relevant image until all the scattering pieces fit together.

I remembered her now with perfect clarity.

She was the same haughty lady seated in that magnificent motor car in front of the European store where my father and I had come upon the very same day he had lost his life.

Lek and I stayed behind when all the neighbors were gone that night. At the funeral pyre in that temple, we stood to watch my father's coffin lowered into a small furnace room for cremation. The pulsing heat from the open furnace door permeated the skin on my face. I heard the crackling sound of fire, so I stole a glimpse through the half-open metal door. In terror, I saw tongues of flame greedily engulfing the coffin box and what it contained, licking and devouring them mercilessly into nonexistence. Lek put a piece of sandalwood into my hand, asking me to throw it onto that box as a token of farewell before the furnace door was pulled shut, leaving his body to be burnt to ashes.

In front of that locked iron door, I flopped to the floor and wept that loss at the top of my voice, fully awakened from the surreal, dreamlike feeling that had numbed me since the moment they pronounced his death on arrival at the medical station. It was the loneliest, most heart-wrenching cry of my life. It echoed into the heart of the night.

"Lek, when the bag…that bag–which he put the snake toy inside—dropped to the ground, I was about to run to pick it up myself. But he stopped me," my eyes burning with scalding tears. "He said he would help pick it up for me. That's why I'm still with you, but not…him…"

I was not able to go on. I collapsed into wild sobbing. Lek didn't interrupt. He stood dead still, looking at me. But his eyes were blazing. They fell on me with a strange gaze that almost frightened me out of my wits. What I saw in his eyes was an unmistakable outburst of fury, a naked fury from this most peaceful man I had known all my life.

"Lek… Are you mad at me?" I whispered in fear. "Are you mad that he died because of helping me?"

He calmed down immediately, his massive shoulders still trembling from the attempt to control his rupture. When he raised his eyes again, I saw tears streaming down his face. He was now weeping, too.

"No, Pran, I am not mad at you and never will. Nothing to do with you at all," he clenched his teeth and moaned as if in acute pain. "It's…something else. Damn! Damn it!" his voice almost rose in scream.

"Lek!"

He wearily let go of his hands, which had covered his face as if all his strength had left him. That strange agony momentarily transformed his revealed face into another man, much older than he actually was.

"Don't forget, you've still got me." he said in a trembling voice. His hand finally reached out to wrap around my shoulders. You will never be alone, all right?"

"Don't leave me, Lek, please. I'm so scared," I started crying like a little boy.

"No, I won't. I promise,"

He knew more than anyone that without my father, I utterly had nothing left in life.

Then he said something I never thought a simple man like him could. "Just look this way, Pran, and you'll be happy for him. Your papa was an explorer at heart. And since he already ventured into the other side that had always been fascinating and mystifying him, his journey to that place must now satisfy his hunger. It's a hunger for clarifying the mystery of life after death. Now he knows. He finally knows things that are still utterly unknown to us. Therefore, why don't we feel truly happy for him instead of grieving like selfish ones?"

Then he sighed heavily and patted me on my shoulder.

"Now, time to say a final goodbye to your papa. Say in your mind you will let go of him so his body will return to where it originally came from."

He began to say aloud, making his voice as clear as possible for the last farewell.

"*Khun Than*," never had I heard Lek address my father with such an honorific title. "You are returning to elements; to earth, to water, to fire, to air, save for your pure soul that will transcend your flesh and rise above all to sublimity. *Sadhu…*"

As he said, we folded our hands and raised them to our foreheads to bid farewell to the man who meant the world to the two of us.

The location of that temple was within a short walk to my bungalow. Therefore, around midnight, we headed home, guided by Lek's dimly lit lantern, amidst shadows and silhouettes of trees and bushes along the meandering walk that cut through the grove and led to my house.

The noises of a million insects on bushes and treetops deafened my insuppressible sobs. The thin crescent moon hung feebly in the bleak, immense sky, and infinite stars glittered like millions of tiny shards of ice, cold and indifferent to the existences of all insignificant earthly lives far below them. Without Lek's lantern, we must scramble our way through the heart of darkness.

Soon, we entered our perimeter marked by that lone tamarind tree, which stood forsaken and forlorn near the barbed wire fence. The tree branches rattled, and the leaves rustled in the night breeze, perhaps the whispers of things beyond our eyes that were rendered from my imagination.

"Are you hearing that? Listen."

My prolonged sobs gave way to a stir of alarm. I gazed in the direction where I believed the sound came from. But it was too obscure to make out the outlines of anything or anyone, only blotches of blackness looming around us.

"It sounds like something or someone moaning and tramping under that tamarind tree's canopy," I whispered.

But when my eyes began to familiarize themselves with the ambient dark, the obscure outlines loomed gradually, giving the murky illusion of a figure in a white bundle standing under that tamarind tree facing us. After blinking, it had swiftly gone. All the darkness now enveloped that spot.

I felt so fear-stricken that I couldn't open my mouth and tell Lek what I saw. All I could do was point to that spot under the tree.

"Shushhhh… I didn't hear a thing, only insects' noises and the far-off hooting from some barn owls,"

Lek shook his head vigorously, yet his eyes wide open as he jerked his head around. Finally, his gaze fixed on the direction to where I was pointing. He strained his ears to listen carefully and suddenly gasped as he urgently told me.

"Come on; let's hurry up now."

He took my hand firmly and almost dragged me with him while we ran as fast as our feet could carry us, as if we were being stalked, toward my sheltering bungalow that stood snug and warm among clumps of trees within our view.

"Wait for me. Wait—"

I was out of breath while we struggled on the steps to the veranda. After the unlikely sprint, we were finally home. He quickly opened the bedroom door and nudged me inside. I watched him latch the door, locking us in.

"So, you heard it. You saw it too and heard the footsteps following us…"

"No, I didn't hear or see a damn thing. I didn't, really," he refused fervently and excessively. Yet the tone in his voice and a certain look on his face showed me otherwise. Then he said in his more sober voice, "You can't live here. You know it's not safe for you anymore."

"Why? I want to stay here, Lek." I cried in protest. "It's Papa's home. I don't want to leave him and our home."

"All by yourself here at night?" he cried out. "No, I won't let you on your papa's behalf. This place is also ridden with those damn snakes." He was shaken again when he inevitably had to mention those creatures to me. "You have to move out of this place."

"Where?"

He turned and gave me a grave look.

"Your papa wanted you to stay with his own elder sister, Lady Rumpai. You already met her. She came with their father to the funeral today."

I was aghast.

"No, no, not with that awful stone-faced woman, Lek. I can't. I won't," I burst into sudden tears. That thought immediately shook me up with dread. "She was so-o outraged she could tear me into pieces when she caught me coming to sit close to her father's body. She took a lot of nerves, showing her open spite in front of everyone as if I were…" I gulped, "…some cockroach."

Then I told Lek about a brief episode of encountering her the day before.

"They were so shocked at the sight of each other, Papa and that woman. I didn't believe it when Papa insisted he had never known her. And yet she looked wealthy and haughty, so, so different from my papa. I never imagined she could be Papa's own sister," I paused. "I want to stay with you, please…"

I couldn't continue due to a sudden shudder. That woman's icy stare immediately flashed in my mind. They sent a message straight from her heart, telling me how my father's flesh and blood felt about me, whom they had just met for the first time. Had they ever known about my existence for all these years? Or, if so, ever care?

Lek looked at me. I never saw his face so tender and yet so agonized.

"I…wouldn't have been happier if I could have brought you to stay with me. But as you saw it a day before, it's the worst place to live, surrounded by dirt and despair. It doesn't provide a good future for any youngster. It would be best if you did what your papa wants. He knows what is best for you."

"Can you live with someone who hates your guts? Can you? Not only that, you don't even know why either."

Why? Until today, I had no idea that the old man and that lady existed. So, what had I ever done to trigger a rupture of rage severe enough to stop the old man's heart?

Lek immediately became silent. He couldn't deny that fact. It was as plain as day. Finally, he sighed as if in defeat.

"Let's talk about it tomorrow. We have to get up early to take…your papa's ashes from the caretaker. At least you can keep part of him with you for your comfort as long as you live."

"These people in his family…who are they?" I did not give up. So, I continued. "Why did their presence almost rock all the guests at the funeral?"

After another long silence, Lek began to speak in a low whisper.

"Your neighbors always suspect your papa must be somebody, a runaway from some upper-class, genteel family. Until they saw his old man, they never had the slightest idea that your papa did come from one of the wealthiest noble families in our country. When this was revealed, it was a real shock to the entire neighborhood. His father had in decades maintained the most important and powerful role in the Siamese military."

My mouth fell open. I was speechless for a long minute. To me, this was even far more inconceivable than Papa's unexpected death.

"I am the one who sent this message to his family. But honestly, I never expected they would come to attend his funeral. Not in the least… Apart from that, they paid for all his funeral expenses. Whatever it comes out…"

Lek's voice suddenly trailed off. His eyes gazed into the darkness outside the barred window as he murmured something to himself rather than speaking to me.

"The old lord's health had drastically declined since his wife, your papa's mother, passed away some years earlier. He retired from that powerful role recently due to his failing health. They have only seen him wear black since then. They said he mourned the loss of his wife. But some said the mourning was indeed for his most beloved son, your papa, who, however, was still alive at that time."

Lek hunched his shoulders as he began to mutter under his breath.

"The family must have been under a curse; the father dropped dead suddenly amid his son's funeral. That's what I overheard people whispering today."

"How do you know all about this, Lek? Why? Why did Papa never breathe a word about him to me?" I cried exasperatedly.

He was hesitant. Yet, he responded only to my first question and ignored the latter.

"I know because when I was young," he said carefully. "I was chosen by Her Ladyship, his mother, to wait on your papa as one of his servants. My parents and the parents before them served his family with great loyalty for generations. However, both my parents died when I was very young. So, I was under the care of my aunt, who had also been his nanny since your papa was an infant. Since your papa and I were only a couple of years apart in ages, besides attending to his personal needs, I became his playmate when he was a small boy, kept him company when he grew up, and shared all his joys, his losses, and pains as no one else had ever done for him. I respectfully called him *Khun Than,* a high honorific all his inferiors and servants called him. But later on, he forbade me from calling him that title. Just called him by his name *Ananda*, he said…"

Lek's voice faltered. So, he paused and collected himself.

"He even taught me, his humble servant, to read and write so we could share our points of view. He opened different perspectives for me to perceive things. I learned from him to look into things deeper than their face value. In my eyes, your father is so close to being a saint."

Then I saw tears filling his eyes as he tried to blink them away.

"Wherever a man goes, his shadow follows him. That was us: he is that man and I, his inseparable shadow."

Their mysteriously unique comradeship suddenly came to light. Now, I understood why he never got tired of visiting my father as often as he could, always with small woodcrafts made for me and with groceries and our favorite tasty tidbits. He knew my father's cooking was bad, if not terrible. That always included his never-ending dedication, concern, affection, and companionship, which he gave to my father through all those years as early as I could recall.

After a moment, I let the breath I'd beeen holding and hastily asked him.

"Lek, the young lady in the old photograph, who is she?"

"What lady?" He blinked.

Though he did not tell me, I knew that after giving him my father's keys, he must have opened that drawer and gone through all my father's belongings. Until this moment, I had lost all enthusiasm for knowing what Lek would manage with my father's personal belongings, which I used to be so curious about.

"One time, Papa forgot to lock his drawer, and I found some old photographs inside. One was a picture of a young lady, maybe fourteen or fifteen, in a European dress. She has the most unusual smile," I began to waver. "Tell me. Is she... Is she my mother?"

Lek stared at me with a strange expression before letting out the sound of astoundment.

"My goodness!"

"Is she? Tell me, please... Papa told me my mother's name is Siri. Is the young lady in the picture Siri?" Hot, scalding tears stung my eyes again.

He abruptly turned his back on me. I didn't see his face now, but as I waited desperately for the answer, which I was sure he must know, I saw his back was slightly trembling. Then I heard his flat and hard voice as he turned back to face me.

"The whole thing is way too complicated to tell you now. Your papa always said what's so good about the truth if it kills you and what's so bad about a lie if it encourages you to carry on. I promise you, Pran. One day when you begin to understand life, I will tell you everything you need to know."

"When? When will I begin to understand life, I asked him hopefully and perhaps naively. "Maybe in a few months?"

Though my voice was as serious as it could be, it must carry words that enabled him to let out a soft laugh for the first time. He squeezed my hand and said, his eyes glowing warmly.

"How old are you now, young man?"

"Um…I'm seven going to eight soon."

"Oh, no, not in a few months, no way. Not even in five or ten years. But when I'm sure you're ready, I promise you'll never miss a thing to which you're entitled, Pran."

"One more thing, Lek," I grabbed the golden opportunity before it would be gone forever. "I also found another picture of some *Farang* man. He must be kind of important to my father. Who's he?"

"You saw a picture of an American man the lord hired as your papa's private teacher. If your papa's parents gave him a life and soul, this gentleman probably gave him a mind that made him what he is to us."

Lek and I shared the bed in my father's bedroom that night. I pretended to fall asleep because I didn't want to create more worry for him. But I was not able to, and so was Lek himself. Yet we tried to fool each other by feigning sound sleep.

He wasn't aware that through my half-open eyelids, I watched him sneak out of bed. He silently stood facing the bar window, gazing out into the dark for hours. The slightest movement and the faintest sound from outside alerted him.

Several times, it was only tree branches rustling from rainy wind and old floorboards creaking.

His act reminded me of my father's: looking out this same window in challenging in the dead of night. He kept watching and listening, anticipating the presence of something, imagined or not, lurking in the dark—perhaps a sinister shadow behind that old tamarind tree.

Lek was holding my father's old pistol, which he had found kept in the drawer, ready to fire out at any moment.

I must doze off in the wee hours of the night. When I woke up at daybreak, he was nowhere inside the bedroom. I rushed to the veranda and found him kneeling, gazing at the floorboards. The wooden floorboards were still damp from last night's shower. After my father was gone, I did not expect to see Lek's smile. But at this specific moment, his face looked grimmer, his eyes following a faint trace of mud blots that started from the corner and down the plank steps leading to the ground.

"Lek, what are you doing there?"

He seemed so absorbed with his intent gaze that he didn't give me a reply. So, I stepped toward him to take a closer look.

"Do you have any idea about these mud blots?" He abruptly asked me without looking up. The tone in his voice made my uneasiness grow.

"Oh, we always saw mud blots after the rainy night. Papa told me they were just the footprints of some stray dog. That's all." I assured him. "I always helped him scrub up the floor and washed them out."

He nodded, but his grim and dark look did not disappear. I saw two dark circles from his sleepless night around his eyes. I wondered what became of Lek. Why, all of a sudden, did he make such a fuss over some mere mud blots?

Late in the morning, when we entered the temple hall to take my father's ashes home, now contained in a small brass urn, from the funeral undertaker, I was dumb-struck at the presence of the same haughty and stone-faced woman Lek had mentioned as my father's elder sister, a Lady Rumpai. She sat aloof on one of the seats, apparently waiting for us inside the empty, deserted hall.

"Nai Lek, I wish to speak with that boy alone. Can you leave him with me for a few minutes?"

She asked him with that same quiet yet authoritarian and distant voice. This was the second time she merely mentioned me as *that boy*. I wondered if she had known my name. If she hadn't, it wasn't difficult for her to ask. Therefore, it conveyed that she chose to ignore my name only to make me aware that she preferred to keep a remote distance from me.

Without speaking, Lek lowered his head in consent. It wasn't hard to notice that he had regarded her quite highly. My eyes followed him as he began to walk silently to the other corner and settle himself far enough to be out of earshot.

That lady kept staring at me for a minute. At least I saw no fierce hostility from her, as I had seen yesterday. Yet I detected neither warmth nor concern in that gaze, only complete nonchalance, like you found in the eyes of any strangers when they come upon you on the street somewhere. Or if there was one thing to signify her awareness of my presence, it was probably the curiosity flickering in her eyes as she silently watched me.

At a closer look, I noticed some resemblance that the two siblings had shared. A sense of loss attacked me abruptly. Oh, my father and his sister had the same handsome features. I could see a trace of beauty on her face. Yet she was only my father's cold version, the ice maiden who must be once upon a time gorgeous and full of passionate desire. I wondered what had drained the zest for life from her.

"Before I left yesterday, Nai Lek had given me my brother's letter, which he had written to me sometime before he died."

She initiated the conversation, speaking in a voice reserved for inferiors—cold, superior, and impersonal. It was more fitting for a stranger than an aunt addressing her nephew. She mentioned my father only as 'my brother' instead of 'your father.'

"In his letter, he asked me to be your guardian if he happened to meet his death before you become your legal age. Since it's his last wish, I feel the commitment to do as he had asked me," she paused. "After all, he's always my baby brother."

As if her last sentence possessed a spell, her voice suddenly faltered. I could trace a tremble in her ever-steadily stolid voice. Her cold and barren eyes, like the ones seen on a mannequin's face, were now softened with a human feeling—a touch of sadness and grief. She must have loved him—I was assured of it. And yet, for some obscure reason, her love and affection for her brother did not extend to embrace me.

She swiftly regained her composure.

"My brother left his money in his bank. Not much, but good enough. He wrote that you will have his money when you reach your legal age. But for now, you will be under the care of my brother's old nanny, Nai Lek's aunt. During your stay with her, I will send you to some decent school or, if you can make it, later to a college. I will provide financial support for you, as my brother had asked. I was hoping you could do your best if I give you this opportunity. After you are twenty, you will be on your own because I will wash my hands off the whole business."

She suddenly rose to her feet to finish our brief conversation. Then she said with finality.

"Tomorrow, Nai Lek will bring you to Bangkok, where she resides. You will stay with her until you finish school or college if that's what you want."

Then, her voice was as icy as her glowered.

"And bear in mind that you won't cause any trouble to people who put a roof over your head and meals on your plate. That's all. I must leave now."

Before she left, she had done another unexpected thing: She asked one of the caretakers to bring my father's urn to her. The brass urn was meant to be my most precious keepsake, to preserve a memory of him. She made it clear to us that she came today to bring her brother home to the bosom of his family.

"Where's his urn? Bring that to me now."

Her demand was promptly met. The dismay must be written clearly on my face. When she noticed it, she turned toward Lek and went on. She didn't bother talking directly to me.

"Don't you think it's more appropriate to rest my brother's remains at the place where he truly belongs? I will change his urn to gold and place it on the altar in our sanctuary room, surrounded only by the ones who truly love him—his parents and the rest of his long-gone ancestors' urns."

As she engaged in conversation, her face slowly turned to me, staring at me. I knew her message now was direct to me, cruel and cold like a piercing ice blade.

"Honestly, I must admit that I feel grateful for his death. If life took him away from us, now death brings him back to me, to his own family. Our Beloved is at last coming home."

Lek only lowered his head as if surrendering to what she just declared. I had never seen him so meek and defenseless.

Since I met her, I had seen her crack a smile for the first time, a flicker of a smile that did not hide her insidious satisfaction. It was out of the question for her to inflict physical pain on me, so she injured me with menacing words. There was no doubt left now in my mind that she despised me to the core and did not care to let the whole world know it.

"After our father's grand cremation ceremony, which will be held in six months with His Majesty and more royals coming to attend, I will put our father's ashes to stand side by side with our mother's and Beloved's."

Finally, she walked away with her head held up. The sun was now so hot she protected the urn with the cover of her soft silk handkerchief. Her hands were tenderly snuggling my father's urn against her bosom as if she were carrying a fragile newborn son. The pang of envy hit me hard. How could someone I'd never known—an utter stranger—have a right to snatch Papa, my papa, from me?

I recognized the same grand motor car I'd seen the day before, waiting for her nearby. When the chauffeur in his neat uniform saw her approaching him, he got out of the car, bowed his head, promptly opened the door, and held it gently for her to get in like a royal highness.

I had never seen her again, not even once, after she left the temple hall that day. I had no idea whether she was now dead or still alive. I still wondered if she'd ever known my name after all.

Or maybe not.

* * * * *

Part 1: Chapter 6

Lady in Yellow Skirt

" *If Khun Than told you that your mother was already dead, I want you to know he made that up for some reason that I cannot guess.* "

I could hardly believed this was a greeting from my father's nanny as she met Lek and me on my first day staying with her in this house in Bangkok.

I quickly glanced at Lek, startled. That was the last thing I expected as a welcome speech from my new guardian, whom I had met for the first time. But Lek just remained silent.

As she spoke, this fifty-year-old nanny never took her eyes off me. Her mouth, stained deep red from constantly chewing betel nut, now grimaced in slight disdain. An image of Kru Riam, that preschool teacher, suddenly flashed and superimposed onto this woman in front of me. How could I ever forget Kru Riam? How could I forget that horror nightmare, with her blood-red saliva from chewing betel nuts drooling down her gaping mouth and dripping on the floor while chasing me around in that dream, aiming to cut my left hand with a sharp cleaver in her hand? I must do my best not to be frightened by some distinct resemblance I found between the two women.

Nanny Sook had strong features with prominent jaws, and large cheekbones, contrasted with her thin, salt-and-pepper hair, tightly pulled back into a bun. There was no trace of any pleasant attraction on that cold face. Her small pair of penetrating eyes were set deep in their sockets, sharp and hawk-like. And now, they seemed to bulge out from glaring at me. It puzzled me how my papa could have taken her on as his childhood nanny.

Despite her enormous breasts and overweight body, her movement was surprisingly brisk and authoritarian. She pointed at the floor, gesturing to us to sit there while she dropped on a sofa and put her walking cane aside.

"When I'd asked Lek before he brought you today, he told me otherwise, and I believe him more. He said that woman had left *Kun Than* and you for good since you were barely two weeks old."

Another puzzling thing was that she didn't speak to him directly. She spoke about him as though he weren't even in the room. I believed Lek must have felt she intended to humiliate him by implying he was invisible to her.

"No one has heard about her whereabouts or known whether she's still now kicking somewhere or was already eaten by worms in her hole," the tone she stressed on the word *that woman* brazenly told me how she felt about the person alleged as my mother.

She'd never opened her mouth to tell me more. And I was too scared to ask. That was why the cold and cruel stare she greeted both Lek and me on the first day vaguely reminded me of when I'd first met Kru Riam. The nanny seemed unhappy to see even Lek, her nephew, whom she hadn't seen for a long while.

He must have sensed his aunt's hostility, so he spent time

in her house as shortly as possible before leaving me alone under her single-handed care.

"For your papa's sake, be strong, Pran," his eyes were reddened. "I promise I'll come to see you when I can."

"Lek," I'd whispered before he left me to that woman. "She said my mother is not dead." That news was shaking me to the core, yet it mixed with confusion and doubts. "Isn't it true? Why do what you tell her is different from my papa?"

Lek said slowly. "This is between her and me. And if I were you, I would believe that way too. I will choose hope over everything under this circumstance."

"I don't understand, Lek."

"You will later. I promise. For now, behaving like a good boy in her care must be the priority you must be concerned about. Let all the unnecessary go."

Before I had a chance to ask more, he was gone.

Nanny Sook put me to stay alone in a small, dank, one-room shack far behind the main two-storied house where she stayed with some of her folks. My place was so isolated that no one could hardly come near it. I believed it must have been used as storage before I came.

A dank smell hit my nostrils so hard that I almost gagged when I stepped inside that small, empty room for the first time. I found cobwebs draping on the ceiling and dust covering everywhere on the dirty floor with a worn sleeping mat, an old blanket, and a flabby pillow set on the floorboard at one corner. Since my first day here, everyone in the main house completely ignored my presence. Even a few children in the house, probably her relatives, never paid attention to me, let alone came to talk to me.

A few days passed, and I stayed in my room all day except when I had to take my meal. For every meal, I had to come and enter the main house by the backdoor. I had my meal alone in the kitchen, where food on my plate, mainly rice, grilled fish, and chili paste, was left for me in one corner of the kitchen floor. I had to sit down and squeeze myself as small and quiet as possible. I couldn't help picturing myself as a little mouse, sneaking out from a hole in the wall to eat some scraps of food people accidentally dropped on the floor.

Once, when I came for dinner, I found it was already gone. I was afraid to ask but assumed it was probably because I came a little later than usual. I had to go back to my shack and wait with an empty and rumbling stomach all night until my next meal was put on that corner again.

I had to learn it the hard way without anyone in the house coming to warn me that I must be promptly on time; otherwise, my meal would be thrown away a few minutes after I didn't show up.

Moreover, although I always tried to offer a hand, they never asked me for help with household chores. It wasn't hard to start realizing that they deliberately made me feel like a 'freeloader' who shamelessly came only to take advantage of all accommodations in their house.

But all these were nothing compared to this cold torment I had to endure with dread every week. I had to come into the nanny's room and meet her face to face; she was on the chair, and I was on the floor. Apart from receiving my weekly meager school allowance, I had to let her read the list of miscellaneous stuff she spent on me at Lady Rumpai's expense, all to the details. She never missed a penny that Papa's sister had to pay for my meals, clothes, school stuff, etc.

"Lady Rumpai wants me to make this list, together with my monthly report on your behavior and your study in school. So, she can check whether or not you deserve all she has to spend on you."

I began to realize that the three women I'd met—Kru Riam, Lady Rumpai, and my new guardian, Nanny Sook—had shared their open hostility toward me almost in equal measure.

But the worst was that all three of them never told me

why they thought I deserved such humiliating and spiteful treatment from them.

The one thing that made this place tolerable was a dozen photos of Papa I found in almost every room in this house. It seemed so unreal to see the face of my papa everywhere in this very unfamiliar and hostile place. She put many of his photos on those walls, all I'd never seen before. They were taken at different ages: as a toddler cradled in the nanny's arms while she was beaming at him, as a young boy with two older girls smiling by his side. Those two girls looked very similar to each other. So, I guessed they were twins; one of them must be Lady Rumpai.

The most recent photo was taken when he was a very handsome lad at sixteen in his student uniform. In that photo, his nanny held him in her arms while she heartily kissed him on the cheek. I never expected such an ecstatic smile to pop up on the nanny's usual grim face. This particular picture alone could make me feel their intense attachment to each other.

And like Lady Rumpai, the more she devoted herself to him, the more her hate flared up on me. She must have been so possessive of my father that she harbored hostility toward anyone she believed stole my father from her, including the one who was my mother.

Yet I could find a way to sneak in for a few minutes and wrap myself in his presence in those photos when no one was around. So, I could cry in front of his pictures and tell him I missed him so much I could die.

But very soon, I was chased out and firmly told I was not allowed in that room or anywhere else inside the house except the kitchen at the back, where I could come to have my meals and leave as soon as I finished. The shack at the far end of property was the only place I was allowed to stay.

I missed Papa so much that I once broke that rule and sneaked inside her house again while there seemed to be no presence of anyone. All I needed was to take a swift glimpse of

Papa's pictures and then tiptoe out before someone caught sight of me and rushed to report to the nanny of my intruding.

As I stood focusing on one of his pictures on the wall, oblivious to the ambiance around that room, I suddenly heard the fierce growl of some animal behind me. No sooner had I turned my face to see what the growl came from than a massive black dog jumped on my face with all its force. I was so damn lucky I impulsively put my hands to cover the whole face just in time, only to sacrifice both my hands and arms to the ferocious bites. Somehow, I managed to shake myself off that beast and fled from that room while blood from my arms was dripping and trailing all behind me.

While I tried to make a hasty retreat, running off toward my shack, once I turned around to see if that dog was still behind chasing me. I found it had gone now and was nowhere to be seen. But after I'd turned around, even facing that monstrous dog must be more merciful compared to what I was catching sight of, instead.

On the veranda of that main house stood a shadowed figure of someone in the act of intensely watching me. I would never forget the look on that cruel face that made a shiver run through my spine. Only someone who hated me at the depths of her heart could give me that dead look as she stood in silence, one of her hands clutching her cane to support her fat body so that she could take a better view watching me being attacked fiercely by her dog.

But the worst was that she kept staring at me even though she noticed me turning around and finding her watching me. My eyes had met hers for a few seconds before I fled for my life. This time, it was not from fear of that beast but of the glare she sent from her eyes without a wink.

The dog's sharp teeth sank deep into my arms and left two nasty gaping wounds. I was afraid to ask for help from anyone in that house. What I could possibly have in return must be a cold stare. So, to help myself, I washed the wounds and tied a towel around my wounded hand to stop the bleeding. That night, I ran a high fever that caused me to be absent from school the next day. I was left alone the whole day to curl up, shivering with pain and fever on my cot, too feeble to come out to have any of my meals. If I showed up in the kitchen late or didn't show up at all, they would never wonder what was happening and look for me. They only took my untouched meal to feed that damn dog. I believed they couldn't have cared less if they had later found me dead and bloated inside my small living hole.

Late in the day, I heard someone knocking on the door and saying she brought me a tray of food and some painkiller pills and bandages.

"The nanny wants me to warn you that if you sneak into her house again, no one can guarantee your safety from her dog. And if it happens again, no one will bother coming to bring the food to you like this time. You must crawl to the kitchen by yourself. It doesn't matter whether you are still in one piece or not,"

I'd heard that warning voice before she walked out and left that tray at the door without stepping inside to check me up.

I was lucky enough that the wounds weren't infected and eventually healed. However, it left some permanent ugly scars on my arms that kept reminding me of one of the most merciless incidents I had met since my father was gone.

I'd sensed Nanny Sook's unwelcome demeaner since the first day I moved to this place. But after she'd let her vicious dog maim me and then she stood watching that attack in cold blood, it was the day I began to realize that the hatred she had for me must be much deeper than I could count up.

Since that day, I'd never edged close to that house again except when I was called to show my school report to her. It was pretty hard to use either of my hands in handling things, especially the left hand when I wanted to write. Although the wounds were healed, the dog's fangs went deep into the tendon area, which affected the hand flexibility control. It was Lek who brought me to check up at a medical center for more treatment with his scant money.

Although I didn't find any photo of that mysterious girl with an unusual smile in the nanny's house, I had never forgotten her smile in the old photograph, which Lek had now taken with him along with my father's journal.

I believed it couldn't have been anyone else but that girl who had brought me into this world. However, her face, which I quickly saw in that old photo, was of a barely fifteen-year-old teen girl. That picture must have been taken years before she gave birth to me.

Lek was right. It would feed my hope if I clung to Nanny Sook's version that my mother was still alive. And if so, my mother must be a mature-aged woman today, at least in her thirties. Her face must have changed so much from her old picture that the chance to recognize her must be slim. If I ran across her on the street, I would never know the woman who had accidentally bumped into me—and even apologized, *oh, I'm so sorry*—could be her, the woman of my childhood dream.

But once you let hope stem into life, it starts growing, flourishing, and sustaining your own life. So, no matter where she could be, I set my mind to find her.

At least Lady Rumpai sent me to school as she had promised. It wasn't that famous Catholic school my father had intended to send me to. The nanny said it was too far from where I was living. But that new place was enough of a decent school for boys where I could get there within a few minutes' walk. I didn't mind going to my new school, not because it was a pleasant place but because I believed every other place would welcome me far more than the one where I lived. It had never provided any sense of belonging for me as long as they put me to sit and eat my meal on the kitchen floor alone while the rest of the nanny's family had a decent place all together on their dining table.

Since that day, I'd never sneaked inside her house to see my father's pictures, and I avoided staying at the nanny's compound during the day. I must be eye-sore to them whenever they saw me around their house. They neither needed my help nor wanted me to join any of their activities. It meant I was absolutely on my own and was free to live or to die.

I had two favorite places to hide; one was the school library, which became my haven. I had read many books to enliven and widen the horizon of my bleak present world. I constantly borrowed books and brought them to the shack to relieve my loneliness at night. As a result, I was doing well in my class, keeping the nanny away from me. Her stern eyes scrolled up and down my report card but found nothing to her advantage.

My other favorite thing after school was to spend the afternoon sitting alone on the sidewalk near where I lived, watching people pass me by. My utter loneliness drove me to search for a single woman among the sea of faces of the passers-by.

That was how I looked for my mother.

Thousands of footprints helped make the sidewalk dirty and dusty. The morning heavy rain made it slushy and muddy, and the afternoon hot sun baked it until the slush and the mud dried and turned into crust. The following day, the rain would again melt and dissolve hardened mud into puddles, waiting for the afternoon merciless sun to bake it again, like a never-ending cycle.

I skipped all the males, grownups, and boys alike, including all girls of school age who walked past me, not bothering to raise my head to look up. I always bent my head down to protect myself from the glaring sun. Their shoes at my eye level—working shoes, school shoes, sandals, slippers, and so on—were good enough for checking and screening the right ones.

What I had on my mind was to single out only women, any grown-up females whose age seemed to match someone for whom I was desperately and secretly searching. As soon as my eyes caught sight of female shoes, I became instantly alerted and abruptly raised my head to gaze up at their face, making them a little startled and sometimes offended by such blunt rudeness. As I stared into their eyes, I wondered if that face had possibly been the one who was my long, long-lost mother.

Of course, no matter how desperate I was, I never dared open my mouth to ask this crucial question to any of them. After a split-second encounter, I just let them, one after another, walk straight past me and vanish from my sight. Sometimes, I was so frustrated with my cowardly reluctance that I could throw myself and cry.

How many of them each day slipped by without me asking that life-and-death question? What if one of them had turned out to be her? That thought tortured and gnawed at me day and night. But I never gave up the search, and it was because I could not afford to give it up.

The reason I was afraid to ask was that their appearance and posture did intimidate and discourage me. Most of them ignored my presence completely. They did not even notice my pleading stare with a huge question mark on my face. They just strode past me, their body poised, their chin up, their eyes looking straight, and their makeup face impassive. Probably, it was not their fault because from what they were wearing, I guessed they were working women on their way to work. Once in a while, some of them slowed their pace and gave me a meager half-smile, somewhat acknowledging my presence. And then, they quickened their pace again.

One mid-afternoon, the sky was so cruelly bright and cloudless. The sun was burning so fierce I had to nudge myself under the stretching shade of one of the small young mahogany trees lined up along the sidewalk. Yet, the sun's white glare still pierced through these thin limbs, mockingly playing light and shadow to dapple my face. I had to sit with my knees up and my head bending down to avoid the pulsing heat. As the hot, faint wind swirled on the sidewalk, a few crisp, dry leaves dropped from the scrubby tree and skittered around my feet.

Usually, on cloudy days, when the sky was softened and the heat was not threatening, I watched the overcast sky with fascination. I enjoyed huge, floating, fluffy balls of clouds moving and shifting their peculiar shapes right before my eyes. Any shape could inspire me to conjure up countless daydream stories. A dragoness ferociously puffing out a ball of fire protecting her dragon eggs from a wicked wizard; a flock of white sheep grazing peacefully at the foot of the fluffy white hill—mother and baby lamb safely huddling together. Once, I gasped as I found a beautiful cotton-white cloud shaped like a mother's profile holding up her child. My eyes were transfixed on it, attempting with all my efforts to imprint that picture into my reminiscence before that particular cloud would swiftly shift its shape to something else completely different from what I had seen earlier.

Since there were no apparent big cotton ball clouds today, only wisps of icy cirrus clouds so high on the mercilessly deep, blue sky, I bent my head down to shield myself from the sun and looked for anything to pass the long and tedious hours.

As I looked down at the surface of the heat-glistening black asphalt-coated street in front, which seemed on the brink of melting from the noon-white heat, something immediately caught my eye. Its presence was out of place, and it was hard to decide whether it was funny or horrid. It was a humor that was too cruel to laugh at, like a clown at a circus, still having his huge red paint smile fixed on his face, dying a funny death in front of his audience.

It was one small rubber flip-flop, children's size, stuck permanently to the street, melting surface like someone had coated some glue on its sole. One of the kids must have lost one of a pair while hurriedly crossing the boiling street, and one of the flip-flops accidentally stuck to the oozing surface. The poor kid could not pull that one from the gruel-like sticky surface.

So, he had to leave it behind and hop-hop-hop like a bunny hop dancer. With only one of his feet supporting him, he hopped across the inferno path, dragging another of his bare and burnt feet with him.

I glanced down at my own pair of shoes and let out a long sigh of relief. My shoes were old and nearly worn out, but they fit perfectly. I could run half the world, tramping and trudging across the field of fire at one hundred degrees with my shoes sticking firmly and faithfully to my feet.

Suddenly, I heard footsteps.

Not wanting to miss out on any, I quickly raised my head and squinted hard, catching a sudden glimpse of a woman walking toward me. The sun was shining all over that figure, making her body and face shimmering and her long dark hair iridescent as if she were putting on a glowing aura. All the peculiar effects from the noon glare made her look so otherworldly to me. My mouth gaped. To my eyes, it was as if she had just descended from somewhere far, far above the clouds, probably heaven.

I still vividly remembered her wearing a cream linen blouse and a bright yellow skirt. As my eyes met hers, some particular expression on my face probably made her slow down her pace. She then stopped before me and gently asked. *What are you doing on the sidewalk alone? Are you lost?* Because her voice showed concern, I timidly confirmed that I was okay. I was sitting there looking for my mother.

She looked surprised, her eyes a little widened, before asking me. *For how long has your mother gone? Just yesterday or a few days ago? Oh, and when will she come back?*

I told her I had no idea because she had gone since I was born. But I believed one day she would come back and find me waiting for her right over there. Of countless people walking by, I was sure I could single her out at first glance, said I proudly.

Oh!

She uttered a single 'oh' word and seemed startled this time, almost speechless, before asking again.

Aren't you afraid of sitting all by yourself? Someone at home might wait and be anxious about your absence.

I said no. I came to sit there almost every day for fear that missing even a single day might mean I'd miss her forever. Since I had just lost my loved one, who was my papa, I couldn't afford to lose another.

I remembered she stared at me for one long minute. As her gaze fell on my face, no words formed on her lips. But her eyes stirred. Something was welling up. My answer moved her to tears. She blinked them away before her eyes brimmed with them. Then she reluctantly stepped toward me, slowly raised her hand, and gently caressed my hair. Her other hand was dipped into the handbag she was carrying.

With an amiable and warm smile, she reached out with a handful of milk toffees and gingerly put them onto my palm.

That smile was so unusual that I was thunderstruck. It transformed her plain face into something sublime, above and beyond female mundane attributes such as beauty and charm.

Before she walked out, she had said to me in a cheerful, soft voice.

You will find your mother very soon. She will show up. Any mother cannot help coming back to such a sweet, caring boy like you.

She assured me with another smile. It crossed my mind in that instant. I knew it. I had found her at last.

She had the smile of the girl in that old photograph.

I watched her as she slowly walked away from me and finally turned left at the corner ahead. Just before she disappeared forever from my line of sight, I decided to run after her, run, run, and run. She had been moving ahead of me as a saunter along the sidewalk, which gave me quite an advantage in that I could catch up with her in no time. Of course, she was never aware that I was following her. What I was doing must have been an act of impulse.

My loneliness screamed out at me.

Never let her go. Never.

I lost sight of her once. I panicked and was on the verge of tears. This was inexplicably strange. I couldn't figure out why I did miss her despite her slow pace and my sprinting right behind her. I couldn't comprehend. But as every second trickled by, I could not afford to stand and only wonder; I had to do something swift. I had to. So, I decided to turn left at the next corner.

As I emerged to that corner, I immediately found a group of four or five schoolboys clustering ahead of me. They were walking at a leisurely slow pace, blocking my way to pass through. I shouted at them to get out of my way, but no one responded to my urgency. They seemed to be having a good time after school, dawdling, chatting, and giggling while heartily munching the ice cream cone they held, oblivious of the realm outside their world.

So, I decided to do the unthinkable.

In a flash, I started to push and shove, using all the strength of an eight-year-old boy, jostling my way to proceed ahead. Two off-guard boys in the group staggered and lay sprawling on the hard sidewalk, their ice cream slipping from their hands and plopping on the ground. They tried to stagger and scramble to their feet by getting hold of one another, still howling and wailing.

With neither time nor heart to apologize, I kept on running, leaving those stunned and angry boys far behind. After I ran a few blocks trying to catch up with her, panting and gasping for air, my shoes clattering loudly against the hot, solid sidewalk like a moaning animal as I kept racing down.

The prolonged heat and exhaustion from sprinting quite a distance suddenly attacked me. It blurred my vision, spun my head, and stopped my movement. The crowd seen in the fierce sun now appeared to me in double vision with hazy, dazzling, and indistinct forms.

Suddenly, it seemed to me that almost all the women walking past me were now wearing outfits with slightly different hues of yellow. I saw one over here, another over there, and three or four more yonder. The swirls of yellow, from lemon to amber to saffron to sunflower to canary, began to drown me. They blinded and suffocated me to the point that I was about to throw up. I could die at that moment from the explosion of sobs.

As my tears started to well up again, I spotted her. It was unmistakably her; I just knew it—no one else. My thought and vision were as clear as a clairvoyant's crystal ball, perfect for reading the immediate future. This one was not as deceptive as I had seen seconds ago. Even from a distance across the street ahead, I instantly recognized her from her radiant yellow skirt and her glowing aura as bright as the sun, which stood out from the dullness and grayness insignificance surrounding her.

Like a glowing beacon for the shipwrecked souls lost in the dark and stormy sea, she was standing amid the crowd at a crammed trolley stop on the other side of the street.

My heart almost exploded from a strange, nameless feeling, unknown to me, yet so intense, so powerful, so overwhelming—which I realized later in my life that what I had been experiencing at that moment was an outburst of euphoria. Believe it or not, that was the first moment of true happiness I had ever experienced—the moment of miraculously sighting my lady once again.

I started shouting across the street at her. *Wait. Wait for me. Wait-t-t-t...* But the din from the traffic drowned out my voice. So, I shouted again, this time at the top of my lungs, trying desperately to raise my voice above all ambient noises, my feet jumping up and down, and my hands waving wildly.

Mama! Wait for me. Please don't leave me, Mama-a-a-a!

I was unaware that the most magical word in our language was slipping from my mouth.

Mama...

Flooding with exuberance and anticipation, I barely noticed

a trolley with two compartments running along the track across the crossroad and pulling up at that stop to pick up passengers. The whole length of that trolley blocked the entire view, and she was completely obscured. I set up my mind to be the daredevil. I raced across the street as fast as I could toward that trolley stop to stop that lady, or more precisely, my long-lost mother, regardless of the red-light sign flashing angrily ahead of me.

All the sights were blurred. All sounds muted. Immediately, I heard a car screech to a stop, and then it lunged toward me. As I lost my balance and stumbled onto the street, the wheel grazed the skin of my leg, leaving some scrapes and bleeding. The halt almost forced the driver in the car to hit the steering wheel on his head. He hollered at me furiously as he managed to gain his balance. *Get lost, you rascal. I hope your mother will beat up your stupid sense for running amok on the street.*

Just like I cared for my nearly causing his and possibly my fatal accident, I started to pick up my speed again toward that trolley stop. I was oblivious to the bleeding and the scrapes on one of my knees and a blister from burnt skin caused by the fall to the street heat on the other knee

Halfway through the wide and busy main street, I suddenly saw the trolley slowly pull away from that stop. It speeded up again along with the conductor's bell ringing *clang-clang-clang* beneath his feet and then swiftly ran past me, letting me come to be aware that the crowded trolley stop was now almost deserted.

Mama…

Now, she was nowhere to be found.

I felt my heart beating in my throat. Yes, as I came as close as nearly a few steps toward her, she just stepped into that trolley, gone forever. I thought I was going to faint and slump into the middle of the traffic and heat-ridden street again, but I did not. Instead, my feet were transfixed to its surface by the sheer horror of seeing the empty trolley stop. A tremendous sense of loss was unbearable.

I crawled back home like a wounded bird with broken wings to face a harsh punishment awaiting me: this time, Nanny Sook asked some man in her house to punish me with a long switch for idling on the street and causing my clothes to be torn and filthy. She ignored my bruises and bleeding. She never asked what happened. All she was concerned about was how much my new clothes would cost my benefactor, Lady Rumpai.

For a month after that day, I faithfully repeated what I had done, risking more possible punishment. However, I knew they did not care whether I was absent or present or whether I lived or died as long as my absence and my death did not cause them trouble. They never checked if each day I was absent from school or if I missed my meal. They never wondered if I was sick and needed a doctor or at least some medicine. I shuddered every time the dog attack incident came to my mind. If I didn't show up at the kitchen's corner, they would have dumped my meal into the garbage. And that was all they cared about me. One day, I rushed to the kitchen in the nick of time only to find one woman who was a cook in the kitchen sweeping everything from my plate down another big bowl. Although she was well aware of my presence, she acted as if I hadn't existed. A rule was a rule. If I came one minute late it meant I was late and deserved to go hungry until the next meal. She walked past me to the door with that bowl in her hands and then put that bowl for that horrible black dog waiting hungrily outside. It kept growling and barking relentlessly at me when it saw me, frightening me to death. But it didn't attack me as long as I didn't intrude inside the house. Nanny Sook must train it that way.

With this bleak acknowledgment, I had ritually come every day, rain or shine, and settled myself on the same spot on the sidewalk, waiting very patiently. My fingers groped inside my shorts pocket for one last milk toffee, kept safely in my pocket, melting and sticky to my touch.

Until I met her again, I vowed I would never put that toffee in my mouth to savor its sweetness. The rest had been spilled along the sidewalk, lost forever, while I raced after her the previous day.

My eyes worked vigorously, catching all thousand pairs of legs pacing, striding, strolling, trotting, and strutting past me. I then scanned the faces of the people wearing those shoes, trying to single out only one face, that angelic face I believe with all my heart must belong to my long-lost mother.

I believed she must also be anxiously and feverishly looking for me after we had missed each other the day before. If only we had met again, I would have run and thrown myself into her arms, sobbing and laughing, then crying and laughing again with a feeling of utmost happiness spreading over my being. This time, she would have brought me with her wherever she had been living, and yes, with a promise she would have never left me again, never, ever for the rest of her life. And we would have lived happily ever after.

Now, the one and ultimate hope I had held onto was that she had known the very spot where I was waiting for her every day. So, she would come back to find me. She would show up. If not today, it would be the next day. If not the next day, it would be the day after, and so on. That hope sustained my being.

The whole reason to live.

Day after day on that sidewalk, my ears perked up whenever I thought I heard some familiar walking footsteps approaching me. And suddenly, out of the corner of my eye, as my heart nearly jumped out of my chest, I thought I caught sight of a flash of bright, bright yellow color on someone's skirt.

But I had never found her again despite my long, tireless search.

Yet, shortly after that day, I still clung stubbornly to my flickering and diminishing hope. Out of the utmost desperation, I started a secret habit of glancing up the open windows of every house I had passed—luxurious bricked houses, run-down plank board houses, new houses, old houses, green-painted houses, yellow houses, etcetera—and wished I could have been able to peek inside those window curtains and blinds to check which of these she had been living inside.

However, as the years passed, I eventually gave up this childish and absurd idea of searching for one single woman amidst the sea of strangers.

It was better—or somewhat worse—that as I grew up more, I came to fully understand that the lady in a bright yellow skirt, who had by chance crossed my life path for merely ten or fifteen minutes, was not my mother and never was able because it was simply too good to be true.

The mother I had had abandoned me before I was two weeks old; they told me so.

To be honest and truthful, as the fully grown man I became today, I could not eliminate that lady in the yellow skirt from the core of my consciousness. Throughout all those years, especially as my drinking habit was getting more and more uncontrolled, I had been constantly glimpsing a ghost, a shadow of her somewhere, somehow. At one corner of my eyes, I often believed I caught sight of her, her bright yellow skirt swirling in a flash among the crowd, then vanishing before my eyes could focus.

Sometimes in the late afternoon, as I walked along a quiet road, another existence beside me was only my own dark shadow moving soundlessly behind me. I believed I heard a faint sound, a leisurely walking footstep as if I had someone constantly stalking me. When I stopped, my shadow stopped, and so did the footsteps. Once I resumed walking, the footstep resumed its existence. Every time this strange incident happened, I could not help but hope and turn to see behind my back because I sensed the presence of either someone or something, but I had never caught a soul there.

Only a void, a total emptiness that had been stalking me ever since.

But sometimes, when I tried to imagine a woman who had given birth to me, though a decade had already passed, I still helplessly chose to see her in the borrowed image of the young lady in a bright yellow skirt—her face, her voice, her smiles, and most of all, her kindness.

And let it be seated at the deepest corner of my heart as my most cherished reminiscence.

* * * * *

Part 1: Chapter 7

The Doll Face

I *always wondered how I was able to tolerate staying in the nanny's house for ten years under all the humiliations she inflicted to me.*

One of the main reasons was that I didn't want to disappoint my father, who had done so much to secure my future. I had to endure those mistreatments only to stay with an opportunity to finish school so that I could leave this place and stand on my own with pride.

I remembered the day I faced Lady Rumpai in the temple after my father's funeral. She told me my father had some money in his bank. She would take care of that money, as he had asked her, until I reached the legal age to receive it. She was the one who would approve my legitimacy for the money, which depended on two conditions: an academic good grade and also a decent behavior. Otherwise, that sum of money would be thrown into some charity instead.

My school grades so far, although not at that top grade level, were high enough to guard me from all kinds of malice in this house. It wasn't easy when you knew Nanny Sook had been waiting for a chance to throw you out of her house for whatever accusation she could find. But while she couldn't find that opportunity, she kept putting pressure on you, hoping it would eventually drive you out of her house for good.

One of the problems the nanny raised was that she said Lek didn't lead a decent life to set a good example for me. In short, she didn't want Lek's drinking habit to influence me. So, Lek was not welcome to visit me at her house. That reason upset me, but Lek only shrugged and complied with her. There must have been something deeper beneath that reason. Why did the aunt show open hostility to her nephew, whom she had taken care of when he was a boy? But as always, nothing came out of Lek's mouth when I wanted the answer.

"How come Nanny Sook can have such a big house?"

I asked Lek one time when I saw him. But this time, he answered me promptly.

"I don't blame you if you think this house is hers. The way she put on airs to everyone!" He smirked. "Actually, it's one of Lady Rumpai's properties. She inherited this house after her mother, Lady Pearl, passed away. The lady sent my aunt to look after this place. I guess she wanted to return a favor for my aunt's loyalty to their family, especially for her doting on your papa." He chuckled, emphasizing the word 'doting'.

However, he tried to see me every week after school. He would patiently wait for me in front of the fence wall of that house and talk with me for ten to fifteen minutes before I went inside.

One late afternoon, I went home late and still found Lek waiting for me at the spot where we usually met.

"Lek, I can't talk to you today. I have to hurry to get inside."

"Why? Ten minutes doesn't hurt you," my breathlessness puzzled him.

"I…I can't be late for my meal. Otherwise, they will take it away."

"What?" A perplexed expression on his face was genuine. "Can't you ask someone to save it for you later on? Just ask. It won't hurt."

When I reluctantly shook my head, Lek clenched his jaws without saying a thing. Then he sighed and let me go.

From that day on, whenever he came to see me, he would slip some money into my hand and pat my shoulder.

"You need it for a rainy day."

It wasn't much, but that was from some of the hard-earned money he always saved for me. I tried to force back my tears and swallow a lump. He knew my meager allowance from Nanny Sook alone hardly helped me make ends meet, and I was too scared to ask her for more.

Since Lek was not welcomed into that house, after I got familiar with the directions, I took the trolley to visit him and sometimes stayed over in his place when it wasn't a school day. He still lived alone in that rundown slum where my father had brought me to visit him many years ago. I didn't mind a swarm of mosquitos and the awful smell of the stagnant ditch by his house as long as I felt Lek's warm presence.

At least the nanny's negligence on me gave me the advantage of going in and out anytime without their watchful eyes. I hardly complained to Lek about whatever I had to put up with to keep him from worrying about any of my problems that he couldn't help. After my father's death, for better or worse, I felt closer to him. I always caught his eyes brimming with caring and affection while he looked at me. It was unmistakably the same affectionate expression I had from Papa when he was still around.

During my last year of high school, I announced to Lek that I planned to attend law school to follow in my father's footsteps. I'd never seen Lek acting more buoyant since my father's death.

"I know your papa must be so proud of you. Oh, you make me so happy for him."

Then he paused and carefully asked me. "Have you talked

about going to law school to the nanny?"

"Um…I will. You remember? Papa's sister once told me that if going to college was my goal, she would support me as Papa had asked her. After all, I am still…" my voice trailed off, "…her brother's son." I felt more comfortable using the phrase 'her brother's son' rather than 'her nephew.'

He nodded to me and changed our subject into something else.

"Now, time to celebrate. Have some drinks with me."

When I came to see him this evening, he was drinking alone. Despite his aunt's disapproval of that habit, he still drank every day to relax after his strenuous carpentry work.

Then he poured the rice whiskey from the bottle into a glass and handed it to me. I was reluctant. He knew I'd never tasted liquor before, but he only laughed and coaxed me.

"Pran, you are almost eighteen now. You're not a boy any longer. And being a man, from time to time, you can't avoid getting drunk. So, to be safe, learn how to get drunk as best as you can in front of me."

It was the cheap rice whiskey from a bottle Lek could afford. I tried with all my force not to spit it out on my first gulp. It burned my stomach as if I was swallowing a liquid fire down my throat.

"How is it?"

"Why! I'm absolutely fine." I didn't want Lek to poke fun at me because I didn't act like a grown man enough. So, I asked him for more to prove my maturity—or, in other words, my manhood—to him while keeping a straight face and averting my eyes from his knowing smile.

But after one more glass from Lek, I started to choke and cough and rush to empty my churning stomach. I ended up slumping on the floor, barely conscious of Lek dragging me to his cot, and left me there to pass out like a log through the whole night.

"Now you have experienced how awful it is when you get drunk and will surely remember that feeling anytime you go out drinking. Your father never loved drinking or wanted me to drink. You know what? Even your saintly papa acted horrible like everybody else when he was drunk. I know he got drunk once in the moment of crisis, but he never did it again."

"But despite that, you still *love* drinking," at last, I could find a chance to talk back.

"Well, it doesn't hurt to spark a pleasant mood. I never go too far to lose my marbles. That's the point," he winked cheerfully at me.

I couldn't sleep well at night waiting to see Nanny Sook and make my intention to attend law school known to her. When that moment came, I was a bundle of nerves while waiting for her response, which could be anything beyond prediction.

"This law school for commoners was newly established last year as an open university for any high school diploma students who want to enroll without passing the entrance exam. This new one is different from the loyal law school my father attended, which required only the exclusive elite group. After graduating with a law degree, I will take a bar exam to become a law magistrate. It's…my father's wish to see me going this path. I promise to do my best so that Lady Rumpai will never be disappointed."

It was the first time I had such a long conversation with the nanny. Before bracing to ask permission to come inside the house and talk to her on this subject, I had kept reciting this speech to convince her for all it was worth. So, relief shot through my body when she simply nodded to me without creating a scene and answered me in her casual voice.

"Well, I'll acknowledge the lady on your request and let you know soon. Now you can go."

After my sleepless nights for the whole week, the nanny asked to see me. I never expected it to be that fast. I broke out in a cold sweat as I entered her room. This was the first time I didn't trace any hostility from this dreadful sixty-year-old, grim-faced woman. Instead of a usual sitting on the floor, she even asked me to be seated on the sofa near her and spoke promptly to me with a flicker of a smile at the corner of her lips.

"The lady has no problem with your request. She said it was a good decision you made. We will discuss all the details later to prepare for your law school enrollment, all right?"

I walked out of her room as if floating in the air. I'd never felt more exultant in my life. Oh, I couldn't wait to announce my best news to Lek. I would tell him with all my swelling pride that I had come a long way to have this day of triumph after ten long years of my ordeals, one after another. With all my forbearance, this day finally came, the day I overcame Lady Rumpai's prejudice and proved to her that I had the heart, brain, and willpower to pursue my goal.

All my fortitude now paid off in the end.

I noticed another significant change in her treatment. The following two weeks, I heard a faint knock at the door of my room. When I opened it, I stopped dead to find a girl from the main house carrying a tray with some dishes in front of the door.

"Khun Pran…"

The girl spoke to me in a soft, modest tone. Her use of the honorific *Khun* conveyed some respect that partly surprised and partly embarrassed me.

"Nanny Sook said you don't have to come to have your meals in the kitchen any longer. I'll help carry meals in a tray for more convenience. And from now on, I'll come someday to clean up your room and wash clothes for you. She wants you to have more time to study."

I became tongue-tied for one full minute.

"Um…I…really don't know…" I stammered.

"Leave it to me," she then walked out with a timid smile. "I'll come again."

The girl's name was Took-ta. I'd heard she was a distant relative of the nanny, a sixteen-year-old who had recently come to live under her roof to help with household chores. One thing about her bothered me: of all the girls in the nanny's house, Took-ta's pretty face outshone everyone. Since she was new, most people didn't know her name yet, so they simply referred to her as 'that doll-faced girl.'

Early before she came to introduce herself, I always averted my eyes from her whenever I walked past her outside. Not because the sight of her displeased me. On the contrary, a single glance at her could make my heartbeats boom. If she heard my heartbeats as loud as the sound of a cannon and let the nanny know, that could bring real trouble to me.

So, to avoid her face-to-face and to save myself from showing too much interest in her, which was somehow growing beyond my restraint, I made up a new habit of peeking at her without her awareness. Whenever I had a chance, I wandered near the nanny's houses, most of the time oblivious of all the risk of being caught by that damn old dog if it eyed me sneaking around that house. I hid behind a bush and put all my efforts into stealing a glance at her while she was too occupied with the house chores to notice me stalking her. She usually came outdoors in the late afternoon to tend the plants around that house. A swift glimpse of Took-ta tending plants and humming a song to herself was enough to elate my spirit all day, as much as missing out on the sight of her could dim and dampen my entire day.

After the day she came to introduce herself, I didn't have to take my own risk to peek at her anymore because Took-ta regularly came to my room to clean and wash my clothes, as she had promised. However, I often missed out on those chances since she came in while I was at school.

Anxious to be close to her, I rushed home from school every day, never letting anything stand in my way in the hope of finding a fortunate moment to talk with her. At the weekend, instead of seeing Lek at his place, I stayed in my room the whole day, my ears perked up for only one sound I was dying to hear: a soft knock on my door.

But at least I could see her briefly in the evening when she brought my dinner and sat patiently and quietly on a wooden bench outside the door. After I'd finished the meal, she stepped inside and carried out the empty plates. We hardly talked. But I wished I could hold back my heart from jumping off my chest during her stepping into my room, even as swiftly as one or two minutes.

She blushed and looked embarrassed because today she caught me stealing a glance at her. I forced myself to take my eyes off her, fearing that all the feelings I attempted to hide would flare up at any moment.

"Hope you like the fish green curry… I cooked it myself."

In her shy voice, she made a conversation for the first time to break that embarrassing moment.

"Oh, that's why it's so good," hearing what she said, my heart was swelling. "Thanks for cooking for me…"

She smiled timidly and looked around the small room cluttered with my books.

"Um… I heard you're going to study law," she said softly. "Oh my! They said lawyers make good living."

"I'd rather want to be a law magistrate," I said, struggling to keep my voice steady as I saw her sweet face in close-up. "I wanted to follow my father's wish."

"Um…they said Nanny Sook was your father's wetnurse. I saw his pictures all over her house. They're just everywhere. Oh my! I can tell how much she has adored your father."

She hesitated and stopped. I believed she must be wondering why the nanny had sent me, his son, to this isolated and shabby place at the far end of the main house. Then she added, "I never go to school. I have to ask someone to read aloud for me." She cast her eyes down and said, "It amazes me when I see someone can read. I hope it's not that hard to learn."

My heart was beating so frantically now it could have leaped out of my chest.

"I can teach you how to write if you want to learn…" I nodded to her vigorously, "and with all my pleasure."

"Oh, thanks. You're so nice," she looked meek, bowing down her head, "maybe it's too hard for me. My head is always muddled up."

"No, it's easier than you think. Believe me," I held my breath as I tried to coax her but yet tried not to be too obvious. "I could teach you little by little each time you come to bring me dinner. Sounds good?"

"I...have to ask Nanny first,"

Suddenly, she cried and looked around in alarm.

"Oh, time to go now."

"Stay with me for just one more minute..." My heart sank from her abrupt departure. "...Can you?"

I didn't realize that I had grabbed her hand to stop her until she quickly freed it from my grab.

"Let me go. The nanny doesn't want me to be outside after dark."

She took the tray and ran out. Her body disappeared into the dusk, but her girlish giggle still lingered.

I looked at the hand I'd just grabbed her. Before I realized it, I slowly raised that hand and passionately kissed it

When you started having a crush on a girl for the first time, it was impossible to stop this strange fever that had begun inflaming you night and day. And since you found nothing on earth could stop that crushing feeling, you welcomed it with a wide-open heart and let the bursting fireworks spark in full bloom. Oh, what a sweet, sweet agony of falling in love and afloat in that trance at every instant you breathed in and out.

But the next day, when I heard a knock on my door and flew to open it, I found another girl at the door, bringing a tray of food for me. My smile faded.

"Where...is Took-ta? Why didn't she come today?" I made all my effort to control my alarmed voice.

That girl shook her head and bluntly told me. "I don't know. She's gone, and the nanny asked me to carry this tray for you.

"Will...she be back?" I held my breath, forcing my voice to sound casual, but she shook her head again.

"I'm not sure. I think you better ask the nanny."

She eyed me curiously after that reply that didn't help me at all with any clue. I felt so shaken at Took-ta being gone out of the blue that I had to hold the door frame to support myself.

During the most tormenting week of her clueless absence, I sank into the infinite depths of despair. I sprawled on the cot all day, refusing to do anything except brood over that doll-faced girl. I couldn't even picture what to do next if there was no chance to see her again. Even though I moved heaven and earth to search for her, what chance could I find her out of millions of people in the whole wide, wide world? The sad, sad feeling I once had for the lady in the yellow skirt now came back and overwhelmed me again...

The next afternoon, I heard a faint knock on the door. Still disheartened, I dragged myself to open it and found who was there. I had to blink several times, so afraid that what I saw in front of me couldn't be real.

After the spell was broken, I heard myself cry in exuberance.

"Took-ta, where were you the whole week?" my voice trailed off, "...I think you left this house for good."

"Oh no," she giggled and smiled. She seemed glad to see me, too. "I had gone to take care of my sick grandmother. She's good now. So, the nanny asked me to come back here."

"Don't disappear again..." I just couldn't control my shaking voice and tears from great relief. "I'm....when you were gone, there's no way to know what happened; I'm so worried to death."

"I would come back," she smiled at me again and laughed, "I know how messy your room will turn out. So, I have to come back."

When she entered my room, I noticed she held a broom and a rag in each hand. It was the first time I was alone with her in this room when she came for a clean-up. I didn't want to make her feel uneasy in my presence. So, I tried to focus on my homework and pretended I didn't pay much attention to her.

However, I stole a steady glance at her while she was dusting and cleaning the room, her back now on me so my eyes could follow and be transfixed by every sway of her flowing movement while she was busily working on each of the room's corners.

To ensure her presence was real and not a shadowy image born from my own desperation during her absence, I tiptoed from my desk toward her as if under a mysterious spell, my trembling hand reaching out, closer and closer. *Oh, please, please, please stop...* I begged myself for the impossible. *Please stop...*

Instead, I felt my fingers grazing the nape of her neck. Now, I knew she must be real. She slowly turned her face to me, and our eyes met. Oh, what a lovely nymph she was turning into under the aura of the afternoon sunlight coming through the open window. It made both cheeks on her doll-like face glow in a rosy radiance so alluring that it was hard to avert my eyes from that image before I completely lost myself to that spell.

Trying to come to my senses, I swiftly withdrew my hand and quickly took one step back, receding to my desk to stop that startling compulsion to touch her. But before I could restrain myself, Took-ta slowly pulled me into her, and we together rolled down onto my cot on the floor.

Every night before falling asleep, I always fantasized about her in bed with me without her clothes on. I imagined caressing and kissing every part of her body over and over. So, when this wish-come-true moment occurred, it seemed more like some surreal dream than a solid reality. Yet, it must be real because I felt her soft flesh burning my own while our aroused bodies crushed and almost blended into one. The sensual, sultry scent on her bare body was arousing me in full-blown. I shuddered and winced when my groping hand finally found one of her stout breasts. It was so firm and yet soft in my trembling hand before I slipped it into my clenched lips and cherished every drop of its sweet juice.

One could not stop the earth from moving as much as I had no power over the mysterious nature that was taking its course in this small room.

Our amorous act was spiraling to its peak as I felt my raging ecstasy bursting with a suppressed scream. *Oh, oh, oh.* I'd never imagined that such a euphoric heights could exist until this very moment. Its extreme rapture made me oblivious to all, whether heaven or hell. All I heard was her racing heartbeats as I put my face buried deep in her breasts, moist and glistening with beads of sweat.

Love you... Oh, oh, love you so-so-so much I could die...

My whispering, moaning, and gasping breaths resonated with hers. They seemed to be the only sounds I was conscious of. I was unaware of any other noises, whatever they must be, which seemed to keep coming from so far away.

No sooner had I been alert that those noises came from someone frantically banging the door than it was suddenly thrown open. Three women stormed into my room; one was Nanny Sook, and the other two were her relatives who had forced the door open.

"You animal, what are you doing to my girl!"

The nanny shrieked as she rushed toward me and hit my face several times. Each strike was so forceful my nose started to bleed, and yet I hardly felt that pain compared to the shock when I saw Took-ta still nearly naked, bursting into a frenzy, sobbing, and rushing to kneel in front of the nanny, her arms wrapped tightly around the old woman's lower limb.

"I...I tried to run out, but he grabbed me... He threw me on the floor and jumped to rape me. He threatened to strangle me if I didn't let him... Help me, Nanny..." As those words were torn from her throat, her whole body was wracked with choking sobs.

As if being hit with a lightning bolt, I stood in paralysis while staring blankly like a dumbass at the girl I was falling head over heal with.

All words so desperate to utter were frozen in my throat. *I didn't force her. I swear she started it…* No one would believe it whatsoever. The nanny was acting as though she was going to tear me into pieces. She came to slap my face again and again until all her fury seemed finally let out.

"You ungrateful, filthy, vile animal! Is this what you gave Lady Rumpai and me in return? I sent Took-ta to help you around so that you can have more time to study. Now what? You downright raped her in broad daylight."

The nanny turned to Took-ta and asked her to put on her clothes and leave the room. When she fled outside, the nanny turned back to flare up at me.

"Pack your things right away and then leave my house. And don't even think of coming back. I'll give you ten more minutes. If you're not ready to go, I'll let my dog out to get you. And you forget about your law school," she emphasized the word 'law school' with a sneer at the corner of her mouth. "You don't deserve all the good support from the lady anymore because of your vile behavior. Now hurry up and get the hell out before I send some men to throw you out of my house!"

That'd happened out of the blue before I found myself kicked out and now wandering on the street, too numb and confused to put myself together. The only place on earth I could think of now was Lek's house in the slum. I took a trolley to his house after dark, carrying all my belongings. In this world, I had scarcely more than a few stuffs, most of which were my school books.

Lek listened intently to all I told him with no interruption. After a glass of rice whisky was gone, he clenched his jaws and suddenly said in finality.

"It is a setup."

"What!" This was worse than a thunderbolt striking me.

He looked at me gravely. "Don't you notice things changed right after you told my aunt you intend to attend law school?

They, I mean Lady Rumpai and herself, couldn't find any sound excuse to deny you. So, they started a conspiracy to burn your future to the ground."

"Conspiracy! Why?" I gasped. "No reason they hate me that much, Lek? I'm nobody. It doesn't make sense why they took so much effort only to ruin my life. Whether better or worse, my future doesn't mean a thing to them."

"They don't hate you out of nothing. They have a reason, all right? And it's a good reason they do believe you deserve it."

I never expected that in a million years. So, I became silent and listened to every word he said.

"That girl Took-ta must be some loose girl they hired to work for them. They looked for a pretty young chick who knew all the tricks to get a greenhorn like you hooked on her. Tell me, you found that girl moving into the nanny's house right after you'd let the nanny know about your plan to go to law school, right?"

I grudgingly nodded to him.

"That girl is bait. They watched your every move and waited for a ripening time to strike you. And when they saw you take a dare prowling around Nanny's house for a chance to peek at Took-ta, they knew it was a perfect time to deliver her at your door and just waited in participation for what they calculated would happen—to have her spark your groin—and then use that consequence to kick you out."

"I swear I didn't force her…" I stumbled and cried out, almost in tears. "She…started it, yet I just couldn't resist."

"That's it! That proves everything was schemed, as I said."

"Lek, you assume without a solid proof. What if she's not a loose girl? Took-ta would get punished if she told the truth she indulged me in…doing her? That's why I'm so worried about what she must face now." At that point, tears started to well up in my eyes. "I couldn't take it, I couldn't, if I'll never see her again. And what…what if I make her pregnant?"

Lek stared hard at me and then laughed as if I were telling him a joke.

"Let her get pregnant a hundred times by all men on the street for all I care. If you know one girl of this sort, you'll know every single one of them. Now answer me this. The nanny had never set foot in your place since you came ten years ago, not even once, am I right? So why did she suddenly show up in your room precisely to witness that scene if it wasn't Took-ta herself who must send a signal? All things add up to the point you can't deny they used her to seduce you. But what? Do you still lose your head over this girl?"

Then his expression softened into a pity.

"Don't cry, Pran. I know it's damn hard to forget her. Kicking the girl happens to be your first love out of your life is not easy. But too bad, she doesn't deserve that genuine affection from you."

"I can't forget her, Lek. I don't know how I can do that."

"The shock makes you still in a state of denial. But deep down, you know, with all pieces of evidence. And you should be smart enough to know what a waste to brood over a girl who is hired to damage your future and never gives a shit in doing so."

After this, he let me cry to my heart's content. Yet he never left my side. He waited until I was calmed down and began to tell me softly.

"You are welcome to stay with me as long as you want. I never wanted you to stay in that awful house in the first place. I can foresee how they were going to treat you. But I must respect your father's last wish to see you under his sister's care. Of course, he trusted her because she was his sister. So, he was unaware he was sending a lamb into a tiger's cave. Although I understand their motive, I am so outraged at what they've ruthlessly done to an innocent boy like you. So, I can't help feeling so relieved to see you out of their claws and come to stay with me," he patted my shoulder and smiled kindly. "It's your home now for all it's worth."

A few days later, after I was back from school and straight to my new home, I found Lek a little drunk as he was awaiting me. He looked up at me, his eyes so bloodshot I became startled at that sight.

"Lek, what's up?"

"It's the last thing I want to tell you… Haven't you got more than enough? But you need to know this. Sit down, please."

Oh, what is it again? I began to close my eyes. My hands were shaken terribly while bracing myself for whatever was awaiting me.

"I got the mail from my aunt Sook today. I'm going to read it to you."

He began to read with a flat, dead voice.

"*I wrote this letter on behalf of Lady Rumpai. She wants to let you know that she had withdrawn all Khun Than's money from the bank, including all the accrued interests, and donated all she mentioned to some non-profit charity—*"

"What!"

"You heard it right," he sighed and continued.

"*...So that this donation will merit her beloved brother's soul in celestial heaven. I enclosed that charity's receipt as proof of her transparency, stating that she did not take even a penny from her brother's bank and put it into her pocket. Her decision was made due to Pran's hideous behavior towards one of the girls in my house, which devastated the lady to the point that she decided to disinherit him from Khun Than's will. She wants me to announce to everyone residing in my house to acknowledge to them that the boy Pran has disgraced Khun Than and his whole family beyond her forgiveness.*'

He let that letter drop from his feeble hand.

"I'm so, so sorry, Pran. Although I understand why, I've never thought they could be that ruthless to you even though they know damn well you have nothing to do with whatever happened in the past. But at least, what they've done has laid bare some truth to me: they've never found peace for even one moment of their waking hours. Even to these present days, the two pitiful women are still tormented by their grudge that keeps burning them alive perhaps till their last day."

I sat there, too shocked to make sense of their intense hatred toward me.

"My aunt can't write something that elaborated," Lek said. "I believed Lady Rumpai wrote this letter herself. She used my aunt's name only to keep her distance from us," Lek forced a laugh, "Just like we are some cockroaches too filthy to risk a contact with."

The day I stumbled to see Lek, at least there was a thin thread of hope to dangle from. Although they had thrown me out, I was still entitled to my father's assets as his only son and beneficiary. I planned to use it to pay my tuition fee until I graduated. And if some were left, I would save it in time of need. But after listening to this fateful letter, my last hope that I was hanging on was completely cut. The cut sent me free fall down and down into the bottomless pit.

"My poor child," suddenly I saw him forcing back his tears. "Who would believe they make the blameless like you the main target and victim of their rancor?"

"The main target and victim? Do you mean all this happened because they've held grudges on a certain person but released them all on me? So, who's that person in question?"

"Your mother," unexpectedly, his answer came out in a dead voice.

First, I was too stunned to speak. But at last, I forced myself to ask.

"Had...had she done something terrible to them in equal measure?

"No, but they claimed she had done a thing no less than a serious crime," he paused before blurting out. "They condemned her for wrecking your father's life."

"Please, Lek," I begged him. "I don't want to go insane. Let me—"

I grabbed Lek's whiskey glass and, without thinking, poured myself a drink and slugged that liquid fire down my throat. I gagged. That hellish burning from a big gulp gave me a new, strange, satisfied feeling that somewhat drowned out the terrible reality of the past that kept surfacing one after another.

I expected he was going to snatch that glass from me, so I prepared to fight back. But he just watched me keep slugging down the liquid alcohol as if I were drinking plain water. His eyes were filled with tears as he watched.

Finally, I began to ask him. I tried to steady my slurred voice. "Lek, tell me. Had you…had you done something bad to my father, too? That's why even your own aunt has acted so hostile to you?"

The pain in Lek's eyes intensified. He was silent. Suddenly, he blurted out.

"They've believed his downfall started because of me. Maybe it's true…but I never meant it…not in a million years. You know he is everything to me."

"You try to hide from me what had happened to him. Whatever it is, it turns out to be me, *me* only, who has received and absorbed the worst impact from them. Seeing me having no future, they took all my father's money and dumped it into some unknown charity. That money was meant to support my school tuition. It's not fair, Lek. It's not fair."

I stared hard at him for one long minute with tears in my eyes. What I'd blurted out must hit the bullseye. It seemed to have shrunken him and kept him silent for a while.

When our eyes met again, to my great surprise, he began, for the first time, to unearth the story of my father he had buried inside him for half of his life.

The story started at sunset, went on all night long, and finished at sunrise the following day… the story of Beloved, the boy who was born with a golden spoon in his mouth.

A story of my father.

End of Part One

PART TWO: BELOVED

Part 2: Chapter1

The Golden Spoon

Many, many decades ago, in 1896, the year of Monkey on the zodiac calendar, a boy whose name meant Beloved was born with a gold and silver spoon in his mouth. He was a member of one of the most prestigious aristocratic families, a pure-blooded noble.

His ancestors had been in close servitude to the monarchs and the royal court for generations. His father, as well as his grandfather and great-grandfather, was an authoritarian military officer at eminently high rank, a formidable and overbearing figure who took his honor and pride so seriously: pride in his country, his pure noble lineage, and, above all, Beloved, his heir. *Chao Phraya*, or Grand Lord *Abhibal Bhuvanathnurak*, was his father's title, one of the highest nobility statuses.

His father was also a great landlord of almost ten thousand acres of feudal estate bestowed on him by his monarch. A large number of those lands were used for rice agriculture in the rural areas where he annually reaped a colossal profit from his tenants, who were peasants and commoners. The lord had his secret storage room built deeply underground to secure his treasures. There was a rumor that if one ever had a chance to peek inside that storage, one would gasp at the stunning sights of rows after rows of solid gold bars stacked up so high until they reached the ceiling.

His mother, Than Pu Ying Mook, or Grand Lady Pearl in short, also came from another equally wealthy and prominent noble family. After six daughters in a row, his forty-six-year-old mother finally gave birth to him, a long-awaited and almost miraculous son who would inherit their vast fortune and uphold their family's pride and glory.

At the time of his birth, his father already had twenty male and female children born to his concubines, some of whom were his waiting maids. However, they were counted as second-class children, incomparable with their significant siblings whose mother was the Grand Lady, his official, hence most important wife, and the matriarch of his huge household.

Rumor had it that Lady Pearl had declined her night shift in his bed since her first grandchild was born, leaving her husband alone to enjoy younger flesh. But one night, after quite a heavy booze as his wife was at his side to wait on him, his desire suddenly erupted. He couldn't wait to summon his other younger concubines to walk from their quarters to the main building where he had been living only with his wife and daughters. So, the rumor said, as a consequence, Beloved was conceived that night.

The story ended with the lady's unexpected pregnancy, stunning and yet amusing the household and embarrassing her grown-up daughters, especially her fourth daughter, who was just newlywed and also in her early pregnancy. However, nine months later, Beloved was born: a perfect infant boy as healthy and handsome as his mother had prayed for since she realized in blissful surprise that she was carrying her last-born child and her last hope. Though very late in her life, his arrival was finally a godsend for her.

Had she not given her husband an heir, his eldest son, born to one of his minor wives, would have been entitled to the lord's inheritance.

However, there was another covered version of this episode secretly told among her husband's concubines that his birth was her set-up plan from the beginning. Beloved's mother, out of her sheer desperation and frustration, deliberately set up the cunning scheme to be impregnated.

A fortune teller and also her consultant, whom she trusted, had prophesied a perfect son if she bore her husband another child. It's pretty hard for a middle-aged woman who was already several times a grandmother to arouse a romance and sensual flame in her husband, especially in a man who was nightly surrounded by his voluptuous concubines as young as his own daughters.

So, her consultant gave her some rare herb powder used to arouse acute sexual desire in men.

Rumor said one night she had laced his liquor with the herb, leaving him senseless and stunned enough to sire a son in his wife's womb, which he had long abandoned. It said those coupling acts, aroused by that powerful herb and encouraged by her, were carried on through the whole night; each time that he performed on her meant more promises for her to conceive a child.

After nine months, the midwife pulled a newborn out of her womb into the world. But a stigma of the newborn's virginal was unmistakably shown between the frail legs. After putting the infant to lie down beside the mother, it was neither moving nor breathing, and its skin was as pallid as death, a sight that made Lady Pearl scream her head off from shock. The midwife muttered that the grand lady was far too old to bear a child. That's why she gave birth to a stillborn.

While the whole delivery room was in extreme turmoil, everyone in that room heard another blood-curdling scream from the lady. The midwife found another baby emerging, alive and kicking.

His loud wailing, claiming his right upon this earth, suddenly silenced all ambient noises. His unexpected arrival even shocked his mother more than the death of another one.

The news spread like wildfire; the twins were born to Her Ladyship. The girl was stillborn. But the boy was alive and as beautiful as a divine reincarnate.

The celebration for the arrival of the family heir lasted three days.

His mother named him *Ananda,* which meant Beloved.

By the time Beloved was born, his eldest sister, who had been married into another wealthy family, was already twenty-five years old and had five children of her own. His second sister had three children, and the fourth was on its way. A few months earlier, both his third and fourth sisters had their baby boys within the same week. All his sisters seemed to compete with one another in making more babies to keep their husbands bound in their beds rather than stray into the arms of their rival concubines.

All his sisters were married off except his twelve-year-old twin sisters, *Rumpai* and *Chandra*, or Sun and Moon, who joyously helped her mother raise him along with his wet nurse and several attendants who watched over him nights and days.

It was said no one had ever heard him cry or wail, not because he was an exceptionally calm baby. On the other hand, Nanny Sook, his wet nurse, and her extra never let him have the slightest chance to open his mouth and hungrily cry for the rich milk. They took turns to suckle him around the clock.

Beloved was the apple of his parent's eye and of his twin sisters' who always fought over taking him in their arms and cooing over him as if he was their little doll, which they refused to share with anyone. When Beloved was a young boy, the sky was the limit, except for whatever in the sky that his family was not able to bring down for him as his playthings. And since they could not give him these celestial objects to compensate him, nothing else was impossible if he just opened his mouth and asked for it.

He had a partition in the house to play with his expensive toy collections, mostly imported or purchased from the British and American stores opened in Bangkok's downtown. There was a whole set of wooden building blocks, a box of crayons, a set of tin soldier toys, and a whole set of miniature clowns, acrobats, and animal figures like one could see in a circus, so popular among rich children at that time.

But the most amazing and fascinating of all was his Victorian cast-iron locomotive train sets paint in black and red, which actually ran on live steam power. The locomotive engine was a real live train in every aspect, only on a miniature scale with exquisitely and painstakingly minute details. This set of toy machines with passenger figures boarding in each car ran in circles around and around his large playroom at full speeds on its track network, passing along miniature houses and men figures standing by the railroad track, then crossing a tiny narrow bridge and going through a small long tunnel before the engine whistled *Choo-Choo-Chuck, Choo-Choo-Chuck* as its wheels gradually reduced its speed and finally came to a complete stop at the terminal train station.

All the boys in the household, including his half-brothers, rarely had a chance to glimpse this fascinating toy. On a rare occasion when Lady Pearl was in her high spirit, she would allow them to enter that toy room, the heaven-on-earth place that existed only in a dream of all children, and watch the train operated with their mouth hung open and themselves turned green with white-hot envy. However, when Beloved was not playing in that room, it was kept locked up at all times under the watchful eyes of his nanny Sook, who would see to it that none of his half-siblings would ever intrude on that room.

His nature of empathy and compassion for others began to emerge when he was seven years of age.

That year, his father gave him a birthday present: a first-class bicycle imported from Germany, a hot stuff of that period. Of course, his mother protested in alarm. When Baby Beloved reached his toddler age, he hardly had any chance to practice his walk. He was always carried in Nanny Sook's arms, his head well protected under the shade of a white parasol held firmly by another, for, as his mother proudly called, 'taking a morning walk'. And on a rainy day, the five-year-old Beloved sat cocooned in the cozy, warm corner, looking out the window to see other children—most were his half-siblings—romping, frolicking, and laughing boisterously behind the thick white sheet of rain.

No sooner had he poked his head out the window and stuck out his tongue to suck cool droplets ravenously than his Nanny Sook rushed in alarm to pull him into her arms, away from such a calamity. *Oh, my precious! You're getting wet and catching pneumonia. No, no, no!*

Therefore, the bicycle became a big issue. His mother and his nanny could not stand the picture of any imagined scrapes on Beloved's skin. Finally, his parents settled on a solution to this problem. The first rule was that he was not allowed to venture with his bike outside the perimeter of their estate. Apart from that, as he enjoyed riding his bicycle inside his courtyard in the late afternoon, his attendants, especially Lek, would never leave him out of their sight.

His doting mother had warned them that if he tumbled down his bike, they would all be responsible for every scratch and black and blue he suffered. Since they were not able to stop him from riding, they followed him on foot, quickening their pace while watching their young master's every movement as his bike capriciously meandered along the long, shady path cut through a grove of tall old trees that shrouded and secluded the mansion from the outside view.

The path led him to the vast square green lawn; its edges lined up with dwarf trees in valuable white and blue china pots.

From the far end of that lawn, one of the most magnificent European-style buildings of that period stood lofty against the sky. Its front—which was separated into two long curved wings with an elegant porch in the middle, two bay glass windows, and two balconies on each side of the mansion—faced the lawn where a fountain and a large marble basin full of swimming gold carp stood gracefully in front.

There, in the courtyard flanked by two curved wings of the building and surrounded by flowering shrubs and two paralleled long beds of roses in white, soft pale pink, bright yellow, and crimson, he stopped his bike right in front of the round basin and sneakily climbed into the waist-deep water inside with all the thrills of the world. He waded toward the fountain and opened his mouth, letting the cool water from the fountain sprinkle his face and run down his throat to quench his thirst for some adventure.

I'm now in the rain. Rain. Rain. Rain. No one will stop me from playing in the rain.

Oh, how he yearned to stay and walk in the rain like all the other children he had seen from his window. Oh, it seemed a world apart between the gloomy indoors and the outside, where rain and sunshine were for everyone but never for him.

After refreshing himself, Beloved soaked up from head to toe, climbed down the basin, and sprawled face down on the grass, his face gleaming wet with small beads of water, his nose smelling the damp earth, and his dreaming eyes darting around looking for his favorite tiny creatures that had never failed to fascinate him.

Aha! Finally, he caught sight of them scurrying along the patch of grass, moving to and fro. He closed his eyes, imagining himself turning into Lemuel Gulliver, a hero in his favorite storybook that his sister Rumpai always read to him, standing towering over the tiny citizens of the island country of Lilliput. *One, two, three, four, five, six, seven*, and many more emerged from their mysterious hole in the ground. To attract them, He fumbled for his handkerchief in his pants pocket, unwrapped it, cast a handful of the grains of cooked rice he had stolen from the kitchen, and stuffed it in his handkerchief. His heart beat with delight as those tiny black ants, his Lilliputians, started to hurry toward him as soon as they traced morsels of food.

Then he lay down again and let those tiny black ants crawl and climb across his chest in an amazingly single straight line. He lay so still, almost breathless, for fear of scaring away those tiny insects who were busy themselves, each carrying one grain of rice—its size bigger than their body—on their tiny backs. Their unfaltering unity, unyielding strength—compared to their wee body—and heroic efforts to cross an unknown vast land of his body stirred his heart. He suddenly yearned to become one of them, for absorbing their joy, experiencing their hardship, and sharing their comradeship.

He always dreamed of joining their camaraderie in their line throughout their adventurous journey back to their nest, and perhaps he would live among them down, down the dark and deep labyrinth underground. Never again going back to be Beloved, under the crushing affection and choking protection of his mother, his sisters, and his nanny. Free, free at last from the human burden that he sensed weighed more and more each day on his shoulder.

Drifting deeper into his reverie of the imaginary realm of ants, he was so oblivious to the world outside that he was startled as he abruptly caught sight of his attendants, led by Lek. They now caught up with him and rushed to him with their alarmed faces. In one instant, they noticed his clothes soaked with water from the fountain. He immediately rolled himself and turned up his body to face them as his response to their approach.

"*Khun Than*, how did you get all wet, sir?" Still panting noisily, Lek asked him nervously, too anxious to keep his voice courteous. "Her Ladyship and your nanny won't be pleased to see you in such condition, sir. You might catch a cold, sir."

"Well," he sighed, "while waiting for you, I felt so hot and thirsty I needed to drink some water. Then I found that basin…"

Now, all faces turned pale.

"Please, *Khun Than*, please don't do that again," they begged him. "The basin water is not clean. You might fall ill from stomach upset and, no! Even from dysentery! And if so, what shall we do?" The more they lamented, the more terrified they grew.

The impish smile lit up Beloved's face. Today, he felt mischievous enough to reveal his little secret, which he knew would make them worry to death instead of relieving their excessive worry over him.

"Why not? So many times, I've tasted the basin water. How fresh and c-o-o-l! Only one thing I have to avoid is to swallow some tiny fish or tadpoles alive!"

As they gasped, Beloved's jolliness abruptly changed. He sprang to his feet, aghast, looking so terrified.

"Oh…no! My friends, my tiny friends…" he wailed and moaned.

"Your friends, sir?" Puzzles were in their eyes.

"Yes! What have I done to them? They're all dead by now… I snubbed their life. I just squashed them when I rolled over…"

His voice dissolved into sobs, stunned and this time appalled his attendants. What happened to their young master? They rarely saw his tears or witnessed his temperament and other ardent passions. He always stayed composed, placid, and amiable to everyone in the household, his attendants included.

"*Khun Than*, where's your friends? I don't see any of them, sir," to please him, Lek's eyes darted back and forth nervously around the lawn, trying desperately to find the presence of his friends or whatever he took for his friends.

"They're just right underneath me, all dead and pulpy. I didn't mean to kill them, those poor ants… Believe me. Please believe me."

He whispered, his eyes pleading helplessly with his

attendants to believe him. His tears welled up again, but this time, he managed to hold them back. Oh! If only his imperious father had caught him shedding tears and showing his 'weakness' in front of others, especially his servants. He closed his eyes as he shuddered, trying to swallow his sobs as best as he could. "Poor, poor little ants…"

All his attendants looked at one another in absolute bewilderment. They couldn't believe their own eyes; right before them sat the heir of one of the most potent Siamese aristocrats. Oh! Look at him. See how he hung his head very low, and his teardrops dripped on the grass. Didn't he look so heartbroken and so guilty of the meaningless death of those worthless insects that he had caused?

Indeed, he must be thinking he had just annihilated the entire world with his own bloody hands. Their astoundment slowly dissolved into profound pity. Not only the heir of a nobleman his young master had been but also a small, vulnerable boy in a cold ivory tower whose lonely heart yearned for friendship from someone regardless of what someone or something might turn up to be, and in this case, the swarms of ants on the ground.

Lek felt a strong urge to rush to him, hold him tightly in his arms, wipe out his tears, soothe him, and comfort him until he made sure his master's silent agony was gone. But each attendant was always aware he was unreachable for them. They were forbidden to lay their hands on their young master unless in the matter of life and death circumstances. Between this vulnerable golden boy and themselves, there was a thousand-year perpetual wall of social status, so immense, so towering, and yet so deep-rooted into the bottom of the heart that the thought of climbing to breaking it down had never crossed their mind. All they could do so far was kneel beside him, silently and anxiously watching their great young master, their *Khun Than*, wrapped all alone in his strange misery that no one was able to reach.

Yes, It was such a ludicrous yet daily scene for any onlookers:

a long wriggling tail of humans trailing behind one little boy pedaling his bicycle around his father's mansion.

What does her ladyship think of her son? She must have thought he's made of an eggshell.

In this large compound, which consisted of nearly a hundred people—members of the family as well as servants—Lady Pearl's authority was second only to her husband. Therefore, all they could dare was gossip in whispers behind her back, shaking their heads in silence. However, they adored their young master as much as they dreaded his mother.

One day, Beloved asked them to leave him alone to ride his bike. He didn't want them to exhaust themselves by running after him. Reluctantly, they told their young master they had to protect him from a fall that could have caused him some minor cuts.

Suddenly, one of them, Lek, said in a low voice.

"A scratch on your knees meant a lash on my back, my honorable *Khun Than*. Additional scratches meant additional lashes."

His reply puzzled and startled the boy.

"Why should my mother punish you? If I fall, it's all my entire fault, not yours. This doesn't make sense to me, does it?"

He frowned; his young face suddenly looked serious and thoughtful, like a grown man. No one could provide a valid answer for him, or if they could, they would better keep their mouth shut.

The following day, when the same group of attendants brought his bicycle to him as they had done every afternoon, they kept waiting for him in vain because he never showed up.

After that day, the young boy gradually withdrew from riding his bike and spent most of his leisure time in his playroom, playing with his toys and reading the pictured storybooks his father had ordered for him from a foreign store. He might not understand the meaning of 'injustice,' yet he could sense that his fun and pleasure had caused trouble for someone else. And he knew he had never felt good about it.

Every morning after the breakfast Nanny Sook made for him, Beloved routinely and dutifully spent an hour or so with his mother in her private wing, one of the most exquisite parts of the grand mansion.

This wing included her living room, her bedroom chamber, her twin daughters and her son's bedrooms, and his famous toys playroom. Beloved's bedroom was adjoined to his mother's room because she could come to see him anytime during the night. No, his mother wouldn't let him sleep alone. His nanny Sook would share his room, sleeping on the soft mats on the carpeted floor, alert to any of his whimpers and cries when he was afraid and woke up from a bad dream. His nanny would climb to his bed and soothe him with his favorite lullaby song until he fell asleep again in her arms.

Mother Cuckoo, Mother Cuckoo,
Sneaking your egg in a crow's nest,
Fooling Mother Crow to hatch and care—
your creepy egg as her own flesh
Oh, Mother Cuckoo, sneaky Mother Cuckoo...

There had always been many hearsays in his large family. One was about his father, the Lord of this mansion, who took one of his waiting maids into his bed one night when he was not himself and still stupefied from the long-lasting effect of the herb his wife had doped him the night before to beget her a child. In his restlessness, he found a maid he hardly recognized crouching at his bedroom door. It was her turn tonight to wait for whatever he needed. So, he blindly took her into his bed to quench his sexual urge.

However, after that sex act was over and he became himself again, he found her face far from pleasant, and her body was too bulky-built, or, in other words, too fat to attract the lord any further. So, when a daughter he had unintentionally sired on that single night was born to her, that maid was sent to Lady Pearl to be Beloved's wetnurse because her swelling, fat bosoms could give bountiful and rich milk enough to feed more than one hungry mouth simultaneously.

That was why Nanny Sook became Beloved's wetnurse from the first day he was born. Except for her, he refused all other wet nurses his mother sought for him. The nanny's daughter was born less than a week before him. So, she nursed them side by side; one breast, the more swollen and more abundant in milk, devoted to her *Khun Than* and the other for her own daughter, who was entirely ignored by the father since birth for his shame of having even a fat, ugly maid pregnant. Unfortunately, her baby girl died two months later, prompting Beloved to become the whole world to her.

While other babies Beloved's age turned to solid food as their other source of nourishment, she kept suckling him and enduring his growing sharp teeth, which always left painful bitemarks and bleeding on her soft teats. But nothing mattered as long as he clung to her milk so much that he turned down most of the other foods he was offered.

The fact that the toddler was too grown to be breastfed was ignored. She kept feeding him to the last drop. However, at the time he had reached three years old, she had to give up nursing him because all her milk had dried up. Not a drop that he could squeeze from those empty breasts under his vigorous sucks. When he threw himself on her lap and wailed nonstop, demanding her milk that didn't come anymore, his wailing nearly broke her. All she could do was hug him and cry with him.

Although he no longer needed her as his source of nourishment, he still clung tight to her for his other needs. Whenever he felt fear and lost and needed to feel safe, he would quitely sneak into the nanny's room while she was alone. He was grown-up enough to know he was not supposed to, and yet he couldn't stop his urgent need to throw himself on her lap and snuggle his face into the warmth of her breasts, which he fondly called *nom-nom* until his trembling mouth found the familiar fat teat he missed so much. She never scolded or turned him away. On the other hand, she pulled him into her arms, her eyes brimming with blissful tears while she indulged him in suckling her milk-less teat to his heart's content.

While on her lap, during their silent rapture bonding moment, she always covered him with a blanket to protect him from all the curious eyes that could take him from her. That habit had prolonged without anyone's notice until the boy reached the age of six when Lady Pearl found out in alarm. She stopped his nanny from indulging her son's immature habit of clinging to her nipples as his security blanket. The lady even brought him a new nanny, but it never worked. Her son threw a tantrum and cried all night until his mother gave in and allowed his old nanny to return to him. No one could separate them or weaken their fierce bond.

Every morning in her living room, her ladyship would sit idly on a couch covered with an exquisite Persian carpet, leaning comfortably on three or four large embroidery silk pillows with her gold inlaid betel box always by her side. The furniture in that room was a mixture of European and Oriental. Everything in the room was larger than life. It screamed power and wealth. In short, the room represented its owner. If someone entered the room, first, he would gasp at an elegant crystal chandelier hanging from the ceiling and catching the bright sunlight from the window and flashing sparks of fire.

If the guest dashed his eyes around, he would see in plain sight a set of grand sofas with golden embroidery used for receiving her guests at the left corner and a mahogany tall gleaming grandfather clock with soft tick-tock, tick-tock sounds from its faithful pendulum at the right corner.

Or if he looked straight and focused his eyes on the middle of the room, he would marvel at a large ebony table inlaid with iridescent mother-of-pearls in painstakingly elaborate designs with an antique China vase filled with a bunch of beautiful rare orchids setting on it.

Yes, that room immediately awed any person who strode in as her guest as much as intimidated anyone who crawled in as her inferior.

As idle as she could be on her cozy favorite couch, Lady Pearl still held herself with a grace that radiated from her inner strength and self-righteousness. She looked so elegant in her gold brocade loin cloth and her shoulder-green silk wrap. A pair of her waiting maids crouched behind their mistress, steadily waving a large iridescent peacock feathered fan in their hand to ventilate the cool, fresh air for the lady's comfort.

In contrast, the others prostrated quietly on their heels before her, their eyes downcast but their ears constantly perking to respond to their mistress's fluctuating moods and whims. The sweet scent of jasmine flowers mixed with the fragrance of red rose petals and deep yellow magnolia champac flowers in a large silver bowl permeated the room as they helped her ladyship embroider dozens of jasmine garlands prepared for the incoming Buddhist Sabbath.

Despite her elderly age, in her mid-fifties, Lady Pearl still had a small, delicate figure in contrast to the strong and sharp features on her face. Her porcelain skin grew so silky and glossy that it shimmered in the morning sunlight that slanted through the open glass window as her body basked in it. Even at one swift glance, no one could deny the trace of outstanding beauty on that face, the face of a living female deity.

Yet when their eyes met hers, they were startled and intuitively withdrew from that penetrating stare immediately. Those eyes did not match the owner's feminine, soft, and ladylike appearance. It would have been perfect if they had been removed and set otherwise on the severe face of a man in absolute power.

Yet, all severity and austerity had instantly disappeared when she saw her son. His stout nanny carried the nearly seven-year-old boy in her arms as if he were still a little boy.

Once the lady caught sight of him, her face lit up, and all

her unpleasant moods were gone. All the lady's maids released a sign of relief at his presence. They knew they were safe now from her unpredictable temperament.

They knew he was her source of joy, her greatest pleasure. She beckoned him to come to her and opened her arms as he approached her with his disarming smile, which always melted her steel heart. After he settled himself snug and cozy on her soft lap, his mother greeted him with numerous hugs and kisses as she mumbled to him affectionately.

"Welcome here, My Beloved, my baby, my darling, my precious…"

After that lavish greeting ceremony had been over, the time for a lesson of 'Our Ancestors Study' promptly started. She would proudly recite all the names of their noble ancestors, paternal as well as maternal, their heroic deed, and their significant contribution to Bangkok's establishment and prosperity when the new capital had been founded by this recent dynasty a century ago.

Then, he would repeat those names after her, spelling and writing them in calligraphy. He knew she expected only accuracy and perfection, nothing less. His exceptional memory and his excellent command of calligraphy deeply pleased his mother. After a very short period, he could memorize all those lengthy and challenging names and titles of his predecessors.

It began with his paternal great-grandparents, *Chao Phraya Abhai Dhamrongritthi* and *Grand Lady Montha*, both long deceased.

His maternal great-grandparents would be next. Their names were *Chao Phraya Siharaj Sansongkram* and *Grand Lady Nuan*, both long deceased.

Then came his paternal grandparents, *Chao Phraya Chaninthorn Dhammanuchit* and *Grand Lady Kulaab*, both recently deceased.

The following would be his maternal grandparents: Lady Pearl's father and mother, *Chao Phraya Akkhradej Dechochai* and *Grand Lady Sri.* The wife recently died, but the husband remained, though in declining health at the age of eighty-three.

The family tree list went on and on as if it had never ended; with less but still respectable status as *Phraya*, it included his great uncles, his uncles, and his distant relatives on both sides of his parents.

"In the future, we will welcome another Chao Phraya into our distinguished family. Guess who he is, my Beloved."

His mother asked him, hinting something to him with a sly laugh. He shook his head in a genuine puzzle, making her laugh even more heartily and drawing him closer to her bosom—and, therefore, her heart.

"It will be you, my darling. You! That's why your father and I have to prepare you so early for that significant status you will receive in the future. Ah…" she sighed deeply; her eyes burned with intense determination. Then she softly murmured. "I know it's still such a long way. I would be long gone before you achieve that status. So, Beloved, promise me you will put all your efforts into carrying on our family's honor."

"But Mother," he frowned as he protested in his usual subdued voice, "there are so many of our ancestors and living relatives who are already Chao Phraya and Phraya. So many of them! Just look at their names on the list I wrote down. On the other hand, there is only me in the world. What's wrong with being *me,* which is the one and only in the whole world? And what's so unique about being just 'another' Chao Phraya among the whole bunch?"

His naïve question stunned her. She was nearly taken aback. For seconds, it seemed she could find no words to respond. Had he been anyone else in this household not her Beloved, that person would have been immediately punished with a slap on the face for taking a dare to offend her. Without a second thought, she would also fling right on their face a box, a tray, a scalding hot tea from her cup, or whatever was within her reach. Finally, all she could do to her son was to collect herself, steady her voice, and pat his shoulder.

"Darling, who put that nonsense into your head? Any of your attendants?"

Suddenly, Nanny Sook crawled to her and whispered something to the lady. Only her favorite was allowed to do that.

That whisper made her gasp. A sudden suspicion fiercely flashed in her eyes. She raised her voice almost in a shriek.

"Sook, you are right. It must be one of those boys. Darling, I told you many times don't play with them or even talk to them. Don't you know those boys and their mothers neither have goodwill for your future recognition nor achievements? Now, darling, tell me which one put this nonsense into your head. You're just too young to fancy this idea yourself."

She coaxed the truth out of her son, but he had already witnessed the trouble his mother could cause to those under her power. She always used the collective term 'those boys,' which she stressed with contempt, to mention her husband's other sons. She never bothered trying to learn their names individually.

"No, mother, please don't blame them. It's nobody, not any of my brothers," he replied firmly with his usual gentle demeanor.

The word 'my brothers' that her son uttered so casually infuriated her. It pierced her heart and stirred all the hatred embedded there for so long. Yet, she could not hurt her Beloved. All her blazing anger instantly shifted to all her husband's concubines.

Suddenly, the peaceful episode, moments ago, twisted into an unexpectedly war-like atmosphere. In front of him, she immediately summoned all her husband's concubines, so far twelve of them altogether, to be present. And as they all soon hurriedly prostrated themselves before her, she hurled all her anger at them, accusing them and their sons of brainwashing her son and abetting him in behaving against her. Meanwhile, Beloved sat stiff and frozen, eye witnessing the scene of humiliation his mother had created before his eyes.

"Where's the new girl? Where? Why don't I see her face

among you?" With her thundering voice, her eyes swept across those faces, one by one. "She knows she has no privilege not to show up when I call."

There was a moment of silence. Then, one in the group replied with hesitation.

"Your Ladyship…" she paused. "That girl has just given birth to a baby boy this morning. She isn't able to get herself up here, for now."

The woman lowered her head, trying with all the effort to conceal a faint, almost invisible smile of satisfaction at the corner of her lips that she could not control.

Every sound fell into silence. This large chamber would have been deafened if all of their heartbeats could have been heard outside their chests. They expected the thunder to clash on them any minute, but after a long silence, all they heard was a chuckle from the grand lady.

"You want to see me howl and scream, right?" She snickered again to let her nonchalance be seen. "Why do I have to pay attention to such a petty thing? Another piglet born into the pigsty crammed with female pigs that my lord has feasted on. It isn't worth my time even to piss off. I am concerned that if you want to live peacefully under my lord's roof, tell your children to stay away from *Khun Than*. Tell them to stop feeding my son all those weird and hideous ideas. I know what all of you are up to. It doesn't and will never work."

But the tone of her voice eventually betrayed her words. As they listened to her shriek and scream of anger, they sat so still as if they were carved from stones, their eyes downcast, their face expressionless and fathomless. It was hard to tell what they felt under such an attack.

Perhaps the matriarch's blame and accusation that did not need proof or evidence became a norm in the household, and they did not bother or even care. Yet, they did not dare to overtly challenge her, let alone show their resentment and unconcern on their faces. Everyone in this household, except her husband, was under her supervision and authority.

Their meals, their garments, their beddings, their monthly allowance, and all their extra expenses relied alone on the matriarch's judgment, which in turn depended on her whims rather than explicit principles. The lord of the house left all domestic affairs to his wife only in exchange for his indulgence in younger women. However, from time to time, after hearing some complaints in whispering from his women, he would see to it that the way she directed the household was decent and fair.

Suddenly, she turned her back on them and resumed her work on flowers as if the sight of them was not worth her time and attention any longer.

"Oh! Beloved," she shifted all her attention to her son as if only two were in that room.

"Guess what? Your sister Chandra told me last night that after she read you the bedtime story of Snow White, you wanted to taste some fresh red apple, the one the wicked witch lured her to take a bite of!"

After peals of laughter, she went on, raising her voice with full awareness of the concubines' pricking up their ears.

"Your father said the steamship from Singapore will arrive at the port in two weeks. It will be loaded with all kinds of overseas fruits from Europe: apples, grapes, pears, and apricots. You can try them all, whatever you wish. Can you wait, darling? You might be fed up with dried persimmon and pickled lichee from China." Then she frowned, peering at his face, her eyes flickering with concern.

"What's wrong, baby? Do you not feel good? Something upsets you?"

He shook his head without saying more to his mother. He just wanted to save those poor concubines from his mother's slashing words.

The concubines waited patiently while mother and son were engaged in their seemingly trivial conversation. They waited but did not dare to move if they could not leave without her permission. It must be worse if they did it against her will. The next time, they would be punished with what they called among themselves, 'the cold blood torture.'

They all still remembered the last time she had asked Nanny Sook to summon them up to her wing without any particular reason, or if there had been a reason, it was to enjoy watching them crouch aimlessly before her for an hour on end, humiliated and entirely ignored by most of Lady Pearl's waiting maids, who had been ordered to cram the room as the lady's supporters and audiences. Their acknowledgment of the presence of these concubines had been so subtle, almost untraceable: only the scorn on faint smiles that played on their lips or sideway glances with a hint of mockery and contempt. The nanny's unhealable wound caused by the lord's downright rejection of her always flared up in the presence of the whole bunch of his favorable concubines. Therefore, nothing would please her more than having a chance to watch them being humiliated. No wonder Nanny Sook could make her way to become the grand lady's favorite. They both had one thing they strongly agreed on; it was the resentment they both felt in equal passion for those concubines.

A full hour had been trickled down, and those women still crouched, perplexed, in the silent presence of mice in their hiding hole, waiting for the usual outburst of the lady's temper followed by the predictable yelling. But that time, they had heard nothing, only the absolute and cold silence, which seemed far worse for them to respond. Why did she summon them in the first place if she didn't open her mouth? What should they do in response to such humiliating treatment? Was this an innovative way of punishment? And the most puzzled of all, they wondered what had they done wrong to her after all.

Yes, they all did something deadly wrong to her. Their existence wronged her. Their sons' existence wronged her. Her husband's open affection and concern for them wronged her.

Absurd and childish as it seemed, Lady Pearl wanted the most effective revenge—an act of revenge in any possible method as far as she could figure out for crushing their worthless beings and their pathetic pride into a mere speck of dust that she could stomp under her feet.

At least the meeting this time was considered more tolerable because there was a reason for it, though trivial as it seemed. When it was apparent that the lady exhausted all the topics that she could find to criticize them—or, more precisely, to abuse them—she soon let them get out of her face. With her cold stare, she pointed her finger at the door as the grand finale of this drama scene.

"You can leave now. But remember what I said. Go! Get out of my face!"

They started to inch away from her on their knees and elbows until they were quietly out of her sight, at least safe and sound this time. Yet, the lady's burst of satisfied laughter, accompanied by her choruses led by Nanny Sook, followed them as they stepped down the flights of stairs, echoing down the hallway. Hearing the fierce laughter behind them, though they could not fly, they wished they could have wings and fly away.

Fly. Fly for your life before that bitch tears you to bits.

There was a talk that when Lady Pearl was young, she had been sent to stay among the great ladies in the royal court, the tradition for the noble families to refine and cultivate their young daughters. It was the best place for girls within the elite circle to learn what was best, from culinary to music to dancing to handicrafts to literature and poetry and all kinds of arts, enabling them to be the most sophisticated group of the Siamese high society.

Soon enough, Pearl's blossoming rare beauty attracted the eyes of the monarch himself. This meant she was offered the highest honor of becoming one of his consorts. But she had vowed to choose her own path rather than become another insignificant figure of a royal concubine among the numerous females in the royal harem.

Before any arrangement was made, she had found her prince charming, a minor military officer then, during one of her home visits.

Her elder brother had introduced Mongkol to her as his classmate when both were in the military academy. His strikingly handsome face and masculine appearance, with his elegant and sophisticated manner, attracted her in equal measure, as her remarkable beauty almost stopped his heart at first sight.

The second time they had met, he started to court her, then confessed boldly to her that she had swept him off his feet like no other girl he had ever laid eyes on. He was unaware that the admiration and the praise to the sky for her meant only to melt her heart had planted a seed of conceit in hers. And the conversation ended with his brave proposal. Since both of their families were considerably on good terms and equally wealthy, they had been engaged and soon married in a perfect and fabulous grand wedding ceremony. The couple was celebrated as the perfect bride and groom of the era.

With the couple's perfect match in their striking good appearance, wealth, and love spell that they had cast on each other, they could have lived happily ever after as in a fairy tale, but they could not in reality. Maybe they could have if only the mistress of the house had been less possessive of her spouse and the patriarch less womanizing.

Year after year of her giving birth continuously only to daughters, her husband started bringing home under her nose new faces of young girls, one after another. Those girls could not be compared to her in every aspect except for their young flesh, their only advantage over her. And soon enough, the worst news came when one of his concubines bore him his firstborn son, which nearly shattered her into pieces.

That boy was born only two hours after Lady Pearl had

given birth to her twin daughters, Rumpai and Chandra. The lord didn't come to see her and his new daughters until late the following day because he couldn't wait to hold his firstborn son in his arms and stayed there overnight to care for the baby and its mother.

Her pride and vanity were as formidable as a wall built to withstand any attacks against her sense of grandeur. However, as invincible as it appeared, her towering wall was so immense that it stood awaiting crumbling and collapse, for it could not withstand its own enormous weight and gravity. Her overweight pride became her own vulnerability, creating numerous cracks and holes as opened wounds, and having been stabbed time and again by a sense of humiliation and despair of her incompetence in keeping their intimate relationship, which by degrees caused failure in their marriage. She had never gotten over this unbearable fact even though she eventually had her Beloved to shift all her dedication, her hope, and her affection to him.

If the lord's hobby were collecting young women to expand his harem, hers would be raising hell to them, the way to avenge his betrayal. Their house was perpetually on fire. It burned night and day, charring every soul under the roof—including the one who set the fire, the ones who were the fuels, and the one who threw those fuels into the heart of blazing flame.

* * * * *

Part 2: Chapter 2

The Forbidden

T *he living quarters where all the lord's concubines and other children had been dwelling were the immediate area behind the mansion. There were two long, parallel rows of small, single-story houses crammed closely together, with a narrow brick path cutting through them.*

The air was always filled with the aroma of cooked food and firewood smoke, the scent of sun-dried clothes, and the sounds of laughter, quarrels, children playing, a baby's cry, a distant lullaby, and other everyday activities.

At night, his women would take turns coming up to his father's chamber at his separate wing of the mansion, or sometimes, the lord himself would come down to spend the night with some of his favorites in their quarters, depending on his whim.

When Lady Pearl, accompanied by her twin daughters, went out once a week to visit her aged father whose health now was drastically declining, or when she was busy with her handcraft works, receiving her guests, or taking her afternoon nap, Beloved always sneaked out and ran into this compound, his pocket stuffed with imported sweets: chocolate bars, lollipops, striped gumdrops in red, green, and yellow, and sugar candies he had smuggled from the pantry, reserved only for him and his little nieces and nephews on their weekly visit.

Those sweets were a special treat for his little brothers and sisters, who, each like a puppy with so many wagging tails, squealed and jumped with joy and delighted at his sight. They swarmed around him and trailed after him wherever he went. Their faces showed admiration and pride for strutting alongside him and openly calling him Brother Beloved instead of Khun Than, as they had been taught to call him.

One day, he dropped by after he heard that a new baby boy, his father's youngest child so far, was born to his current favorite concubine, the one who had not shown up at his mother's room. He wanted to see that baby because they said the new baby looked just like him. Apparently, at first, his new stepmother was reluctant and uncomfortable, almost to the point of dread, to welcome him into her room, yet she did not dare to refuse his regard.

As promised, he sat quietly, watching with wonder as the young mother nursed her newborn.. He saw the tiniest creature he had ever laid eyes on sucking its mother's nipple greedily and noisily, regardless of the new world into which it had just emerged, its tiny face turning so red with its ravenous hunger, and then still in its mother's cradle, it abruptly yawned and closed its eyelids, falling asleep like a docile little kitten.

She carried him to his crib nearby and put him in there. As his mother's lastborn, it was the first time Beloved had watched an infant so closely.

"Oh! What the cutest thing I've ever seen!" He cried, his hand reaching out for the baby and gingerly patting his tiny head with the soft, silky black hair. "What's his name?"

"The lord told me he will find an auspicious name for him according to his horoscope. Meanwhile, I call him Baby Boy."

"Hey, Baby Boy, open your eyes. Your big brother's here. Welcome to our family," he greeted his new sibling softly.

Because of his eagerness and tenderness toward her baby, she soon turned disarmed and eagerly let Beloved bend his head to kiss its cheeks and tiny hands as she tried to teach him how to sing a lullaby to soothe a cranky baby. She seemed to be the youngest among all his stepmothers, barely fifteen, a child herself, cute, young, and so full of life. Even his youngest twin sisters were five to six years her senior. She looked so girlish that it was odd for him to see that what she held in her arms was not a doll but her own baby.

Soon, they started laughing together—like two young playmates sharing a favorite living toy—at his attempt to imitate her crooning, which he disastrously failed. She giggled, and he made a face for her.

"Now, listen to this one. It's so funny. I bet you'll love it," the adolescent mother giggled again and excitedly started her new lullaby song with her fantastic, sweet, silky voice.

> *A slave boy paddles*
> *Up, up the raging river*
> *While his master rumbles*
> *That the boy dawdles*
> *The boy is furious to his core*
> *He hits the master's head with his jumbo ore*
> *Bang! Bang! Bang!*
> *And his master ever grumbles no more.*

"Is it a lullaby?" Beloved asked, incredulous. "The lyrics sound very weird, not like my nanny's lullaby I heard when younger. It's about a mother cuckoo laying her egg in a crow's nest to fool mother crow."

She wiggled her nose and shook her head.

"Nah, that's too old and too boring. My mother has sung it a hundred times. Oh, by the way, I saw your fat nanny once. I saw her outside carrying you around like you're still her baby." A giggle slipped from her lips.

Oh, that made his face as red as it were catching fire. How often did he insist that he never felt exhausted at all while doing his walk? But just like his stubborn, doting nanny cared to listen. So, he quickly returned to their previous topic.

"Did you make up that lullaby yourself?"

She shook her head vigorously with her girly giggle again.

"No, It's a folk lullaby. But it's so funny. I sang it to my younger sisters and brothers every night to keep them quiet. Oh! How they loved my voice! They were willing to go to sleep to listen to their favorite lullaby. But sometimes, when they were so peevish and started whining, do you want to know what I did along with that song?" Her eyes now were gleaming mischievously.

"What did you do? Tell me now!" he urged her with his boyish enthusiasm.

"When the song came to the bang part, I knocked their head with my knuckle. *Bang! Bang! Bang*! A complementary act. And it worked! They stopped bubbling over and hurriedly shut their eyes at once!"

Then she abruptly sighed, a saddened shadow clouding her lively eyes. "I'm the eldest. I had to take care of them all. You never had the idea what nuisance they were, but oh…I missed them now," she sighed again.

"So, why are you here?" He asked curiously.

"My family is dirt poor. So last year, my mother sold me to the lord."

"Sold you?" His mouth hung open in disbelief. "Your mother?"

She replied with her nonchalant nod.

"According to the slavery abolition act recently effective, slavery now is illegal," he announced, frowning like a grown-up man.

"That is the law, not life," She shrugged. "But when I entered the lord's household, instead of doing backbreaking work like laundering, dishwashing, sweeping, and scrubbing the floor, I was chosen to be trained as one of the vocalists in his private string assembly. They all said I have lovely features and a voice as a chime of a silver bell," another coy smile from her. "A few weeks later, the lord ordered me to wait on him in his chamber at night, giving him a good massage. It has been my duty almost every night since then. A few months later, when I noticed my belly was getting swollen, I was scared to death. Then they told me it was the most promising sign. I was carrying the lord's child." She giggled again.

"So, a woman can have a baby by massaging someone," he concluded in wonder. "Now, I get it."

"You silly boy! Are you serious?" She burst into a hearty laugh, looking at him strangely as her body shook up with laughter.

"What's wrong? Did I say anything wrong? No one has ever told me. Why is it so secretive about the way women have a baby?" he asked her with a series of questions, puzzled at her peals of laughter, which were so irritating and senseless for him.

Shaking her head, she shed her tears from a prolonged laugh, yet still in her laughing fit as if she would have choked herself to death. "You silly, silly boy…" She managed to talk through the ripples of her uncontrollable laughter. "You don't know a thing. Oh, I can't believe it."

Her laugh abruptly came to a stop, as abruptly as it had started a minute ago. Her eyes shone like a cat's sneaking in the dark as they darted around, searching for anyone who might appear unexpectedly at her door. Then she turned to him. Her jet-black eyes glowed with something even more mischievous, almost sinister.

"Let me show you, silly boy," she grabbed him by his hand as she hastily untied a long cloth strap. In a flash, it slipped from her breasts and dropped to the floor.

"Don't you see? Don't you see how it starts—the making of a baby?" She hissed.

He gazed at the sensual flesh on her large and voluptuous breasts with his blank eyes while she guided his hand toward her until his fingers glazed one of her breasts.

"The lord just came to see me last night, and oh, he said he had no patience to wait till I recovered from childbirth, for no other concubines can satisfy the urge in his groin."

"No, I don't get it," he shook his head and frowned, starting to be annoyed.

"Press your hand on it. Cup it in your hand! Feel it!" Her eyes gleamed as she whispered. "Now, suck it with your mouth! You'll come to understand what I mean."

"No," he shook his head again, blinking, perplexed. Her mischievous and dark smile faded as he withdrew his hand from her in disdain. "I don't want to suck it. A woman's teats are only for a baby to suck. I'm a grown-up now."

Her open bosom reminded him of himself as a petite boy in his nanny's arms, hungrily drawing the milk from the swollen nipple of her huge breasts. And even after he was weaned, she still used her milk-less nipples to comfort him so he could fall asleep. Yet, he never felt the presence of his nanny's nom-nom and of all other women in this world could arouse his interest, and that definitely included this girl in front of him.

He then stressed his words with indignation.

"Who still needs a wet nurse?"

Beloved stood as erect as a man and looked as solemn and proud as he could while trying to reason with her.

Again, her smile returned as suddenly as it had faded an instant ago. A mocking, defiant smile a female would give when her feminine pride was hurt. Then she hastily wrapped the cloth to cover her bosom, shaking her head as if in deep pity at him. Oh, what she tried to hint to him was still far beyond his experience to grasp. He merely felt what she had secretly shown him struck him as odd, making him rather uneasy, embarrassed, and even more mystified.

"Oh! You're a grownup! You, a big-g-g man now!" She snorted. "How old are you? Nine?"

"I am ten," he declared, his shin up.

"A grownup man of ten-year-old!" She feigned excitement and giggled. "But how dare you claim you're grown up if you are so sure women's breasts are for babies only? Just go ask your father himself." She finished with a shriek of laughter.

"Oh! Really!" cried Beloved, his eyes still dull and blank from this very new acknowledgment. The particular topic she brought up in their conversation started to bore him, yet she enjoyed much of it.

"Yes, it's true," she insisted defiantly before dropping her voice into a whisper. "I'll give you a few more years; this time, when you return, we'll see if you've changed your mind. Don't you know your father fell head over heels for this?" Her hand caressed her ripe breasts, which were quivering heavily from their weight of plumpness. "Yes, this turns me into his favorite, making all of his other women green with envy." She held her head high in triumph, flashing a haughty smile as she uttered a punch line. "...Including your pathetic mother."

"But my father is old enough to be your father! Some of my brothers and sisters are way older than you." He protested, puzzled at her apparent pride.

"So what? Look what he gave me last night," she proudly and excitedly showed him a pair of sparkling large diamond studs on her earlobes and a thick gold bracelet on each of her wrists, the new toys for a barely fifteen-year-old mother. "Those are the gifts from him because I bore him a son. A son whom everyone said was a spitted image of the lord. Oh! Why! My baby looks just like you, too. I've just noticed." She clapped her hands, pleased and excited. "It guarantees he'll grow up to be a very handsome boy like you!"

"Does he look like me? Really? I heard some said that too." he started to be excited, too, peering at the tiny red face still sleeping peacefully in the crib.

"Yes," she nodded to confirm her remark. "I can see that you're the image of the lord himself, your face. Except that you have eyes so soft and dreamy like the eyes of a fawn, but the lord's eyes are like those of a powerful tiger, so fierce he makes me gasp when he pounces..." She said with another giggle.

Then she started to sense his annoyance. She sighed in

defeat, and suddenly, to please him, she changed the subject.

"Do you want to know my name?" She coyly asked.

"Oh, Yes," said Beloved promptly and eagerly.

"Lin Jong," she said proudly. "That's my name."

"Lin Jong…Why! It's a water lily… My favorite," he cried with delight. "Water lilies bloom every morning inside a row of earth basins lining up the front garden. They're so lovely I like to pick some for my mother. She loves them too."

"Do you call those scrubby and scraggy cultivated things water lilies?" The scorn in her voice was obvious. "If only you could have come and seen the real ones, the sea of water lilies at my home."

Her voice suddenly trailed off; her eyes softened. She suddenly transformed into a dreamy young girl before his eyes.

"In the rural area where I once lived, there's always an expanding body of water. Water everywhere as far as I could stretch out my eyesight when our rice paddy field was under the flooded water that came every year. Fat fish were so abundant I could jump into the water, hold my breath, and then dive down. And in an instant, I could catch one of them with my bare hand."

"Poor fish…Why did you catch them? Don't you know you took their life?" he cried in protest.

"Why not? If they don't die, we will," replied Lin Jong flatly. "Aren't we wrong if what we can eat is the thing that breathes? No one can eat pebbles and sand. Or can you?"

This time, he sighed, defeated.

"And then one morning…" she continued. "When I looked outside from our shanty, millions of water lilies were blooming all at once in pink and white, so lovely I couldn't resist paddling our boat to pick them. Out there in the open, vast sky, I could shout and whoop and holler as far as my voice could carry. The sun was so frizzling, but the breeze was so cool, and so was the water. We stopped paddling and let the boat idly float and gently penetrate thousands of their green pads. The faintly sweet fragrance of water lilies drifted through the open air. You could hear music from a flock of birds and crows squawking and cawing, flying over your head and circling your boat. Their cries echoed in the air. Those birds hovered just barely above the water to catch fish. When I threw a dead fish in the air, it never splashed into the water. In mid-air, one of those birds always caught it in time with its big beak and soared away."

Her story now nearly took away his breath. Of course, it was a lot more interesting than talking about her boring breasts. He listened with his wide eyes, beginning to see what she had seen and feel what she had felt. He even heard her wild whooping and the thousand birds' squawking echo in his ears. The bright blue sky, the golden sunshine, the cool, soft breeze, and the sweet smell of water lilies in the open air.

"What fun…" he murmured and sighed deeply.

"Well, it was. But you never know what was lurking beneath that murky water. Have you ever seen leeches?" Her voice sounded thrilled, as if she were about to tell him some hair-raising ghost story.

"Leeches?" he shook his head promptly. "What are they?"

"Oh! I heard you are so smart. But you don't know women's breasts are for, and now the leeches!" She sneered, then excitedly said, "They are a kind of tiny worms the size of a needle living in stagnant and murky water. Once they smell your presence, they swim in a large swarm toward you and feast on you. You will never be aware while those creepy things are sucking your blood. And in just a few moments, their bodies are getting so fat and enlarge tenfold."

Beloved shuddered, yet his eyes shone in thrill.

"Once my little brother had surfaced from the water, I saw leeches, yes, a dozen of them, clinging and wriggling on his back and upper arms. I tried to pull them off his back, but they stretched longer and longer as I put all my force into pulling them one by one. Not a single one let go of him. So, I brought him home with those bloodsuckers still clinging to his back and still sucking and devouring his blood. Oh! What a horrid sight!

It made my little brother scream his head off all the way home."

"No one could help him at all? Do you still let those things stick to his body until now?"

"Don't be silly," she chided him again for his obvious ignorance. "My mother just poured the dissolved lime water on them, and they all started to shrivel and die. She said we shouldn't try to pull them because they could stretch up to a foot long and never let go. Ewww...What a creepy and disgusting creature!"

They both shut their eyes tightly and shuddered, sharing the thrill and terror of her childhood episode.

"You never mention your father," he abruptly reminded her. "How is he?"

"My father?" she blinked, her voice faltering. "Why? He was just some dirt-poor peasant. He went fishing on his boat one early morning and never came back. The next morning, some neighbors brought him home, well, actually not him but...his body."

Beloved felt his heart was sinking. Death, so far, existed only in story books that he had read in fascination. Yes, death was unknown to him. The closest image of death for him, in reality, was in the remote form of gold urns lining up the dark and shadowy sanctuary room in his house, which all the children avoided. Those urns contained his ancestors' ashes, long deceased before he was born. And on every Songkran Day, the Siamese New Year's Day in April month, he and all his siblings had to be inside that dim room to burn incense and pay the highest respect to those ashes. That was what *death* meant within a boundary he was allowed to conceive by his adults.

"They told my mother they had seen his boat drifting on the water, alone but without him. So, one of them had dove underwater and found him already drowned. Well, he could beat a fish with his ability to swim, but they suspected that morning he might have an acute cramp. They said they had found a wound on his head as if he were hit by a blunt object. So, they guessed before he fell into the water, his head had probably hit the edge of his boat. I saw two or three men helping drag his body as his head hit and bounced along the plank floor, and then they dropped him in front of us as if he was just some heavy sag. He had quite a dark skin, but that day, his skin turned so pallid, as white as an eggshell. His belly was so swollen, as if he had drained every drop of water from that pond into his stomach. His eyes were wide open, and his eyeballs almost plopped out his eyes. Water kept on leaking from his mouth for an hour on end while my mother left him there as she tried to find a wood coffin to put his body in."

Her detailed and vivid description now shook Beloved.

"Well, the coffin cost some money. She had to save money for more necessary things. And for us, everything was necessary. So, she decided to wrap his body with one of our bedding mats before bringing him to cremate the next day. And that's all."

Her voice as she was describing her father's death was toneless, a matter-of-fact tone as if this tragedy had fallen to someone else's life, not her own. And that "someone else" turned up to be Beloved, whose soft and innocent heart opened to absorb its impact to a degree that somehow her family's tragedy seemingly became his own.

Until now, he never had any idea that people could be dying so easily, so abruptly, and so meaningless without any chance or any sign of premonition. Why was life so worthless in the eyes of its creator if there had been one in heaven? Merely one speck of dust among zillions that were floating meaningless and purposelessly on the surface of this planet.

"Please, skip this part. Let's get back to the water lilies…"

He swallowed a hard knot in his throat, suddenly feeling forlorn from his own reflection.

"It's all right if you don't want to hear more of it," her voice softer, a big sister's soothing voice to a small brother. "Let's continue on the brighter part. Where am I now? Umm…are you sure you don't want to hear more about women's breasts?"

"N-o-o-o!" Beloved almost screamed. Then he realized that Lin Jong was teasing him.

"All right, let me go on. On the way home, our small boat was loaded with hundreds of water lilies. The neighbors laughed at us, thinking we were off our heads because their boats were loaded with fish and prawns instead. At least during the flood, we did not starve to death since their long stems, either raw or cooked with coconut milk, could turn into our meals alongside smoked fish and chili paste. But the more we pulled them from the water, the faster they grew back as thick as weeds. Growing denser and denser until it's hard to paddle through. So, later, we were satisfied just to look at them from a distance and cherished and preserved the image of the sea of water lilies in our heart..."

"What a good life you had spent in the sun when you were young," he sighed of plain envy. If he were caught playing under the full sun without someone holding an umbrella to shade the sunlight, his mother and nanny would freak out for fear that he would fall sick within minutes of exposing himself to the sun's heat.

"A good life?"

She repeated as she glared at him, trying to detect any possible sarcasm. What she caught in his naïve eyes was only his outright honesty. She then forced a laugh.

"There was a price to pay, though. The flood that nursed such beauties simultaneously destroyed our rice paddy field, and soon enough, we found ourselves penniless. That's why my mother brought me as collateral when she begged the lord for the loan. My goodness! Are you crying?" she cried in surprise. "Wait. Hold your tears until I tell you the real and darkest story that occurred to me. What I've just told you is nothing compared to that. Absolutely nothing! But no, I think you're too young to listen to it."

He hurriedly wiped his easy tears before she could make more fun of him and said firmly.

"If you don't tell me, I'll never have any chance to hear such things from anyone."

Lin Jong narrowed her eyes, estimating him. Then she smiled her mischievous smile.

"Maybe some other time, or maybe tomorrow if you come

to see me again," she toyed with him. "Are you still crying? Come on."

"No, I'm not crying," he said, raising his voice nearly to a shout from embarrassment, which quickly turned to indignation.

"Yes, you are. What a baby you are!"

"Stop teasing me, or I'll tell…" He paused, trying to find the most dreadful figure in his world to scare her. "Or I'll tell my mother!"

"Oh! Just like I care," she sneered and made a face. "You should know how your mother looks in the eyes of everyone. Look now!"

This time, he couldn't help laughing. He knew he should defend his mother, but Lin Jong's exaggerated imitation of her posture and voice was so precise it was almost perfect.

It was the image of Lady Pearl sitting so erect and graceful, her eyes haughtily and slowly sweeping around as if demanding every ounce of attention, respect, and honor from every one of her inferiorities who were crouching before her. Lin Jong's face was now wearing his mother's austere and cold expression, and if a smile had ever appeared on that face, it had never been a full, pleasant smile but perpetually tainted with slight scorn and contempt at the corner of her lips.

"How do I enact your mother? Poor? Well-done? Exceptional? Any comments?"

He couldn't resist laughing until tears were filling his eyes. "Wait! Just wait until she comes to see you're making fun of her. Oh!"

Suddenly, he cried in alarm, springing on his feet. "I have to leave now. It's time to study with my teacher." He then hesitated, "Can I come to see you and Baby Boy tomorrow?"

She nodded and smiled sheepishly, showing some hesitation as she gestured at her breasts.

"Of course, just…don't let your mother or anyone at all know what I've just shown you."

He sensed an unhidden fear in her voice. So, he promptly

promised her. Letting him see her breasts must be a really bad thing. Otherwise, she wouldn't ask him to keep quiet. After all, she was still afraid of his formidable mother.

In that brief moment, they were no longer master and concubine, stepson and stepmother, or strangers meeting for the first time. Odds as it was, Beloved seemed to find a friendship he had longed for from another soul who had one thing in common with him: a life in a pampered imprisonment.

"Lin Jong, when I come tomorrow, don't forget to tell me your darkest story as you promised. The darker, the better! If you don't, I will tell my father that you tried to coax me into suckling your boobs."

He shouted to her as he sprinted from her door.

"Shush…" she hushed him in alarm, but he was already gone.

That night, he tossed and turned in his bed. His agitation made his nanny climb on his bed to see if he was all right before moving back to sleep on her cot, leaving him still wide awake. No, he knew enough never to slip a word to his nanny about his sneaking into the forbidden quarters and came across that girl Lin Jong, who had so many things that mystified him. If she knew, his mother would know in no time.

In his ten years, he had never met anyone like Lin Jong. She was raw, untouched by the careful grooming of society—a wild, unpruned tree flourishing beautifully on its own.

So familiar with immaculate female figures from head to toe, Lin Jong's candid, daring, whimsical, and childish nature attracted him from the beginning. And in just a brief moment, her wild, lively spirit started to intrigue him as her chatty and witty talk made him laugh hilariously in one minute and moved him almost to tears in another.

In short, she was totally different from all his sisters, other female relatives, and his mother's friends within her elite circle, who were all perfect and refined ladies.

What frightened him the most as much as it had drawn him

into her was her spontaneous mischief that, even though he did not know what harm it could bring, he could sense its vague and yet impending dark danger. He was not sure what he felt more between dread and fascination. Her eyes, which gleamed with mischief, had repelled him, and yet it had strangely and strongly allured him.

Oh! It must be the first time in his life that he felt a pang of an unknown feeling so peculiar to him he could not find a name to define it. It was an adolescent feeling of the ten-year-old boy to an older girl who threw open the door to the wild wide world beyond his lavishing yet locked-up life. He was so envious of her past, of her adventurous yet colorful world of poverty, of her bittersweet memory that he did not have any part of it. Oh! He wanted to live in her past, to swim with her under the hot sun across the spans of water over the green rice paddies and help her carry home those loveliest pink and purple water lilies far more beautiful and elegant than those craggy ones grown in a small basin in his grand courtyard. Had life given him a chance, he would have imitated every step of hers, laughed every laugh, felt every joy and pain, and touched the deepest part of the mystery that made her so enticing to him.

He was probably too young and naïve to know that his immature passion for her had a name. It was simply called an infatuation. Oh, knew it or not, he did not care as long as his heart felt it.

In the afternoon of the next day, Beloved waited until his mother and his twin sisters left the house on her elegant horse carriage with her driver and one of her maids, heading for his grandfather's house. His father was busy, either at his administrative office or spent the whole afternoon at the routine meeting in the Grand Palace. His nanny, the last but not the least person he must be aware of, also started her usual afternoon nap. He would be as free as a bird until she woke up and began to look around for him.

Lately, most of his mother's attention was shifted to her gravely ill father, whose life could pass any day. Beloved knew that she would not come back until late afternoon. And his nanny would never have figured out where he would be, so it must take hours for her to find him. No one else in the house had authority over him.

He sneaked out of his toy room and headed for Lin Jong's quarters as soon as his mother was out of sight. As usual, he did not forget to grab a handful of imported chocolates and candies from the pantry room if he found some of his half-siblings on his way. He was starving for more tales about her exotic countryside home where he could joyously slip in and live her life as long as her story lasted.

This time, after Lek's pleading, Beloved grudgingly allowed Lek to tag along. Never mind, he trusted Lek as someone trusted his own shadow. When his *Khun Than* acted mischievously over his dead body a word would slip from Lek's mouth.

"I know you'll come back, *Khun Than*."

She greeted him at her door. Her half-amiable, half-mischievous smile played on her lips, the kind of smile he dreaded as much as he longed to see.

He stepped inside while he told Lek to wait outside by the door to watch around in case someone unexpectedly passed by.

"I hope my Baby Boy brings you here, not me," her meaningful smile deepened.

There was no need to reply. He flushed and gave her a sheepish grin as he turned his eyes to Baby Boy, now cuddled in her arms.

"I hope you don't mind. It's time to nurse him. You can walk out and come back later when I finish."

He gulped, avoiding her eyes.

"Oh, I'll wait here…" he stammered, forcing himself to look casual.

Now, her grin infuriated him. What was wrong with his reply that made her grin? But the sight of Baby Boy suckling noisily and greedily on her lap compelled him to keep watching. As tiny and soft as it looked, Baby Boy's hungry mouth could force her firm and plump breasts to quiver as the fluid source of life flew generously into his mouth. Somehow, the sense of fascination began to creep into his mind, unaware. The sight he was watching began to carry him into his vague, almost lost childhood memory of the dripping nectar from his nanny's ample breasts that he knew he would never have a chance to savor again; only her dry teats now his nanny gave to help him drift into sleep. Oh, what if it was him, not Baby Boy, whose lips hungrily clenched her teat, drawing the nectar of life into his trembling mouth? He felt the surge of such an impulse so strong it frightened him to the degree that he wanted to dart out and lock himself inside his playroom as his refuge. Yet, he just couldn't withdraw his eyes from that sight.

At last, the obscure and disturbing atmosphere was lifted. Beloved became more at ease when the nursing was done, and Lin Jong's breasts were covered. After Baby Boy's tummy was full, he was awake and alert. His eyelashes had fluttered at Beloved's sight before he started to gaze intently at Beloved's face with his wide eyes and his serious frown for one long minute as if trying to study and figure out what on earth looming in front of him with a humongous face and two huge goggling eyes.

Then Baby Boy swiftly darted his eyes around. His pink mouth hung open now as if in wonder as he tried to make sense of an alienated new world surrounding him. An instant later, his eyelids abruptly drooped shut. He started yawning and falling asleep once again in Lin Jong's arms. Probably, the new world began to bore him, so he decided to let his dream gently carry him back to the better and more comforting place, the only place where he had known for his entire life: his mother's womb.

They both laughed together at Baby Boy's sudden change in his gesture, so cute, so endearing he believed the infant's cuteness could break his heart if he had prolonged his gaze at this little creature just for another minute.

"Can I hold him for a second? Can I?" he begged her breathlessly.

She smiled eagerly and encouragingly, putting the napping baby into his arms. "Just don't wake him up. It will make him cranky and start wailing."

Oh! How he loved this baby, who was sharing flesh and blood with him. His heart swelled with fierce love as he clumsily cradled the infant, struggling to hold its fragile body as securely as possible. He sank his nose and buried it into the baby's soft skin, deeper, deeper and harder, harder, irresistible to the juiciest and sweetest smell of the newborn little creature.

Without warning, Baby Boy woke up and opened his mouth, releasing a wail that quickly rose to a deafening pitch.

For Beloved, it was the loudest ear-splitting sound he had ever heard. So helpless and frightened, he was about to give Baby Boy back to Lin Jong. Then the fierce scream let up a little. He drew a deep breath and blew it out with relief. Wasn't it so unbelievable a creature this weenie size was able to produce the highest pitch from its lungs so threateningly and powerfully that he believed the voice could shatter a mirror?

He startled and jumped up a foot when Baby Boy once again unexpectedly let out another deadly shriek; this one was not only capable of smashing a mirror but also his eardrums, causing his hands to jerk violently on impulse.

It happened so swiftly he did not comprehend what was going on.

All he was aware of in the next instant was hearing a hair-raising scream from Lin Jong. He blinked, trying to make sense of Lin Jong screaming her head off as she darted to her baby, whom Beloved had no longer seen in his arms but sprawled on its back at his feet on the hard floor. His stare remained fixed on the baby, sprawling in sudden silence and unmoving, as Lin Jong instantly scooped him into her arms, howling and howling and keeping on howling.

In that split second, it was clear enough for him what had

happened. Baby Boy's sudden scream made him cringe, and that caused the baby to slip from his jerking arms and fall with a thump onto the hard plank floor. It happened so swiftly that his eyes could not even catch that critical moment. He felt his blood rushing through his head. An enormous hand of pure terror clutched his throat, blurred his vision, and tore his heart.

This couldn't be happening. It just couldn't.

He tried to take a step backward, but he could not.

Finally, he wobbled and collapsed onto the floor. Everything turned into an enormous black void as the hysterical scream from Lin Jong continued.

Beloved found himself fully awake on his bed, so surprised to find himself surrounded by the familiar faces of those in his family: his father, his mother, his two sisters near his side, Nanny Sook sobbing loudly at his feet, and even Lek himself crouching not far from her. His body ached, and his head throbbed with pain. A middle-aged European physician with round spectacles on his grayish eyes stood among them by the edge of his bed.

"You were in deep shock and hence passed out. Nothing is serious except a little bump on your forehead when you collapsed on the floor. You're good now, son. Just a dull headache for a couple of days. Take the medicine I've just given to your mother, and you will rise and shine from bed very soon."

The doctor said brightly with his soothing voice, contrasting with all the darkened faces surrounding him. Sensing the tension among the hosts of this house, the doctor patted his young patient's clammy hand and cheerfully winked to reassure the boy that tomorrow would be a bright and beautiful day again. Then he turned to the patriarch of the house, who had stood beside him as big and tall as the Caucasian doctor himself.

"Your Excellency, please ensure her ladyship gives your son adequate rest for a day or two and restricts vigorous activities. And please don't let anyone disturb him with any questions that will upset him. He is such a well-brought-up young gentleman, so intelligent, so courteous, so graceful, and yet so, so sensitive to whatever he has perceived. Things that hardly affected anyone else can either bruise or move his heart tenfold."

"Thank you, Dr. Sheldon, for coming to check up on my son. I appreciate it."

The lord nodded grimly and thanked the doctor for the advice and concern for his son. With his last words, the doctor said goodbye, with his promise to visit the young master of the house in a few days. He exited his bedroom, leaving Beloved with his grim-faced father and his tearful mother.

As soon as the doctor was out of his sight, Beloved tossed his head, uttering a choked cry.

"Baby Boy…the baby… I dropped Baby Boy… I don't mean to hurt him. His cry startled me…"

But his mother hushed him as she stroked his hair and patted his cold cheek.

"Shush…darling, the doctor said you need a rest. Did you hear him say that? Go back to your sleep. Nothing matters now. Nothing at all, my darling. Only your well-being that counts."

So, Beloved closed his eyelids, feigning asleep, finding the escape from his mother's superfluous concern that embarrassed him to death. Wasn't she aware he had dropped Baby Boy? Instead, the lady turned her head to her husband while her son was still in her arms. She was looking the Lord in the eyes, fiercely defending her son.

"Except for our son, nothing else really matters. Do I say it right? My lord?"

Her eyes were on fire as her voice remained icily cold. Her fierceness reminded her husband of a Bengal tigress, roaring, pouncing, ready to sink her deadly fangs into any living flesh, tearing into bits whoever she suspected came to harm her cub.

As everyone predicted, Lady Pearl immediately took her son under her wings. She blamed the baby's mother for being so senseless as to let a ten-year-old boy hold a newborn infant.

It was his concubine's fault that inevitably led to the accident. Furthermore, the lady fiercely accused Lin Jong of causing her Beloved the shock and trauma due to such foolishness. She would also never forgive that stupid girl for a bump on her Beloved's forehead. Could the lord assure her their son would not permanently suffer, externally and internally, for his entire life from immeasurable damages caused by that bump?

It was hard for anyone trying to detect and read the mind of this great man. His calm composure hardly changed under any force of circumstance, his face, an image of a handsome warrior, so impassive and stoic with his eyes sunk deeply below his thick eyebrows, shrouding all the human traits ever lodged inside him. So different from his wife, he had never let passionate emotions, especially anger, take over his prudent and dignifying appearance. They hardly heard him yell or use harsh words to intimidate anyone inferior to him. However, if they had a choice, most people chose to face his wife's explosive rage rather than stand in front of the solemn lord and let the lord's eyes pierce into their naked core.

A pair of his eyes were like two small cracks on a massive wall, which he had skillfully used to watch and observe the world. With a pair of shrew-piercing eyes, nothing could slip from his keen awareness; no one could conceal their thoughts from him once he had focused his eyes to detect them. On the contrary, no one could read anything through those eyes. They were shuttered perpetually by the owner's cold and impassive look, which sealed off the possibility of every man—except for his wife—peeking into the inside and exploring his mindscape.

The handsome features and the formidable figure of the lord of the house met their match in his spouse.

Their eyes met for one long minute. Yet, a towering, formidable figure as he was, he finally averted his wife's eyes. The lord peered down at his feignedly sleeping son for one more time with his troubled eyes, which revealed his anguished and frustrated feeling between his anger and yet his deep concern for his son—a rare occasion he had ever shown his emotions for anyone to see. Then, he regained his poise and quietly retreated from the room. Only his mother still hovered over his bed, her eyes fixing only on his face, loving him with all the love that could move heaven and earth.

Lek had a chance afterward to whisper to his *Khun Than* that his baby brother had had a seizure and run a high fever that night. No one had expected him to live another day, but he had miraculously survived that fall and was now under the doctor's good care, the same British doctor who had come to visit him. Probably, the injury that afflicted the baby was not critical. Maybe he had not fallen head-on. His baby brother would return home as soon as he recovered. Maybe in just a few days or so, sir. He kept reassuring his *Khun Than* until he saw the color returned to his young master's cold and pale cheek.

"If you see Baby Boy returning home, can you tell me, Lek?" Beloved's dull eyes brightened a little.

"A minute that I hear his ear-piercing cry, sir. Your servant promises you." Lek bowed his head.

However, as a week passed, no one could give him any update news on his baby brother or on Lin Jong, its mother. He kept asking about them, but his attendant's reply was vague and incongruous—the kind of answer that, in turn, created more questions.

"Nai Lek, it's time now. He's supposed to come back, isn't he? The baby…"

"I think I heard …a baby crying from that direction, sir."

"Oh! Can you go to Lin Jong's quarters and check her for me?"

"Actually…Sir, I have no permission to enter that compound. However, I will ask someone over there for you, sir."

That answer seemed plausible and calmed down the young boy for another day.

And when the next day came, his inquiry started all over again.

"Have you asked someone about that baby yet? And…and his mother's doing all right?"

"Your servant is so sorry, sir. Today, her ladyship ordered me to do some errands for her. Maybe tomorrow, sir."

"So, you actually don't know whether the baby came back or not," the tone of his voice could not conceal his growing anxiety and impatience, "your answer went around my question in a circle. It never gets to the point."

"Yesterday I heard a baby crying, sir, I did." He repeated his answer once again in a circle.

"How do you know that cry is from Baby Boy? You know there's more than one inside those quarters."

"I'll ask some servant in that compound, sir," he replied cautiously.

That was all Beloved could squeeze from his trusting attendant's mouth.

After the third day of increasing ambiguity, he almost gave up his dim hope.

"Nai Lek, you tell me what really happened to my baby brother. *Now*! I want the true answer once and for all. Don't ever fool me!" his voice rose in an angry wail, a scarce scene to witness such an outburst that sprang from a young person with a gentle demeanor like him.

"I'll ask someone for you, *Khun Than*. Please be patient…."

Lek lowered his head, his voice so strained and his eyes downcast. With the same reply as the previous day, he could not bring his eyes to meet his young master's.

Especially when Nanny Sook, his aunt, stepped into the room in the middle of their conversation to give Beloved medicine, Lek would close his mouth and leave that room immediately as his aunt's suspicious eyes followed him until he was out of the room.

* * * * *

Part 2: Chapter 3

Seeing World in Blue

*F*rom that day, Beloved stopped inquiring about his *attendant. Let alone the grown-ups—even a child his age could sense something was wrong with Lek's hesitant and evasive answers. If Lek, his most trusting and closest attendant, could not tell him the truth, it was useless to ask anyone else, especially his family.*

As days passed by into a week, he was more frustrated to the point of despair being trapped inside the grandiose yet hollow building, surrounded by his doting nanny and other servants who breathlessly rushed to him at the slightest crack of his coughing sound and pampered by his twin sisters, who took a turn to read his favorite storybooks at his bed. His parents did not allow him to step outside due to his prolonged illness. Besides his mother's and sisters', many other eyes were now watching him, although out of pure concern.

Beloved also knew from Lek that all his attendants except Lek himself were punished for negligence in their duty. At least Lek was spared because he was Nanny Sook's nephew and also his young master's favorite. They inattentively let *Khun Than* roam around his father's concubines' quarters, where he did not belong. As a penalty, the lord sent them out of his residence and replaced them with a new group of more responsible attendants who made the young boy feel as if they had been a pack of well-trained watchdogs that could smell him for a mile no matter where he tried to hide from them.

After that day, Beloved began to realize that as he was a source of joy for his mother, he was equally a source of trouble for others in her household. His presence always signaled danger as if they had been treading on a hazard zone. *Stay away from him.* They might be warning one another. *He is the untouchable. Anything he has done, any words he has said, intentionally or not, can cause our real trouble.* After that day, he could sense that his father's concubines, all of his half-brothers and half-sisters, younger and elder alike, did every possible way to avoid him.

So forlorn and friendless was his world.

Therefore, before he could plunge deeper into insanity, he'd sought his solace in books. After finishing the lesson from his Thai and English teachers in his father's library, he spent the rest of the afternoon in that room. Countless volumes were put neatly on the shelves for him to enjoy with no end. He spent most of the time there in reading. Yet sometimes, he merely sat quietly, absorbed in his thoughts.

As Beloved immersed himself in a book, Lek would sit undisturbed at his young master's feet for errands he might request. While he quietly waited on him, Lek always grabbed a book and gingerly touched it with great wonder. As he flipped the crispy leaves and peered at each of them, he couldn't figure out how his young master could understand the meaning in those curves and lines called letters.

So, Beloved, out of his kindness and desire to have at least someone to share what he had read, began to teach Lek, who showed enthusiasm for learning to read and write. Once Lek could read and write, Beloved never felt disappointed in him. They became almost inseparable, spending time together contently in the quiet library that transported them into a world of wonder and imagination far beyond the library walls.

Soon, Miss Francine Spencer, his austere English teacher who had taught him reading and writing since he was a small boy, had to leave for her country. The person who replaced her was an American gentleman who worked in the American Consul and whom his father was hiring as Beloved's new tutor. His father told him he was interested in hiring this American man because he heard of his notorious reputation as 'Mr. Omniscience' and 'the walking encyclopedia.'

Beloved was so fascinated with his eccentric and funny character he decided to be fond of this gentleman at first impression. It was hard to tell Mr. Aaron James's precise age, as he was bald except for some salt and peppered tufts of hair above his ears. He had an upright body, a friendly face, and extraordinarily rosy cheeks, perhaps caused by the tropical heat. Though it was a hot and humid day as it usually was, he wore a straw hat and a navy-blue jacket with two rows of buttons down the front, and inside that jacket was a light blue vest and a silk necktie with the matching color.

As his new teacher entered the library room, he winked at Beloved as if he had already known his student for life. But his intense china-blue eyes were so vividly blue that Beloved wondered if Mr. James would see the whole world—the trees, the moon, and even the sun—only in blue color. It was so hard to avert his eyes from Mr. James as he walked, extending his hand for a handshake to the startled young maids waiting in the room.

"Just give him your right hand for shaking. It's the way of the traditional *Farang* greeting."

Beloved explained to the young maids. "And even when he asks you for a kiss on your cheek, you can't turn him down. It isn't polite if you don't let him kiss you. That's because, in the

Western culture, a kiss is a courteous greeting from a man to a woman." He tried to hide his mischievous smile as he said.

"Lord Buddha!" They gasped in response and protested in whispers. "No, no. Over my dead body."

Lek was the first to be willing to shake hands with Mr. James. Then, the waiting maids finally let him shake their hands with some nervous giggling. What a relief for them when Mr. James did not kiss them as their *Khun Than* had warned them.

After the introduction ceremony had passed, Mr. James cleared his throat and said abruptly,

"Umm…What's wrong with my eyes, my dear Beloved?"

"Oh, I'm sorry, sir," he tried to withdraw his gaze from those mesmerizing eyes, "I…just wonder if you see things only in blue color."

"Pardon me. What makes you think that way?" Mr. James asked in his amused tone.

"Your eyes are so intense blue they must alter any color on anything you're looking at into blue only."

Mr. James began to laugh heartily and thus reddened his ample cheeks.

"How I love your question! It's a good remark. Can I ask you something, too? I notice you have very dark eyes, just like a pair of shiny black beads. I wonder if you see everything in black only."

So, Beloved and Mr. James introduced themselves to each other in this fashion.

"I really like that blue-eyed American, Lek. You too?"

Lek, who followed him everywhere, including inside that class, eagerly nodded in agreement. It was no problem for him whoever and whatever his *Khun Than* liked; he felt obliged to like them also.

The second time Mr. James showed up late in the morning, he carried a small wood crate about a square foot with him and with great care. He winked at Beloved again as if it was his favorite greeting. His fierce blue eyes glittered as his mysterious smile spread over his face.

He put the crate on the desk and announced it in the manner of a magician to his audience.

"I have a surprise for you, the biggest surprise you have ever experienced. *Ta-da*!"

Mr. James dramatically removed a mysterious cube-shaped object from the crate. Beloved had no idea what it was supposed to be because it was covered with sawdust.

"What on earth?" He whispered.

"Can someone bring me a bowl of clean water and a hammer quickly, please?"

Still in a puzzle, Beloved asked Lek to do Mr. James a favor. As soon as Lek put a large glass bowl and a hammer on the desk, the teacher put that cube into the water in that bowl and scraped out all the sawdust from it, revealing a transparent solid cube with a wisp of white steam rising from it. Mr. James put that thing back inside the crate, and with the hammer, he broke the whole cube into small pieces. All eyes in that room were wide open while they watched his every move.

"Beloved, take a piece, please," Mr. James handed one broken piece to Beloved with his mysterious smile.

"Ouch! It's so-o-o cold!" he exclaimed in astoundment. "My hand is tingling."

"Now, put it in your mouth."

He hesitated but did it obediently.

"My tongue...my tongue..." He moaned and, almost on impulse, spat it out immediately. That lump dropped to the carpet at his feet. "O-o, my tongue is burning now."

That startled Lek. He rushed to his *Khun Than* in alarm to help.

"Calm down, calm down. Your tongue is fine," said Mr. James soothingly. "That feeling will be gone very shortly. Tell me how you feel."

"It...it's like I slipped a glowing charcoal into my mouth.

But it burnt my tongue cold instead of hot. I have never felt so freezing; my tongue is numb now. What on earth is it?"

"It's simply water—water which has turned into ice, as solid as a rock."

Beloved eyes widened in bewilderment.

"Impossible! This couldn't be. Only a wizard with a magic spell could conjure this up!"

"If you don't believe it's just water, please look at the spot on the floor where you spat it on," said Mr. James gently.

Beloved scanned his eyes cautiously on the carpeted floor, but the lump seemed to disappear. He saw a small drop of water that quickly dissolved into the carpet on that spot. He stared at that spot in disbelief.

"Nature is that wizard you just mentioned. You are witnessing the ice melting into water," he explained to his bewildered student. Now, you see that with your own eyes," Mr. James added. "Do you want to try some more? This time, you won't feel that shock. You will even enjoy chewing it, I bet."

After a pause, Beloved reluctantly put a small lump Mr. James offered into his mouth. He blinked his eyes shut, resisting his impulse to spit it out again. He winced and cringed as the ice slowly melted, making his gum and teeth tingle before its incredible coldness ran down his throat and prickled his spine.

He opened his eyes widely as his tongue started savoring that wonderful cold from what Mr. James called ice.

"Ah, you like it," announced Mr. James triumphantly. Beloved managed another smile before he winced again.

The next fifteen minutes passed, and everyone in that room had their share of ice: Lek, the waiting maids, and even Mr. James, who seemingly enjoyed chewing ice more than anyone else as his life-saver on such a sultry day in Bangkok. There were some screeches and screams from his maids while chewing ice.

Then, the lesson began.

"In Europe and North America, when the temperature drops to the freezing point in winter, water in oceans, rivers, and lakes changes into ice, like the water you just put in your mouth. The whole lake surface can be frozen, so solid and smooth like a large mirror pane people can walk and slide and even dance with their skates on the frozen lake."

Beloved was speechless. It was something so otherworldly as if his American teacher and he did not share the same world.

"In deep winter, we can even travel by riding in a wagon drawn by horses across a frozen river or a lake to the other side of the bank as if it were an ordinary road."

Beloved blinked—still more surprises to come.

"Yes, in the winter, it's so cold that not only does water on the ground turn into solid ice, but those water vapors high up in the sky can also turn into tiny ice crystals and fall as million flakes of snow. Snow blankets the whole landscape with its soft, wonderful white fluff—house roofs, chimneys, fences, tree branches, and grounds. It turns the lush green woodland in summer into a winter wonderland. If it has snowed for so many days or if we have a snowstorm called a blizzard, the snow will drift so high that it can bury small houses. We have to use a shovel to dig our way from our doorstep through the deep drift of snow, like a long tunnel out. Otherwise, we will be trapped inside that ice cave. What a back-broken labor!"

"Tell me you did see the snow with your own eyes," cried Beloved.

"I spent my childhood with my parents in a small town in New Hampshire State. We lived in a big white clapboard colonial house with black shutters and whitewashed picket fences in the front yard, a typical house in New England, the northeast part of my country. There were two huge oak trees in our front yard, and beyond our backyard were woodlands with white birch trees, sugar maples, elms, hemlocks, white pines, and other evergreens. In winter, my sister, brother, and I couldn't wait to go skating in a small lake near our house on the weekend. We slid and swirled in circles on the ice sheet until we felt so giddy and warm. Oh, nothing on earth that gave me more fun…

except riding a sled down a snow-covered slope our face against the icy wind. Ah! We even made a snowman…"

"A snowman?"

"Yes, we made a snowman from the thick snow carpet that was so abundant under our feet. I'll show you how he looks. Here's his small round head. Here's his big, round, and fat body. American children love to have a snowman in their front yard as much as to throw snowballs at one another."

As he talked, Mr. James earnestly used his fountain pen to draw a picture of a funny snowman on a sheet of paper and handed it to Beloved, who peered at it breathlessly.

"The snowman's eyes are made of two pieces of black coal, his nose an orange carrot, his teeth a broken rake, and his arms two dry sprigs. My little sister Emily always put a wool scarf around his neck because she didn't want Mr. Snowman to get sick from a bad cold. Once, she even fed the snowman a cup of hot apple cider to warm him up. She said she felt sorry he stood so lonely and freezing amid the snow-covered ground, which stretched as far as our eyes could see. Only seconds later, the part supposed to be his mouth started to melt, and she cried her heart out. She thought she was killing him, poor little thing…"

Mr. James laughed softly and then stopped abruptly, apparently from a pang of his childhood nostalgia as his tiny beads of sweat started to grow on his forehead on a humid and drowsy afternoon. He fumbled into his pants pocket for a handkerchief to wipe them out. One of the waiting maids, who crouched quietly on the floor at his feet, started to fan him vigorously with a big fan.

"Thank you, Miss. I appreciate it," he smiled gratefully and courteously at the bewildered maid as if she had understood what he said.

Beloved found out he was looking forward to seeing his teacher, Mr. Aaron James, the next day.

He finally found the miraculous hand that pulled him out of the abyss of despair and loneliness and opened a new world.

It was the world he had never thought existed, so otherworldly yet so wonderful: Ice, snow, sled, and the Snowman!

And no, that didn't seem enough for all the wonders of this world. When Mr. James returned the next day, it seemed the ice was not amazing compared to what he was listening to this time.

"Today, I'm going to tell you another phenomenon so unlikely you will, again, ever believe."

Yes, I do believe. I do. He said without slipping a word, holding his breath in anticipation.

"It's a Midnight Sun."

Mr. James smiled triumphantly as Beloved's mouth hung open, thunder-struck. "It means there are some parts on earth, far, far from the Kingdom of Siam, where the sun stays on the horizon for 24 hours, even at midnight."

"Holy Buddha…" Beloved whispered. Though it was simply impossible to comprehend such an upside-down idea, he knew better now it must be true. "How…far away from here?" He stammered.

"At the North Pole and the South Pole," Mr. James replied in a matter-of-fact tone, then he got up from his chair and trotted to the small globe on the desk, "Look, the North Pole region lies above this Arctic Circle line and the South Pole lies below that Antarctic Circle line. Do you notice the earth's axis tilt slightly? As the earth rotates around its axis, the tilt allows the Poles to stay in full sunlight for the entire summer. In far north countries such as Norway or Finland, the sun starts to go down at midnight. It almost disappears from the horizon, making the whole sky ablaze with red, gold, and orange flames, just like the ordinary majestic sunset scenery. Then a miracle happens; instead of sinking, the sun ascends again an instant later and then higher and higher, the greatest spectacle on earth."

"But…why does it never happen *here,* Mr. James?" Beloved's voice showed unhidden disappointment.

"It's because your country is located just slightly above the equator line where day and night split equally all year round. Don't be upset, Beloved. Nothing is fairer than Nature. People in those parts of the world with eternal sunshine all summer will never glimpse their sun again for three long months when the winter comes since the pole tilts away from the sun. Imagine, while having lunch at noon, you look out the window but see nothing outside, only the pitch darkness. And when you look up at the midday sky, you'll see not the blazing sun at its zenith but millions of stars shining so coldly and dimly on you. Imagine three months in eternal darkness without a glimpse of daylight! After three months of darkness, when the sun emerges from the horizon for the first time at dawn, Eskimo people hold a ceremony expressing their great gratitude for the return of the sun, their god of light."

"Here, we as well believe that the sun is not a star but a divine god named Surya," Beloved said hesitantly. "From dawn till dusk, he will be in his golden chariot, riding his horses across the sky, providing light for all humans. If any mortal man tries to approach him, that man will be vaporized instantly into nothingness."

"You also share this belief with ancient Greeks and Romans. Their sun god, Apollo, rides his chariot across the sky to give humans light and warmth. You will find the same sun god only in different names in different cultures. What does it tell you? Think!"

Beloved shook his head slowly with some abashment on his face.

"Don't be ashamed, Beloved. Rather, feel glad that there are always a million things waiting for you to know and learn. You will never be bored if you are always hungry to know. And most importantly," he lowered his voice and looked around this grand room. "Wealth and power will someday be exhausted, but knowledge will never."

Suddenly, Mr. James peered down at his pocket watch and frowned.

"Oh, today I must leave early. I have some errands to finish. I enjoyed talking with you so much that I completely forgot the time. Next time, we will start with the same question I just asked you."

"Mr. James, I hope one day I will have some chance to see snow and walk on ice."

"I'm sure you will," Mr. James nodded more solemnly. "Your father has discussed sending you abroad in a few years with me. He wants to enroll you in one of the best law schools in the United States. That's why I come here three times a week as your tutor, preparing you for your future education. He told me he has the vision that after the American naval victory over the invincible Spanish Armada a few years ago, our flourishing country will exceed the old United Kingdom in every aspect, including education. Yes, it is the turn of the century, the modern world. So much change, so many new ideas and unprecedented inventions—electricity, railroad, gasoline, the engine car, the camera, the telephone, and even the flying machine in progress, and yet…" he sighed heavily, "same old greed, mass oppression, savagery, imperialism, power-seeking, and war after war remain as if we have never been out of the Dark Ages… Our brain advances incessantly as century after century passes, yet our instincts have remained unchanged since prehistoric times. What's so good for our brain to be more advanced and sophisticated if it has to serve our primordial instincts and raw desires? No, that sort of progress never makes our world a better place."

What Mr. James muttered to himself did not quite interest the young boy as much as what the American gentleman mentioned about his father's plan to send him aboard to the land of snow!

"Oh! I want to skate on the frozen lake like you and your sister. By the way, how is she now, your little sister?"

Mr. James stared blankly at Beloved, and then he blinked. The tone in his voice strangely changed.

"While Emily and I were skating on the lake one winter,

the ice sheet was broken through, and in one instant, we plunged into the icy water underneath. I survived, but she didn't."

Beloved was aghast.

"My six-year-old sister slid under the ice sheet and was trapped beneath," Mr. James' voice faltered, yet he continued. "When some adults found some equipment to pull her out through that hole, it was too late. She drowned, and her body froze to ice. It's my fault, after all. At that time, it was almost a Spring time. Winter was almost over. I warned her that the ice was getting thin and it would crack soon, especially near the shore's edge where the water was shallow. But she insisted on going skating. I shouldn't have let her go… I should have run to our mother so she could stop her in time… But instead, I cheerfully followed Emily and brought her to her death as a consequence. I couldn't resist her disarming smile. Once I fell in, I was able to grasp the edge of the ice sheet with one hand while my other hand tried frantically to clasp her hand, but hers had just slipped from mine. She kept screaming, *Aaron, Aaron, help me…* as she sank deeper into the water underneath the ice sheet and got trapped there,"

Why did terrible things have to happen? That little girl's story started to crush Beloved's heart. Terrible things could happen to anyone anywhere around the globe, not only here.

Why?

"My parents, especially my mother, never got over this tragic loss. She was their youngest and favorite child. Although they never blamed me verbally for her death, I could see the accusation in their eyes every time they turned to look at me… Oh, their eyes. Their cold and unforgiving eyes have still haunted me up to today, worse than the image of my sister's frozen and lifeless body lying in her coffin. So, after graduating from Harvard School, I decided to leave home. I traveled half the world to unfamiliar and hot climate countries, Egypt, India, and Burma, and finally settled in Siam for almost a decade. One of my reasons is to wipe out that haunting memory of that horrible winter. But how can you escape your own shadow, which constantly stalks behind you as long as you walk the earth, hot or cold?"

Mr. James' cheerful manner drastically changed. He sank heavily into his chair again and looked at least ten years older. After outpouring what Beloved expected the least to hear, he seemed to lose himself in another time and another place that Beloved was unable to share with him. Yet, what he shared wholeheartedly with this gentleman was the feeling of guilt and self-loathing, to which he felt almost identical.

"Mr. James, I know how you feel, honestly—" he paused, searching for words to represent his heart. "I…I had dropped my newborn half-brother by accident while I was holding him, and he…fell hard on the floor. You're luckier because at least you knew what happened to your sister afterward. But I…" he tried to swallow a lump in his throat, his eyes reddened with stinging hot tears. "No one in my family let me know what happened to him. No one. All I know is that since that day, my baby brother and his mother have disappeared from this house. I've never seen them again. I never had a chance to ask for her forgiveness and tell her I could do everything with my life to atone for what I'd done to her baby. Can you tell me what you think about what happened to him? Please?" He begged Mr. James not only with his words but also with his anguished eyes for the answer.

"Poor child. Poor, poor child."

Beloved heard Mr. James murmur and felt his hand being firmly squeezed. However, he did not hear any answer from his tutor. The gentleman's mouth was clenched tightly. Maybe he didn't know, or perhaps he did but chose not to answer.

"Why do terrible things happen to them, Mr. James? Your little sister and my little brother both have never done anything wrong in all their short lives… I don't understand."

"According to my people's belief, it is God's will, and for yours, it is each individual's Karma. They choose to believe what comforts their souls best. Yet, the truth, the absolute truth, still waits for us to discover. Whatever it might be that causes such horrible things, I was determined to uncover a long time ago. And that is what I have been doing all along until my time comes..."

"To find out?" Beloved repeated, puzzled. "Find out what?"

"Yes, to find out," Mr. James emphasized, "why terrible things happen for no reason to everyone, young or old, rich or poor, good or evil. My words are as simple as that." He frowned at the boy's puzzlement. His face showed he wondered why everyone, including Beloved, did not understand what he had just declared. "This is the simplest task yet the most urgent: to find that answer. Life is just too short to delay this task. Every minute counts."Then, he abruptly sprang up from his chair as if on fire. "Oh God! Now, I am late, way, way beyond, I must run. Good day!"

Mr. James swiftly put on his hat and rushed to the door, mumbling something almost inaudible. Then he was gone. The more peculiarly he acted, the warmer Beloved felt toward him. Their camaraderie flourished, bonded, and tightened by the similar life's trauma each of them had gone through.

When Mr. James showed up again, he did not forget his question from the preceding day.

"Why do people from every culture believe the sun is their deity?"

"Why?" Beloved muttered.

"Well, that isn't a good answer because you answered me with a question," his teacher protested good-naturedly. "A good answer doesn't always mean the right answer. It means an answer that carries your point of view even though it might not be correct. There is no such thing as absolute right or wrong. So, don't be self-conscious when answering any question. Now, do you want to know what the answer is?"

"Yes, please."

"It shows a unique nature possessed only in humanity. It proves that humans always hunger for explanations of things unknown to them. They are rather satisfied with the ambiguous and unproved answer than knowing nothing if that answer comes from someone they have faith in. In this case, it will be their spiritual leaders, oracles, or prophets. It's because they need not a truth or a fact but a comfort. In fact, very few among us want the truth more than the comfort and a search for the answer themselves."

Abruptly, Mr. James asked.

"Now, prepare yourself for the most famous question of all time. Why were we born, Beloved?"

This time, Beloved felt too ashamed to remain ignorant. He concentrated so hard on finding the answer. Luckily, once a month, his father sent him to study Buddhism with an eminent abbot at one of the numerous Buddhist temples in Bangkok. There, he learned Buddhist doctrine and spent time practicing basic meditation.

"In our general belief, if there is no sin—no Karma, in our term, there is no birth. Karma is the debts we made from our precious lives. We're born to pay for them. Yet, instead of paying off all debts at once, we always add more debts to our present life and are reborn repeatedly into this endless cycle to keep up with the never-ending accruing debts. All in all, Karma works systematically and naturally without God. Does it make some sense to you?" He asked timidly.

"Oh, yes, it does. It does a lot. Though, for me, it's quite a pessimistic view. But I can't deny the logic of cause and effect in Karma. Good work!"

"Do you mind if I ask you the same question? In your Christian belief, why were we born?"

"Well," Mr. James paused, "I'm a Christian by birth but an agnostic by choice, which means I'm skeptical about things that have never undergone any tangible proof. But because you asked me, I can't refuse to give you the answer. We believe God creates every existence in this vast universe, including this world and all creatures. We believe He is omnipotent, which means He is all-powerful; omnipresent, which means His presence is everywhere, including in our hearts and souls; and omniscient, which means He knows all. Most important, we believe He is infinitely *good,* and His love for all of us is boundless. Is it clear enough?"

Beloved hesitated.

"I…don't think you answer the question why we're born."

"I can't fool you," Mr. James laughed heartily. "We believe we come to this world to find some salvation from our original sin that we inherit from our first ancestors, Adam and Eve, whom God created as a first mortal couple and then put them to live sin-free and suffering-free in the paradise called Garden of Eden. Somehow, Lucifer the Evil, the Falling Angel, disguised Himself as a snake and lured them to be rebellious against God by eating a forbidden apple in the garden, which would destroy their immortality and bring guilt and suffering to them. In consequence, God showed His wrath by chasing them down from paradise Eden to be on their own on earth. That's a birth of sin, the sin that since then has caused misery and chaos for all humankind who are the couple's descendants. But perhaps God has some compassion after all. He gave us a chance by sending his son, Jesus Christ, onto earth to redeem our original sins by sacrificing his life by being crucified and suffering to his death on the cross. The Christian believes if anyone has unwavering faith in God and Jesus Christ, his soul will be purified from his sins and be with God forever in Heaven. If not…his soul is still tainted with sins and will be burned in infernal hell for eternity."

"Does that mean Jesus also suffered and died for cleansing my sin?" Beloved asked doubtfully. "I have nothing to do with Adam and Eve. Both aren't my ancestors," the row of his ancestor's gold urns on the sanctuary room's altar popped up in his mind.

"According to them, yes, you are. They are the first pair of humans God created. And yes, Jesus Christ can purify your sin only if you become a Christian; that's the quid pro quo." He smiled. "But right now, you are considered an infidel, a Non-Christian. And so, he cannot save your soul."

"But…it's me who sins, and yet I can get away and go sin-free, unscathed because I have someone so benevolent like Jesus who suffers my sin for me. Isn't it too easy and convenient?"

"Remember what I just told you? Humans need comfort, not the truth. Why? It's because comfort gives them hope, but truth, most of the time, *doesn't…*"

"And if God's power is absolute and he also loves humans, as you said, why do we always see bad things happen to people, especially little children like my baby brother and your little sister? Does it mean either he is not that powerful or he does not love us? Otherwise, he will use all his supreme power to protect us whom he claims he loves and cares for."

"If you ask a clergyman, he will answer this: God always works in His mysterious way, beyond human's capability to comprehend. Are you satisfied now?"

"And if I ask the clergyman if God created everything, who or what had created him in the first place. Can someone create himself before he exists? What answer is he going to give me?"

"Unfortunately, the same answer will be applied: God works on everything in His mysterious way, including working on Himself."

"Oh my!" Beloved sighed. "What is the point of asking if the same answer always comes back, like walking in a circle?"

"That's why the Church declares you cannot question God, only have faith in Him. Faith is all God wants from you. A person with a skeptical mind can be a profound thinker, but he can't be a devout Christian due to his rebellious nature."

"But such a dogmatic answer doesn't clear away my doubt. Instead, it increased more."

"Let's talk about some Buddhist beliefs. I need some precise answers as well. If the reason for your reincarnation is to pay for your karma, which you committed from another life and another life before, how do you have your karma in the first place to make you be born for the very first time? I presume before your first incarnate, you do not exist. You are in a state of nothingness. So, logically, before you exist, there couldn't be a sin to be committed by you. In short, if you are born for the first time, you have to come into this world empty-handed and Karma-free, right? My question is; if you are Karma-free, what sends you to be born for the first time?

They looked at each other for one long minute, then laughed simultaneously.

"My religion teacher, an eminent and high-ranking monk, told me that Lord Buddha called any existence beyond our human sensory grasp *Ajintai*. Lord Buddha compared a single tiny leaf in his palm to things we are capable of understanding and then compared the rest of the foliage, millions of leaves, still on a tree to what he called Ajintai, the unknowable. Probably your God's existence and the law of Karma are parts of Ajintai, extremely complex matters for us humans."

Mr. James beamed at the young boy.

"Ajintai, Ajintai! Aha, that's the term I'm looking for," he shouted excitedly. "The Buddha is amazing. Even people in the science circle declare the same as him. With the help of science, we still know less than one percent of all existences in the infinite universe, which means more than ninety-nine percent is still our big mystery. But at least now, science sheds some light on some mysteries. Before the invention of the microscope in the seventeenth century, no one on earth had any idea that organisms called bacteria, which are invisible to our naked eyes, exist and that inside our body is their world. Imagine the world within the world within the world down, down to infinity! The breakthrough leads people to the new concept what they can't see, hear, or touch doesn't mean that that thing doesn't exist. It only means human senses alone are limited and not sophisticated enough to detect all the trillion existences that share our world, let alone the entire expanse of the universe. Ajintai!

"Now, I can be both Buddhist and Christian," Beloved declared.

"Beloved, learning has no boundary. Keep your mind open not only for all the possible but also for the impossible. An atheist who fiercely denies God's existence can be as blind and ignorant as a religious fanatic who shuts his eyes on everything and sees only his God."

"So, does everything have or have no meaning?"

"Let me wrap up like this. In Hindu belief, back in ancient times, before the birth of other religions, Hindu gurus believed that Good and Evil were not as authentic as the balance and harmony of all existences. They pointed to men's inability to make sense of the complexity and the ambiguity of our cosmos and the mystery beyond. So, men played down and simplified its abstract complexity to a level they could comprehend by simply putting a label of Good and Evil to judge all deeds and things they had done. The concept of Good and Evil may be necessary, but it can obstruct your understanding of the ultimate truth. I believe this is the best answer I could find so far."

The lonely boy drank every word into his thirsty soul as if his soul were the parched desert working on absorbing every drop of rain into every grain of sand. The true friendship Beloved had searched for so long was ironically found in his foreign teacher, who had come from a different part of the world. Mr. James almost made him believe that God must be real because Mr. James himself was a godsend to him.

Every time Mr. James came, he added new topics to their conversations. It was not a formal teaching class but two friends discussing things and ideas together. There was no limit to the subject they chose as long as those topics enkindled Beloved's curiosity and sharpened his mind. His teacher even encouraged him to have different opinions and perspectives out of the norm, under one condition: Beloved must find his own reason to support and fortify his points of view.

"You have to distinguish fact from opinion. The fact stands the test of time; therefore, it never changes. However, we shouldn't forget that every fact used to be a mere opinion till it undergoes proof and stands proud as fact. That's why opinion is no less important. Who knows? Your opinion will one day emerge as the fact that will change the world."

"In my opinion, your opinion about my opinion is right!" Beloved exclaimed.

Even the discussion on sex was welcomed, explicit yet matter-of-factly, as if in the biology textbook.

Now, Beloved clearly understood the significant nature of being a male and a female and of what Mr. James called 'the sexual intercourse' that led to conception and childbirth. He couldn't help letting his mind drift away, back to the day with Lin Jong inside her room. He felt his cheeks flushed and hot as he started to visualize her. Oh, how could he forget the moment she had grasped his hand and guided it to caress one of her breasts? *You silly boy*, he heard her hissing, laughing softly. *Touch it. Fondle it now. And you will get what I mean.* His eyes were still wide open, but all he visualized in front of him was her gleaming eyes, glowing like a pair of cat eyes in the dark. They did not reflect only mischief but also something he realized now that was closer to being insidious. He flinched when he felt the warm, soft flesh of her breast quivering between his damp and trembling hands.

He forced his hand to let go of it, but his hand seemed to start its own life and boldly declared independence. It refused to listen to him. *No-o-o-o-o-o-o-o.*

Suddenly, he jerked back and emerged from the trance-like daydream, rescued by Mr. James's voice.

"Beloved, are you all right? Is something disturbing you? You've just shouted no."

He blinked several times, trying to focus. "Yes, yes, I'm

fine. I feel…a little bit tired and let myself drop off. But I'm fine now."

Mr. James looked over at his nervous student. Then he asked carefully. "Beloved, you'll be fourteen next month, won't you?"

"Yes, that's correct."

"Oh, the coming of age is around the corner. We call what you're about to go through the state of puberty, a transition from boyhood to manhood. Soon enough, you will start to experience some queer feeling that you never dream of. Don't feel alarmed or ashamed if that stir happens. It only means you are as healthy and normal as every good male. Don't suppress it. Let nature take its course. The best way for now is to help yourself because it saves you from troubles and also venereal disease, which can be transmitted to you during sexual contact. Remember, an intimate relationship with a girl leads to sexual intercourse and, in turn, causes pregnancy. And that result can ruin the whole course of your future. You are not ready for a try. Promise me, please, for your own sake."

He had no idea why that urge was such a big deal for Mr. James, but he promised his concerned teacher whatever he was asked for.

But that night, that strange trance his teacher had mentioned came back as a dream after he'd drifted asleep. Suddenly, his eyes jerked open, too afraid to sleep. He didn't feel safe from that mysterious dark trance. That made Nanny Sook, who insisted on sleeping on the floor near his bed every night as if he was still a small child in her care, wake up at his steady toss and turn and groan; *Nanny, I'm scared. So scared.* In limbo of half-awake and half-sleep, he wailed at her just like when he was five years old and wanted comfort from her warm flesh. His desperate act hustled her to climb up his bed, pulled him close to her, and rocked him in her arms. *Don't be scared, darling. Come to be cuddled on my nom-nom.* He softly murmured with closed eyes before turning his head to her. That made her hastily drop her chest wrap and pull him into her chest, waiting for him to take it into his quivering mouth. It was their die-hard habit that she had been indulging him for all these years behind his mother's back to calm him down whenever he couldn't sleep or had nightmares.

But this time, it could not calm him down and help him return to normal sleep. The more vigorously his mouth squeezed her nom-nom, the more it seemed to arouse every pore of his tense body. Every part of him was suddenly turning stiff and half-paralyzing except his frenziedly trembling mouth while working around her nipple.

As he lay helpless and tortured, he became little by little oblivious of the present moment and started drifting into his favorite dream with that young female he had been keeping in secret in his reminiscence. He felt his hands start moving agilely, like two hungry snakes on the prowl, groping in the dark for the voluptuous, ripe flesh in his bizarre dream. Suddenly, his hands found and pounced at what he wanted like a predator. The hands started to squeeze and crush his prey with all his strength, squeezing and squeezing; he never got enough of squeezing it into a pulp.

That heated trance blinded him, hustling him to climb onto a body that was readily sprawling close to him. He felt those heavy limbs of a female begin to spread out and suck him in. He couldn't see that face in this dream-like state. His sense of vision had been weakened and blurred. Yet, his sense of touch was aroused and intensified tenfold. He heard the female's soft and shuddering moan as his trembling hands took turns with his quivering mouth savagely devouring her fat breasts. Her moaning set off his instinct to flare up, leading him to that juiciest part of her body he was wondering and dying for. He frenziedly thrust into that deep, soft cleft and gasped with all his shooting rapture. He screamed in silence while she gasped and moaned until he felt a volcanic pressure churning inside his groin suddenly erupt, spewing hot, slimy, flowing fluid to overflood everything in its way.

Startled by that violent eruption, the lad wondered whether he had wetted his bed but found out it was not the urine. His body then turned limp, yet the feeling of rapture he had just experienced was still pulsing and radiating all over his body. What a hideous, malicious, and, oh, delicious dream he'd ever had. It made him bury his face deep into his pillow and cry silently in surrender for an unquenchable fire in his groin that the female in his wildest dream had kindled.

But when his eyes opened again, even in the dark, he was aware that the flesh he had devoured in zest didn't belong to that young female he had always secretly dreamed of since she was missing from his life. Instead, the familiar scent of a juice from betel nut his nanny loved to chew lingered so close to his nostrils. He'd felt a familiar hand caressing him and heard a voice he was so familiar with cooing softly into his ears, coaxing him to drift back into a sound sleep as if he had become a baby once again rocked in her arms. *Ah, sleep well, my darling. I won't let that bitch to bother you in your dream again. Darling, you have me now…only me ever…*

When he woke up again, it was late morning. He was alone. There was no one in his room. Everything from last night seemed to blend and blur until he couldn't tell which part was real or a dream. But he hoped the whole thing was just a dream, the bizarre and most sensual he had ever dreamed.

Then he smelled that familiar smell of chewing betel nuts following his nanny into his room. She was carrying a breakfast tray to him. She dropped herself on his bed, touching his forehead, and said last night she'd found he had a fever. So, she had told his mother he needed to rest for the whole day without anyone coming to disturb him. His nanny spooned the pork congee soup to him herself. Alone with him, she crooned to him in triumph as she took off his dirty night pants and washed his body thoroughly with a warm, soaked towel to make him rise and shine again. While she dried him with a soft, clean towel, she planted her passionate kisses everywhere on his lean and young body. With each kiss, she poured out every ounce of her fierce affection to him.

"Come to me, darling. No one will bother us this moment."

She slowly unwrapped her chest wrap, her lips quivering. "Come to me now. Come like you did last night, darling."

"No, Nanny, no..." the lad whispered, weakly shaking his head.

But she coaxed him, pulling him into her arms. And a moment later, that quiet room was alive with their soft moaning.

* * * * *

Part 2: Chapter 4

The Isle Where Time Can't Find Us

*E*veryone in his family, particularly his mother, had noticed Beloved's change since Mr. James came.

Color reappeared on his pale cheeks. Smiles came back to his once-darkened face. Talk and laugh more easily flowed from his sealed lips. A sense of wonder and joy shone again from his somber eyes.

All in all, life returned to his existence. Being alone was not lonesome anymore for him but a joyous time to contemplate and explore. He had to ask all his attendants, including Lek, to leave him alone for a while, which he rarely did.

Now, every insignificant thing he came across as he took a walk all alone brought him big and small wonders as if he had discovered a hidden magical place of those overlooked by the rest of the world: the sight of the unwanted weed claiming its right to live by struggling to grow in the tiny crack of the moistless old brick wall: a single dead leaf about to drop to the earth and be forgotten forever: a tiny, almost invisible grain of sand he carefully put on his palm and pondered over some hidden reason of its bare existence in the whole universe before he blew it into the air, never be found again. Yet, it made him sad with a strange sense of loss. Because if he had indeed seen it again somewhere, there seemed no way he could recognize that particular grain of sand. Yes, he tried to find some hidden meaning among small things. It was his homework that Mr. James assigned for him for that week: searching the meaning of the meaningless existence and finding beauty in the unsightly.

He never discussed what he had been learning in Mr. James' class with anyone else, least of all his mother. His father might somewhat understand because he was the one who had chosen this eccentric scholar for his son, but his mother never would. Practicing English conversation at home with a foreign teacher, apart from going daily to the most prestigious Catholic school run by a group of French brothers, was all she knew, and she felt satisfied with her son's best education that they provided for him. That would be good enough to prepare him for further education in the United States in a few years.

She would freak out if he bluntly told her what his latest lesson was. Of course, he could imagine she would jump and scream: *A dead leaf! Absurd! Your father didn't mean to hire this crazy Farang to teach you how to squeeze some nonsense out of a dead leaf! I should discuss this with your father*! He couldn't help smiling as he tried to picture his mother's fuming response if someone had the courage to translate Mr. James' recent lecture to her.

"Beloved, imagine yourself as an extraterrestrial being from a distant star an infinity away. You have absolutely no concept about the blue planet you will enter. The earthling's values, such as beauty and ugliness, good and evil, love and hate, don't exist in your mind. Therefore, whatever you find while exploring—a diamond or a pebble, a rotten body, or a beauty queen—will bring you an equal measure of curiosity and awe. Thinking as if you were an alien, you can peel off the human dualistic thinking that hinders you from accessing the truest nature of all things…"

As Beloved let an earthworm he found in the soft soil wriggle on his palm and peered at the little creature with interest and respect (Mr. James told him earthworms make the earth inhabitable: they are the soil makers), his mother sent her maid to bring him to see her at once.

With this new spirit, reciting the names of his ancestors and memorizing their immortal glory in front of his mother became more tolerable. But when he entered her room, he saw his mother among her guests, all sitting idly in a circle on the carpet playing cards, his mother's favorite hobby, while his nanny was crouching right behind her. All ladies had their maids fanning vigorously at their mistresses while the afternoon tea was now served with delicacies and sweets as if for a much grander party.

He could tell his mother was in her most pleasant mood, a rare phenomenon. All of them except for one lady were his mother's regular visitors whose faces were quite familiar to him. He saw an unfamiliar girl his age sitting on the carpet by their side, her head bending on a book in front of her without raising her face to the noises and babbling, which grew louder all around her.

"Oh, Beloved, darling, come here," his mother greeted him excitedly as if she hadn't seen him for ages. Then she turned her head to the new lady by her side and announced proudly.

"Lady Ubol, this is my Beloved!"

That haughty and gorgeous lady immediately put aside her cards and turned all her attention to him for almost one minute with an air of being swank and showy. Instead of chewing betel like the other ladies, including his mother, that lady put one imported cigarette between her lips, lighting it with a match and slowly letting out a ribbon of the blue smoke as her eyes moved up and down, overtly appraising him. Then, she gave him a generously approving smile.

"Lady Pearl, you have such an awesome, awesome son. Oh, look at his sculpture-like face, the image of the great lord himself. He must be your greatest pride," then she called the girl. "Grace, come here, sweetie. Beloved, here's my lovely daughter, Siri. They said that you are a bookworm, one of a kind. Now you're probably facing your perfect match, my daughter."

Now, he was able to see the girl in plain view. Siri, meaning Grace, slowly raised her face from her book after she had heard her name called. What struck him was the feeling of disappointment. No, he had some sense enough not to expect a face of a rare beauty that seemed so close to impossible. (Though he knew rare beauty did exist after seeing a photograph of his mother at her grand wedding day she had taken with his father.) He didn't even expect a lovely face or a sweet face. He merely expected at least a cute face with deep dimples on her cheeks.

So, it took him by surprise as his eyes caught sight of a girl with a plain face, so plain she could be easily blended with a crowd of a hundred thousand girls whom he could see everywhere without bothering to turn his head to look back, ready to be forgotten the minute his eyes withdrew and turned somewhere else, that plain.

And yet, it wasn't fair to call that girl ugly because she was not. She was just perfectly plain, reminding him of spotless wall paint in plain gray—no blots, no stains, no streaks, no blemish—not a single thing either attractive or repulsive to arouse any attention whatsoever. Yet, her plainness oddly aroused his curiosity.

"Mother! I'm not that good, please."

Moments later, he heard the girl whisper in protest. She blushed, apparently embarrassed at the blatant compliment her mother showered her.

"Why not?" Lady Ubol said between her laughter. "Grace, do you remember? I once heard your voice out loud on your bed. I was surprised and concerned because it was already late at night. So, I sent a maid to check you up, and do you remember what the maid rushed back to tell me?"

Lady Ubol had paused, ready to send out a punchline.

"She came back and told me not to worry because you were reading something aloud in your bed. She found no book while you were reading, and besides, the room was dark. That was odd. So, I sent her back to see you again. This time, she returned and told me you were reading while your eyes were closing."

Now, all the ladies laughed heartily, apparently enjoying that joke—all except the girl.

"Good grief! She was dreaming of reading a book! What a smart girl!" another lady exclaimed.

"Beloved," Lady Pearl chimed in, "remember Grace, your playmate when you were a toddler of three? Oh, no, I don't expect you to recall that scandalous scene. That day, Nanny Sook carried you to meet Little Grace while she was playing with her toy stuff, um...I think it's monkey stuff. Then, all of a sudden, you slipped from your nanny's lap, jumped on her, and snatched that toy from her, leaving her to scream her head off. Good heavens! You two fought tooth and nail over that toy like two puppies fighting over a piece of cookie. But at least you were a little gentleman enough to hand it back to her, of course, still with your sulky face. It's now time you two should forget that old grudge and come to make peace with each other, once and for all!"

His mother's story ended with peals of laughter. Of course, he didn't have the faintest memory of the fight, let alone recognize this girl, his childish foe.

"A few years ago, she had left Siam with her family to stay in England. At that time, her father, Praya Pairach Rajamaitri, had been sent over as one of our Siamese ambassador member groups. Then, after he'd served his term, the whole family moved back, and Grace is now attending Ma'am Cole's school where all your sisters used to go," his mother referred to the most exclusive private school for girls from wealthy and well-established families.

"Grace, darling, I heard from your mother that you are excellent not only in your classroom but also in piano. Aren't you something?"

Her mother nodded, promptly verifying his mother's statement.

"I'll let my Grace show her talent shortly after if you won't mind," Lady Ubol, unable to conceal her delight, pointed eagerly to a huge grand piano at the far corner of the room.

"Why! It's my pleasure to listen to her playing nice pieces of music. My Beloved loves music, too. He is now practicing the violin. He's quite good at playing some piece of...of... what's his name? Ah, yes, *Taikobsky*'s violin concerto."

Of course, her mispronunciation of the great Russian composer, *Tchaikovsky*, was completely ignored. Bruising her vanity was beyond anyone's thought. Instead, another roar of laughter filled the room as Lady Pearl beamed at her son.

"What a match! Just like the old saying said, a gold branch would only match with its jade leaves. Do you think so, Lady Pearl?" Lady Ubol winked at Beloved. She had opened her expensive, brown croc leather purse and taken a small black velvet square box out of it before eagerly handing that small thing to him.

"Oh, I have a present for you. Open it. I bought it myself from Harrods store in London."

It was a luxurious, handsome gold pocket watch with an engraved gold hunter case linked with a long gold chain. It was the work of exquisite craftsmanship.

"I..." he stammered. To receive such a pricey gift from this over-familiar lady he had met for the first time made him somewhat uneasy.

"Why not? Beloved," she smiled at him meaningfully as she dropped the box onto his palm. "Aren't you my son now?"

Lady Pearl, who now apparently felt so compelled to start her own scene, asked Grace to come closer to her. She took her solitaire ruby ring off her finger and put it gingerly on Grace's. That ring perfectly fitted the girl's finger, creating another meaningful ooh and ah from everyone.

"This exceptional-quality ruby came from Mogok mines in Burma, the best ruby source in the world. Do you see six-ray legs stars crossing the gem? This ruby was cut in a cabochon shape to render the deepest pigeon blood color rarely found. How deep and brilliant it is when it reflects in sunlight. Why? Though you have money, it doesn't mean you are lucky to find such an ideal quality. However, only the best ruby is for the best girl," she declared in triumph as she eyed the girl's mother, who was beaming and exclaiming excitedly.

"Oh my! What a match! What a match!"

As the conversation went on, the girl looked more abashed. Her growing uneasiness made him give her a soothing smile. Why did those two ladies try to bombard him with their overwhelming praise for this girl? Weren't they sensitive enough to notice how much effort the girl had to put up with that talking? He believed that she would have flown this minute off the open window behind her if she had had wings. He looked at her despaired and timid face and then decided to break in their zestful chitchat.

"Mother, can I bring Grace to take a walk around? She might be bored with nothing to do in this room."

The response was immediate and overwhelming as if they were waiting for this moment.

"Why! Beloved darling, what an excellent idea, and a thoughtful young man! Yes, yes, bring her with you for a couple of hours if you want. How about enjoying the afternoon tea inside the gazebo in our rose garden? It's the most splendid place, quiet and cool. I'll send someone over there to serve tea and scones to both of you. I'm sure you children will have a wonderful time together."

"Thank you, Mother," replied Beloved gently yet shortly.

Before his nanny got to her feet, Lady Pearl frowned and stopped her routine for accompanying him when he stepped outside.

"That's all right, Sook. Let the two children have a good

time alone without us around."

Though Nanny Sook complied with the lady, her eyes still followed Beloved until he tip-toed out of the noisy room, followed by the girl he had rescued. She quietly followed him downstairs, apparently relieved, and out to the sun outside. At least he felt thankful to his mother for allowing them to stroll alone without the watchful eyes of his nanny or any of his attendants trailing behind.

"Do you feel all right now?" Beloved asked her gently as they walked along the path under the cool tree shade.

"Yes, thank you so much," whispered the girl gratefully, then reluctantly added. "I am so sorry about…my mother."

Before Beloved opened his mouth, she continued in her low voice.

"I…can't stop her from exaggerating her talk about me. Please ignore what she said. She probably means good for me," then she sighed, "regardless of its consequence."

"It never bothers me a bit," he assured her, and this time, with a big grin as big as his heart, he said, "Don't worry. I've already gotten used to that. You accept the fact that we both are not, whatsoever, able to change our mothers. That's all. Don't you notice my mother also shares this trait when she starts bragging about me? I believe your mother is finding her match."

"Oh, really!" the girl cried out loud. His frankness took her by surprise. She tried to bite her lips to suppress the indiscreet giggle but to no avail. So, she let her giggle burst out as Beloved joined his with hers.

"So, we seem to have mutual issues with our mothers' behavior. As far as I notice, none can beat one another in a boasting contest."

Now, he even made the girl laugh openly with bitter satisfaction. Suddenly, the girl's face started to intrigue and then fascinate him; what he was witnessing right before his eyes was the most extraordinary transformation on her face. Oh, that smile, so natural and so honest, that smile of hers had washed out all the dull plainness from her face, just like the work of a miracle,

Before that, he always wondered whose smile among hundreds of thousands could truthfully represent the definition of the word smile in the dictionary. He had seen numerous smiles flash in front of him. Yet for him, none had qualified the term smile. They were all superficial, misused as camouflages to disguise the owners' true feelings that lay behind their masks of smile—fear, despair, anger, scorn, repulsion, or malice. That's why those smiles looked too refined, too courteous, too sugary, too ambiguous, or too mysterious.

Only the genuine smile of the girl named Grace showed what a smile truly meant.

He couldn't wait to show Mr. James the homework for which he was assigned: a discovery of the real thing found by chance in the most unlikely place.

Why! The true beauty of a smile was found on that girl's insignificant face.

"You have the most extraordinary smile ever," he managed to conceal his excitement, yet he couldn't help slipping his remark.

"Really?"

Instead of being impressed, she looked surprised, even perplexed. It was his fault. He desperately needed her to know what he told her was a pure and simple fact, not praise. Yet, he couldn't find the precise word in his lexicon to match her smile. Therefore, what he just blurted out sounded, even to him, too bland and hollow, almost to the point of simply flattery.

Yes, people said *oh, you have the most beautiful smile* to one another, a convenient sentence for social talk—forever losing its original meaning—when they couldn't think of any better phrases to please one another. So, after one minute, he firmly told himself never again to contaminate her pristine and original smile verbally. He now realized it was too risky to reveal his disclosure even to her. To protect that, he shouldn't even let her be aware of what she had been possessing so that her smile would be protected as it had always been. No flattery would corrupt it.

"How is England? I heard it is unimaginably cold. Do you like it?" he abruptly changed the subject. "With all the snow and ice in winter, I wonder how you manage to get on," he still remembered with a chill and shudder when he first tasted Mr. James's ice cube.

"My family lived in a big flat by the River Thames in London, and I went to a private school for a couple of years. The weather was always wet, gray, and foggy. It rained so steadily that I rarely glimpsed the real bright sunshine. Some days, the fog was so dense even when you stepped outside and raised your hands in front of you, you couldn't even see your own hands. So eerie. Its density seemed so solid, as if a permanent wall was standing before you, and you had to use a hammer to break that wall so you could walk past. But it was just an illusion playing on your eyes. In fact, you could walk through that wall of fog as easily as you walked through the air."

"The fog must be soft to the touch like a cotton ball," Beloved said dreamily, "If only I could have felt it."

"No," she vigorously shook her head. "It just dampened your clothes and made you feel creepy as if a monster was breathing its cold breath on your neck. Some even call this kind a pea soup fog for its strange-looking thickness. Yet I love the villages of Kent and Sussex in the countryside along the south coast not far from London. In the spring, my father always brought my elder sister and me there on the weekend to picnic under the cool tree shade on the green meadow peppered with yellow daffodils and blue wildflowers. It was so picturesque, with quaint thatched roof cottages and English gardens with rose bushes and lush green trees everywhere, exactly like the idyllic landscapes I always see on the oil paintings masterpieces in the museums. Anyway, as they say, there is no place like home; now I know how true it is when I can walk in the hot sun every day and smell the scent of jasmine again."

Then, he noticed her still holding her book firmly against her chest.

"What are you reading?" he curiously asked her.

The girl didn't answer but shyly showed him the book. Once he glimpsed the cover, he cried.

"Robinson Crusoe! You do surprise me! It's a novel of exotic adventures. I thought you would enjoy more delightful books like Little Women or Jane Eyre or Pride and Prejudice…. something like that. Why this one?"

As they talked, the girl grew more at ease with him. That smile of hers came back, shining all over her face again. This time, a hint of secret played on her smile.

"Promise me you're not going to tell anybody."

Beloved nodded earnestly. "Never would I breathe a word!"

"I always dream of living on an isolated island alone, maybe with two or three of my cats, just like the shipwrecked Crusoe, learning to make my own shelter, my own tools and utensils, growing my own plants. My life would miss nothing. What a self-sustained life! Oh, no…" Suddenly, the girl looked like she had just missed out on something crucial, "I almost forgot to bring a huge trunk full of books into my island."

"Don't you want to bring people to live with you too, maybe just a few people you like?"

"People?" she sighed deeply, telling him quietly, "The main reason I want to live on a remote island is just to be away from them. All of them. Their gibberish and blabber bore me to death, making me feel even lonelier among such a chatter-box crowd. They surround me most of the time, even a moment ago."

The tone in her voice vaguely touched him.

"Can I come with you? I also want to be away from them… Someone in particular…" his voice faltered. Sudden shame stopped him from thinking of that *thing* behind the shadow at night.

The girl searched his face, hesitant. Her subdued face made

him go on more eagerly to persuade her.

"We can help each other with all kinds of chores," he frowned, his tone becoming serious. "Are there any coconut trees on your island?"

The girl nodded earnestly.

"Yes, as many as you ever imagine, thousands of them, or a hundred of thousands, all right, or even millions!"

"Good! We can survive on them alone—their meat and juice for our food source and water supplies, their shells for utensils. I can carve spoons, cups, and pots out of coconut shells. With their sturdy trunks for making the floor and walls and their long, abundant leaves for our roof, I can build a snug and cozy shelter for us. Oh, I can also make a raft from those lightweight trunks and bring you on the raft and row around the shore to explore different landscapes of the island and search for fresh water. I'm sure we will find a cool waterfall deep in the heart of the island somewhere so we can swim in a gurgling creek and catch some fish," he paused and said meekly, "Maybe we will um… eat them in case we can't find anything else to survive."

"Don't worry. We can live on plants alone if you don't want to take any life," she assured him, "we have abundant seaweeds for our protein source, and we can dig underground roots like yam and taro for starch and sugar. I'm sure there must be wild plantains and fruits everywhere for minerals. We can live happily like two sovereigns co-reigning our pristine kingdom."

"And in the evening," Beloved chimed in, "I can bring you out on my raft to the open sea to watch the blazing fireball of the sun slowly dropping into the dark ocean. While the sun is sinking, we can tell the borderline where the horizon and waters meet. And then we will let the night gently blanket us with its ink-black darkness to hide ourselves from the world. We let only the millions of stars see us from afar. Never would people come to bother us any longer. You have only me for your companionship, and I have only you. How is that?"

There was no answer, but this time, he saw her on the verge

of tears as she gazed at him; a million thanks shone in her eyes.

"I can make a sundial from a flat stone plate and make a gnomon cast a shadow onto the plate surface so we will know the time of the day by the movement of its shadow that circles that plate."

"No, don't drag *time* with us!" Grace's sudden alarm startled him.

"Why not?" he asked curiously. She gazed at him strangely.

"Where I'll bring you to live is so remote. Even time can't find its way to reach us. Don't you know time is the most ruthless hunter? It has devoured every single existence since the beginning of its existence. It can devour us into bones and devour bones into dust and keep on devouring dust into nothingness. Nothing! Beloved, don't let time know where we are. Promise me. This way, we will be safe to live forever out there."

It was his turn to be stunned and fascinated by her fierce remark. To her, time is the most ruthless hunter of all lives.

"Oh, yes, you are right," he said finally. "Where we'll go to live is humanless and timeless. How is that!"

They didn't know how long they had spent together planning their castaway adventure until one of the maids came and crouched in front of Grace, telling her mother to ask her to be back because it was almost time for them to leave. They turned their faces to look at each other, fully awakened from the reverie spell they had shared moments ago.

"Can you come back, Grace?" he whispered.

"I hope so, but I don't know. It…depends on my mother. And what if she says no?" She started to wring her hands in frustration.

"I'll ask my mother to invite your mother and you again. I can ask her for anything, and she rarely says no to me," as he assured her, he saw that smile swiftly return to light up her face as she cried out.

"Really? Really? Thank you!"

The following morning, his mother summoned him to her bedroom. He found her sitting alone, on a rare occasion, in front of her ivory-carved vanity table, with varieties of perfumes and powders in pastel-colored crystal bottles, green, indigo, and red. She was sipping hot green tea from a bone-china teacup in her most relaxed posture, also a rare sight.

"Beloved, darling, how is Grace? Are you fond of her?" she kissed his forehead, fondly stroked his hair, and opened a smile to him.

"She is a nice and intelligent young lady, mother," he replied honestly yet cautiously. He had no idea what his mother was up to.

"You get along with her, don't you, when you two got together the other day?"

"I do enjoy her company," another concise yet honest reply from him.

"You don't mind if she isn't conventionally pretty, do you? Her complexion is not fair, and her features are somewhat..." she paused, trying carefully to choose a word—a word that was toned down yet still carried some weight of truth. "Umm...sort of homely."

Now, her eyes were studying him, testing his reaction. "It's too bad she takes after her father. He is very brilliant but far from a good look. Her older sister is way prettier; she takes her mother's looks, but that one was already engaged to marry next year."

"Her being pretty or not has nothing to do with me. Anyway, what is it all about, Mother?"

After a bombardment with odd questions, the truth finally unfolded. His mother suddenly turned more solemn. "Beloved, yesterday we've just arranged a future marriage between the two of you. Grace's mother, Lady Ubol, is wholeheartedly fond of you. She told me she had decided to turn down all other proposals and embraced ours when she first saw you on her visit yesterday."

Beloved was too astonished to respond as his mother kept convincing him eagerly.

"Well, they've raised their daughter in quite an untraditional way because they spent a lot of time in foreign countries. She might lack some qualities of a perfect housewife, which I expect from my daughter-in-law because one day, she will take my place as the matriarch of this great house with hundreds of people under her care and supervision. Then I realized this shouldn't be a serious problem because she can learn first-hand from me. On the other hand, her family is one of the wealthiest, just like ours, or perhaps wealthier. Besides, her father never has other women," she paused and sighed heavily, "therefore, he had only three children to share his immense fortune and estate. She has only one brother, who is now attending some prep school in England. I heard that Grace is the youngest and her father's favorite. They said her father spoils her and puts some fancy notions in her head, encouraging her to talk and act strange. Yet, overall, I found her a refined and prudent young lady. But the most important fact is that her father had great influence in the royal court, and her mother was my good, old friend from when we were in the royal court. With such in-laws with such wealth and status, I can rest in peace when my time comes, for your bright and secure future will be guaranteed for life with her parents' unwavering support. Oh, Beloved, I love you so much. All I've done is always in your best interest, darling."

Grace was appraised and approved by his parents as the most suitable for him due to her family's immense wealth, high social status, and political power, as he was for her, with the same standard being applied by her parents. Their betrothal was more of a business-like contract between two of the most prestigious and influential families, with many deals and bargains involved until mutual benefit emerged.

She dreams of living all alone on the most remote isle, where time—the most ruthless hunter—cannot find even her shadow,

Mother.

No, he had enough sense not to crack a word about Grace's 'dream island' to his mother.

His silence was interpreted as his acceptance. His mother went on cheerfully.

"The marriage will be arranged after you finish law school abroad, which is still far ahead. And your wedding is planned to be the greatest one of that year, no less than that. Now, you two still have plenty of time to get acquainted. For now, take good care of her, darling. She is your betrothed now."

That night, he couldn't sleep well, not because that news brought him distress; he was so fond of Grace, but because he couldn't picture Grace as a wife to someone, let alone to himself. He grew up enough to understand well what a wife was for, apart from the role of a lady in the parlor and a maid in the kitchen. Oh, after all, being a sex slave in her husband's bed was what a wife was actually for, to produce children for her husband as many as she could as his other four sisters faithfully did. No, no, no, not that way for an immaculate and fragile girl like Grace.

If his father didn't have a whole bunch of concubines, he couldn't imagine how many more children his mother might have borne, beyond the eight she already had including his stillborn twin sister, who had died nameless.

How did he dare to drag Grace down into the sensual dark world and contaminate her flesh? At least for now, he wanted to lift Grace above all filthiness and let the other one in his secret delicious dream do all the dirty work.

Maybe he didn't want Grace that way, not yet, because when nature mercilessly called him in the dead of night, someone else knew and climbed up his bed to release him from that intense torment.

After that first night, it happened too frequently to dismiss as mere dreams. Almost every night in the dark, a shadowlike female figure climbed onto his bed as stealthily as a move of shadow. The boy still told himself it couldn't be real when that act started. And yet it was so real that he cringed and winced when his hand scrambled in the dark and found the part most familiar to his touch, his nanny's fat *nom-nom*. But her hushed voice could compel him as if he were still a small boy in her care. *Shush... I am feeding you, darling. When you were a baby, I fed you what hungry baby needed. But you are big now; I am feeding you what a big boy craves.*

"*Please...*" He whimpered to her weakly. But she coaxed him, leading him inside her, letting his orgasm, together with hers, shoot up to the sky.

The fourteen-year-old youth was unsure how to handle what had been happening to him at night. He was only aware that heaven and hell were rolling into his bed when she climbed up on him. While she was frenziedly on him, heaven spun him up into a soaring euphoria, but hell hurtled him down into a pit of shame after it was done, and she climbed down to her cot beside his bed, leaving him alone with that burning shame. He must keep it to himself. He must. Because their frequent acts in his bedroom were too bizarre for anyone to believe, most of all himself.

Refusing to believe helped him feel better because not believing meant it wasn't at all real.

However, as months passed into a year, whether he wanted it or not, that nightly act in his bedroom turned into a routine while at the same time, the friendship between Grace and him also steadily grew. As he was possessed by that nocturnal demoness at night, he needed Grace to purify his soul during the day. He felt as if she were the sunshine that could chase away that dark spirit from him.

They saw each other almost every week now, sharing dreams and little funny secrets. She was thrilled whenever he told her what Mr. James had just taught him. He never omitted anything because she loved savoring otherworldly details like a dream-starving child. They understood the very thought of each other like two Siamese twins whose souls were conjoined. Once, he proudly introduced Grace to Mr. James, who greeted her warmly and excitedly.

"Hello, my young lady. It's the greatest honor to meet Beloved's soulmate." Then, with a simulated alarm, he added, "Oh, sorry. You are not just each other's soulmates. You two are twins inside out!"

Amazingly, they found out that they had even shared their birthday. Beloved was born at dawn in the zodiac sign year of Monkey, barely an hour before Grace's arrival. The day before their sixteenth birthday, she had shyly slipped an envelope into his hand before she left, saying it was his birthday gift from her. When he opened it with shaking hands, he saw a poem she had written for him in her beautiful longhand handwriting.

> *O, Bountiful Heart*
> *Beating, bleeding,*
> *Bestowing all your existence*
> *Beneath the bosom of someone*
> *But so little have you known*
> *The one whose life you sacrifice for*
> *Able to wreck the heart of another.*

Another phase of Beloved's life came when one of his twin sisters, Chandra, died of acute pneumonia. That year, the usual mild winter turned unusually cold. His sister began complaining about having a sore throat and fever, which hardly anyone paid much attention to. She was always the first in the whole family to succumb to a cold whenever the weather changed slightly.

Two days later, she died, leaving Lady Pearl to collapse in utter shock. She tearfully blamed herself for her negligence of her daughter's illness. She should have asked a doctor promptly to check Chandra's symptoms. Instead, she still enjoyed playing cards with her friends, unaware that her daughter was lying in bed in a coma. Though the funeral had already passed for months, the lady never got over her overwhelmed guilt and grief. Her health drastically declined physically, mentally, and emotionally in particular. Consequently, she sought solace in the only person she loved more than any soul.

Now, she stayed in bed most of the time, losing most of her vitality and enthusiasm to her grief, trying grudgingly to listen to Rumpai, her leftover twin, reading a Dharma book for her. Nothing mattered to her except for one singular thing. She pricked up her ears to the only sound that enabled her to come alive again: Beloved's footsteps.

As the first thing after returning from school by the family's grand automobile driven by Nai Lek, Beloved would go straight to his mother's room to sit on her side and devote at least an hour to her. He would kiss her cheeks as his mother hugged him so fiercely as if it was the way to keep him in her womb again, safe and secured from peril and uncertainty outside, which had just deprived her of her daughter. Beloved would take the book from his sister, who could eventually retreat to her private room, and with his soft and resonant voice, started reading to his mother her favorite poetry or some religious text to comfort her.

This time, she would cling to every word he uttered, her eyes fixing on his face and her hand clutching his. Nothing more in the world, even the presence of her husband, whom she always yearned for his care, could lift up her gloomy spirit.

The doctor diagnosed the symptom of her deterioration as chronic heart failure due to her growing stress as she was approaching old age. She would possibly face a mental breakdown or a life-threatening heart attack if she had one more major stress.

Beloved asked his father to postpone the plan to send him abroad next year after his mother had desperately begged him not to leave her for now. Due to her fragile health, she was so apprehensive of never seeing him again if he was out there and of dying alone on her deathbed without him at her side.

"There are only two people your mother genuinely cares about—herself and another one she has seen whenever she looks into the mirror," his father said contemptuously during their argument. Of course, his father vehemently disagreed. "There is no room in her shallow heart for anyone else. She doesn't care about you. All she cares about is her feeling, her injured feeling of losing you."

"Father, my mother's peace of mind is my priority," he said quietly, "because you are rarely there for her whenever she needs you, I feel I should compensate her for your absence."

His father stared at him for one long minute. Yet, with Beloved's undeniable fact, his father finally gave in. After a long pause, the lord started again. This time, both his eyes and his voice softened.

"Beloved, be fair with me, although you might be right. You have always witnessed my nonchalance to your mother for so long, but you seemingly don't want to know whose fault it is. She is the most headstrong and overbearing creature I've ever known. Yet, no matter how much she has given me hard times and heartaches, I always forgive her. Do you know why? I still owe her one priceless thing I can't figure out how to repay. Therefore, I found a way to repay her through my tolerance and submission. I always let her win," he sighed, and Beloved witnessed a weary look cracked on his father's usually impassive face for the first time.

"You must remember Lin Jong and…her baby son, yes, my own son too. And that also, I let your mother, under her whim, do it her way just because of what I've owed her."

Beloved's heartbeat quickened. He hardly believed what he had heard. The Lord had never discussed personal matters with anyone, let alone mentioned them.

"Father," he held his breath, his voice almost turning to a

whisper as he collected all his courage to interrupt. "What had happened to them?"

Another long stretch of silence. Then his father said bitterly.

"Your mother had thrown her out of this house."

Beloved gasped, and then he breathlessly added one more question before that rare chance might be gone. "And...Baby Boy? Where is he now?"

The fear he had tried so hard to suppress crept back to his trembling voice, which couldn't escape his father's observant and keen eyes. Probably because of this, his father didn't answer him. He must know his son's long agony over that accident. He merely rested his hand on Beloved's shoulder and gently patted it, a sign of affection and tenderness toward his son that was rarely shown, even in privacy. Instead, he said.

"Lin Jong is the hardest case for me. I'm so fond of her more than any woman of mine. But even today, I still have no clue where she is. I only heard a rumor she's in some place that's not for decent women. Well, it's not all her fault. She needs to survive. Perhaps if I can find out her whereabouts, I might bring her back to make up for your mother's unfair treatment of her," then he sighed deeply. "Do you know what I've owed your mother and therefore let her get the upper hand for so long?"

His father stroked Beloved's hair as he went on.

"Your mother gave birth to you, my son. *You*. Because of this, nothing else matters."

Beloved was stunned. He felt hot tears sting his eyes. *Be strong, Beloved. You are almost seventeen now, and you can't show such a sentiment in front of a figure like your father.* Yet, for all those years of distance between his father and him, he had never been aware of how much his father loved him. And out of that love, the lord had sacrificed so much.

After his sister's death, Lek, who was his master's shadow, noticed that Beloved had become preoccupied with mysterious matters he had rarely paid attention to before.

"What is a ghost, Mr. James? Do you think such a thing exists?"

"Do you?" Mr. James raised his brows. "What about you?"

Beloved paused for some seconds, then shook his head regretfully.

"No, I only wish I could see one. To see is to believe, right? Sometimes, I thought excitedly that I had seen or heard a ghost, but I found out later that it was only a moving shadow of some tree branch, a window slammed by the wind, or the creaking sound on the old staircases. That's it. I was so disappointed none were ghosts. But tall tales about things out of the ordinary thrill me. Those supernatural tales always ended up with someone coming face to face with a ghost, screaming his head off, and flying for his life. It's fun to listen to, giving me a good creep. But, had I been them, I wouldn't have fled and missed out on the golden opportunity to unfold this mystery. I will stand my ground and confront what we assume as ghosts."

"Ah, that's my student!" Mr. James beamed. "Who knows? You might be the first person who officially interconnects with a ghost and reveals to the world what ghosts truly are. It could be a big surprise that ghosts may not be what we think they are."

"So, it means you also believe in ghosts, don't you?" asked Beloved excitedly.

"Unfortunately, I've never seen one either." Mr. James shook his head sadly as his voice softened. "Anyway, my answer is either yes or no. I experienced something so bizarre shortly after my sister's funeral. That night, I cried myself to sleep because I missed her so terribly. While I drifted into half-sleep, I heard someone calling me in a soft whisper. When I opened my eyes, it seemed like it was already in the morning, warm golden sunlight flooding all over my bedroom. I saw Emily sitting by my side, wearing her Sunday best and her favorite bonnet with the big bright yellow ribbon. She smiled brightly at me and laid a small bunch of wildflowers in her arms onto my pillow. Everything I saw in the room was golden yellow, her favorite color: the radiant sunshine, her clothes, her bonnet, her flowers, and her long curly hair, except for her eyes, which were brightest blue. Oh, if you could see her eyes, mine, which you said were so blue, would fade into insignificance. My heart nearly burst from the overjoyed at the sight of my little sister, so much that I could die…"

Beloved was almost in tears.

"I truly believe at that instant that I did wake up from my nightmarish sleep and found my sister by my side, coming from her bedroom to wake me up as she usually did on Sunday morning so we could join our parents in a short walk to church. Everything was absolutely normal and yet so wondrous. I heard the birds twittering outside the window, smelled the fresh summer flowers she had laid on my pillow, and even felt Emily's warm and soft hand stroking my face. Suddenly, she exited my bed and started walking toward the door. A splendid bright light at the door was so bright it nearly blinded me. I shouted, calling her desperately to return to me as she was about to enter that light. An instant later, my own shouting startled me awake. This time, I opened my eyes to face the bleak darkness of the freezing winter night. I saw the heavy snowflakes swirling in the blowing wind outside the windowpane. Strangely, the fresh smell of the flowers still lingered, so, so sweet…."

"She had come to say goodbye. She wanted to console you by showing you she would be a little divine angel in heaven. I'm positive." Beloved abruptly interrupted. He could no longer bear Mr. James's heart-wrenching story.

"I never wished anything more in my life to be true. After this incident, I understand why people need desperately to believe in a controversial yet comforting concept like the existence of heaven, the best place ever for their loved ones to go after they left them forever. I began to understand why we need a religion. It's because a religion, any religion, ensures the existence of heaven. Maybe after all, being in existence of ghosts is better than becoming utter nothingness after death if we have to choose what we want to believe."

"Yes, it's true. Yet, I don't believe in the dead who can drag their body out of their graves and roam around to hurt or kill the living. It extremely violates the law of physics you taught me the day before."

"You're right, Beloved. If the deceased can still command its body into action as much as we, the living, can do, that means it doesn't make any difference whether to live or die. And if we believe it could be possible, anything can also be possible—people suddenly having wings to fly, gold suddenly growing on trees, and so on. List of such unlikely and impossible things can go on endlessly with no boundary and respect to the law of nature."

"I can't figure out how people here will react to our view," Beloved laughed sheepishly. "People claim they always see ghosts everywhere. By their standard, I'm afraid the ghost population in Siam probably outnumbers us humans."

Mr. James laughed. "Well, at least the superstition among your people sounds milder compared to the one in Europe some centuries ago. It led to up to sixty thousand women's violent deaths from around the fifteenth to the eighteenth century; most of those victims were innocent people."

"What!" Beloved exclaimed. "What is it all about?"

"During that period, people's apprehension of witches led to the witch-hunt frenzy. There was a strong belief that the devil empowered witches to harm people through their spells and witchcraft practices. Therefore, a large number of women were accused, on trial, convicted, and punished either by being burnt alive in a bonfire or lynched to death. Their execution was held in public where town people, adults, and children alike, were allowed to watch and celebrate their gruesome death."

"How did they know who was or was not a witch?" Beloved hunched his shoulder, "Poor, poor souls. What if they had accused the wrong ones?"

"One method was to search the suspect's dwelling place. If

they found a black cat in any woman's possession, that's enough for the proof. If she had two, the evidence was double."

"Good Heavens!" Beloved rolled his eyes and sighed hopelessly. "Last week, my sister's black cat just gave birth to a litter of five. Four of the kittens are pitch black like their mommy. Since losing her twin, Rumpai has been so lonesome that she has started having pets. These two twins were just like a shadow of each other. If you saw one, you instantly saw the other. Now, I spend more time with her, letting her know she is not alone."

"I can see you are always her little angel, always a little doll to her," he teased him and went on.

"Your sister should thank her lucky stars that she was not born in Europe a few centuries ago. In history, people's irrational fear of witches back in the Medieval Age led to felicide, meaning the mass slaughter of cats, which in turn led to the major outbreak of bubonic plague. The epidemic, called the Black Death, spread like wildfire and wiped out at least half of the population in Europe. Why? Almost no cats were left to kill the real culprits: the flea parasites on the rats—the plague's carriers. During that period, the whole continent was infested with rats and rats. What a pity! They had to pay for their superstition caused by their ignorance with twenty million lives within four years."

"The funny thing about ghosts is it's always someone else who saw it, a secondary source," Beloved pondered. "A cousin saw it, a neighbor saw it, a friend saw it, or an uncle's friend's sister saw it, et cetera, but why do we never see it ourselves? They recently said one of the housemaids had come to clean my late sister's bedroom as my mother ordered. Mother wants her room immaculate as if the owner were still living with us. All her clothes and belongings are kept intact. Mother even ordered her maids to bring my sister's favorite dish and put it on the table in that room daily. As that maid entered the room, she said she caught sight of my dead sister sitting on her bed and staring at her. But when I pinpointed which maid who had seen my sister, they started to be elusive and unsure."

"Very elusive indeed, like trying to grab a smoke with your hand. Yet, I still open my mind to all possibilities of the spirit in the form of energy that so far can't be detected with our ordinary senses. If there's a way to contact these spirits, they might try to correct our view about them. What if they argue that they are more alive than we are? Why? It's because they, the spirits, are purely in the form of thinking entities, able to live independently without the burden of breathing, consuming, and excretion. At the same time, more than half of our energy, the living, is constantly used for serving our physical needs— hunger, sickness, and deterioration of our body."

"What if we, the living, are, in fact, all dead and remain in 'the world of the dead' and on the contrary, the spirits of the departed are the ones who do transcend us into the true form of life?"

"Well done!" His teacher gently touched Beloved's shoulder. "Keep working on this perspective. Make it a fact and disclose to the world what you find out," he beamed at his student. It is worth all my efforts to see how your mind works."

"Thank you, Mr. James," he grinned and then sighed. "My people's belief in such things the way they have believed for generations is so deep-rooted. I can't so far expect them to see such things your way. They interpret all phenomena they don't understand as the work of the supernatural. They dread the paranormal harmful power to the point that it affects their state of mind and shapes their way of life. In some cases, when you believe some spirits closely watch you, the way to hide yourself is to disguise your own identity, such as your name and your gender, so they aren't able to find and hence harass you. In some extreme cases, when you are severely sick, you could try to trick some watchful and malicious spirits by setting your own funeral to fake your death. Once the spirits assume you are no longer among the living, they will turn their attention to someone else instead and leave you alone again."

Mr. James was amused. "Poor ghosts, with those ingenious tricks, it's impossible for the ghosts to find the slightest chance to harass you people."

"You bet. All walks of life need protection, especially the children. Compliment for small children is forbidden for fear that it would stir ghosts' malice. In some severe cases, if a baby were born to perfection, which means he was born without one single blemish, parents would make a scar on his body to save him."

"Well, you are that perfect human, Beloved." Suddenly, Mr. James's voice grew solemn. "I mean physically and spiritually, a human being close to an angel in my eyes. Now, I can see that your people's beliefs make some sense. Naturally, we humans are supposed to have flaws, more or less. But, in your case, you are unblemished, Nature's masterpiece...or on the contrary," he paused, "Nature's worst error. Had I had some ounce of superstition hidden in my mind, I should have worried about the flawlessness of being you. The Ill-Will One looks for the one like you out of his spite."

He paused again, then said quietly. "Watch out, son. Please watch out."

"No," Beloved averted eye contact. " I'm not flawless."

It made the dark things behind his closed door started haunting him again.

* * * * *

Part 2: Chapter 5

Life Long Pursuit

*B*eloved was thunderstruck by Mr. James's abrupt farewell. In fact, he felt as much as the sky was falling after
Mr. James told him the most unexpected news.

"Why?"

His head went numb and dumb, and his hands and legs went
limp, unable to think of anything else to exclaim.

With his grim expression, Mr. James fished a letter from
his pocket and showed Beloved.

"I received a letter from my elder brother, Theodor, yesterday. He urged me to go home immediately. My aged mother's
consumption disease has come to the last state. The doctor
warned him she would live only for another three months. Ted
stressed that it is her wish to see me before she passes and have
my forgiveness for her unfair treatment, which she has given
me since my sister Emily's drowning accident,"

Mr. James wiped the tears that kept coming down his cheeks.

"She has not seen me for over twenty years since I left
home... Now you know why I have to leave. The steamer

will take me at least one month to arrive home, let alone the unexpecting delay during that long trip in the open sea."

Beloved bowed his head in utter surrender. That was settled. They were now in the same boat when it came to the obligation of their mother's illness.

"Will you come back? Will you?" he asked feebly with flickering hope.

Mr. James sighed heavily, "I wish I could. But nothing is certain in life. I'm not rich and young enough to travel as far as I can afford. It's about time I should settle down in my mother's estate in New Hampshire, which my brother said will legally belong to me, according to the will she wrote."

Beloved struggled to swallow the lump in his throat. If he let it come up, it would burst into sobs, the most childish, disgraceful sobs he hadn't shown for years.

"So today will be my last day with you. Let me tell you something. I am tremendously proud of you. I always tell your father you are my best student and best friend ever."

Before he left, he promised Beloved he would write as soon as he arrived home. They could become pen pals for life across the world. Why not? Time and distance could not be in between their close and strong friendship. He handed him a book. It was not a new copy. Its brown leather hardcover looked somewhat worn, but it was still in good condition.

"My favorite book is the collected poems by William Blake, the most beloved English poet. I always carry this book with me as my solace. Read it, and you will never miss me again."

Then he opened his arms as widely as he could.

"Now let me give you a good hug, my son. Hug me like you will never let me leave you."

"Don't forget to write to me," Beloved whispered. "Ever."

"No, I won't. Remember, we have a lifetime project to work together," his teacher whispered back. "Help me discover why terrible things happen in our lives for no reason. Can you? That's for my poor sister…as well as for the sake of your baby brother."

For the first couple weeks of Mr. James' departure, Beloved took his teacher's farewell so seriously that he started again withdrawing from everyone around him. After a couple of months, he was not any better. When Mr. James sent his mail with the news of his mother's death, his father decided to write back to him. Apart from his condolence for the loss in the gentleman's family, the old lord asked him to return with the promise that he would pay up all the trip expenses, including all the accommodations that Mr. James would need during his stay in Bangkok, no matter how long it would take. All he needed to do on his part was only to show up; he begged him. His son needed his mentor back so desperately to help support his strength and morale.

Mr. James' reply surprised yet profoundly moved the old lord. After all, this stubborn-headed, peculiar-minded American had never disappointed him a bit. Every word in Mr. James' letter was indisputable.

Your Excellency,

I highly appreciate your benevolence and am deeply concerned about your son. I must admit that right after receiving your letter, I was so anxious about Beloved's state of mind that it compelled me to be with him as you requested. And yet, after having second thoughts, I decided against that urge. Your Excellency may never know how I missed your son since I was back in my country. I put his photograph, which he had taken with me, on my desk so I could look at it daily. Yet, I am afraid that my presence will not do your son any good but weaken his inner strength.

He needs his unshaken confidence and a strong belief in himself more than he needs me. Those inner qualities so essential for his future success would never have a chance to grow if I kept watching over him and never gave him the independence to judge and pursue a dream his own way. I wish to see him as a mighty eagle soaring up the sky, not a squab bird in a cozy nest and perpetually under my wings.

This is one of my most painful and difficult decisions, but because I genuinely care for your son, I would rather take that pain than indulge both of us in being together and see him become otherwise.

Yours Truly
Aaron William James

"Your teacher cares about you this much."

His father said solemnly after letting Beloved read Mr. James' refusal letter. They were in the lord's office room, a big and spacious room with an austere and military atmosphere, while Lek crouched behind his young master. The single luxurious decoration on the wall was a larger-than-life gold-framed oil painting of the new monarch, King Rama the Sixth, and under it stood a set of gold altars arranged with candles and flowers.

"What can you do for him in return? Or feeling self-pity for his farewell is how you bestow your gratitude on him. Why don't you choose to show him your strength in the face of his absence as he wishes? Don't let your heart overrule your head. Don't allow your sentiment to cloud your senses. Otherwise, not only your father, who you fail, but also your revered teacher."

Beloved listened wordlessly, no expression on his face. However, his son's stoic expression satisfied the old lord. At least he could assume it was the sign of strength his son began to show in the face of pain and despair.

"You can go now and ponder on this issue. And remember, of all the children I have, you are my sole heir. My son, you will carry on all I've owned, my fortunes, my honor, my pride, and our family's long, glorious name."

After Mr. James had left, Grace tried to lift his spirit by coming to see him more often and keeping him company. To encourage their relationship to flourish, Lady Pearl allowed them to spend time together without Nanny Sook present as a chaperone any longer. The nanny had never left the couple alone while they spent time together in the library room, their favorite place. Although Grace always showed respect to her, the nanny's silent and threatening presence unnerved the girl. Beloved's nanny would sit in one corner, her watchful eyes following their every movement, making Grace increasingly uncomfortable. It was the eye of a she-hawk watching her chick she knew would soon fly away from her nest.

So far, under more independence, Beloved had never shown any inappropriate or indiscreet manner to her other than holding her hands. On every visit, Beloved brought Grace to see his mother and gave the old lady company, the delightful thing that made her day.

Today, after spending time with his mother today, they lolled leisurely on a mat under the deep shade of a large tree in the late afternoon with a dozen books scattered around them. Bushes and shrubs were enshrouding them from all nosy eyes. It was a hot, slow, and lazy afternoon, not a stir of soft breeze. At least a shade of the tree cooled them down a little. Grace had chosen this particular poem, *Auguries of Innocence*. She found it interesting because the verse was underlined with Mr. James' thick black ink.

To see a World in a Grain of Sand
And a Heaven in a Wild Flower,
Hold Infinity in the palm of your hand
And Eternity in an hour

"Now, I know what he meant, Grace!"
Beloved cried excitedly after Grace had finished it.
"Tell me, please," she urged him.

"Yes, he told me that the connection between all existences in nature from the biggest to smallest scale that Blake wrote in this poem intrigued him and inspired his thinking. No wonder he asked me once to look for significant meanings in all the small things that are always unseen or overlooked. He is right, Grace. If your small palm can hold infinity and one small hour on your clock can hold eternity, why can't your plain eyes also perceive the divine smile on a face everyone overlooks?"

"Have you ever seen one, that divine smile?" His tone, which carried some mischief, stirred her curiosity.

"Yes, I have," his smile widened. "Not once, not twice, but numerous times..."

"Really! How do you know? Is it different from ours? What does it look like?

"What does a divine smile look like?" he repeated her last question and looked cunningly into her eyes, "what are you going to reward me if I tell you?"

"Whatever pleases you," she shrugged and said carefully, "because I know you're sensible."

"Promise?"

"Of course!"

"I'll take that deal. If you want to know what the truest smile looks like. To see it, just stand in front of a mirror and smile your casual smile into it,"

The best way to trick and fool her was simply to tell her the truth. He didn't want her to believe him, not now, and the trick indeed worked.

"You silly!" she giggled. "Anyway, thanks for making my day."

"So, you don't believe me, don't you?" He narrowed his eyes.

"Yes, yes, I do believe you," she stressed. Why don't I believe what makes me feel so special?"

"Are you sure you want to believe me?" his voice faltered.

There was a trace of disappointment in his voice that started to puzzle her.

"Beloved, what's wrong with you? Make up your mind. You want me to believe you, or you don't," her voice grew slightly upset, mixed with amusement. He grabbed her hands and held them against his chest.

"Honestly, I did tell you the truth about your smile. But for some strange reason, I don't want you to believe me. I know it sounds a little too weird, but this is the truth from my heart. Do you believe me now?"

"What a dazzling way to flatter me!" she laughed, averting his gaze. From her laughter, he knew, with some relief, that she didn't however believe him, yet that flattery pleased her. She couldn't help. After all, she was naturally a girl. Nothing lifted a girl's heart better than a bit of flattery from the boy she was so fond of. The corners of her lips moved gently, reminding him of a pink rosebud about to open to the sun to lure a swarm of bees. He held his breath as she lit up her face with her unique smile. He gasped. He never got used to it, especially at that very moment when the transformation of her face was about to complete.

"I want your promise. *Now*."

Her dangerous smile suddenly stirred a volcanic desire that had lain dormant inside him in her presence yet was ready to erupt at the slightest tremor. He held her hands more firmly. "Remember? Whatever I ask for, you will give me."

The girl widened her eyes; her smile was slowly fading. She sensed an impending danger not only in his voice but also in her own heartbeats.

"It's just a kiss," he said softly. "I give you a truth. You return with a kiss. It's a deal."

"No...Beloved. You know we can't..." she whispered; her face paled. "We can't do that..."

"I can't resist your smile, Grace...please."

His breath over her face was so feverishly hot, melting her body inside out. She grew so feeble that her body was stopped entirely defending against his approach. Surrendered, she let his lips crush her trembling lips. He kissed and kissed her until her fragile whole body quivered. Like a lone chick shivering helplessly under the heavy downpour, so frightened and yet so irresistible to the burst of his intense passion.

"Beloved, I love you so much I could…die."

She murmured between her breaths as they were in each other's twisted embrace, his body fervently entwining hers. He kissed her passionately and violently like there wouldn't be the next day, "Oh, I love you, Grace…my darling…oh, oh…" he groaned and agonized.

She gasped. She felt his hand feverishly move under her blouse, caressing and fondling her soft-budding breasts. And in a flash, it wasn't his hand but his mouth that kissed and fondled soaking her breasts with beads of sweat and a pool of saliva. She suddenly felt the tear of her flesh and gasped at a sudden surge of sharp pain as his thrust went deeper and deeper into infinity. His breath sparked a fire on her flesh, his thrust thrilling her pulse, making her moan softly in pain and yet in complete sweet surrender…

She grasped his hair, gritting her teeth, trying to endure what she now intensely felt. If it was heaven she was reaching, why so much pain? If hell, why such a blissful rapture?

It stopped as abruptly as it had started. Beloved suddenly withdrew his approach, leaving her to draw back with a big puzzle in her eyes. He sat up straight, shaken and frightened.

Oh, that damn, damn thing that took him at night… It crept out and gripped him in this broad daylight before he could be aware.

"I'm so sorry, so-o sorry…" he put his hands to cover his face and murmured. "So sorry, Grace."

Then he drew her close to his chest, gingerly kissing her on her cheek, his hand tenderly stroking her hair, whispering. "Oh, what if you're going to..." It was too dreadful to continue that thought. "What a monstrous beast I turned into."

There was still some puzzle and even a tint of hurt in her eyes. Now, she sobbed, gasping for air from the pain that he had left to her.

"I'm bleeding… It hurts."

She whimpered softly between her sobs. He peered down in dismay on the mat at the spot blotched with mucus blood in a pool of his own semen, which also soaked up between her legs, where her body was sprawling helplessly. He froze, fully realizing what he had done. He had torn her hymen, that piece of vulnerable tissue which signified—and more importantly—glorified a maiden's virginity. He could tell by her startled look that she did not understand what had just happened to her.

He sank and crushed her to him. She probably thought something was wrong with her that didn't please him. That was why he stopped. She had no idea how a woman could conceive a child. Poor Grace, a well-educated, profoundly insightful girl who read hundreds of books, was raised in quite a liberal and moderate family. Her parents allowed her to speak her mind like a modern girl, yet she was as naïve as any girl in a more conservative family when the subject of sex was involved. The sex issue was obviously beyond her ken, for it was still considered indiscrete and thus forbidden to discuss at any rate openly. And now he betrayed her mother's whole-hearted trust in him just because he couldn't in time stop his dark and explosive urge, which had been locked inside him and waited for a chance to break out.

At that moment, he understood the old saying that he should not put an open jar of honey near an ant and should expect it not to crawl into the jar and gorge itself with that nectar.

"Grace, don't cry, babe," he gingerly wiped her scalding tears with his trembling hand, trying to keep his voice steady. In fact, he was as frightened as she was, but he could not show it to dishearten her, "whatever happens, let it happen. I will never let you face it alone because all are my faults. But only in a couple of years will you be my bride, and we will live happily together. We will set off for your dream island and spend life there until we get old and die. How is that?"

Her drooping eyes brightened up a little at the picture he had verbally painted for her.

"I love you so much, darling, so-o much," her tears started to roll down again, trying to talk between her sobs, "I know I just can't live without you. Whatever…you've done to me, I don't care if Mother finds out."

"No, Grace, you'll break her heart. What we've just done could bring scandal to our families if anyone found out. I'm going to pray every night. Please don't let anything happen to you, and I swear I won't let that happen again to save you. But promise me. Don't smile at me again. And if I try to kiss you by force, you have to run and hide from me. Will you?" He paused and then added. "Do you believe me now when I tell you about your uncanny smile?"

"But you don't want me to believe you at first. Why?"

"If I make you aware," he met her eyes, "you might show your smile all around to captivate everyone's heart and I am afraid of losing you to some other men."

"Oh, Beloved, if only I had known my smile means this much to you."

She threw herself into his arms again, trying not to choke on her blissful sobs.

That made Beloved break his promise. And Grace hardly restrained him. For the rest of the afternoon that they spent together, alone and enshrouded by the thick foliage of trees, time and again, she surrendered herself to him and took in his wildest thrusts into her, each time through her soft groans and hot tears until not an ounce of the couple's strength was left. Finally, they let themself linger on kissing and caressing each other while wondering about the extreme and otherworldly bliss they had found in one another.

It almost released him from his pain and guilt from the pleasure he was having nightly.

"Tell me. Have you ever done…this with somebody else?"
She asked shyly.

"No," he looked her in the eyes. It must be true because he was determined to believe in what he said. "You are and will be my one and only," he gulped and collected himself to ask, "Grace, did you…enjoy *it*?"

She nestled her face on his chest. "I…can't find a word to say…" then she closed her eyes, wincing and whispering. "Just like…being pierced by an arrow dipped with honey." She paused again. Then she timidly asked. "What about you?"

"Like I was venturing deep into a virgin grotto in a sublime paradise," he said with a soft groan as he stroked her hair.

Spending too much time alone, they began to be aware that someone—who couldn't be anyone else but Nanny Sook—might be suspicious of their absence. She thought of Nanny Sook's strangely cold and stern eyes, which always made her uneasy and even guilty whenever she came to see Beloved. She usually found him with his nanny, who hardly left him alone. Although she never asked him about his nanny, she sensed their strange attachment and was afraid to ask.

So, she hurried him back into the library room to occupy themselves with books. Grace was right. She found Beloved's nanny already waiting for them inside. The nanny watched the couple tiptoe into the library room as if watching two furtive thieves in the middle of their conspiratorial act. The couple didn't talk much to each other under his nanny's accusing, fierce stare. So, before Grace left, she'd stealthily handed him the note she had just written and hurried to her grand motor car, where her father's chauffeur was waiting to bring her home.

The love of my life, Ananda,

Before that destiny came upon us today, my love for you had stayed in its purest form, with the freedom of a flying bird that sang its song to bring joy everywhere, regardless of the absence of audiences.

But since our moment of intimacy started, a new face of love has emerged. It has lost the selfless spirit of the songbird and turned itself into a blazing wildfire that devours your love as if your love were fuel to keep its existence alive.

Please forgive me for the distorted love that begins to damage my soul. I can find no cure for this incurable ailment. So, what I could do is let it kindle in full-blown, demanding more and more of your love to its last bleeding drop to keep feeding my insatiable hunger for it.

Without you, I must die like a fire that dies out with no more fuel to feed.

I must.

Your Soulmate
Siri

His eyes were damp with tears as he absorbed every passionate word she had written. Oh, this was how a sophisticated girl confessed her love to her sweetheart with every drop of fiery passion bleeding from her heart. He intended to preserve this note with him for life. And maybe to prove his steadfast love for her, he planned to show it to her again at their twentieth wedding anniversary, surrounded by a dozen of their children.

Miraculously, what Beloved had dreaded did not occur. After some sleepless nights and a poor appetite, he found out with great relief that Grace was safe.

But now he knew better that he could not fool mischievous and volatile Luck to stay on his side twice. Mr. James had warned him of the consequence of a heedless 'sexual intercourse' that could change the course of his future if Grace was pregnant.

For Grace's sake, he couldn't any longer afford to be alone with her and risk spontaneous temptation. He didn't trust himself as much as he didn't trust her for the strength of her will to stop him.

After he'd been sure he would have only Grace in life, he decided to tell his mother that he was a young man now; he didn't need his nanny to look after him in his bedroom, prompting his mother to move her to stay in another separate room nearby. He let his nanny hysterically cry and scream at his ingratitude for all the selfless devotion she had for him night and day for so long.

But after a few weeks of trying to keep a distance from her, he asked his nanny, almost begging her, to come to him at night, to which she responded in triumph. She knew all along this would happen, probably more than he knew himself. She knew he couldn't turn his back on her for long. He needed her to satiate the ravished hunger she had sown and kept nurturing it.

Over that triumph, he did not let her know the real reason he needed her. He needed her to drain his groin and save Grace from himself.

People then always saw Lek, his confidant, as the solution, followed the couple at some respectable distance. Lek adored his young master's fiancée almost as he adored him. Grace always showed her good nature and thoughtfulness to Lek. Sometimes, when they had some heated argument, and no one could convince the other, they asked him to be their judge. Beloved was confident he would get the upper hand because he declared Lek his own shadow. Naturally, a shadow's movement resonated with its owner. But how wrong he could be when Lek decided sometimes to speak his mind and considered Beloved wrong. As Grace smiled as proud as a peacock as if Lek's opinion were as sacred as the Holy Scriptures, Beloved sulked and declared Lek a traitor deserving only beheading. Within minutes, they made peace, and Lek's head seemed to be spared.

What a perfect match. They were godsends for each other, intellectually and spiritually. Both were born at the bosom of the wealthiest family and yet, despite their awareness of such privileges, they seemed to have no sense of superiority to others below them. They were down-to-earth and true to themselves. Only their families' wealth had brought them to meet. They both were aware that their future marriage would unite and strengthen their powerful families together, but what drew them together had nothing to do with that circumstance. It was the uncanny and unique nature they both shared that bonded them to the core.

After that, Beloved's life went on as contently and peacefully as he could manage. His mother's illness seemed stamped on her permanently. Her health slowly declined; her hair turned more and more gray, wrinkles and lines appeared mercilessly on her face and skin and only a few steps of walking exhausted her. Age had chosen to pay regular visits only to her while leaving his father alone to sire more offspring steadily. Each year, an average of two children were born into his huge family.

Once, as he and Grace were taking a walk along the path in the garden, he heard a faint, shrill voice from a distance. His ears pricked up to catch its direction until he was certain it was the voice of an infant wailing so persistently from his father's concubines' quarters. He stopped short, feeling a pang of terror running through his spine.

"Oh, I think I heard some baby crying. Listen, Beloved, it must be a baby boy," Grace guessed as she laughed, "so persistent, so demanding. Whose baby is?"

Suddenly, she stopped talking and gazed at him.

"Beloved, you look so frightened. What happened?" then she grabbed his hand with more concern, "Oh, you are shaken now."

"I'm fine…" he managed a wan smile. "I don't feel good today. Maybe I'm catching a cold."

She looked over his face, which was now turning blanched and glittering with tiny beads of sweat.

"Let's go inside. Can you rest? I'll make you some hot herbal tea."

Lek dared not lift his eyes to meet his young master as he helped support him in walking. He was in a terrible dilemma. He could throw himself into a fire or jump off a cliff for his *Khun Than* but what he couldn't at any cost was to unfold to Beloved some truth that he believed far worse if he revealed it. He would rather see Beloved go on in life with the weight of that doubt because as long as there was doubt and uncertainty, there was still a thing to hope for.

Apart from that, the lord and her ladyship had forced Lek to take a vow he would never speak a word about the fate of Lin Jong's son to his *Khun Than*. Because he had kept his promise so well, the lord let him stay close to his young master, whom he idolized with all his heart and soul.

During this period, his father dutifully visited his mother at least once a week, but only under one condition. Beloved had to be his company during each visit. He knew Beloved's presence could calm down his mother's temperamental moods to some degree. After his first visit, he told Beloved he would give up because of her icy welcome, which caused big embarrassment for him in front of everyone, as her means to get revenge on him.

"Beloved, I'm sorry. It's such a waste of time to see someone as disagreeable as your mother."

"Father, please. You told me you owe her one thing you cannot find worth enough to give her in return. I think you are able now to return what you still owe her. It's so simple you somehow overlook it. I know she's so desperate for your care. Yet, her pride keeps her from letting you know. She responded hostilely in your presence only to conceal her true feelings, which she always believes is her weakness. Please rescue her from that."

The lord turned to stare at him for one long minute. Beloved held his breath and averted his father's eyes. How dare he preach to his father and even refer to himself as a gift from his mother his father had to pay for?

The hearty laugh broke his tension.

"Beloved, I know what your future career is. A diplomat to make peace between two nations' disputes,"

Lady Pearl's health thrived significantly as the couple's estranged relationship began to reconcile. The lord spent time more often with his wife. In the morning, he brought her for a short walk in the garden, which usually included dinner in the evening. No one else was more joyous than Beloved and his sister Rumpai, who declared she would never marry because nothing could bring her contentment other than staying with her parents and her dear brother.

As his mother's health grew, the plan for sending him to school abroad was brought up again by his father, and this time with his mother's consent. The lady asked him to marry his fiancée before the trip started. This way, he was able to bring Grace with him to the United States. His mother couldn't stand to see him alone in such a foreign land, and the idea of having Grace as his companion greatly relieved her worry. Even the lord planned to buy real estate in Boston under Mr. James's name for a couple to reside in until Beloved finished college and went home. The Lord planned to have Beloved attend the school in the Boston area because it was not far from New Hampshire, where his teacher had been living since he left Bangkok.

"Oh, Beloved, I feel like I am walking on air now,"

Grace whispered to him after Beloved told her the news, her voice trembling with unhidden joy and anticipation. Despite Lek's presence, she threw herself into his arms and cried out.

"There will be no one else, only you and me walking hand in hand around the Bay State. After reading American history, I always dreamed about visiting Plymouth Rock, where the Pilgrims had set foot for the first time since their Mayflower ship arrived in the New World. Oh, we'll go to every place where our heart desires. We'll take a trip to New York to see the Statue of Liberty and spend a few days in a resort at Catskill Mountain where legendary Rip Van Winkle had fallen asleep for twenty years, and when he woke up again, America was no longer a British colony. But the most fun in New York is the big amusement park in Coney Island where we can watch the circus and take a roller coaster thrill ride. While staying in the USA, I would also like to enroll in some reading and writing courses. Oh, oh, and you know what? I read some books about the Red Indians of the Great Plains and the Wild West frontier. Oh my, they've always fascinated me…"

"Oh no, Grace! How come you forgot our dream Island where time could never find us," he feigned his frowning and held his laugh when she was so excited she could hardly breathe.

"That can wait," her voice became more solemn. "We will come to live there forever when our time in this world is over."

"I'll bring you to the top of the world if that's what you want, my love. And nothing will ever come between the two of us. That's my promise."

"All I want in my life is to be with you, for better and for worse. I need nothing more," she said gravely. "Remember what I wrote in that letter? Without you, it's no point to go on living."

Beloved smiled and pulled her into his arms.

"Me too."

Dear Beloved,

How glad to see you soon. I received your father's letter with great delight. Congratulations on your most recent news. Not only has Grace been your soulmate, but she will also become your significant other soon.

I am currently writing a book about my years in Southeast

Asia. I plan to finish it in a few months and publish it by the end of this year. I want you to know that I will dedicate this book to my beloved Siamese friend, Ananda Phuvanathnurak.

While they were busily preparing for that trip, the lord brought the current international news to his family that a war had just broken out on the European continent between two sides, the Allies and the Central Powers.

"In fact, there had been some long and deep-rooted conflicts among the three Empires: the German Reich, France, and Russia," the lord told his son gravely. "These powerful empires perpetually fight among themselves to rule over all other parts of the world, especially Asia and Africa. Luckily, Siam can remain a sovereign state while our neighboring countries, such as India, Burma, Laos, Cambodia, and many more, are being colonized by those Western powers."

Beloved rarely saw his father sigh as heavily as he did now.

"Yet, what sparked this current war is the assassination of the Austro-Hungarian heir to the throne while he was visiting Sarajevo. And now most of Europe has become involved by taking sides with their ally nation. Today, the battles had already spread to both the Western Front and the Eastern Front, with higher casualties reported each day. It was forecasted to be a prolonged and most brutal war ever, with unimaginable and gruesome weapons that each side introduced into this war."

The grooves on the lord's forehead deepened.

"Who's ever thought of living long enough to see unimaginable things like a submarine or an airplane or a tank or a lethal machine gun that fires into a whole group of humans and kills them all at once?"

Beloved was holding his breath as he listened.

"None of those events has anything so far to do with Siam. We are in quite a safe corner, half the world far from the war zones in Europe. The warfare would never intercept your plan because the United States has stayed neutral since the war started."

"But Father, you still look worried."

"Well, there's one thing that's worrying me," his father admitted. "I heard that Britain recently declared war against Imperial Germany after her ally Belgium had been attacked by Germany. So far, Britain has the mightiest navy and the largest colonies from nearly every continent. I believe you might know the saying that the sun never set on the British Empire. I'm quite afraid if Britain gets involved, it will absolutely grow into a full-scale war which draws many nations to participate."

"And?" Beloved was holding his breath.

"Including the United States," the lord's face hardened. "Even after winning the Revolutionary War against the British and declaring an independent nation a little more than a century ago, America still takes Britain as her motherland."

Beloved felt his heart sinking.

"Well, we shouldn't jump to the conclusion yet, my son," his father comforted him. "America is a new and growing nation with quite different ideas from the Old World. European people are always aroused to glorify nationalism and imperialism. However, American forefathers escaped oppression and injustice from the Old World in search of the ideology they believed was the right to life, liberty, and the pursuit of happiness in individuals, which they generally call the American Dream. The country has been shaped since the day of her independence to serve that purpose. Naturally, I believe the last thing the Americans want for their country is war and violence. That's why they have been steadfast in becoming neutral."

"Father, have you ever heard of Mr. James? He hasn't written to me for quite a while. I hope he's all right."

"Yes, last month I received his letter. He was all right but busy finishing his book about his journey to Asia. I thought he would tell you about that also. Now, he is a little worried about his brother, who married a British lady and moved to Great Britain after their mother passed away. The couple are now running a textile business in Liverpool. His brother's business is going well, but Mr. James is afraid the war will have some impact on it. However, he told me he believed the United States would not be involved in that war. So, he said you still have a good opportunity to study there."

Yet, Beloved's hope had crumbled due to the latest news his father brought to his attention after some months had passed.

"Beloved, be prepared for the worst. Now, a circumstance creates more tension between the United States and Germany. Only a week ago, the British luxurious ocean liner named Lusitania was sunk by a German U-boat during its voyage across the North Atlantic from New York to Liverpool, England. Germany accused the British government of smuggling war ammunition on that civilian ship. More than a thousand civilian passengers perished, among them a hundred Americans. International outcries are condemning Germany's atrocity. Some people have already called this expanding war the World War. The World War? It sounds so unprecedented. I'm afraid that, before long, this sentiment will force the United States to declare war against the Central Powers. And, my son, I'm afraid that your plan to go abroad has to be postponed for the priority of your safety."

Beloved hunched his shoulder. He suddenly felt a cold lump in his heart. The postponement had disappointed him enough. Yet, there was more that genuinely terrified him. He had never experienced any discomfort or hardship in his daily life, let alone the cruel nature of war itself. Yet, he could imagine the calamity and loss on a staggering scale that war could bring to men.

By closing his eyes, he saw corpses of dead soldiers sprawling on top of one another in a trench wall somewhere in a vast battlefield as far as his eyes could see while the soil beneath them was soaking with red blood gushing from their ghastly wounds. Some were fortunate enough to lay silent, their body motionless, and suffered no more. And yet some were still moving feebly, their mouth quivering from unimaginable pains as their breath still clung desperately to the diminishing hope for their survival.

Those dying soldiers truly believed they, no matter which side they belonged to, were fighting righteously for the noble cause—for justice and for saving the world from the other side. Each clung to their steadfast belief that only their opposite side took on the role of villain and evil. Yet the irony lay in the fact that the ones who killed might not be more wrong than the ones who were killed. It seemed both sides of soldiers dying on the battlefield were the victims in equal measure. There must be a real culprit somewhere who had caused destruction on such a staggering scale. If so, who was the real culprit? Maybe some monarch on the throne or some tyrannical leader who exploited innocent men in fighting and destroying one another under the name of patriotism and nationalism for the benefit of his own glory and power.

Beloved never felt more desperate to search for the valid reason for all the wars' eruptions. The only person who was able to shed some light on the mystery of humanity was Mr. James. Time and again, his teacher had proven to be capable of simplifying complicated matters in less than a minute.

"What about our Siam, Father? If joining that war is inevitable, which side are we going to take?"

Beloved heard his father go on with another heavy sigh.

"To be honest, the British and the French are our two big bullies. Do you remember I told you how audaciously both attempted to colonize Siam decades ago? You must remember Aesop's famous fable in the Wolf and the Lamb episode, rendering tyrannical injustice of the more powerful over the weaker. It cost Siam an arm and a leg to remain an independent nation, while Indo-China, Burma, Malaya, and even India could not escape that fate. We had to settle the unfair disputes by sacrificing big chunks of our land to keep these two superpowers away from the rest of our country. On the other hand, the Germans have always been on good terms with us. So far, we are still neutral. Hopefully, it will stay that way until the end of this war. But when a push comes to a shove, they said I will be chosen to be one of the consultant committees who help His Majesty make that crucial decision which is based on only one fact,"

His father paused and sighed.

"It is sad to admit that in politics and warfare, being a saint or an evil is not the essence to be discussed. The only rule that counts, no matter what, is…" The great lord looked at his son. "Might makes right."

"Which means…" Beloved gulped. "When push comes to shove, we must take sides with our bullies."

"Moral is only for the world of fairy tales. But benefits are for the real world of politics," his father chuckled. "In this case, it will count on who will benefit us more."

As bleak and unsettled as the war situation remained, Beloved felt the growing trust that his father gave him. The lord treated his son as a grown man now. As the head military man, he always asked Beloved to come to his office in their home and confidentially discussed the ongoing warfare with his son.

One sunny afternoon, Beloved was urgently summoned to see his father immediately. He, followed by Lek, his faithful shadow, entered his father's room with his pounding heart. The lord had already settled himself in his leather armchair, his face as expressionless as a carved stone. He gestured to his son to be seated on his side while Lek crouched at their feet. Beloved noticed that under his calm and composed bearing, his father's hand was slightly shaken as he handed Beloved an envelope with foreign stamps on it.

The sender's name shown at the left corner of that envelope was Mr. Theodor James, whom Beloved recognized at once as his teacher's brother.

"Read it, my son," he told his son in his dead voice, adding more sense of alarm to Beloved himself.

He obediently took an enclosed letter out of its envelope and tried to concentrate on every word written in that letter.

Your Excellency,

Aaron M. James, my beloved brother, was one of the US citizens who boarded the Lusitania liner on May 1st, 1915, due to my request for our family reunion during the war. Near the end of the journey in the waters of the Irish Channel on May 7th, the ship was attacked by the German U-boat and sank, bringing with her the lives of 1,195 innocent passengers and crews, including my own brother.

There would be no funeral for him since his body had disappeared under the treacherous waters and could not be found under such circumstances. Yet, a special memorial ceremony will be held to honor his death this week by our family.

At least there remain two comforting things in a time of our great grief. First, his soul will enter the Kingdom of our Lord, where he will rest for eternity. Second, his name, among the fallen victims of this unspeakable and atrocious act, will be remembered by all American people for an immeasurable time into the future.

Furthermore, we all have a strong belief that my dearest brother did not lose his precious life for nothing. He had sacrificed his life to prove to the world that wars have brought none but the massive and utmost destruction to mankind as a whole.

I am afraid my mail might not arrive on time due to impending dangers along specific European sea routes in the Atlantic that have been declared war zones. However, I do not want you, whom my brother had regarded so highly, to keep wondering about his unlikely disappearance without being informed of the true nature of this matter.

Yours Truly,
Theodor W. James

Beloved's stare remained transfixed on the letter even though he had finished reading it a moment ago. He heard his name echoed repeatedly as if someone were calling him from afar. He was half conscious that his father's alarmed voice must keep calling him, returning him from his sudden shock.

But he was not able to respond. All words froze; all feelings turned hollow and dead. Even the afternoon bright sun suddenly disappeared behind immense and ominous dark clouds. The heavy rain started pouring outside the window, and soon, thunder cracked and deafened all other sounds. Giant teardrops from the weeping sky splashed the earth as it wailed and moaned for Beloved's most tremendous loss.

"Father, I don't understand. What…what is happening?"

After a moment of struggle, Beloved heard his voice escaping from his parched lips. He started looking around, blinking his eyes repeatedly as if emerging from a trance. "Please, tell me the truth, not the lie his brother had just made up in that letter."

The lord's hand almost touched Beloved's to give his son comfort and tenderness in time of his son's utter crisis. But he abruptly decided against it. Instead, he slowly rose to his feet, his face once again a cold stone.

"Listen to me, Beloved. Now, your teacher is dead. He is *dead*. Nothing can bring him back. Face it, because in years to come, you will witness the deaths of more and more of your loved ones. You can't afford to cry your heart out each time his or her final day comes. Don't you think how your teacher would have been disappointed had he known you wasted your life crying over the dead ones like him who could never come back?"

The starkness of the word *dead* from his father shocked Beloved. That word pierced through his heart like a sharp dagger. How cruel his father was to him. How heartless. Beloved recoiled from his father. After a long silence, he slowly raised his head to meet his father's eyes.

"You're right. I can't waste my life on that sentiment," his dry voice carried a dead tone. "Before he left me, Mr. James had asked me to do him a favor on one almost impossible task."

The Lord couldn't help raising his eyebrows.

"One almost impossible task? Define it."

"He wanted me to find out," his voice became more assertive. "Why do terrible things happen for no reason to all, good and also wicked ones? It seems no one can escape terrible fates coming to them anytime, at any moment, without warning signs. And Mr. James's unbelievable death has proved this fact."

He paused to suppress the painful lump in his throat, then continued with a more determined voice.

"This is what I will do for him, even if it may take a lifetime to find that answer. So, I must start my task now. Yes, you are right. No more wasting time crying over what and who will never return."

Beloved rose to his feet and walked out in silence, hastily followed by Lek, leaving his father behind in utter puzzle.

* * * * *

Part 2: Chapter 6

When Silence Screams.

" *So, after that, your father decided to attend the law school in Bangkok while waiting to study abroad. He would marry his fiancée Grace as soon as the war ended and bring her with him.* "

Lek continued with his drained voice.

"After the tragic Lusitania incident, the United States promptly joined the Allied Powers, and the tide of war began to turn, making victory over the mighty German increasingly possible. With that prediction, their wedding plan was fixed, and their wedding preparation was underway. Apparently, nothing would come to change what Beloved and Grace had waited for quite a long."

Abruptly, Lek stopped and looked out the window. He looked surprised at the arrival of the daybreak.

"Holy Buddha, I can't believe it took the whole night to finish only half of the story. I promise to tell the rest. But now, I need some sleep…"

"Oh, please. When are you ready again? Tomorrow?"

"When? Whenever I see you prepare yourself for law school."

"I'm not a fool!" I burst with anger at his reply. You're using my father's story to bait me into attending school."

"I tricked you, yes, I admit it. But only for your own good, Pran."

"School? You know, not a penny in my pocket." I cried out in frustration.

"You have an outstanding high school grade. Don't you consider applying for a scholarship or a financial aid grant? As long as you stay with me here, no one can any longer come to harass you. You'll have time in the world to devote yourself to study."

I lay down without sleep that night, listening to Lek's thundering snores in the other corner. Nothing was more torturous than waiting for Lek to finish my father's story, which I knew would somehow lead me into an ever-darkening journey into human minds. But I must take it for all it was worth. Following the tactic my father had always used when he faced a dilemma that he couldn't handle, I blotted that part about Nanny Sook from my mind as if it had never happened at all. So far, I couldn't take that ugly part, and I believed either of Lek. But he had no choice but to let me know.

A few days later, I came home to tell Lek the news I knew would make his day.

"Lek, I went to ask for my high school principal's advice about the financial aid needed to study in that law school. He promised to write a good reference letter as his approval of my academic performance. He was positive I qualified for that grant. Just wait. Aren't you happy?"

"Happy? That word isn't even close to what I feel now. I can close my eyes and die peacefully this minute!" he exclaimed loudly. "Now, come with me."

He led me to the room we used to sleep in. He rolled up his sleeping cot, revealing a small square-shaped hole cut through the plain floorboard beneath it. He fumbled down and fished one old envelope out of that hiding place. He opened that envelope, took out what was inside, and handed it to me.

"Remember? You told me you were nosy enough to peek into these three photographs when you were a boy?"

I remembered them all in a flash.

"I kept these photos for you as a keepsake. These photos show your father's most loved ones in his short life: his mother, his American teacher, and his fiancée."

I pointed at the photo of that girl with a unique smile and asked in half a whisper. It was a moment of life and death, the end of my journey searching for the mystic lady in a yellow skirt who, a long time ago, I'd seen disappearing into a trolley, out of my sight forever.

"Grace… So, she's not my mother…" My voice cracked. "I asked you once, but you've never answered. Isn't she?"

"No," I heard his flat voice. "She is not."

That was it. That kind-hearted young lady with such a sublime smile in the photograph wasn't my mother. Yet, I was quite surprised I didn't feel the sky fall when acknowledging that fact. Perhaps deep down, I'd already known that answer. My mother couldn't be her because it was plain as day that an angel girl like Grace couldn't be the same woman Lady Rumpai would hold a grudge against.

I drew a long breath for my next question.

"How's Grace today? Do you know she's all right?"

But he said nothing, only slowly shaking his head.

"I've made believe she was my real mother since I pried into Papa's drawer and found this photo of hers. And since then, Grace's image has been kept in my mind and become my only solace when I had to fight my utter loneliness while staying under the nanny's roof."

I began revealing to Lek about that lady in a yellow skirt,

about her resemblance to Grace's smile and her kindness to a lonesome boy who kept waiting for his mother day after day at the same spot on the scorched sidewalk, only hoping one day his mother would happen to walk by and recognize him.

When Lek saw my eyes filled with tears as I went back to become that lost child once again, he couldn't hold back his own tears. Then, he swiftly wiped them out.

I braced myself one more time and then blurted out.

"If not her, then who is my mother? Who is she? Please, Lek, I beg you… Is she dead, as Papa told me? Or if she's still alive as you told Nanny Sook, where is she now? Tell me the truth."

He did not answer me, only observed me for one long minute with a strange, indescribable expression. It was the intense, fierce look I had never seen in such a subdued and placid character like him before it slowly dissolved into concern and pity.

It took another moment for Lek to swiftly flip the same cot and pull out one worn black leather journal book I'd also found in my father's drawer. He was now holding it in his shaken hand.

"You aren't supposed to read it," he said solemnly. "But I let you, against your father's will. What you told me about your lady in the yellow skirt moves me to the point that I can't take it anymore. Some parts of the journal are illegible from rain-soaking damages, especially the final parts. So, I tore those parts off and threw them out. But what's left is still in pretty good shape."

"Why?" I cried in anger and bewilderment. "What made my own father think I have no right to know?"

"The main reason I decided to let you read is that you will learn who your mother is, so it will finally bring peace to your mind. But the other reason is I want you to know about your father's ordeal that took him so close to ending his own life. Yet, he didn't do it."

He then lowered his voice.

"And the sole reason he didn't choose a suicide is you. You!"

He never took off his hurtful eyes from me.

"Believe me; not everyone, or, to be more precise, very few, can endure the fate your father had faced. In his case, had he chosen to take his own life, I wouldn't have had a heart to blame him. Because if I'd walked in his shoes, I might have chosen differently…"

Lek's voice was trembling from a surge of emotion. It now moved him to tears.

"You are a grown man now. Remember I told you when you were only seven I would give this journal to you when you grew up and understood life better? Now, you have your own experience of life yourself. So, you are strong and sensible enough to face this very complex matter of your father. Take it." He handed that journal to me.

I was stunned.

"Suicide? Him?" I raised my voice almost to a shout. "No, you're wrong. Once, when I was a boy, I saw a hideous leper. I remember how frightened I was when he approached us and begged for money. My father then told me to try to picture that poor soul when he had been just a baby in his mother's arms. It's unlikely that whoever could see the bright side of this world and could even find beauty in a beast is able to take any despondent view into his heart, let alone suicide."

"That's only because you had popped into his life during his crisis," Lek said. "You are a reason he didn't spiral down into his misery and so, get on living."

Now, that old journal book was in my trembling hand.

I tossed and turned at night, dreading and yet dying to read that journal. I was too young to understand any words when I first found it in the drawer. As soon as Lek left the house for his carpentry work in the morning and left me all alone, I darted to take it out under my pillow and, with uncontrolled pounding heartbeats, flipped all the leaves still left. I'd never expected that the moment I'd been waiting for such a long time would arrive.

Lek never warned me that some parts of his journal contained shocking graphic descriptions and vulgar language. There must be only one explanation for that: it was written as his confession and self-punishment to express his 'self-abhorrence' and to tell the world how one sole weakness of a golden man could lead him to meet his doom.

And that weakness was lust.

Oh, I never realized until this minute that Lek was so right. Now, I understood why My father kept warning me not to harbor hatred. That was because he loathed himself like hell, and throughout his short life, he suffered tremendously from that hatred.

In the beginning, all the letters scribbled in black ink on his journal became blotched and blurred from rain soaking. Rain must have leaked from the roof and seeped inside, damaging what he had written so that the beginning of his journal was ruined and barely readable. I anxiously flipped past those unreadable pages and sighed with great relief. Though worn out, the following pages were still intact and in relatively good condition.

And the lines of his orderly and handsome handwriting suddenly became alive before my eyes.

....
....
....
....
....
......................*was late in the afternoon. I heard the baby wail in my room, and she was nowhere to be found. I rushed to his crib and picked him up in my arms. His face reddened from screaming, his tiny mouth quivering from hunger. Why did she leave him in the room alone? Then, I heard some unmistakable*

giggles outside the window. I leaned out and saw her chatting with a young lad barely fifteen years old whom I recognized as our neighbor's son.

The lad was teasing her, whispering something in her ear, making her giggle. She was in a loose sarong wrapping precariously around her voluptuous body. Apparently, she just finished her bath from the canal and was on her way home with that lad by her side as her companion.

She had fully recovered from childbirth and resumed her daily life, which now included one favorite part: chatting with the males around our neighborhood.

I cleared my throat to let them know I was there. They looked up and startled. Then, that lad hurriedly walked out.

"Hey, what's the matter with you?" she frowned, obviously displeased at my interruption.

"The baby is hungry now. Don't you hear him howling?" As I said, I tried to soothe the little creature by rocking him gently in my arms, but he did not stop.

She grimaced and snorted.

"I'm not his slave who waits on him around the clock. It's so damn hot today, and I need to be in cool water."

Her reply took me by surprise. It was true she wasn't Pran's slave. But she couldn't deny the fact that she was still his mother.

"This is not the first time you leave him to cry," I said calmly. "He's barely two weeks old and needs all your care. I try to help you whenever I can, but I have some outdoor chores to do, too."

She stomped up the bungalow steps and stormed into the room, fuming.

"I need a house, not a hole. Why? I'm a human being, not a mole." her eyes swept around the room in disgust. Her gaze stopped at the baby in my arms for one second or so and then swiftly turned away.

"You know so well why," I said in a low voice. "So, no need to outcry. But at least we have him..." then I hesitated, "and...

one another."

We had hardly been at peace lately. She was always the one to start the brawl, and I gave in to her whim. During the day, she wore me out with her ceaseless and trivial complaints. At night, she exhausted me with her enormous appetite in bed. Yes, I couldn't blame her alone. At night, we were an equal match. I neither got enough of her nor she of me.

And yet, I knew now I could not satisfy her in bed. She reminded me of a tiny kitten with the appetite of a huge mammoth. Some nights lately, after draining me of all my energy in our bed, I found her slipping out, disappearing into the dark outside, and not returning until daybreak.

"Why!" she replied most casually when I asked her. "I have my thing to do."

"In the middle of the night?" I let out the breath that I was holding. "I wonder what kind of thing?"

"What's the matter with you? That's some of my nocturnal business," she raised her eyebrows as if so surprised at my upset. "Now, let me have some sleep. Stop babbling and get out of here."

The next afternoon, I found her with that lad again. They were seated together on the bamboo bench outside the bungalow while she was suckling Pran and over-familiarly laughing with him. One of her bare breasts that fed the baby was exposed boldly as the lad's eyes were gluing on it, apparently encouraged by her giggle. That unexpected scene took me by surprise. I had stood numb for a minute, stunned by their bold and explicit act in the broad daylight.

Suddenly she jerked Pran away from her while he was sucking her milk greedily. That sudden force made her exposed breast quiver, urging the lad's trembling hand to come to the verge of groping them in the middle of her giggles mixed with the angry screams of my baby son.

A spark of memory struck me as if it was happening this instant. I suddenly saw the image of myself superimposing this

lad while I watched her nursing Baby Boy in my father's
concubines' quarters when I met her for the first time twelve
years ago.
    And so began all my dooms—

What the hell? What?

I snapped shut that journal with such force it slipped from my hands and fell hard on the floor. Terror gripped my heart. I felt like I was having a heart attack. To support my shaken body from collapsing, I leaned on the wall, gasping and screaming a silent scream.

That woman mentioned on the page I just started reading was no one else but *Lin Jong*, Baby Boy's mother, and also, the very same woman who was feeding me while flirting with that lad.

Was this Lin Jong my own mother, the mother I'd moved heaven and earth to find since I started to remember things? None in my life could ever have shocked and terrified me more.

A long moment had passed, and I forced my hands to stop shaking and collected myself. Now, I clearly understood why this journal was forbidden for me.

I held my breath, let it out, and again coerced myself to continue that fateful journal.

    "Get out! You get out!" I heard myself shout frantically to
that boy. "Go away! Go!"
    The lad, alarmed by my outburst, fled and disappeared
swiftly into the thick clumps of trees.
    A strange relief flooded over me. Although I had been unable
to save myself, at least I was able to save that boy. But for how
long, I wondered. How long could a puny ant resist its greedy
nature from crawling into a pool of syrup and being drowned?
    For two days, her sullen silence had hung ominously around

me. During that time, she disappeared again after hearing a voiced signal of a mimicked hoot that came from outside of the house, giving me a sleepless night with the terrible void of hours to count. I was positive it was the signal from that lad.

I got up and tiptoed to peer down into the baby's crib. My eyes rested on the sleeping little creature with deep concern. Intense love for my son rushed to wrench my heart as I gazed at his peaceful, tiny face. Oh, poor, poor baby, where is your mother now? Perhaps she was copulating with the same lad somewhere behind thick clumps of trees in the dark. She must be feeding sexual pleasure to him and turning him into another fool. After all, a whore had never changed from who she always was.

For Pran's sake, however, there's no other choice. I had to salvage our shaky relationship, at least until he was grown enough to be weaned from her nursing, maybe in another six months. It wasn't that long. I would wait for the time to set myself free from her for good.

But to free yourself from her is like forcing yourself to wean opium that contains high addict power. Night after night, you feel so powerless to her wild appetite that you just let her climb on you and keep you howling and whimpering like a tortured animal in heat, making you feel both heaven and hell are at the same time being violently churned inside your groin over and over by her.

That must be what Lord Bhuvanathnurak, my father, felt. That feeling of helplessness as he had to surrender time and again to this kind of sex she kept feeding him.

Lately, as my life was being trapped deeper, I couldn't help thinking of my nanny, the one who had molded me into what I was shamefully becoming now ... a sex addict.

That morning, Lin Jong appeared at the doorstep, bearing herself coolly as she swaggered to where I was sitting patiently, guarding her approach.

"Please..." I started cajoling her. "The baby needs you, Ling Jong."

She didn't answer me, but her voice softened when she began to talk. There was no trace of her previous tempestuous mood.

"Beloved, do you remember when you were young; you were so fascinated by my childhood story? Remember? You urged me to tell you about a big pond by my shanty full of water lilies. And you remember this also?" She laughed softly. "You urged me to tell you the darkest part of my life, which I never had a chance to tell you..." she opened a smile, "until now."

That struck me as odd. It was the least I expected to hear from her at this very minute. So, I said cautiously.

"If you don't feel comfortable, you don't have to bring it up now. We better bury the past that doesn't do us any good."

"No, you're wrong. Now, I've never felt more ready. Let me tell you about that part—it's a hundred times more engrossing.

"What part?" I was still reluctant.

"The missing part, the part about my father. Remember I told you he drowned in that pond?"

A zealous look gleaming in her eyes added more uneasiness to me. She was eying me like a she-wolf staring down a lame, defenseless lamb. She knew I always gave in to most of her whims, including this time. Since we had lived together almost seven months ago, I've hardly refused whatever she wanted.

Against my will, her gaze forced me to sit down, my ears grudgingly capturing all her nightmarish story that gurgled through her mouth.

"My father was a chronic drunkard. I only saw him sober when he was asleep and snoring like thunder. But even in his sleep, he probably dreamed of nothing else but being drunk, for it seemed the only thing he ever knew of in his useless life. I don't know what caused that curse. But it seemed like he led his life in a cycle, over and over. His problem came like this: why *was he a drunken man? He was because he hated himself, so he punished himself by making himself a drunken man. And why did he hate himself? He hated himself because he was a drunken man instead of a decent one. If he could hate himself this much, imagine what he would feel about the rest of the world, including his wife and his own children. It's worse. A lot worse. The more deeply he hated himself, the more severely he got himself punished. Do you know what kind of self-punishment he enjoyed most?"*

I wished to turn my back on her. But her eyes kept hypnotizing me to stay.

"No, not by hurting himself or ending his own life as he really should, but by beating and torturing someone else senselessly and severely until that person—anyone in the family, especially my mother—was as good as the pulp. No, he left his own body intact, not even a scratch by his hand. He even went on devouring more foods meant to be our scant rations and still forcing my mother to quench his lust night after night and hence beget more and more mouths to be fed as the by-products of their coupling...

"In short, he demanded only the best of everything as far as we could drain from our sweat. Maybe he just loved himself too much. Therefore, all problems sprang from this root. Loving himself extremely must be the true answer as to why he hated to see himself in the life of a miserable and good-for-nothing poor man, as he bitterly and inevitably saw every time he opened his eyes. I always wondered why he beat us for no apparent reason whenever his eyes caught our sight. Now, I know. It's only because our presence never allowed him to deny the reality he dreaded. We were the living proof of his failed life...

"Yet my mother had a far more miserable life, from her own and his, but it did not stir her self-pity and hence her hatred. Maybe she was luckier because she didn't love herself as much as he loved himself. So, it did not destroy or corrupt her soul as it had completely done to his. She didn't have time to whine

about such nonsense, I guess. All she was concerned about was putting her foot down to bring her family through all the hardships. She didn't need anything more on earth as long as she was content that none of her children went hungry. However, as strong and patient as she was, I found her a weak spot. She was naturally born a giver with a bountiful heart. So, she let him feast on that weak spot like a leech. A parasite that sucked every drop of her blood and never went off her. I don't know what I felt between love and contempt for her. Or maybe both in the same measure. Maybe she's born unlucky after all. Why? She's born a giver, making her defenseless; hence, the perfect food for her predator, who was her spouse...

"The day I turned thirteen, my mother was, once again, in labor. That night, she gave birth to her lastborn. Yes, the so far total number of her children was ten; two had died stillborn and two in infanthood, leaving a total of six to be fed. We were so poor we couldn't afford a midwife. So, it was I who routinely helped her deliver her child, cutting the umbilical cord with sharpened bamboo, washing her newborn with warm water, bundling him, and then putting him in the old and worn crib all her children, including myself, used to sleep in. Then the baby cried, and I carried him to her so she could nurse him. Hours after the baby's arrival, my father stomped into the room, staggering from his heavy drinking habit. At first, my mother thought, with a pleasant surprise, that he had come to visit his new child. Suddenly, he chased me out, never taking the slightest glimpse of the new baby. Then I knew I couldn't leave him alone with her. His eyes shone strangely and wildly, like the eyes of hungry carnivores, as he stared at her while she was nursing the infant. I knew right away what he was up to because I knew his capability of indulging his urge for sex, especially when drunk, regardless of time and circumstance and my mother's consent...

"There was nothing abhorrent and shocking for us children anymore to wake up sometime in the middle of the night and accidentally witness the noisy and nasty coitus scene between my father and my mother. We couldn't avoid that scene because everyone had to be crammed into that stuffy room to sleep at night, for it was the only spot in our shanty where we slept, cooked, tended our chores, or in short, did everything, including where my father fucked his wife every night...

"A lot of times, the hideous noise abruptly woke us, my mother's sudden scream or my father's snort and grunt and loud squeal. Yes, the room was so dark it was hard to make out much of anything except for some moving silhouettes in one corner. We didn't see, but we heard him slapping her, hitting her, choking her, and even biting her while he was busy fucking her. We just froze in fear and tried to cover our ears to have some sleep. We prayed this act would be over soon. We hold our breath, hold it tight like being underwater while straining our ears, trying desperately to catch a blessing signal: his snores. They meant everyone would be blessed with a peaceful sleep once again...

"Sometimes, when their act turned so rough and savage, I wondered if she could get through this time. When morning came, the first thing that I always did was rush to check with dread whether or not I would see her body cold and rigid. Then I sighed with relief to see her still in one piece, only with bruises, black eyes, and swollen lips. Soon enough, we would surely see another dreadful sign; her flat and empty belly began to swell with another baby, another mouth to feed, another burden to carry...

"This time, my mother begged him to leave her alone because she still suffered from childbirth and needed a recovery. Yes, whenever he was drunk, he craved sex, more hearty sex to satisfy his morbid appetite. He dragged her with him while the baby was still sucking her breast. She screamed, but she was too feeble to fight him back. I was so frantic I blindly rushed to her, pushed her behind me, and told him to go away. So, you can guess the rest of it, can't you?"

She laughed, yet no trace of amusement was shown.

"He snarled and darted at me as if possessed by a demon, then punched me on my stomach real hard; I thought I was going to pass out. I gagged and collapsed. He was a male beast in heat, standing stout and strong over my collapsed body. Then he raped me brutally right in front of my mother, who screamed and shrieked, trying to use all her strength to pull him out of my body but in vain. Just like he had acute diarrhea, an urge to release his shit before it exploded in his pants, that was precisely what he was doing between my legs as he grunted and squealed like a pig. Remember a leech I told you. That was him, too, never let go until he couldn't drain the victim's blood any longer...

"After he was done, he staggered out as casually as when he had staggered in, never giving us the slightest sign of remorse or even any awareness that he had just committed incest. My mother cried her heart out. She kept moaning and murmuring she had been living with a monstrous man. It was entirely her fault to feed and shelter this monster for so long, but not a single drop of tears I shed while I was listening to her lament. I just calmed her down with my soothing voice and dry eyes and reminded her that the baby was crying and needed to be nursed...

"Like a predator who had once tasted the soft flesh of a young prey, he couldn't resist his urge to return. I knew his ravenous appetite because he came to rape me again the following nights. Drunk or not, it didn't matter any longer to him. He had left my mother alone for the first time but instead raped me over and over at night...

"At the corner of the shanty nearby where I slept lay a mortar made of granite stone with a heavy pestle inside. We used it to pound chili and garlic to make chili paste for our meals. But one night, that pestle was missing from its place. It lay hidden on the mat beside me instead. The crescent moon shone dimly through the window. I lay down quietly in the middle

of the night, my eyes opened in the dim moonlight, my heart in my throat, waiting for any sound and movement approaching me. So, when I heard the plank floor creak, feeling a hot, sour smell and noisy panting on my face, and hoarse hands groping under my clothes, I held my breath, shut my eyes tightly, and did what I had my mind set on...

"I waited until he exhausted all his energy in raping me and slumped beside me with his roaring snores. I grabbed that stone pestle with all my strength and hurled it at him as hard as I could. I saw him howling while his body convulsed. My mother let out a scream. She darted to me and shoved me to the floor as he kept howling and squealing like a pig in the middle of being throat-slashed...

"But she couldn't stop me. I couldn't stand his squeal. I had to stop it. My hatred of that beast who just happened to be my father was now so intense it could burn me alive. I was on my feet again and swiftly gave him another blow with the pestle right on his skull. This time, I heard the croaking sound from his throat before he had become silent. My mother rushed to him. I saw plain terror crossing her face as she knelt, pressing her ear on his chest, checking him frantically. 'Help me carry him into the boat, Mother.' I dropped the cold pestle and forced myself to stay calm as long as I could manage. 'I'm going to drop him into the water. They will think he's drunk and then falls from his boat and gets drowned'. 'No, she shook her head firmly.' I raised my eyebrows as a gesture of question. Then, with a low voice, almost a whisper, she told me. 'His heart's still beating. I can feel his pulse.'

"I told her flatly. 'Don't worry. I'll make it stop in no time.' She was so shocked by my reply she couldn't speak. What I heard was only a choking sound, as if she had tried to utter some words but still struggled with it. 'After all, he's your father, Lin Jong. You're committing the utmost sin no one can ever imagine, the patricide, and down to the infernal hell you will go and be burned for eternity.' Finally, she said feebly and put her hands

to cover her face, crying bitterly. 'Condemn me if it makes you feel like a saint so the heaven gate will throw open for you, but I don't believe in such crap.' I forced a laugh. 'I neither demand nor ask to be born in the first place. So, why must I feel indebted to this man for bringing me into this world? It's him who has to pay me back for the hellish life he caused. Mother, he paid me pretty well with his own life today...'

" 'One always finds a fallen fruit not far from the tree it fell from.' She murmured an old saying. 'You are your father's daughter inside out.' And I forced my bitter laugh. 'I've done this for you too, Mother. For us.' I didn't avert my eyes as my mother gave me a hard stare for one long minute, and then she let out a long, heavy sigh and simply surrendered. No more whimpering or bewailing; she hurriedly helped me carry him to the boat and silently watched me paddling away the small boat that carried his unconscious body into the middle of the pond...

"The dim light from the crescent moon eerily illuminated the dark pond, leading my way as my boat ventured into the bosom of the night. It was desolate and so utterly silent that the chirping from a million insects seemingly deafened all sounds. The other sounds that at least kept me company were the rhythms of the oar on the water's surface. Suddenly, I jerked. All chirping abruptly stopped at once. Amid enormous silence, I heard his faint moan, then another and another as his body slowly and slightly moved. He began to get conscious, that monster, which I wouldn't let him. So, before he was fully awake, becoming upper-handed, I had hit him with the paddle and with all my force before pushing and shoving him into the dark-ink water. The water splashed. Oh! What a heavy man he was, heavy and stout from being fed with the blood of the others. In my boat, I sat so still, so tense, holding my breath, watching the ribbon of bubbles floating up from where he had sunk. My clammy and trembling hand clutched the paddle tightly, preparing to attack if I glimpsed his head surface...

"*Suddenly, my scream disrupted the dead silence of the night as I saw something in silhouette emerge to the surface accompanied by a whirlpool of bubbles. Damn it, he isn't dead yet. It was impossible that he would never die. Oh, or maybe in his case, it was possible? So, I feverishly grabbed the paddle and pushed that thing underneath again with all the force I still had. How long does it take to drown a man? I wondered. One minute? Five minutes? Or forever? I should think ahead or ask someone beforehand. I kept holding the paddle that way until my hands were so numb and aching as my heart drummed rapidly. But never let go of it. Never. My eyes couldn't penetrate the dark water to see underneath. So, I gleefully imagined him wriggling, gasping, choking as more and more volume of water gushed into his gaping mouth and his flared nostrils, and finally filling up his lungs and down, down, down his body went until it hit the bottom...*

"*Soon enough, I saw fewer and fewer bubbles, and once again, the surface of the water lay as smooth as a large mirror reflecting the pale crescent moon and some dim stars from far above. It was so serene and calm like it had never swallowed any soul into its dark and deep belly. The insects started their music again to celebrate what they had just witnessed...*

"*For quite a moment, I sat as if being absorbed in a reverie, then I jumped into the water, abandoned the boat, and swam back to the shanty. I had to leave the boat there to convince people that he had brought the boat there by himself. The water was chilly at night, but I was bold, strong, and elated. I never felt that I was swimming in the cold, dark water. Instead, I felt like I was flying home with two large wings over the sunny sky, just like a bird, free, free at last... Beloved, darling, do you still remember the lullaby I sang to you when we first met twelve years ago? That very song was echoing in my heart all the way home...*"

Suddenly, she sang that lullaby with her dreamy, silky voice.

A slave boy paddles
Up, up a raging river
His master rumbles and grumbles
But the boy can't go faster
So he bears up no more
Bang! Bang! Bang!
He hits his master's head with his jumbo ore
Till his master babbles no more.

After a pause and a long, blissful sigh, she continued that heart-stopping story.

"...When I reached home, the dawn was about to break; the sky turned hushed pink, and the pearl-gray light barely showed up. The flock of birds started flying over the sky. What a beautiful morning. My mother still waited for me, standing so stiff, holding a lantern to guide me. She was so terrified of what I was to tell her—no matter what it would come out—that she didn't dare to open her mouth to ask. However, the answer she dreaded and secretly hoped was printed on my face. She hugged me for so long as she wept hysterically. I didn't ask her either the reason for her sudden burst into tears, maybe from her genuine grief for his death or, who knows, maybe from her dread that he might be somewhere out there and still alive while heading his way home as if he didn't know how to die. But I guess what she feared the most, out of her superstitious mind, was the dead he had become. She feared that he could find his way to come back to take revenge on her in his dead body...

"Oh, I believed she had wished him to die for so long, maybe even before I was born. She might wish every night, if not the coming tomorrow, that something would or should happen to him, whether it was tomorrow after or another tomorrow after. So, she waited patiently and discreetly for Fate to peer at her agony and come to rescue her by getting rid of him for her. I believe every day she enjoyed picturing herself killing him over and over with more and more gruesome and morbid methods

each time. Today, she would love to see herself butchering him, splitting his chest in half and boiling his heart. Tomorrow, she would scalp his head with a large machete like a savage and crack his skull open to feed some hungry rats with his brain. If he never contributed anything to this world when he was still alive, she would make sure he would, at least after his death, with his corpse...

"The next day, she would try a bonfire. Yes, nothing was better than burning him alive. Oh, his screams would be the music to her ears. But wait a minute, wasn't impaling a man on a very sharp and long stick by far the most horror to torture a human to his prolonged death? It took almost three days for an impale to die. And for only one split second that your anus was pierced through the sharp stick, it could be felt as if it lasted for eternity. Do you see she desperately wanted to kill him tenfold more than I did? But as we know..."

She smirked and looked contemptuously at me.

"All the givers like you and her are born suckers and cowards. All they dare to do is to use their imagination to kill people, if not to wait for Fate to do the actual work for them. How pathetic. If I want someone to die, no, I won't wait for Fate. I will become Fate myself. And with my own hands, not with my mind, would I kill. So, I vowed before my father's dead body that I would never let any soul on earth take advantage of me anymore. Do you want to know the best way to protect yourself from predators such as my father?"

"You become one yourself..."

Surprisingly, I heard my own voice coming out flatly. I wasn't even surprised when I blurted out what had lodged in my mind for a while about her true nature.

"Oh! My Beloved, finally, you come to your senses. You've become a real grown-up, babe."

She cried and clapped her hands excitedly. She tried to clutch my hand, but I immediately recoiled from her touch as if on impulse. She laughed again at my strong response, then *dropped her voice into a barely audible whisper.*

"You are absolutely right. You have to become one yourself. But even that isn't good enough, darling. No, no, no. This is the world where countless predators are roaming and waiting to eat people alive. So, even some predators can't survive if they still have a weakness. Ah, what is their weakness? The sheer wickedness always makes their victims recognize them at first encounter. Of course, to beat the shit out of thousands of rival devils, I need to become on top of all the devils, the master of beguiling people into my bondage without leaving any trace of my true self. I must be an alpha predator. Tell me, am I not the one your heart trusts and your groin lusts for, above all women, the one for whom you sacrificed your life, your pristine fiancée, your glorious future, and above all, your mother who can die for you if that means your life will be safe?"

I tried to speak, but no words formed on my lips. All I could do was battle a wave of convulsion that was about to attack my stomach.

"A few days after my father's death, my infant brother suddenly stopped breathing during his sleep. They said it was a crib death. It normally happens to infants, even healthy ones."

Finally, I could collect myself to say. "Lin Jong... so it's you...you again who made yourself his Fate."

"Why not? I smothered him," she watched my horrified face with her playful smile. "I simply pressed my hand over his t iny face to put him out of his misery. And to put myself out of another burden as well. He was gone so swiftly, so peacefully. There was no pain, no torture, compared to when I got rid of my father. You can call that a slaughter, but this was indeed a salvation I had given him. Poor little one..." her voice softened. "I genuinely meant to rescue him, not to hurt him. He was very sick and fragile since his birth, probably born before his full term. The result must come from his father fucking his mother savagely every night, although she had already been so heavy with a child in her womb. I had to strain my ears so intensely

to hear his first wailing, which came out so feeble, like a little mouse, almost a whisper. His day was numbered anyway. I just helped hustle it a little."

Her smile then broadened.

"Since that day, I've found an advantage in death. While weak people shun death, I found out I can use death, the death of someone else, to benefit a life of mine."

"What sin has your mother ever done to conceive you in her womb? Oh, she doesn't deserve that."

Tears welled up in my eyes when I mentioned her poor mother. But this time, her eyes showed a flash of anger.

"I was the one who did all the dirty work. And she was the one who reaped the benefit clean-handed, taking and taking while condemning me that I should be burnt in hell for eternity. And you are shedding your tears for such an innocent one like her, right?"

She mocked him with her smirk and a shake of her head as if in disbelief.

"After my father's death, she kept a cold distance from me. She probably figured out by then her last young one didn't die of natural causes. And it included those other two before that one. Well, at least I let the stronger and the healthier live, the ones who wouldn't dump their burden on me. After all, all of them were nothing but worthless seeds from their old man's lust... including the new one growing quickly and persistently inside my womb, like a parasite sucking my blood to grow bigger and bigger on its way to be born. Perhaps the only mercy my mother finally gave me was a handful of herbs she sought and handed to me to expel that growing monster in my womb...

"And once I got rid of it, she brought me to your father's place. One of her cousins was a kitchen servant there. She wanted to get rid of me so desperately. And since everyone said I was the prettiest girl in our neighborhood. Poor mother, I bet she never thought in her wildest dream I could climb my way to stand tall as the lord's favorite and bore him a son whom he *proudly announced was the most beautiful son he ever had. But you killed him, Beloved. His neck was broken after you'd dropped him. He died in my arms like a broken-winged angel while Nai Lek had hastily carried you out of my room to shield and protect you, leaving me so devastated by the disaster you had caused."*

"You are your father's daughter, only much, much worse," I murmured. "The macabre things you've ever done will shame your father's brute. He is merely a victim of his human flaws. But you are Evil itself in its present reincarnate."

She burst into an exhilarating laughter.

"Oh, oh, that's how you view me. Do you think I give a damn? Who are you, after all, to stand tall and judge me? Just one human blindly judging another, that's it, using one's perspective to make oneself righteous over others. You should expand your view to another horizon, or otherwise, you will be blindly trapped inside your so-called virtue. Well, let's not use the terms vice and virtue to understand things in this world. Beloved darling, that would end up in understanding nothing. Nothing, all right? The truth is that there are simply two kinds of people existing side by side. Let's say I was born free to indulge in whatever urges lead me to go and do things unlimitedly while you are born chained with fear and guilt...

"Listen to me, Beloved. You and I are just human counterparts who are naturally no better or worse than one another. The only difference between us is that your kind is born to embody and sustain the existence of my kind; the same as fish or chicken meat sustains humans' lives, whereas, fortunately, my kind is and will never be born to sustain yours. The sky's the limit for us. But because of your disadvantage being you, that's why you condemn our superiority as evilness or whatever terms you could make up to dehumanize us...

"Why, you can be free like us, Beloved, if you want. No one ever forbids you to cross over to the other side where we stay and then learn from us until you excel in our capability. Fine,

if you switch the role to become my predator, I will be your prey. But it's you that determines to remain who you believe you are—a giver. Can't you come to your senses that the term 'giver' you value as much as your life is, in truth, a loser in disguise? Are you proud of yourself that under the sacred name of a giver, you've indeed lost everything to me? So, don't blame us for what seems to be your own fault. Poor soul, your kind is blind and illusory about this truth and yet too stubborn and adamant to believe otherwise. And you will live and die this way if you are never aware that your world is an illusion, whereas mine is a solid reality."

This time, fascination and awe took me so completely that I could not withdraw my eyes from her face while she was speaking her mind. Who could believe that a street whore who couldn't even spell her name—and was so puzzled when finding me get the meaning out of a cluster of vertical lines and curbs and slants that appeared in lines after lines on every page of a book—was capable of defying my logic with her own? I felt like an enormous magnet was mercilessly pulling me, a small scrap of iron, into its tremendous force. What if Lin Jong had swung open a mysterious door and forced me to look into the new truth behind it? What if good and evil had not existed in nature and hence held no inherent value? And what if this concept was merely a man-made construct serving some meaningless purposes? Maybe the man-made virtue was to comfort all the losers like myself so that they could endure their misery a bit more. And maybe for fooling them and tricking them into more self-sacrifice and hence accommodating the kind of people like Lin Jong to reap more benefits?

It was as if I were venturing into an alien world where all familiar laws and rules were hung upside down. No, I couldn't allow myself to be swept away by this madness and lost forever in her warped world; I couldn't because I knew in my heart that a giver is never a loser. In giving, a giver loses none. But what he gains cannot simply be beholden by eyes or held by hands.

Only his soul can profoundly feel it in the name of joy. And the sources of that joy—the suffering people he can give and help— are found everywhere, far more in numbers that he doesn't need to fight over the prey as predators fight tooth and nail among themselves.

Lin Jong would never have known or understood that this kind of joy existed in the heart of whoever knew the magic of giving. How could one know colors exist if one is blind? How could Lin Jong know that the joy of giving existed if the only thing she had practiced all her life was to take from whoever as many as her bottomless heart could contain?

"I've lived my life, every ounce of it. Not a single minute of my waking hours is wasted," she continued. "How about you? You've only lived perhaps one-tenth of your existence. Your pathetic conscience imprisons the rest. My life opens to all extremes that scarcely a human can ever reach out and taste. The only regret I feel about my life is that it has a limit as a mortal. Oh, had my life been granted eternal, I would have annihilated the world as my offerings to a Being who could bestow immortality on me."

"Now, please tell me, Lin Jong," I cut her off. "All about this; what do you want from me, honestly?"

"Beloved, you have shattered my life. You killed Baby Boy, my precious son, who was my best asset to gain higher status and secure my lavish life. Accident or not, it doesn't matter to me. All I cared about was that his death completely wrecked my dream. The lord came to greet his new son the day he was born. I never saw him look happier. He held Baby Boy endearingly in his arms for so long and showered me with gold and jewelry as his hearty thanks for the most beautiful son he ever had; of course, apart from his Beloved, that is what he said. He even declared proudly that Baby Boy looked just like him and promised me he would provide the best for his new son as close as he did to the children he had with Lady Pearl. Oh, I could imagine my life ahead would be paved with gold—"

Suddenly, her face twisted, a fury busting in her eyes.

"The night Baby Boy was dead, I couldn't close my eyes, burning alive with a grudge while trying to figure out any possible way to make you pay double or triple for what I had lost."

Finally, what slipped out of Lin Jong's mouth confirmed my doubt of her capability of love. She had very little grief over the loss of Baby Boy. What she mostly felt for that loss was rage. She was only concerned that the loss of her firstborn that I had caused would deprive her of all the extravagance my father had indulged her.

I tried to put all my patience into listening.

"So, the following day, I prostrated at the lord's feet, weeping, begging for his justice. I swore to the lord through my tears I had seen with my own eyes that you had deliberately dropped Baby Boy from your arms. Your mother schemed to send you that day as her accomplice to get rid of Baby Boy. Oh, even a dumb could guess the motive behind that act. I told him your mother deeply feared my son would take away what she had tenaciously guarded for her son—the lord's favor and the inheritance of his great fortunes. But I had no clue whether or not he believed me. I could read nothing from his stoic face. As I accused his Beloved of killing my Baby Boy, he just sat like a carved stone figure listening attentively to me yet watching me with his eyes that made me feel as if they were a pair of daggers piercing my guts and swiftly turning it inside out so he could see what lay hidden inside...

"Yes, I admit I had made the most terrible mistake that turned my life upside down. How naïve I was then to overestimate myself on his affection and favoritism for me. I was so young then, just like a small fly whose one-day lifespan limits its ability to understand a time concept beyond the measure of a single day. I had never realized that my Baby Boy could never, ever be compared to his Beloved, no, not until your mother stormed into my room the following day like a ferocious tigress. She ruthlessly ordered five or six of her male attendants to plunder all my belongings until they were torn, broken, and thrashed into pieces. Then, she took all my money and many pieces of jewelry my lord had given me. That day, I never had a chance to glimpse the sight of my lord and ask for a rescue from him. He completely disappeared and left my fate at the hands of this wildly mad woman. Not even one concubine dared or wanted to help me. At least she helped them get rid of their rival they couldn't beat. So, no one didn't bother to help. It was their thrill also to witness the doom of their number one rival. Those onlookers just curiously peeked through their window as if watching a play on stage while I was dragged out of my door and thrown onto the street like a piece of broken furniture hauled to the garbage...

"As I stumbled to the ground in front of the mansion's cast-iron gate, she ordered someone to throw a few coins on me, barking that those little money were not meant to preserve my life but only to prolong it for another day or two so I could taste and suffer the slow death from hunger before dropping dead on the street like a stray dog. She had given me her last words before the gate was shut down perpetually on my face. She declared that justice was done, but it was not for herself. This was for her Beloved—her angel son shamelessly framed by one of the vilest snakes in the grass she had ever stumped on...

"No, I was too young and attractive to starve to death as that old bitch expected. One of the street cleaners found me roaming on the sidewalk in the middle of the night. So, he brought me to stay in his hut, and in return, I gave him what a man wanted from a woman. That made him so madly fall for me he locked me in his hut for a whole week for fear I would leave him. That man was no better than a stinky bum. I shuddered every time his hand groped me. But he made me aware that my best asset for surviving is my own body. And when a chance came, I fled him and found a new shelter in a green-lantern house nearby and soon became a new star in that seedy brothel, fucking more than half the men in town, yes, including... Now,

guess who could be that particular one."
And her eyes met mine with utter triumph.

There weren't any more pages left in that journal. I didn't know whether I was fortunate that the rain had destroyed the rest, as Lek said. As a result, I would never have a chance to know and make sense of why a golden boy like my father chose a whore over a gem who was his true sweetheart and, as a consequence, turned his life upside down from that choice. I wondered and shuddered what turned the impossible possible. Lek must know this answer if I tried to squeeze it from him. But no, I should not venture beyond this point. I doubted if I would ever be able to cope with more possible of the impossible.

Was the stark truth about Lin Jong I learned from this journal not impossible enough?

* * * * *

Part 2: Chapter 7

Naked Truth

*L*ife went on again. Although it was not paved with carpet, it was not bumpy compared to what I had been through earlier. I tried my best to bury all my traumas and move on. But I knew those things never healed, only went down and lodged somewhere inside my mind like a deep wound that had healed waiting for a cruel hand to rip it open.

I was now in my second year in law school, with my goal to pave my future as a law magistrate so that I could redeem what my father had missed out from his life. All were done to honor him and to prove to his scornful sister that my father still had one thing to be proud of. That was his son's achievement.

A couple of years earlier, I was finally able to enroll in law school with the financial aid I had received. I stayed with Lek to save all my money and help him in return with his carpentry job whenever he was hired. Although the house he rented was too small for two people to cram in, Lek seemed happy to have me under his roof and treated me as he would have done to his child if he ever had one. Without Lek and his care, I couldn't imagine where my fate would have led me after being framed and thrown out of that hellish house.

However, when I was ready for a new phase of life, he grudgingly let me leave his place. I had to convince him I should learn to take care of myself. With Lek's help, he searched for another row house nearby. The rent was affordable for someone like me, who had to get by with a limited amount of money.

After moving out, I could find a part-time job in an imported furniture store owned by a European. He wanted a new clerk who was pretty good at speaking English, and luckily, I fit the job. My life, for now, was focused on my law school and the place where I was working. And yet, whenever I had time, I would drop by to see Lek and find him so overjoyed every time I showed up with little stuff that I bought for him.

One afternoon, I visited him as usual. But he had yet to come home from work. I found his room was cluttered. It seemed he didn't have time to clean up. While waiting for him, I came to tidy up his room and saw he left his sleeping cot in a mess. Then I remembered that he had dug under his cot to hide whatever he valued. Out of mild curiosity, I slipped my hand into the hole and groped for the things inside.

I wasn't surprised when I found the missing part of the journal book. He'd lied to me about it being damaged by the rain. In truth, he deliberately tore off that part and hid it from me while handing me only the first half.

I'd fled right away before he showed up, with that part of the journal clutched in my arm. Obviously, he lied to me and even put such an effort to hide it from my sight. It meant I must read it at all costs.

I'd finished the first part almost three years ago and put all my efforts into erasing it from my mind. So, it'd taken a moment to recall some of my father's preceding content before I could go further.

Eventually, the end of the first part began to emerge from my mind; Lin Jong was about to reveal who was the particular one out of her many customers in that brothel, the one who seemed to play a significant role enough to be brought up during the talking.

And this was the continuing part...

"Last year, Nai Lek found me working there. Some of his friends brought him to that whorehouse. When he first saw me, oh my, he jumped a foot as if facing a ghost and did his best to slip away. But no sweat for dragging him back to me. He was too valuable for me to lose him. After the first night with me, he kept coming back almost every night. Of course, most of the time, it's free services. He couldn't afford a top-graded like me."

My body froze, and my heart nearly jumped out of my chest.

"No," it was all I could say.

"Oh, no, no, no," her voice mimicked mine. "If not, how the hell was I able to show up at your law school that day?"

I put my face into my shaken hands.

"Of course, a nobody like him had never dreamed of sleeping with his once great lord's favorite woman. Another fly is lured to the flame. He was a godsend, a direct link to you whom I swore I would move heaven and earth to find. Lek is your Fate. Yes, he is. Though at first, he never breathed a word about his sacred 'Khun Than.' When I showed overwhelming eagerness about you, he only said the bygone shouldn't be any of my concerns anymore. Yet, as Nai Lek often visited me, our relationship grew. So did his trust and lust for me...

"I kept on begging him to bring me to see you. Begging him every single time he came to see me. I said I couldn't close my eyes and rest in peace upon my death without your forgiveness for my false accusation. But he said that you never had a chance to know all these things because your mother had forbidden everyone in her household to slip a word to you about what had happened to us. It's still your biggest puzzle since she wanted to wipe out this trauma from your memory for good...

"He even added that your bright future awaited you after

you graduated. You were already betrothed to a nice young lady of another enormously wealthy aristocrat's family. And soon, you were going to marry her. He warned me I should stay away from you. Oh, this was more than I could take. I boiled with hatred so bubbling that I could die. But one lucky night, he slipped something from his mouth. He couldn't help bragging that he was now your chauffeur, driving you to your law school in the new deluxe car your father had bought for you. Poor Lek, if only he knew that because of his loose mouth, an idea swiftly crossed my mind. Why, if Lek refused to bring me to you, I could bring myself to the gate of that prestigious school and give you a real, real surprise...

"Oh! After ten long, miserable years, it was just like a miracle. I watched you climb out of your lustrous black Mercedes car that late morning in the image of Prince Charming. I couldn't help but gasp at that sight. Oh, how you grew up to be such a striking, handsome lad, just too perfect to be found in real life except in every girl's wildest dream! Your attractive appeal could have swept me off my feet if I had still been a young girl ten years earlier. Of course, I recognized you instantly, for you were the image of the lord, only younger and, yes, obviously more tender-hearted. One thing in you that never changes a bit is your dreamy, soft eyes, the windows of your soul that are always open to see the world with great wonders and love. Had Baby Boy had a chance to grow up and stand by my side today? Oh! I could see his face in yours. He would have been twelve now hadn't he died that day, my Baby Boy..."

Her voice trailed off. After a short moment of her silent anguish, she burst into a shriek of laughter so forceful it distorted her whole face.

"Yes, once I saw Nai Lek drive away, leaving you all alone in front of the school building, I approached you. Remember? You stood thunderstruck, your mouth gaping wide when you saw me only a few steps before you, like a manifest of a long, lost ghost. Ah, you recognized me, you did. You shouted my name *as if you were transforming into a ten-year-old boy who found his long-lost favorite playmate. You kept murmuring, your voice trembling in utter disbelief. 'Isn't it you? Isn't it you, Lin Jong?' Then, your hand reached to clutch mine to reassure my presence. 'Oh, don't cry, Lin Jong, don't cry.' You soothed me when you saw my eyes brimming with tears as if unaware that your tears also welled up in yours with rapture. 'I've wondered where you and Baby Boy are since that day. Long, long, twelve years, Lin Jong. Don't go away, please. Tell me now. Tell me all about you...'*

"But I whispered. 'No, not here, not in a public place. People are staring at us. I'll bring you to a more private place to talk.' So, I hired a rickshaw, bringing us into the Green Lantern brothel where I was staying. The place was dark and seedy and smelled filthy. At first, you stepped inside reluctantly and cautiously. Only a few girls were seated and chatted in the hall entrance, their voluptuous bodies clad loosely in a sarong. I could tell that you had never been in a brothel. You gazed around in perplexity. When those girls turned their heads and saw you following me, your striking face stunned them. They turned all their attention to you as if you stepped from heaven with the brightest halo. One of them roared. 'Look! Here comes our Superstar with her catch of the day.' Then another girl screeched to the group. 'Sorry, Big Fish is not for you girls. It's only for a pussy this-s-s-s enormous size.' She spread both her hands farthest apart to show the size of that thing she mentioned. 'See? This big-g-g.' Their lewd and vulgar guffaws startled you. 'Who are they, Lin Jong? Why is their language so... so unpleasant?' You whispered. At least during the day, the place was quiet and looked decent enough not to arouse more of your suspicion. A huge green lantern hanging in front of the brothel's gate had not been lit yet to signify and welcome the boisterous carnal nightlife that could appall you...

"You meekly followed me up the narrow staircase to my small and dim room as blindly as a moth flying right into the *heart of a giant spider web. Oh, so little did you sense your ominous fate was waiting to eat you alive. You still eagerly stepped into my room, alone with me, and left your life in doom the minute I locked my door...*

"Immediately as you seated yourself on my bed as I had invited, you burst into torrents of questions; 'Where is Baby Boy? How is he now? Why do you stop talking and start crying?' Fear was rising in your voice as you watched me dropping to your feet and bursting into hysterical tears. 'He is long dead, Beloved; He died from that accident. His skull was fractured, and his neck was broken from that fall.' I replied between choked sobs. 'His body was buried in urgency somewhere around your house the same day he died. So, no one outside would ever know he once was born into this world. All were done secretly under your mother's order to save you....'

"Oh my, you jumped a foot from the edge of my bed, shaken so violently. I watched your face shattering. 'Beloved, while you keep wondering where your little brother has been day after day, you are never aware he is merely beneath your feet as you stroll on the ground of your house every day.' And with these words deliberately used as a sharp arrow to hit the bullseye, you collapsed, gasped, and wept bitterly. To share this critical moment, I threw myself into you, giving you the warm comfort from my flesh that I knew you needed at that terrible moment, and we wept together in each other's tightened arms. I put your cold and damp cheeks on my bosom, hoping my soft heartbeats would calm you. I even hum a lullaby to you, the one I used to sing to Baby Boy and let you sink in deep regret...

"'I was so sorry, Lin Jong,' your pleading, fawn-like eyes nearly melt my heart. Well, just nearly, because they never moved my soul. I calmly listened to your whole-hearted lament. 'I didn't mean it. I didn't. It's just a terrible accident. And it has still been haunting me in my sleep ever since. Oh, if there might be anything on earth that I can do to redeem myself from his death.' And I only whispered back. 'No, I don't need anything.

Just don't leave me out there with all my losses. My baby was gone. Your mother threw me into the street, and your father turned his back on me.' I started crying hysterically, clutching you more fiercely into my choking embrace. 'Please, Beloved, I have nothing left now. My life is a complete wreck until I meet you today.' Then, I knew that the perfect time had arrived to confess to you that unfair treatment from your mother drove me into the life of a prostitute ...

"I learned from my harsh and struggling life that each mortal man, no matter how invincible he put on his appearance, has a gaping hole torn by his weakened nature—either greed or grudge or conceit or lust like an armor that a warrior puts on without an awareness of a fatigue crack. The only way to defeat an individual, making each fall prey to my spell, is to find that fatal hole, hit that spot with all the force, and then wait until that man collapses on my feet ...

"In your case, I must admit it wasn't easy because you were different from all the rest. But it didn't matter. If I couldn't detect those normal dark natures in you and use them to my advantage, I could try the other way around. Then I thought of your benevolence—your vulnerable spot that I could worm myself into it. If I declare to the whole world, I am a whore, oh, a repulse and scorn must undoubtedly be those responses. But, no, not from you. On the contrary, it would draw your over-whelming compassion. And it worked. You declared. 'Lin Jong, I will find the way to get you out of this hole, I will. Just let me think. For now, I will come back tomorrow with some money to help.' I started to hold you fiercely and begged you not to leave me to those vulgar men who would soon come to devour my body at nightfall. I held you fiercely as I whimpered into your ears. 'If I must be eaten alive by those animals, it'd rather be by you, my darling Beloved, only you, not them ...'

"Before you got to your senses and perhaps withdrew from my arms, I frantically started kissing you, guiding your hand under my blouse and pressing it on my bosom. Right away, I felt

your trembling hand start to clumsily cup and fondle my quivering breasts while I closed my eyes, anticipating your further spontaneous move. But what was coming in the next instant blew me away. Oh, I had sworn to myself I would move heaven and earth to get laid by you. But this was way, way beyond. I had never dreamt of that rapture of this rawest passion when you jumped on me, beginning to fuck me fiercely in such an explosive force I wondered what had become of you. I closed my eyes, laughing soundlessly as I couldn't help picturing myself as a lone female dog with a horde of wild males incessantly taking turns to mount me for hours on end. I had to clench my mouth not to let out a scream from the most violent ecstasy I rarely got from any male...

"*Finally, thank god, you grudgingly finished and lay sprawling on my bed, gasping for breath, curling up in my arms, groaning, 'Lin Jong, Lin Jong, are you for real? Oh, yes, you are. I need not secretly see you in the dreams anymore. Now, you walk out of that hazy dream to become in real flesh, oh, oh...' Beloved, I let you touch me and explore me over and over to prove I was a reality and I was yours. Then I softly laughed and said, 'Beloved, I know you will return to me one day. And it will be the day you learn women's breasts are not only for babies to feed as you sneered and turned your back on them back then. Am I right?' You didn't even bother to reply, only to keep your mouth busy devouring them. They were merely a pair of large and loose breasts, quite worn out from countless rough hands during so many years in the brothel. But you treasured them and cherished them as if they were your dream toy, your long-missing dream toy that you had miraculously found at last, and so nothing in this world could make you float on cloud nine like that pair of breasts you kept fondling in your hand...*

"*It was still a puzzle after you left my room with a firm promise you would return the next day. What had become of you moments ago? That wasn't you—the timid, golden boy once I knew. Then your murmur rang the bell, your murmur while we were plunging deep in feverish, fierce sex. 'Oh, you are my dream come true.' I suddenly realized that your burning desire, which had permeated through your body and nearly scalded my flesh while you were mounting me, must come from a long-suppressed crush that you had on me since you were a ten-year-old youth. That fiery passion never evaporated... It only smoldered deep inside you during those years of my long disappearance. And my sudden emergence kindled that flame into a blinding blaze...*

"Ah, of all the mortal urges known to humans, lust is proved over and over to be second to none. And you are that living proof. So primal, so utter, so-so raw is the urge to fuck. During the following week, you were on the verge of losing your head to sex. With my soundless laugh, I triumphantly watched you plunging headlong into a thrilled ecstasy of sex, breathing in and out only sex and drowning in our coitus. After school, you took a rickshaw, sneaked inside my room, and spent as much time as possible with me. You thought of nothing but fucking me with only a short repose at intervals...

"Of course, I've screwed my way to master the sex inside-out since I was twelve years old. It started when I went out to help my mother on the rice paddies; a group of older plowboys in my village beckoned me to sneak behind the bushes and whispered to me that they wanted me to join a see-saw game just for fun. They picked me because I was the prettiest girl in that village. Then they took turns to do me with some sweets as bait. The first time, I howled with pain, but they stuffed sweets into my mouth while they were mounting me one by one. Oh, poor mother, she always occupied herself with her work in the paddy; she was never aware the most unthinkable was happening behind the bush only a few yards from where she was working. The sweets were so yummy, but we were too poor to buy any. So, I could take whatever pain in exchange for them. But they didn't bother using sweets to bait me any longer after they found out I had always sneaked behind the bush and waited for them.

My mother never suspected my eagerness to help her in the paddy. She was more than happy to have a regular extra hand for work. In fact, I don't even know who got me pregnant back then, whether my father or one of those boys. Now, you knew why even your old man, who was so experienced with woman after woman, had plunged headlong into my allure like a blind. Why not? A whole bunch of girls in his harem had all come to him as dead, cold virgins. Poor, poor girls, the only cock they had ever glimpsed was his, and some of them came to him with no clue what a man's penis was for...

"Yet, while I was intoxicating a greenhorn like you with our heated eros until you lost all your senses and soul, one single mistake changed the whole course. If only my curiosity hadn't urged me to ask you about your fine fiancée that I'd earlier known from Lek. You didn't slip a word about her when I asked, and your face didn't even change; I only found a strange flicker in your eyes. But the following day you didn't come back. And another torturous week passed without your presence. That was when I realized I overestimated myself and that I was everything to you. Now, I knew the other girl meant much to you, much more than I'd thought...

"But you finally showed up two weeks later, sober and calm like a holy saint. I dashed into your arms, feeling like being born again, but you stopped me. You quietly told me, your eyes cast down, hiding your anguish, yet your voice unmistakably hinted in finality, 'Lin Jong, we couldn't see each other anymore. It's not right from the beginning. Soon, I will marry my fiancée, the girl I've loved for years. But I keep my promise; today, I brought you a good sum of money to help you leave this place and start a decent life. And if you want, you could move to a better place. It's my property from my mother, a small bungalow by a canal in the Old Capital. I called it my sanctuary, where, from time to time, I come to spend a few nights alone in solitude to escape the chaotic life. Over there, you will stay under that roof, safe and sound, with all my support. Or if you find someone you like,

you can settle down with him and start a family in that house for good. The only thing is, from now on, we're not going to see each other anymore ... for the sake of the girl who's going to be my wife very soon ... '

"Oh, oh, oh, a fit of blind rage hit me so hard I could retch in blood when I heard you were leaving me to marry a girl you declared she's your love. All right, it's time to confess that during the few weeks we spent together in that intimate relationship, I let myself savor and cherish those moments. Against my strongest will, I couldn't help falling for you, Beloved. You almost made me forget the cruel fact that I was a mere prostitute. Your overwhelmed desire when we were in bed made me feel there was no one else but me who meant the world to you. Remember? You always pulled me close to you and tenderly stroked my hair. Oh, that moment in your arms, I found I'd never felt more blissful. Don't you know that as each day passed, my grudge melted bit by bit? Whenever I felt that tenderness from you, I had to hold back my tears ...

"For the first time in my life, I started to feel no different from every ordinary female who was head over heels in love with a man she found would protect her for the rest of her life from this cruel world in a cocoon of his genuine love. Yet I tried to stop that wonderful yet forbidden feeling. How could I allow myself to become affectionate with someone who was the cause of my ruined life? And yet I found myself drawn more and more in loving you. That's why the moment you told me you were going to marry a girl you loved, you were tearing me into pieces. You hurled me back into a bare reality that all about me that mattered to you was only that cleft between my legs. Nothing else meant a thing to you ...

"I'd been left to bleed and die from that wound since that fatal moment, to die from you, die from a sublime dream that I put both of us in. They all immediately evaporated. What was suddenly left was a soulless me who vowed to see your future with that girl torn into bits in cold blood by my own hands. So,

I suddenly put forth my plan that I had been prepared but reluctant to put into the act until that moment of unbearable humiliation. I started with a scream and a howl like a fatally wounded animal. 'No, no, no. You aren't going to leave me. Listen Beloved. I've just found out. Something is growing inside me night and day. You seeded a life in my womb.' I saw your face ashen, as white as bone. You staggered like being struck by a hard blow. 'No, don't fool me, Lin Jong, no.' You blindly took a few steps from me until your back hit a wall and slid, flopping heavily onto the floor. 'Yes, I found out during your absence that I've been carrying your child for a month. And everyone here can be a witness. I have never let any man into this room since I met you.' Then, I threw myself into your arms, whimpering. 'Beloved, twelve years ago, you left my firstborn— your brother–dead. Now, you are going to leave my second one—your own this time—born a bastard...'

" 'Give me some drink. I need it, please...' I knew you couldn't handle that dilemma. Fear took over your senses. So, I poured you a liquor I kept in my room to calm you down. After you swiftly slugged it down, you asked for another. I knew you never touched those things. Your speech started to be slurred. Suddenly, you came to me in complete surrender. But, oh my, never did I expect to see you that way. You slumped on my lap; your trembling mouth groped for my nipple and started sucking it while wracking with sobs. That wasn't you that I knew. That was a little child who took a nipple as a refuge against the doom he was never ready to face. However, I let that lost child inside you have his way. But what I doubted began to take shape...'

"Don't try to protect your dearest nanny. I'm not stupid. Yes, I remember her. She was always there when I was called to see your mother. Gross as a fat toad was how she looked. It always made me wonder. I found nothing in her that could draw you in. But the moment you crawled to curl up on my lap, begging with your slurred voice to be fed from my bosom like a child in *famished agony, it was apparent that your disoriented mind took me for your nanny. That told me all about how close you both were. I couldn't help wondering what she had done to you for all those years. It seems it wasn't her milk alone that she fed you, was it? So, I figured out that if I wanted to keep you in my grip, I must feed you the same thing, and it was not hard to guess what it could be...*

"And it worked. From the day we moved to stay in this bungalow together, I kept feeding you what you never dreamed of getting from your fat nanny. The heated lust that kept on each night made you blindly ignore my enormous belly with an almost full-term fetus inside. It surprised me to find I didn't have a miscarriage from those brutal acts at night. Yet from that moment, I knew you completely surrendered yourself to me. You were mine, all mine. I vowed to myself you would never see your fiancée's face again. I guess you might screw her once or twice at least. But her face must be buried, and mine would be replaced whenever you opened your eyes.

"Yet, so many nights I saw you scrambling out of the bed to hide from me at one darkest corner while weeping bitterly. Oh, I could tell you were in extreme agony of losing your fiancée forever. But it wouldn't bother me. Because every morning after your heart-shattering lament, I found you coming back. As soon as you caught me sprawling on the bed waiting for you, you jumped on me and indulged in a desperate fuck all over again. Ah ha, that's you to your core. Your deep, genuine love for that girl of yours gave way to your bursting lust just the instant you began to screw me. But when that's over, you loathe yourself and hate the world, and most of all, despise me to your core for making you become what you've become. Or, more precisely, you loathe me because I am a mirror reflecting on what you've never expected in yourself before. Yet despite that hate, not even once are you able to stop lusting after me. Oh, my morbid pleasure was growing each day as I watched you transform from a noble young man into merely a severe sex

addict who reeked of sex as soon as the sun went down every night."

I'd never imagined the Devil's smile until this minute when she opened her smile to me. Oh God! I could declare her the lewdest creature ever living on this planet.

Why, every word she spitted out is true. Perhaps the Devil from the bowels of hell sent a carnal-arousing demon like her to test my adamancy. And I failed. I failed terribly because that test revealed that I, whom everyone has wholeheartedly believed being born a saint, was indeed worse than a fiend when lust was triggered.

"This day has finally come; the day I stand before you and crush you with my, um... let's say, confession."

As she declared triumph, her eyes turned so icy—a void of humaneness that made me wonder if she was as human as I once believed.

"No, it's not done. I want you to know one more thing. And this particular one, you need to brace yourself, darling. This must be the toughest for you, my last laugh," her words were followed by a peal of laughter.

"When I came to meet you at your school for the first time, I had already carried this bastard for nearly three months."

After a moment of shocked silence, the worst moment in my life, I stepped back from her. I felt a core of myself ceased to exist for some seconds, which seemed to last for eternity.

"No," I got up, stumbled on my desk, and slumped into my chair again. "No! How come you make that lie to hurt me!"

"Beloved, every lie I've told you, you embraced them all. But when the only truth is emerging, you refuse to believe. How ironic!"

"Go away. Leave me alone. Leave me—"

I breathed heavily, covering my eyes with both hands, yet scalding tears still leaked through my fingers and streaked down.

"Why do I need to lie to you? The truth is a plain sight on that bastard's face," she laughed in triumph. "Are you blind?

Have you never wondered why his skin's dark compared to your fair and fine complexion? Your features are perfect, the face of a flawless marble sculpture. But look at the baby's face, so plain, obviously stamped with the inferior peasant blood. Well, you can't blame me. If I have to get laid by half of the men in town, no wonder an ugly face can pop up by chance in my womb."

Suddenly, she faked a gasp, and with a mocking alarm, she screamed through her laughter.

"Oh, no, no, no. It can't be that particular man. It can't, especially if you and him have known each other inside out."

"Please, Lin Jong, stop! Don't be so cruel to me!"

It was supposed to be a good shout, but when my voice came out, it was merely a weak whimper.

"Why! If you think this is cruel, it's only a prelude. The worst is coming now. Ready? That man had come to sleep with me every night before you appeared. You might outdo him in your monstrous lust. But I found no other males able to beat his strength. It wasn't a human but a horse mating me. During each visit, I couldn't take the score of how many times he flooded me with a torrent of his cum. I must confess I became so thrilled I was oblivious to being more cautious. And shortly after, I found a bastard conceived inside me. And when the midwife showed me the face of the child the minute he was born, what I had suspected earlier did become unmistaken. The evidence is stamped on that bastard's face! Have you ever wondered where your baby takes his ugly face from? Or ask yourself if you've ever seen that face before in someone so familiar to you?"

"Go away. Please don't hurt me anymore..." I stammered and was shaken violently. "You are a harlot. A slut inside out." My shoulders were hunched, my body shrunken as I tried to huddle myself in self-defense.

"A harlot? A slut? All the losers like you can do is call me names. Thanks for allowing me to squeeze your zesty marrow for six months to the last drop. At least I left your bare skeleton for you to keep. I spared it so that you can use what's left of you

to crawl back and screw your fiancée girl if she's a fool enough to let you. All right, I'll let you have a good time with your son for the last time while I pack my things and leave you."

And with her broadest smile, she added.

"If you want a downright lie to make you feel as good as ever, you get it now. Listen!"

She was stressing every word as slowly as she could.

"I swear the child is yours alone, plain and simple. Your faithful watchdog, Lek, did not make him. Are you satisfied now?"

"Lin Jong!"

I heard my voice screaming and hers gleefully laughing and laughing.

Those voices seemed to come from far off while a burst of sobbing was choking me. I could not breathe—

* * * * *

Part 2: Chapter 8

At the Bottomless

I let my father's journal slide from my hands after Lek's name was mentioned.

Lek...Lek...Lek.

A violent wave of shock vibrated through my body, as if I were being electrified. It knocked me down leaving me slumped on the floor.

Not an ounce of my strength was left to face whatever awaited me on the next page. After knowing who my mother was, nothing on earth would be more able to shock me.

But I was wrong—damn, damn wrong.

I couldn't imagine how I would carry this twisted truth to my last day.

I threw that journal into the drawer and let out a storm of outrage in a loud howling. I thought of burning that journal into ashes to stop disentombing the ghost of the past to haunt me, the living. Yet, I doubted whether burning it could help me wipe out this most shocking truth, the truth that I was not my father's son. The preceding truth, that I was a whore's child, suddenly paled with this new emerging terror.

Which was endurable between burning in hell and being conceived in a whorehouse during the heated union between Ling Jong and her customer, Lek?

I could hardly sleep and eat from that shock for the rest of the week.

A few days later, Lek showed up in a rush while I was making a fire, preparing to destroy that journal. He must have noticed the journal missing and immediately figured out who took it.

We faced each other like two total strangers who saw each other for the first time. A minute later, he tried to speak as he must have been well-prepared, but it came out awkwardly as much as torturously. He must have known that I'd already found out *everything,* but his awkwardness became alarming when he noticed my distraught and gaunt face in full view.

"What…what are you doing?"

I replied without looking at him.

"Going to burn the whole journal. I have already read some of the parts I have taken from you the day before. But I can't drag myself to finish. I just…can't."

Before Lek's showing up, the deep hollow inside me had left me dry-eyed. I couldn't squeeze a single drop of tear to wash out my staggering anguish. But now, it frightened Lek to see me burst into a wild, hysterical wailing.

He pulled me to him and hugged me for the first time, as far as I could remember. He had never done that before. A massive and strong man he was, I wondered if he could break me to pieces with that heartfelt, crushing hug.

"To me, he *is* your father, Pran," he tried to keep his voice from trembling with a surge of emotion, his eyes full of tears. "A true father can die for his child whereas other millions, like me, merely sire a child but aren't worth being called father. Your papa died from a snake bite, so you were safe from it.

Remember? I can't stop you from burning his journal if you want. But if you put yourself to read till the last page before destroying it, you will see why he is and has always been your father no one can replace. "

Lek was a closed-mouthed and quiet person, but now he was pouring out a torrent of words at me.

"No, I won't lie; you will open a can of worms. As you read more, it will get worse...much worse. Even your father once told me between two hard things: he'd rather embrace a lie that brought hope than take a truth that wiped out all hope from him. Because of that, I intend to hide this part of the journal for your own good. But it's too late now. You've already found it. However, weighing its pros and cons, it's better to face that horrid truth in order to stay proud and grateful to be his son."

I groaned. But he ignored my frustration.

"Whatever happened to him, he never blamed me. He only told me no one else but his weaknesses dragged him down. But I swear that's not true," Lek's voice turned cruel again. "If you finish this journal, you will realize that he has proved himself one of the bravest among us."

Then, his voice was down to nearly a whisper.

"I've adored him like no others. But when he was young, I admit that his weakness upset me. He allowed everyone to abuse him in one way or another, yes, in the name of kindness. So many times, I was mad to see him act like...sorry for my word... like a chicken shit. I was desperate to protect him from those bad hands, but as a mere servant, I was as good as powerless. But the last seven years of his life must change him. It'd changed him a minute he chose to face a life no better than walking straight into hell. He had done that for...do you know for whom?"

Lek's voice fiercely came through his clenching teeth.

"Just for you. He'd done all that for you."

My eyes flooded with tears again. This time, I let them stream down my face.

"After you finish this journal, I hope all the staggering sacrifices he made will not go down in vain… I'm sure you are still aware of his last request before he died in that boat. You told me so, remember? You told me he needed you to find the real cause of his twisted fate. He had never swatted a single fly in his life. I confirm it. When he was a boy, he frightened me and other servants with his heartbroken sobs because he accidentally flattened some ants under his feet he claimed he had befriended. His heart was made of gold, but why did he have to suffer *this* much? Can you pursue that answer for him? Maybe you need to know for yourself, too. I know you never harm a soul. You don't deserve those shits, either. But why? Why you?"

Now, that voice was almost ominous.

"Do it, Pran, do prove your birth is a blessing to your father, not a curse that comes to shatter his life as his family has condemned you. And sometimes I can't help having that doubt myself…"

My mouth went parched as I held his stare, trying to make sense of his sudden, cruel words. His face was distorted with raw emotion, so intense that I was taken aback. Did Lek, not different from the rest, loathe me, too? Did he suppress that hatred for so long, and it erupted right now?

"Don't hate me as everyone does. Please, Lek, I have no one left…"

Perhaps my desperate begging made him aware of his abrupt fit. He tried to collect himself.

"You think I hate you, don't you?" his cynical voice was bitter, his eyes so hurtful. He closed his eyes as if hiding some pain, which forced his mouth to start quivering. "No, you are very wrong, absolutely wrong…"

His last words were barely a whisper before he quietly left me to decide between turning my back on the truth and facing it.

Finally, I chose to face the worst, knowing I would possibly live in perpetual nightmares as a consequence. But I was the son of a man who decided to face his worst with adamant courage. I had to follow what he had done.

After hours of pondering, I picked up the journal again. I'd come a long way from the first page, and now, I was reaching the point of no return, too far to turn back. And so, for one more time, another page of the journal was turned on with my trembling hands.

And the rest of his story began to unfold...

"So, Beloved, let me remind you of the time you accompanied me to meet your old man, twelve years after I vanished from his grand mansion. You must remember his face when I told him I was carrying his grandchild whose father was you. The old man was almost knocked out of his chair by that news. And once his mind registered the fact about our relationship, he gave you a choice between a bright future as his heir and that whore; that's what he called me. Oh, your old man was so blind to the fact that you were cursed with the heart of the giver. You would never turn your back on any soul, let alone a child you assume was yours. So, when you chose your unborn child over your golden future, he declared not a penny he would spare you even though you were starving to death like a street dog. Oh, poor man, all he cared about was his damn honor. All he thought was you had done a disgrace to his sacred lineage. He promptly disowned you and declared your eldest half-brother would take your place as lawful heir to his immense fortune. And the last thing he declared was never to see your face again as long as he lived...

"And your mother, oh, finally, I live to the day her life shattered in pieces. I know you would tell me. But, yes, I heard it. I heard that after someone had reported to her that I was pregnant by you, she collapsed from a mental breakdown and has been locked up inside the walls of her chamber ever since. Yes, that incident also set your father over the edge and almost

gave the old fool a good heart attack. When your mother collapsed without hope for recovery, your old man vowed to spill your guts if you ever set foot in his house again. Oh, compared to what your mother has done to me, she shouldn't deserve less than that...

"And worst of all, you have to sacrifice your entire life for this bastard who is not yours. Since your father cut out all his financial support, you had to drop out of your law school and move out into this shitty hole with me, a fall from grace. Ah! I have to see to it. Whoever hurt me must spiral down into their doom."

As Lin Jong lashed me with her endless, cruel words, my first impulse was to strike her with all my force to shut her mouth from dehumanizing me. But I must be born such a coward and let her abuse reach a crescendo. All I could do for now was picture her being dragged into her grave and buried alive by my own hands.

"I dreamed of the day I stood spilling this confession on your face. And that very day does come."

She strode out of the room, a proud warrior in great victory, while I slumped in my chair, gasping for air like fatally wounded man awaiting merciful death.

Oh! The pain... The pain was unbelievable. How could I manage to push my life through this very moment? How? The pain was so intense it burnt and evaporated the tears.

Some unbearable minutes slowly trickled down, but the pain never went away.

Amidst that searing pain, I heard Baby Pran start to cry in his crib. He was wailing and wailing, hoping his cry would get attention from a tender hand to pick him up into arms and nurse him with rich and warm milk from bountiful breasts. I sat rigid, fear-stricken by that sort of cry.

Oh, that same wailing, that long-lost wail from another infant from another time, suddenly came back, rising to deafen the immediate noise in this room. The old memory flashed, flickered, flashed again, and this time flooded away this present moment, drowning me deeper into the dark bottomless where that recurring nightmare of mine had been lurking, waiting, and attacking.

In that nightmare, I always witnessed myself clumsily holding Baby Boy crying in my arms. The cry escalated, so unbearably piercing it could crack a mirror. An instant later, I heard a thump like something falling hard on the floor. Oh, after the thump, that earsplitting wailing finally ceased. Yet, what rushed to take its place was more terrifying... I always heard a woman's hair-raising scream echoing over and over, waking me up in the midst of the night, my body soaking with cold sweats from those sounds and that scene, which had come to haunt me ever since.

It didn't take long for me to emerge again into the present moment as the wailing of another infant in this room reached its crescendo.

It was the cry of a desperate infant in need of mercy and care for its survival. Shortly after, I struggled to my feet and scrambled to the crib. I held my breath while peering closely at an angry, plain face, so plain it reminded me of the face of the man who had given life to this child. Why Lek? Of all men in the entire world, why did it have to be Lek, this Lek, not anybody else? Why was Life so cruel to me? ... I choked back my sobs and tried to do what I had been doing all my life—denying the truth. Through my blurred, teary eyes, I still saw two tiny fists waving blindly, begging me with a desperate cry to pick it up.

I held my breath as my hands reached down into that crib.

Once the baby was lifted up into my arms, it probably sensed the human warmth. It immediately stopped crying. Shush...go back to sleep, little one. I whispered, my lips softly touching its forehead. Still closing its eyelids, the infant began to rub its face against my chest, its tiny mouth quivering, opening, and keeping moving as it was blindly groping for a nipple from a ripe and ample breast which could never be found on my futile chest. Yet, it kept searching desperately for its mother's soft teat.

That was more than I could take. I pressed my face against the tiny head and broke down into quiet sobs.

Baby Boy, is it you? Suddenly, goosebumps broke all over my body. Baby Brother, do you come again into this world in the body of this new baby to give me another chance to atone for the unforgivable I had done to you? If so, never will I let you slip off my arms again. Never again, my little brother. I promise I will protect you with my own life against whatever and whoever comes to harm you, whether or not that one can possibly be your own mother.

The subtle, sweet smell of the infant's soft skin gradually calmed and soothed me so much that when Lin Jong returned with her luggage, she was aghast. The sight of me cradling the infant, my face against its face, took Lin Jong by real surprise. She quickened her pace toward me, frowning and growling.

"What are you doing to my baby?" A strange alarm was in her voice.

"You let him cry for so long. He's so hungry now," I probably surprised her again with my steady voice and calm composure as I handed the baby to her. "You should feed him now before we go on with our talk."

Lin Jong had given me a hard stare, her eyes narrow, before snatching the baby into her arms. The baby was now squeezed in her choking embrace, so tight, so mercilessly, it started to squirm and cry again.

"No, let's finish our business once and for all," she flared. "He can wait."

"But... but he's hungry. What's the matter with you? A few minutes won't hurt," I insisted wearily.

Icy, cold rage formed in her eyes, so intense I stopped short and took a few steps back.

"What's wrong with you? Why are you so raging?" My jaw tightened, "If you want to leave me, I can't stop you. But just feed him now. You blame your father for your birth, which you never asked for. So, whose fault is it when this child was born?

Whose fault, his or yours?"

"Leave him alone. How dare you force me to feed him? He is my child. He has nothing to do with you," she growled.

"Because he's your child, you admit, so you let him cry and go hungry," I said flatly. "That doesn't make sense to anyone, at least not to me."

"All right, I'm going to feed him now to keep his mouth shut because, after this, we're going to have a long and serious discussion," she lifted her icy eyes to meet mine. "Promise me you will listen to the whole story," she smirked, "And don't freak out."

I nodded blankly and turned my back on Lin Jong while she was busy nursing her baby. He stopped crying immediately as he found his mother's nipple and sucked it noisily and hungrily. My eyes were fixed on the wall. At least I was glad my thought went numb. The last thing I wanted at that moment was to think.

When she finished, she fiercely clutched the baby in her arms, facing me.

"Beloved, don't be so upset you don't father him. For the rest of his life, he has to be so grateful to you. Why not? He owes you his life. Never would he have had a chance to be born had we not met that day at your school."

She said with mock comfort through fierce laughter.

"At first, I was planning to abort him, an accident that wasn't worth any concern, as it had happened to me a few times during the time in the whorehouse. But when I knew from your imbecile servant where I could find you, I immediately changed my mind. I knew I'd better keep him. Why didn't I use this unborn bastard to trap you? It seemed all of a sudden that Luck came to stand on my side by shoving Lek into my life, helping connect me with you, and enabling me to find the best revenge I'd ever thought of. I want to see you blindly taking this bastard as your own—a child whose father turned up to be your most faithful servant."

She moaned softly as if in a euphoric trance.

"I kept my gleeful secret throughout my pregnancy, laughing at you every time you pressed your ears against my swollen belly, listening to the bastard's heartbeats as your eyes were brimming with tears from joy and wonder in a budding life inside me. Once you had lost all you ever had, the single hope that kept you alive was that child in my womb. You anxiously counted down the day when you would peer at his face. When you felt his first kick through my belly, you even told me that we should bury our past for his sake and share our life as man and wife. You would sacrifice yourself to all the hard work so that I could take good care of our child at home. But you never suspected how possible a normal baby could be born after just five or six months we lived together. No one ever educated you on how long a baby should stay in its mother's womb after it was conceived. Oh, I remember how thrilled you were as soon as I started my labor and how devastated after the midwife announced the news of your stillborn child. Poor old midwife, while my eyes followed the grief-stricken father carrying his baby to bury, the gleeful grin on my face that was so hard to hide must startle her to—"

"You..." I interrupted. *"No, you didn't..."* then I stuttered. *Words were frozen. The thought of her newborn brother, whom she told me she had strangled, was suddenly crossing my mind.*

She answered me with a smile that was so insidious that it wasn't hard to interpret that meaning.

"I only needed him while he was in my womb to stop you from going to marry your fiancée girl. Because I knew he was the sole reason you chose me over her. If he had actually died that day, things would have come as I had planned. It's time for me to move on to a new life. Even juicy sex with you bores me to death now. So, no point in sticking with you since what's left of your life is just a hole. Both you and that bastard are just useless junk to me now...

"But that fucking bastard fooled everyone. Even that stupid

midwife believed he was already dead. When she pulled him out from my legs, he didn't move or breathe and had bruises all over his ugly green body from our daily rough sex, more than ready to be buried. But you were the one digging him up because you said you heard his wailing in his grave. Didn't that stubborn bastard intend to give me a hard time by clinging to his worthless life? He's meant to rot and vanish from this world and be forgotten, but you butted in to change his fate. So, it must be your responsibility alone to raise this little monster...

"There's more for you to know. At first, I thought I wouldn't let you know the truth about that bastard. Why? I would have my last laugh watching you as the biggest fool struggling to bring up a child whom you would never be aware was conceived by another man. But I changed my mind. I realized what you don't know will never hurt you; therefore, you will never suffer from what's meant to hurt you. So, before I get out of this place, it's more fun to throw the truth on your face and dump him with you for the rest of your life, a perfect idea to make your life a perfect hell."

She paused, trembling with a morbid satisfaction before it gave way to another sudden attack of rage.

"But a minute after I walked back, I felt a raging fit enough to tear you into pieces. You were ruining everything I'd expected to see. Instead, I saw you cradling this bastard in your arms. And no, that isn't enough. You even urged me to feed him, feed this hideous bastard," she forced a dry laugh, a smile vibrating from her eyes, "I just realized at that instant I nearly made the gravest mistake. How could I overlook the simple fact that for your entire life, you were fed up with being loved and cared for by a whole lot of people surrounding you, so much that such love turned to choke you, wearing you out? So, what you yearned most in life must be the opposite; just a chance to love instead of being loved. You might desperately look for a soul to serve that purpose all your life. Why? It never crossed my mind until this minute. If I am a fool enough to let you keep him, I'll be the

one who bestows a godsend on you—a perfect treasure you can love and cherish and fulfill your life as long as you breathe. Instead of seeing you tortured by the presence of a child you found out isn't yours, that damn bountiful heart of yours will open to embrace him regardless of that stark truth, then making you a man whose ruined life finally finds healing from the love he pours on a child."

A sudden scream from her startled me, revealing she was a mad woman inside out.

"No! No! No! Never will I leave him with you."

Her scream didn't only pierce my wounded heart but also woke the baby in her clutch. And now there were two screams; each rose equally to fill and suffocate this small and stuffy room.

"Shut up! Shut up, you bastard!" She screamed at the screaming baby, shaking his tiny body violently to stop his scream only to escalate it.

"Lin Jong," I raised my voice in alarm. "You can't do this to a mere infant, not to mention he is yours. Give him to me."

"No, don't you dare take him from me? You will never have a chance to lay your eyes on him again."

"Don't...don't take him with you... Lin Jong," I stuttered and then drew a harsh breath to collect myself. "Where and how are you going to bring him with you? Out there is not where he belongs."

"Who said I would take him with me?" She growled.

"Lin Jong, we can talk," her reply made my eyes flicker with hope, "If leaving this place is your decision, I can't hold you back. But... but Pran is not ready for that. He's just barely two weeks old, too helpless, too vulnerable. Lin Jong, I don't think you've prepared for what is ahead of you. So meanwhile, I can help take care of him while you are away. Then, when you think your life settles down, you can come to take him back anytime. If you don't need my help, please let me do this for Baby Boy's sake... for my brother." To bring up that name, I forced myself to swallow a big lump inside my throat. "Lin Jong, please forgive us. My mother and I have paid and suffered enough for what we've done to you, whether we meant it or not."

I hung my head, waiting for her mercy, but only a long silence was what I heard. Finally, there came a sigh, a long mocking sigh from a woman whom I believed was on the brink of insanity.

"Ah, nice try. How impressive! Thanks for spilling a few drops of your caring and concern to extinguish a fire that has long engulfed my life. But no, thanks. Your atonement doesn't amount to anything," her eyes were blazing, burning me. "No, I won't take him into my life. As I told you, I no longer use the bastard; it is only a burden to drag along. But..." she paused, lowering her voice to nearly a whisper, "it doesn't mean I'll leave him with you either. Can you guess what I'm going to do with him?"

Her eyes now glittered like the eyes of a cat one saw in the pitted darkness, only far more sinister.

"I... don't know what you mean, honestly," I blinked.

"Yes, you know what I mean, Beloved. You know damn well what I'm going to do with him. But you always deny things you cannot take."

"Will you give him away for someone to adopt him?" My voice was barely audible.

"Don't play dumb with me, Beloved. You're smarter than that. Can't you figure out why I've just brought up the story of my long-dead baby brother? Can't you?" Her voice escalated into a shriek.

It did not take me long to grasp what she gleefully hinted. Suddenly, once I began to grasp its meaning, I felt my blood turning cold as if plunged into a sea of ice.

So, she would bring her son to get rid of somewhere.

Then, I remembered the day Pran was born. I remembered a frightened look on the old midwife's face as she tried to tell me something after Pran had suddenly stopped breathing. But *it seemed she never had a chance to be with me alone in the room she had delivered him. She must see something, something that caused him to stop breathing.*

So, Pran wasn't stillborn. She repeatedly twisted her tongue to toy me with my frustration and bafflement. Now I believed she had choked him till she saw him stop breathing. But perhaps the miracle existed. He didn't die from that cruel act, causing her to plan to finish him again for good.

Words were struggling in my throat. I must force them out into actual words, some sensible words I could hold on to before she pulled me down with her into an abyss of sheer madness.

"You... don't mean that, Lin Jong," I croaked. "You are sick, downright sick, and sick beyond any hope."

That was all I could think of at this crucial moment.

No, I must force my frozen mind to think now. I must. Merely staring dumbly and standing numbly didn't do any good. I slowly and cautiously took one step toward her, my eyes fixing on the screaming baby in her arms.

"Just come near me one more step, you son of a bitch, and I'll break his neck."

She screamed in my face fiercely, shaking the infant, who was now squirming and screaming at the top of its lungs. "Shut up! You bastard, shut your damn mouth before I'll throw you on the floor!"

I was aghast, almost in shock, watching her glittering eyes turn deadly as she peered into the tiny face in her clutch. Her eyes shone fierily with pure hatred at the wee creature. An overpowering sense of evil rose from every pore on her body.

A creature with an utter void of love. That's what she was.

I had never been so scared of another human being in my life. It was the most primal fear I'd ever known.

"Oh, Lin Jong, what's turning you into a monster? What?"

A shiver started to run through my spine.

"Don't pretend you don't know. It's you! You. You have made me."

She turned her ardent gaze on me with her maniac laugh.

"If I have to burn him alive to torture you to death, I'll do it, I swear," she breathed heavily, almost panting. "I tell you what I'm going to do with him. Yes, I will carry him with me on a boat, which will take me to Bangkok's side, where I will start my new life. During the trip, as the boat is leaving the canal and beginning to connect to the main river, the spot where the current is strongest, I will pass out from the heat of the sun and stumble so the baby will slide off my arms and disappear under the water. I will scream my head off, crying frantically as the boatman jumps and dives down the murky water, trying to pull him out. He may not find him because the rapid current will swiftly carry him down the deep and winding river, which will soon empty into the gulf along with his body. Or if the boatman can bring him back, a two-week-old infant nevertheless couldn't possibly survive. Then the kind boatman will try to comfort me... 'Don't cry, Miss, accidents can happen. It's your poor child's own Karma, not your fault.' And I will thank him through my tears of grief and distraught. A minute later, he will never see me again... Or if he happens to see me after that, it means he will stand as a witness for me to that sad, sad accident."

She was taking a few steps away from me as she still gripped the infant in her claws.

"Accidents can happen, especially to a helpless infant. Right, Beloved? You can't deny this fact because you, too, caused a fatal accident to another helpless infant... my other child."

"Your other child!" I scoffed. "You never feel any creature born inside your womb is your child. If any of them are useful to you, you save it. Otherwise, you discarded them like they were your feces. You've never had affection for Baby Boy, too, never grieved for his death. You're just enraged that his death, which I had caused, ruined your chance for using him to take over my father's enormous fortune. This is the staggering difference between my mother and you. She and you have shared one sacred thing: being a mother. But no matter what, my mother

loves her own child perhaps more than loving herself. But you... *you are utterly incapable of loving even your own child, not to mention other human beings."*

"You are wrong. I am capable of loving," she forced a laugh. "Of course, to love only oneself is enough for surviving. I can't afford to burden my life with extra love for someone else. Therefore, I should warn myself against that absurd feeling when I met you. But I still let it flourish like all foolish girls do when they fall in love. Yet how fortunate I could kick it out after you'd told me you were leaving me for your fiancée. You made me take the utmost humiliation that I was merely a whore good only for fucking. That's why what I feel for you right now is nothing but the intense hatred set ablaze from that humiliation. Are you satisfied now?"

Then, she gave me an amused look.

"Verbal alone never hurts me. Better try some other way to break me."

"Give him to me, Lin Jong. Let go of him. Let go of everything that has ever wounded you. Let go..." I said softly, almost in a begging voice. "Please come to your senses. What you're going to do is the unspeakable crime no one can conceive of. If I bring you to justice, you could get capital punishment for a homicide, a deliberate one. Don't you think I could give my testimony in the court of law?"

"If you think anyone will believe you, go ahead. Tell them a mother kills her own child to torture and avenge a man who has caused all her miseries. Go ahead now. Go!"

As she continued her feverish talking, I slowly inched forward, one small step at a time. They were about ten feet apart—the most treacherous feet apart.

"Don't!!" another fierce scream. I froze midway.

"I already warned you; one more step toward me, and I'll snap his neck. Don't challenge me," her hand feverishly moved to its fragile neck and paused there, then moved to cover its mouth and part of its nostrils to muffle its voice, almost gagging

it. *"Come on; take another step. Come on…"* she coaxed me, *"Die he will, only in a matter of time. If you try to snatch him now, he will die this instant. But if you let him go with me, you help prolong his life, maybe for a couple of hours or so. I'll let you decide his fate, whichever you prefer. Oh, oh, what a day! Never believe this day really comes."*

I still bent down my head to conceal my face, but when I looked up and raised my eyes to meet hers again, she stopped short, staring at my sudden calm and blank face. My eyes were now turning vacant, almost a complete void, while I was looking straight into her eyes with a steady gaze.

"You're holding your own child hostage and threatening to harm him as the means to defeat me," my voice also turned toneless as I was eying her; the corner of my mouth barely formed a smirk. *"Are you losing your mind? No, it doesn't work. Too bad my heart isn't made of pure gold as you believe. Who cares for a bastard who isn't his own? How could you expect somebody else to be capable of loving your bastard child? Even his mother is not capable of loving him. So, go ahead. Strangle him or drown him, or choose whatever method that can thrill you the most. It isn't my concern anymore."*

Then she watched me calmly turn my back and was about to retreat.

Right before I was out of the room, I turned around and calmly said to her.

"Now, you can leave my place with that bastard, Lin Jong. That's all I care. Just go now."

My words did set Lin Jong over the edge. I knew they were knocking her off balance. She gasped, her eyes turning blank for a few seconds to grasp my words. But when her mind registered what I had said, she screamed savagely at the top of her voice.

As swiftly as a flash of lightning, I spun and flung myself to her as she stood off guard, causing her to stumble backward and almost tripped over. Before she could regain her balance,

I twisted her hand and bent her arm backward, trying with all my force to reach her shrieking infant. She kicked me savagely in her defense, trying to pull away, making us both lose our balance and stagger. I fell first, my back against the hard floor, dragging her down and landing on top of me.

My hand snapped the infant just in time before it dropped and touched the hard floorboard. Goosebumps started prickling on my skin. I whispered to myself. "Baby Boy, I once dropped you to your death, but now I save you from it." I could hear her harsh breathing so close to my ear as she fiercely clawed at my face and furiously bit my hand, which was now holding the infant, sinking her teeth deep into my raw flesh like a savage beast. I felt warm blood trickle down my cheek and the sharp pain shooting down my bitten hand, so sharp I jerked my hand and cried out loud.

But I never let go of the infant, still curling intact beneath my protective hug.

An instant later, I felt another forceful blow on my forehead, followed immediately by the impact of another blow and then another. I heard a ring in my eardrums and saw red and green lights flashing and swirling in my sockets. Lin Jong grabbed one of my weighty and thick books scattered on the floor nearby and hit me rapidly and frantically with it. The vibration from each strike made my vision so blurred I barely saw her face but some distorted shadowy shape looming above mine, scary, menacing, and inhuman.

"You'll never have him alive," I heard her voice through her clenched teeth.

I managed to raise my throbbing hand to protect my bruised face from more blows while shifting and hunching my shoulders to absorb any possible impact that could reach the infant whom I tried to shield with the curb of my elbow.

"I'm going to kill him. I am. Now!" She snarled through her clenched teeth.

"Over my dead body," I replied calmly.

"Look!" She screamed.

Suddenly, her hand was pouncing on the tiny face that was slightly slipping from my arm. The instant she was about to squeeze the child's fragile throat, my hand fumbled blindly and reached hers. With all the incredible strength I had, I squeezed her throat so hard with the blind rage I never had a clue I possessed. She struggled and kicked me wildly as she gagged and made a choked sound. Yet, her strong hand never let go of the infant's throat, trying desperately to press more weight on his neck.

During this critical moment, I didn't have any free hand to yank hers from the infant's throat. I needed to use one to cover the infant from her pounce and another to squeeze her throat. Sheer terror knotted my stomach. I could feel the vein on my forehead bulging and throbbing from panic. The only way I could think of during this crisis was to squeeze her throat harder and harder to loosen her deadly grip on her infant.

Oh, how long does it take to strangle Lin Jong to stop her from killing her child? One minute? Five minutes? I panted, gasping, sweating, sobbing, and howling to let out my surge of rage and agony at the top of my lungs. Did five minutes already pass? Should I go on for another minute, or should I stop now? Yet, I went on and on, crushing her throat with all my masculine force, for I didn't trust five minutes would work to get rid of a monster like her.

Suddenly, my thoughts flashed back when she told me how she had killed her father. While she was drowning him in that pond, she said she had to count the time while waiting for his death to ensure he would never breathe again. Now, what she'd done to her father earlier was returned to her by me. What a sick sense of humor life could be.

I dared not withdraw my hand from her neck even though I felt her weighty body on top of me, now lying still and silent. Her hand dropped, her screams and all her movements stopped. It was very eerily as the tremendous silence suddenly had taken over the once turmoil and chaotic room.

I held my breath while my hesitant and trembling hands were nudging and poking her. I shoved her off my body as immediately as I was sure she still lay silent and motionless. She rolled off me effortlessly and lay sprawled on the floor, her face up, her eyes still open wide, facing mine. Her blouse was torn during the fight, revealing those swollen breasts with droplets of milk from her nipples dripping, dripping, ready to feed her baby. I crawled to her, hastily bending down and pressing my ears against her bare left breast, checking her heartbeat. I almost recoiled from that touch, revolted by the thought that they were the same breasts I once kissed and cuddled in blind passion. I shuddered, my teeth shattering from uncontrolled fear mixed with disgust. Then I let out the breath that I was holding. Again, only dull silence and hollowness echoed back from where her heart had been seated.

Silence. The blessing silence at last.

I stared blankly at my hands. All my life, I had never hurt a single living thing, let alone a human being. It's almost impossible for me, who had never swatted even a small fly, to admit that any man, even me, if under a force of circumstance, was capable of killing. Yet, what I had committed an instant ago was a horrendous crime, the murder of another human being. And worse, far, far worse than that, I was astonished and shocked to realize what was flooding my heart at this moment of killing another human was the overwhelming feeling of relief and elation. The long, intolerable weight was at last lifted from my heart. A sex parasite that fed on a man's dignity was gone.

Not a flutter of conscience stirred my remorse. Only the satisfaction that I helped the world get rid of that woman on the floor since she did not deserve another breath.

I feel so grateful to you, Baby Pran. The death of our brother that I'd caused a long time ago is redeemed today because I have saved your life...

After the brief moment of deliverance, another feeling so

despondent was inevitably creeping into my heart. After committing that murderous act, how could I feel as if it were merely an act of removing the cause of the problem that had plagued my life for so long? Or if there was some regret left at all, it was because before ending her life I should wait a little longer, giving her a chance to redeem her mortal sin by making her infant's tummy filled for the last time with her last drops of milk. But as instantly as I felt shocked by my absence of remorse, I forced it down and cursed myself.

Oh, no. Go away, you damn conscience! Not for now. Not for this case. Not for this female creature. She doesn't deserve anyone's conscience, most of all mine. Only death could justify her evil deed.

I hugged the wailing infant so fiercely. It was the first time in my life I felt a scream from an infant was music to my ears. The child who miraculously survived his mother's uncanny cruelty was declaring to the world he was alive with his loud, angry noise. Brave boy, you're a very brave boy, Pran. I kept babbling loudly to the infant, trying to use my quavering voice to wake myself up from the nightmarish mayhem, too surreal to believe it had indeed happened.

I closed his eyes and started to count one, two, three, four... forcing myself desperately to believe that if I opened my eyes after ten, I would miraculously find myself in another place and another time. Way back in the past, inside my luxury automobile in the comfortable and spacious back seat with Lek in the driver's seat, bringing me home from the royal law school as he had done faithfully and daily. When I arrived home, I would see my mother anxiously waiting for me; her face lit up the minute she caught my sight.

I saw her rushing to me, weeping with joy as she kissed and crushed me into her bosom. 'Beloved, my darling, the light of my life, oh! You come home at last. You come home! You're not missing. Please, darling, never leave me again, Beloved Baby...'
I looked at her and shouted in the voice of a euphoric boy,

'Mother, I'm home. Never will I do a thing to break your heart again.' I felt big drops of tears rolling down my cheeks. And we cried and laughed together at the peak of our emotional rapture.

Then I caught sight of another shadowy figure standing at a farther corner, patiently waiting for me to come to her. It was Grace. That's her! She lifted her face and gave me her unique smile while tears of joy filled her eyes. 'Welcome home, my Beloved.' She said timidly. I stepped forward as if in a trance and took her hands in mine as she murmured, her trembling hands touching my face—my nose, cheeks, lips. 'Oh, Beloved, it's you. It's you! Tell me, my eyes don't fool me. I know one day you will come back to share our life.' Suppressing my sobs, I could answer her with only my saddest smile. My hands, which were still holding hers, began to tremble as if my body could no longer contain the growing feeling of intense joy mixed with great sorrow. 'Grace, the love of my life, please hold me. Don't let me slip back into the gruesome reality inside that bungalow. I can't take it. I can't...'

I threw myself in her arms as if they could shelter me against all wickedness. 'Hold me. Hold me, please...' Then I heard her tender voice whispering in my ears, her fingertip pressed on my lips. 'Shush... Now, you are safe in my arms. No one will harm you, my dearest. Just close your eyes slowly, slowly, darling. When you open them again, you will find yourself with me in the heart of our shelter isle, where Time never finds us... Remember we always talked about that place when we were so young and happy together.'

Then I saw a coil of rope in her pale, fragile hand.

'Take this rope. It will take you to our place, dearest. It's the same coil I used after I'd known you had left me.' Her voice was pleading, urging, her eyes glistening with tears, her hands slowly looping the rope. 'It breaks me apart to see you are now living in utter agony; please, use my rope to get your way out and join me forever on our dream isle.' I heard my pleading voice aloud. 'Grace, you are the only love of my life. But not *now. I can't go now and leave this unwanted child to meet his fate alone... Nobody in this world wants him. He is rejected even by his own mother.'*

As I begged her with the sobbing, Grace's hand began to disappear. I saw that the same rope was being held by another hand. When I looked up in genuine surprise, the owner of that hand was a male figure under a shadow so dark I couldn't make out that face. That mysterious figure dropped that rope to the ground, a smile flickering from his dark face as the coil of the rope on the ground started twisting with a quick writhing as if it were coming alive.

'You can't run away from me,' that man said in his warning voice. *'Turn around, and you will see me stalking you everywhere like your own shadow.'*

And everything was gone behind that foggy atmosphere.

When I opened my eyes again after counting ten, I scarcely resisted the impulse to scream at the stark reality. The sudden sight I caught was not my love Grace but the glassy eyes of Lin Jong staring vacantly at me from the floor on where her body was lying sprawled, her neck bruised and swollen from my strangulation, her eyes bulging, her mouth hanging open. Her tongue was slightly sticking out, the ghastliest sight my eyes had ever seen.

I inched my way away from her body, as far as the small, crammed area in this room allowed me, and leaned my body against the wall, forcing down a wave of nausea. Thank goodness, Pran fell asleep again in my arms. His belly was still full from his last feeding. I carried him and put him gently in his crib.

Now, what should I do next?

My first impulse was to report to some authority, confess my crime, and await trial. But seconds later, I thought against it. No, I couldn't. If the verdict on my case came out—though I might not receive capital punishment or life sentence because I confessed and pleaded guilty—I could face at least twenty years in jail for committing a crime of passion. I saved the child's life for nothing if I had to serve my time in prison. I knew no one, least of all my own family, wanted to raise Pran, a whore's child whose birth father was deeply skeptical in their eyes. Without me, Pran was as good as dead.

Besides, had I not already created enough disgrace and scandal for my eminent family? It would certainly become a trial of the decade, so sensational and entertaining, feeding people who had a ravenous appetite for the misery of others.

Oh, I could imagine some lady acquaintances of my mother would be breathless, her eyes sparkling, her gesture excited, as she was about to announce important news proudly. 'My goodness! I heard that the criminal himself is indeed Lord and Grand Lady Bhuvanathnurak's heir!' And as she expected, there were some gasps among her audience in disbelief. 'Yes, it's true, it's true. I heard it from some close friends of the devastated lady who used to come to play cards with her. They whispered to me that a year ago, the great lord had kicked his son out of his house because he'd gone astray, having an out-of-wedlock child with a green-lantern whore who once, the rumor said, had been the Lord's favorite concubine. Oh dear, dear, dear! How outrageous! How obscene! And when Ananda later found out the child was not his, he was in a rage and strangled her to death. It's just like Evil throws a whole bunch of curses and tragedies upon this family, one after another. Then, Ananda's fiancée, the daughter of Lord Pairach Rajamaitri, took her own life. She hanged herself in her bedroom to stop the agony that was eating her alive. Poor, poor girl. I heard she left a note to her parents. She tied it around her neck with the rope she used to hang herself. O-o-h... It made my skin crawl after hearing that. Some said it was a note she wrote to her parents before she climbed a chair to her death to tell her fiancé she would wait for him on some island where time can't find them. Oh my! What a pathetic, pathetic girl! It has just broken my heart to find a young, noble-blooded bluestocking killed herself for the *love of an idiot who chose a street whore over her. Her family just cremated her quietly without the formal funeral ceremony because they couldn't face whoever coming to attend the funeral. Do you remember an old saying that said a son who brings disgrace to his family is as worthless as his mother's feces, which she expelled from her rear?'*

It would be no surprise if the conversation, which was meant to break anyone's heart, ended with a burst of roaring laughter.

Yes, after I'd urged him, Lek opened his mouth and told me of Grace's suicide before he made himself disappear from me. The tragedy occurred the same day I was chased out of my father's house after he knew about Lin Jong and me. But, no, of all the tragic souls whose lives were smashed by Lin Jong, I swear over my dead body that Grace's suicide would be the last thing on earth I would let that vile woman know and add it to her winning scores. After her death, I often dreamed that I saw her standing on a chair with a coil of rope tightened around her neck. I lost no time dashing to stop her. But it was too late. The instant she saw me, she'd kicked the chair she used for her foothold. And I screamed until my screams woke me up.

There was another person I needed in the moment of this crisis. Yet most of the time, my conscience brushed her off, too shameful to recall things that she and I had done with an unrestrained urge behind the locked door. But in the utmost dark moment like this, I fiercely yearned for a comfort that, from boyhood to manhood, I only found in her fat teats and fleshy body, as no others could.

There was no other choice except that I had to dispose of Lin Jong's corpse as fast as possible. Dumping her body into the water was too risky, of course. In a few days, her bloating body would float up, gaining attention from the world by her obnoxious stench. The best way was to bury her. Let her rot alone in the deep hole where no one would ever suspect. But I could not do it in the broad daylight. I hastily wrapped her body with a blanket, securing it with a rope. Yet the length of the blanket was not enough to cover her whole body, so I had to leave her swollen face exposed outside the blanket.

Yes, her eyes still opened as if she were still alive. She gazed up at me with a strange expression I couldn't read, which caused goosebumps to break out all over my arms. I reached out my hand to close her eyelids, but I quickly recoiled before I touched her, as a strong squeamishness about touching her almost immediately took over me.

My stare remained transfixed on her gaze for fear that if I shifted my eyes and looked away, she would start to move, or her wrapped body would sit up and inch slowly, closer and closer toward me. Oh, I always took such things—the supernatural or spirits or ghosts or whatever terms—for the nonsense stuff, laughing at superstitious people who feared the dead more than the living and dreaded the darkness at night more than the darkness in their own heart. Yet, under this circumstance, her strange gaze from her glassy eyes eventually forced me to think otherwise.

If in life she was already a monster, I shuddered; it was not hard to imagine what she would be in death.

What if the unknown and mysterious realm where the dead entered had been a fertilized soil for a dark soul to grow more diabolical? I tried to keep the disturbing thought out of my mind as I dragged that bundle to conceal under my bed, hiding it from the eyes of some of my neighbors who sometimes unexpectedly dropped by.

To avoid being caught up, I waited until nightfall, when the waxing moon started rising above the shadowy clump of trees, flooding the woods with its eerily pale silvery moonlight. Then I dragged her out from under my bed. As I dreadfully expected, her eyes were still wide open, reflecting the flickering light from the small lamp in my hand. She seemed to watch me silently yet intensely, guessing my next move.

Where to bury her? Where? I wondered. I needed to think

clearly. For one thing, I couldn't go that far because I couldn't leave the baby alone in the house for too long.

Then, I recalled the empty, shallow grave I had dug for Pran in the preceding weeks under the tamarind tree that stood by the barbed wire fence. The tree was just a short distance from my bungalow house, and I could see its dark blot from my bedroom window.

Shortly afterward, I carried her bundled body as I wobbled down the steps to the stretch of darkness looming ahead. Yet it took me ten long minutes struggling to drag her through a thick growth of high grasses and reeds as if she was resisting me, still fighting even in death, making every move a hell for me. Besides, I wasn't aware until this minute that the white blanket that I bundled her body now stood out in the dark, making every move more noticeable to anyone passing by.

Finally, in the vast mass of darkness, I laid her rigid and heavy body on the ground, panting, gasping with exhaustion. I intended to put her face down to avoid her stare, and with a shovel in my hands, I feverishly dug the loose ground under the tree until it was deep and wide enough. The ground was still soft and damp from last night's shower rain, easy for me to work on. As I rolled her body into the hole, her body was turned over, and her face was up again, facing me straight from her grave below.

Suddenly, the nocturnal sounds around me seemed to intensify tenfold, the noise of thousand insects, the moan of some night owls huddled with their young ones in a tree hollow, who-o-o-o, who-o-o-o, who-o-o-o, the flapping wings of some bats searching for ripe fruits, and the rattled sound of tree branches against the night breeze, yet the loudest of all seemed to come from my heartbeat.

The silvered moon started to emerge from the dark clouds that had momentarily obscured it, letting the moonlight leak through shadowy and gently swaying foliage above my head and eerily dappled her lurid face, seemingly creating a faint yet *creepy smirk on her lips. The sheen of moonlight reflected in her gleaming eyes, rendering the eerie effect as if she were gazing at me insidiously.*

I tried to withdraw my eyes away, but somehow, her gaze held me against my will. Hours ago, the blankness and lifelessness in her eyes were gone but seemingly ablaze again with intense hatred. She couldn't menace me anymore with her hands, yet she still could with her eyes. I bent down to close her eyes and then turned my back on her to grab the shovel at my side to proceed.

But as instantly as I turned back to her, those damn eyes blinked open again, looking straight into my eyes as if she knew the exact spot on where I had hunkered down. Coincidence or not, it made all the hairs on my body stand on end. However, since I couldn't afford to let such irrational thoughts bother my mind, I was determined to have her eyes closed once and for all.

firmly pressed my thumbs on both her eyes, forcing them to close and waiting for another long minute to make sure they wouldn't have any chance again to crack open. It felt like an eternity doing it. My thumbs sent a wave of shiver along the length of my arms while they were touching her cold, dead, repulsive skin.

Yet an instant after I moved my finger from her sockets, her eyelids began to roll up again, this time so slowly and challengingly.

Almost immediately, I feverishly poured a shovelful of dirt down her face without peering down. Now, I didn't care whether or not I buried her with her eyes still wide open as long as I didn't have to see them anymore.

Yet, either closed or open, it didn't matter now. That nightmarish stare of hers would follow me to my own grave.

I frantically piled down the soil on top of her until her entire body disappeared underneath, then used my feet to stamp on the soil above the grave. The ground looked flat and leveled now. No one would ever know where she was except for earthworms and grubs underground, which her body and her damn eyes would, in a few days, succumb to them as their feast.

Even at the present moment I am writing this journal, I am still in a state of disbelief at what I have done—killing a human being. This must be some joke thrown on me by some diabolical force with its morbid sense of humor.

Why? To save one life—in order to make amends for the death of the other I had earlier caused—I have to end up sacrificing one more life and accrue my sin instead of cleansing it.

I never win. I never win what seems to be my bizarre twist of fate. Life has always taunted me for years on end. Was I born for the reason to turn all the lives of my loved ones into death and doom, including Grace's, the love of my life?

A Midas touch in reverse, I must be.

Never before in my life had I felt so despaired and forlorn as I felt that night. I wanted to weep, weeping for my brother Baby Boy, for dear Father and Mother, for my poor sister Rumpai, and most of all for Grace, the love of my life whom I betrayed in cold blood. If only I could have resisted my spontaneous lust for Lin Jong on that day she had brought me to her whorehouse. If only. And all the sufferings of my loved ones would have never occurred.

And yet I needed my last ounce of energy to walk home to Pran, whose life from now on entirely depended on me, so as not to waste my tears on those mysterious misfortunes that kept falling on me. No, no one will ever understand why things in their lives always happen to them in such a twisted ending, as if they were toys played by some pervert at whim.

'All human beings have flaws, but perhaps except you, Beloved...' Suddenly, it seemed like the voice of the late Mr. James, my beloved teacher, was whispering in my ears. Or was it just a stir of wind? 'You are either the creation of Nature's masterpiece or its greatest error. Watch out, son. Watch out.'

With painstaking effort, I staggered home, dog-tired. After

checking up on my son in his crib, I dropped myself into my bed and slept dreamlessly through the night.

I have become Papa for Pran ever since that night. And we have each other, father and son, against the dark and hostile world.

The sudden belief that my brother Baby Boy had returned as Pran to give me a second chance began to send me a new purpose to live again. Before I had Pran, I dreaded that I had to carry my guilt at causing Baby Boy's death to the day I die. Now Pran has come to help remove that guilt. Out of a broken life that seems beyond repair, I will do my best to put it in whole again to raise him as my own flesh and blood.

Since his birth, Pran was a frail and sickening baby. He always had a problem with breathing, which afterward developed into asthma. I suspected his mother would have some part of it behind my back. I believe she could push down a pillow on his face when I wasn't around. She had done the unspeakable before to one or two of her little brothers to ease up her burden in taking care of them.

Death always awaited Pran at our doorstep. Yet, three times he dodged Death.

The first time, by luck, on the very day he was born, his mother tried to stop his breath, but I rescued him in time out of his grave.

The second time ended with Lin Jong's death, and he survived her attempt to choke him.

And the last time so far was when he was two months old.

I still vividly remember that at that time, the bedroom turned into a battlefield between two sides: a man cradling his baby fiercely in his arms on one side and Death—or probably Lin Jong herself on the other.

As the ominous rainstorm approached, Baby Pran started a fever with irregular breathing that night. He howled and flailed his arms to express his pain. Raindrops the sizes of marble were lashing at the windows as if we were hit relentlessly by a set of bullets. The locals called this extraordinary squall 'elephants-chase-out storm.' Imagine a stampede and chaos among a herd of giant animals in the wild as they try to flee such a storm. Or was there an expanse of the ocean up in the sky, and overnight, the entire volume of water drained out of that celestial ocean and suddenly fell on earth all at once?

I could neither carry him with me in the treacherous storm nor leave him home alone so that I could paddle my boat across the turbulent Chao Phraya River to the Bangkok side. Then, I could seek help and medication among the dense community of floating market people whose floating shops and houses built on their rafts were tied and clustered close to the river quay. If I tried, my small boat would doubtlessly capsize before reaching them.

The only thing I could do was hold Baby Pran in my arms while challenging the presence of Death.

Oh, what a storm! Its roars hushed the world. All stood under the raging sky, bowing their heads in utmost surrender to its force. The trees tossed. Then, the gust of wind and the thundering rain deafened all noises. Yet, at the height of the storm, I was surprised to hear loud footsteps along the veranda. Then, something sounded like a knock on the door.

"Who is that?"

I shouted because the rain almost drowned my voice. But I received no answer. My next-door neighbor's house was some minutes from my bungalow through thick bushes and clamps of trees. No one with a right mind would venture into the challenge of the dangerous storm. The ferocious wind could root up small trees and break strong boughs of the big ones. I tried to believe my ears were deceiving me.

A few minutes passed, and then the knocks returned, this time more persistent and rapid. I could not deny the presence of these knocking sounds any longer.

"Tell me what you want from me?" I shouted again.

There was no answer, only the sound of rain drumming outside.

I slowly opened my drawer and took out my long-kept and rust-eaten pistol. I had never touched it, let alone used it. But this time, the sight of that pistol gave me good comfort. I always put it by my side even though I could not figure out how to use it against something unknown and unseen that threatened me more and more outside.

Thunder crashed as the knock turned to the banging and then rose to the pounding. It was as if someone were using a solid log to force his way through the latched door. Pran's wailing was at its peak. His face was turning blue and the high temperature from his fever made me feel like I was holding a ball of fire in my arms. Terror gripped my heart as I looked at the baby's suffering face.

Stay with me, Pran. You can't leave me.

The pounding became so persistent and loud that I thought the door would break and fly open any minute. Reason and logic I took with me everywhere—as if they were master keys to unlock every closed door and throw light into the darkness beyond—had now apparently left me. On my own, I had to confront the anonymous force that resisted being unlocked by reason.

If I had already saved Pran's life twice, why should I surrender this time?

"I know who you are," I shouted frantically, although the thunder deadened my voice. "Go away!"

Another crash of thunder. The pounding on the door abruptly stopped. The sense of relief spread over me. But no, an instant later, I heard a loud thump on the roof as if something had fallen on it with its full force, something like a giant's footstep stomping on the roof in attempting to smash me from overhead.

I shouted again; this time, I stayed calm and more determined.

"Go away. What are you hungering for? My fear? No, I

won't let you have it to sustain your existence. If I don't feed you my fear, you will be weakened, and your malevolence will die with you."

The wind howled, and the force of the storm escalated. The sudden flash of lightning blinded me for one instant before I heard the loud strike of thunder crashing somewhere so close that the force shook the whole house in its fiercest rage. It must have been one of the trees that stood near my house.

"Go ahead. Trying to frighten me to death doesn't work. Even in life, you weren't able to harm us. How do you expect you are in death?"

Now, I knew that she alone, a mere invisible shadow, could not harm me. The only way she could was to use my fear—which she at this moment tried to create—against me to break me. She herself could not break me so much as my own fear could.

Therefore, the only means to fight her was to fight my own primal fear.

Pran was still in my cradle while the storm's fury played its role. Now, I was in a battle against some elemental and dynamic force. I fought it with the sheer force of will to save a life in my arms.

I closed my eyes and shut off my mind. Let the storm blow off my house. Let the rain flood my room. Let the whole world be drowned. Let her fury run amok. But I would sit there and make sure Pran was safe in my arms. I was used to infant squalling. It wouldn't bother me anymore.

I had to ignore her presence to remind her that she didn't exist anymore.

I might doze off amidst all the threatening sounds. And the stillness probably startled me awake. When I opened my eyes again, there was only tangible silence around me. The only sound I heard from outside was some drops of rain dripping from the eaves to the ground. The storm finally let up, and the pearl-gray radiance of dawn started to spread into the room. My eyes darted around and surprisingly found the door intact *from the unrelenting pounding. So silent, so calm it seemed unreal and distrustful.*

My first impulse was to rush to the door. I unlatched its iron hook, and yet I couldn't pry it open. The door stuck with something so heavy and solid. I forced it until the door panel was slightly ajar. As I peered through the narrow crack, I was speechless.

There, leaning against the door, was a large trunk of an old mango tree that had partially canopied the bungalow since I came in. The lightning bolt struck the tree and fell right on the veranda, breaking some parts of the wood railings and the plank steps that lead to the ground. Some broken branches and limbs scattered and piled up over the veranda floorboards and also on the ground around my bungalow. Thank goodness the tree was not large and heavy enough to collapse the bungalow.

The tree caused some damage to my house, yet I felt some strange relief. Last night, I had lost a rational thought, which was a tangible thing for my life to clamp a tight hold. I had plunged headlong into a bizarre phenomenon that the reason seemed unable to explain. I always deny such existence. Now, at least, the sight of the fallen tree brought some sense and explanation to me; it was the broken tree's branches that had raked and scratched the wall and the windows. So was the pounding from the fallen trunk that tossed and heaved back and forth against the door panel by the gust of wind.

It was so astonishing that under the unnerving and intense situation, a man's eyes and ears could deceive and disorient his mind that much.

Thank Heavens, it was not Her. It was only an act of nature.

I used the back door to carry Pran and rush to my next-door neighbor's shack, where a couple lived with their many children. The wife, Malai, had just had a new baby girl.

When she saw me at her door, she greeted me with a warm smile, showing all her solid black teeth from the habit of chewing betel nuts for so long. She wore a worn dark loincloth and a wrap around her chest. Her sun-parched skin and scrawny body showed her lifelong hard work, yet her amicable smile outshined all.

"I'm so relieved to see you. Last night, we heard the lightning crashing in your house's direction and trees falling. What a terrible, terrible storm! Oh, do you carry your baby to see me? What's wrong?" Her voice turned serious.

"My baby has fallen so sick since last night. I really needed your help or at least your advice."

"Did your wife come with you? Let me ask her about the baby's symptoms. She must know better than you."

I paused, then decided to tell her. I kept my voice as steady as I could.

"She left us about nearly a month ago. Now my baby has become sick, and I have no one to turn to."

"Oh!" She cried in surprise and stared at me before swiftly shifting her attention to Pran.

"I can tell he has a high fever from a croup," she frowned, peering at him with concern. "Don't worry. This symptom is quite common among babies. My older children had it, too, when they were so little. I have some herbs as a remedy for a croup, and I know some basic treatments. I'll boil some water until the steam comes out, and put your baby under a small canopy with the steam. It'll help him breathe more easily," then she added, "Poor, poor baby, he needs to be fed now. Um... How do you feed him now without your wife?"

"I bought cow milk for him."

She sighed. "I have a new baby too, a two-month-old girl. I have abundant milk to nurse a dozen babies all at once. It's better for him if you let me look after him for a few days until he recovers. No, he won't be any trouble to us at all. My children adore little babies. They will help watch over him."

Tears filled my eyes to see my kind-hearted neighbor take Pran from me and gently caress him in her arms. How fortunate for Pran to fall into a good hand after the recent nightmare he had gone through. Her kindness touched me deeply. Though Malai didn't slip a word, her eyes clearly reflected her wonder that the child being abandoned by its own mother was an act beyond her comprehension. Oh! If only she had known the whole truth. If only—

When I returned home, the first thing to do was to estimate the damages caused by last night's storm. It needed a lot of repair work that I couldn't handle alone. I thought of Lek. He's so good at carpentry. Since Lin Jong stayed with me, he has disappeared for good. I used to be worried and wondering, but not anymore. After I had heard the whole truth from Lin Jong. I understood he dreads to face me due to his guilt of bringing Lin Jong to ruin my life, though he has never meant to. Now, since Pran is under Malai's care, I can go to seek his whereabouts. I know some of his relatives can help me find him. When I see him again, I will tell him he doesn't need my forgiveness because whatever has happened is not his fault.

However, I have decided not to tell Lek who is Pran's real father. Let the child grow up as happy and normal as all other children. Unless something happens to me, I will let him read my journal so that he will know the truth.

As I trudged across the debris of broken branches and twigs along the veranda, I caught sight of some muddy blots that appeared along the rain-soaked floorboards. With a close look, it was the footprints to me.

I suspiciously traced those footprints one after another. They ran along the whole length of the narrow veranda that circled the house as if its owner had attempted to find every way to get inside, whether it had to crawl through a hole, a crack, or even a slit in the wall. I also found more receding footprints on the plank steps that led to the ground. They finally disappeared among the thick growth of grasses and weeds that widely spread between the house and Lin Jong's shallow grave under the tall tamarind tree yonder.

As far as I was concerned, the footprints' size and shape

were not of any animal, such as a cat or a dog, which possibly strayed to my house and sought a temporary shelter during the storm.

They were unmistakably from a human. Yet, those footprints were too small to belong to a male.

Who on earth had walked unafraid and unscathed to my house at night amid the life-threatening storm and left footprints all over the veranda floorboards as if to challenge me? Who else?

I felt A shudder as I stared at those footprints in mesmerism and shock.

At least, after the night threat, She had retreated, defeated, and gone empty-handed. I had not given her what she needed most—my fear to empower her.

But who could ever trust a creature like Her?

Pran never became healthier and stronger under Malai's care. The day I came to pick him up, I handed her some money to show my deepest gratitude, but she bluntly refused to take it.

"No! Don't do that!" she cried and frowned at me. "What are neighbors for if not giving a hand to each other in times of need? Don't worry. If Pran falls sick again, let me know. I'll be glad to help anytime."

She kept hugging and kissing him before reluctantly returning him to my arms, following with a lot of advice for infant emergency care. I knew she had doubts about my experience in looking after a new baby, let alone raising him alone until he grew up. She couldn't either read or write. Otherwise, I believed she would promptly list everything she knew about childcare on some scrap paper and hand it to me as helpful instruction.

"I know I should mind my own business," she hesitated, "but I know you can easily find someone good to be a new mother for Pran."

"Thank you. I'm sure I can take care of him myself."

I vowed never to be in a relationship with any woman again to repeat the same deadly mistake. Celibate life is a safe zone I am determined to follow to my death for my repentance of the past.

I said in finality before thanking her again and leaving her house. I felt her concerned eyes follow us until we disappeared from her sight.

As far as I knew, my neighbors were far from a well-to-do family. The couple tended an orchard and picked fruits for their wealthy landlady. I'd known who that lady must be very well, but I would never say a word to them.

During some bad years, they lived from hand to mouth. So, to pay back their kindness without hurting their pride, I gave them a hand when I felt they needed some help in their orchard. They firmly refused my help, but I insisted. I never forgot that without Malai's nursing and care, Pran would probably not survive until today.

The couple had no idea how enormously their friendship and broad sympathy meant to a solitary man who had lost all earthly things, including his family, good reputation, bright future, and most of all, the girl he loved. And the only solace to bury himself from the outside world was deep among those trees along a remote canal.

Like a hermit, I have spent my present life in this isolated place with only Malai and her husband as friends whose act of kindness not only comforts my lonesome soul but also sustains my desperate belief in a more extensive scope for the existence of virtue in human's heart.

They would never know that both of them had kept me from losing faith in humanity.

Of course, I never told them about my past. What they knew about me was what they had only seen at present. Though they never pried into my private matters, I knew they were skeptical and curious about me. No matter how I tried to keep a low profile, they sensed that I was somehow different from them and the rest of the people in this neighborhood.

I remember one afternoon, Malai dropped by, as she did occasionally, to bring Pran's favorite coconut sweet rice and slices of ripe mangoes, which she had prepared for both of us. I didn't realize I had left my bedroom door wide open, letting her catch a glimpse inside and startle at the sight of my room crammed with hundreds of books.

After some pause, she said quietly without looking at me.

"Your soft and genteel-like demeanor and all those books in your room I've seen..." she nodded to herself with more assurance. "There's a rumor that you came from some great noble family. The plot where both our dwellings have stood belongs to a landlady, a great noblewoman who owns most of the vast land along the length of the canal and beyond. Now, I'm sure I know now who you must be. You're her son..." as she whispered, she was slightly shuddering. "I will neither ask you why you live in exile nor let people in the neighborhood know your real identity. But you must keep your library door closed, my young Lord." She suddenly prostrated herself onto the floor as a serf had done to her lord. But before I would act in protest, she was already gone.

However, since that day, the couple had never mentioned that incident. They were keen enough to sense my uneasiness, embarrassment, and, of course, my agony. So, they tried to treat me as they usually did. They also tried to hide their skepticism about Pran's and my lineage since they couldn't find any resemblance between us as father and son inherently shared.

Most of all, I believed they must have some notion about Lin Jong's brazen promiscuousness, which was hard to hide from all eyes. Yet, at least Lin Jong's boldness under the neighbors' criticizing eyes became my advantage. Since her sudden disappearance, it had been apparent that no flicker of suspicion had passed through the mind of any individual in my neighborhood.

They all believed that she had run away with one of her new lovers and left me a child whose real father was still in doubt.

The more Pran grew up, the less his face resembled me. Even a swift glance at him could tell he was the spitting image of his real father. So, I would blame no one, including Malai, if they hardly believed Pran was my flesh and blood.

Yet, despite a skeleton in my closet, our heartwarming friendship grew as a few years passed. There seemed to be an unspoken rule and settlement between us. They would never ask, and I would never tell. Let the past be buried for good.

When Pran could walk, I usually brought him to visit the family and play with Pim, their youngest daughter, who was his age. As a baby, Pran often shared milk from her mother's bosom.

One day, the devastation came to this amiable family; their daughter's drowned body was found under the plank bridge in front of my bungalow. Pim was always obedient to her mother, who never allowed her to play alone near the canal's edge. So, her death remained a mystery until Pran reluctantly told me later that the girl came to ask him that day to go play over there with her as a stranger woman behind that tamarind tree asked her so.

I never told anyone what Pran had told me. Superstition ran deep in this neighborhood. I would not throw the tiny lit match to start a wildfire. I only thanked merciful Fate for sparing my son that day. I knew that he could not stay safe and sound in this place if without me.

Malai could never be the same again after her daughter's death. A few months later, the whole family moved back to their home in the countryside, leaving me more determined to find the answer to the inquiry that had been deep-seated in my mind for years.

Why them? Why do sinless people always meet the worst fate?

So far, I have spent a peaceful and content life with Pran for seven whole years. I loved to call him Baby Boy when he was little. I am desperate to believe he is Baby Boy reincarnated, not as a curse to avenge the death I had caused, but to give me my second chance for redemption. I have vowed to myself to stay celibate for my entire life, which I can make it to this day so far. Night after night, I underwent all those tormenting moments that made me toss and turn in bed so much that I couldn't help dreaming about having sexual relations with those of my women. But, I was dead set on overcoming those deadly desires that could lead me again to my doom. When Pran grows up and can care for himself, I put my mind on entering monkhood for the rest of my life. I must do that for Grace's sake, to atone for my broken promise that led to her suicide.

So far, Pran has survived his death several times. This compels me to believe that if he can survive time after time, it's too bizarre to see them as the co-incidents. He must have been born with an important message.

Hopefully, one day, if I fail the task or die early, Pran will pursue those answers for me and himself as well. This is why I have devoted myself to teaching him all spans of knowledge as much as possible. Under the same method Mr. James had used to enlighten me, I have encouraged Pran the same way to dream, to think, to doubt, and to inquire as much as I have discouraged him from blindly believing. I've prepared him for his particular pursuit in the future.

To make sense of the senselessness of this world.

Yet, most of all, I wish for him to possess what I never had: the courage to fight for one's rights.

That was the last page of his journal I had read.

I also found an envelope inserted between the leaves of the journal. It was a note he had written to Lek.

Lek, my best friend,

Whatever I wrote, please never let Pran know. The last thing I want is to ruin his mother's image I created for him. I want him to remember and carry his mother's perfect image to comfort him through his difficult time. I must admit that I borrowed Grace's image to create the perfect mother for him. It is just a slight fabrication that I don't think will harm him. On the contrary, if he knows the truth about his own mother's morbid and uncanny cruelty, I'm afraid he might shatter into pieces.

Pran is a reason I decided to go on after losing what seems more worthy than my own life. I always imagine that if I had had to endure my agony alone without Pran, I might have chosen my solution: to follow Grace to our secret sanctuary—that human-less and timeless isle where I know she has been waiting for me to join her. Or had I had a child of my own flesh and blood, I was certain I couldn't have loved him as profoundly as I felt toward Pran. Sometimes, I wonder if I turn out to be a doting father who pampers him too much and hence weakens him—just like my own mother had done to me out of her staggering love. However, besides being a thoughtful and enthusiastic child, Pran has shown me he has a trait of toughness, which he fortunately inherits from his real father.

Of all the calamities Lin Jong had created in my life, there is ironically one thing I genuinely feel thankful to her. I am grateful that, after all, the child who was conceived in her womb is not my flesh and blood. I don't want to bring out another gullible and defenseless human into this world if he has to carry on my unfinished task in pursuing the hardest mission—to make sense of the senselessness in this world.

If I lose my life before Pran reaches his legal age, I ask you to bring him under the care of my sister Rumpai, together with my letter to her that I kept together with this one. Hopefully, she will remain the only one of all my flesh and blood who still cares for me. At least with my savings in the bank and my sister as his legal guardian, he will have a decent life and good education without me. Promise me you will watch over him. If someday he feels life turns out to be unendurable to him, tell him to carry on for my sake.

*After reading all these, I am confident you must understand
why you are the one I ask to protect him for me. I don't think it
is necessary to tell you Pran is not my son but yours. (I am sure
you must read my journey before this letter.) But, please, let this
truth be buried deepest in our hearts forever.*

For the sake of our son.

The last I found was another letter neatly folded. The glance
on those willowy handwritings rendered right away who wrote
it must be a female.

According to Lek, this must be Grace's letter to my father
after they started their secretive, intimate relationship. My father
had saved her soulful letter until his last day. I believe he must
have a plan to show this letter to her again after their many years
of marriage to prove his never-changing love for her.

But that day never arrived because my birth had come to
separate them forever.

Lek came to see me the next day and found I'd already read
the rest of that journal. He tried to detect how I felt but found
only a void expression on my stone face.

Finally, he told me with his grave face that there was also
another episode I should know—to bring justice to all, including
the opposite side who stood against me.

I just stared at him without any words but complied to listen.

…Lek began to tell me it happened when I was only a few
months old. My father finally found where Lek was living and
came to meet him. He felt so overwhelmed with guilt he could
not see my father face to face anymore after the family had
found out my father had a relationship with Lin Jong and got
her pregnant. So, Lek made himself disappear from my father's
life. He wept like a child after he'd known my father never
blamed him for causing his doomed life. He briefly told Lek

that Lin Jong left him after she'd given birth to me. And that was all Lek was acknowledged. A lot was left untold.

My father also asked Lek to bring him to see his mother regardless of his old man's wrath if the old lord knew the son he had disowned dared to set foot in his place again. My father agonized over his mother's mental collapse, which he blamed himself for, and therefore yearned to make atonement. Lek tried to find that chance for him, and it finally came when the lord went to spend a few days in the wild for game hunting, which was his favorite.

That night, after my father left me with Malai, his neighbor, they sneaked into the entrance hall of the building and went upstairs, straight to his mother's wing, where she was confined inside her room with no one from outside being allowed to visit due to her mental illness. Lek said he would never forget that night. Whenever his memory flashed back to that scene, it still moved him deeply as if it occurred just yesterday.

It was the first time he had seen the grand lady since my father left that house. There she reclined on her bed, as stiff and cold as a slab of stone, her eyes a pair of voids, her cheeks sunken and her face worn beyond recognition, her fragile, aged body stooping as if it was unable to withstand the crushing weight of distress she had long carried in her life. She was in her mid-sixties but looked so aging that the word ancient had crossed his mind. There's nothing left to trace the grandeur she once carried as a legendary beauty of her era.

The poor lady lay silent, lifeless, and remote under the watchful eyes of three maids surrounding her. Her only move-ment came from her hand; she was untiringly rocking a small wooden crib set not far from her, rocking it back and forth, back and forth, with the same slow rhythm while her parched lips moved a little as if silently crooning a lullaby to that empty crib. She was slipping away from the very present moment. Time to her had stopped entirely at one particular moment of the past, the crucial moment when terror seized and imprisoned her mental soundness perpetually inside its wall.

They said the instant she knew about Lin Jong's pregnancy with a child assumed to belong to her son, she collapsed on the floor, attacked by a seizure that permanently shattered her sanity. The enormous weight of that terror must press down all her awareness of things to the bottom of her consciousness. It was stuck there, too deep and too dark to emerge again to a glimpse of reality.

It was the most shocking sight for Lek, let alone what my father must have felt as he entered her room. Of course, the instant his eyes fell on that crib, his earliest memory must be stirred. He must recall himself snuggling up inside that crib as a toddler boy, and whenever he awoke and began to wail, he would always find the familiar face of his mother bending down, beaming at him as she pulled him tenderly into her arms. And I believe he must remember that, after all these years, after he had outgrown that crib and walked into manhood, his mother kept his crib close to her and in perfect condition at one corner of her bedroom. And that must be the reason he couldn't hold his tears and didn't bother keeping them from running down his face when he approached her.

Mother...

His voice strangled out as a whisper. Yet, he meant to utter it aloud, to get all her attention. Oh, when his mother turned her head to the direction of his voice and her eyes met his, she opened her mouth in a gasp, and with a long, heartbroken wail as if she were a lost little child herself, she cried out.

Come, come here.

She beckoned him in tears, her vacant eyes gazing at his face as she implored.

Young man, haven't you seen my baby? Someone took my baby. Someone stole him. Help me find him, please...

Lek remembered my father's face transformed before his eyes. He gasped in disbelief. And yet, in a flash, as her eyes fixed on his face, the heart-wrenching wail abruptly changed into a scream while she pointed her trembling finger at him in extreme excitement. A dull blankness suddenly disappeared. A flash of recognition sparkled in her wide-open eyes instead.

Oh, I remember you now, she shrieked. *You! It's you! I saw you sneak into this room the other day and snatch my baby from this crib. You monster! You evil! Give Baby Beloved back!*

Then she swiftly turned to the stunned women sitting by her and yelled.

Catch him at once. Hurry up.

Her scream reached the top of her voice as my father, this time, stood paralyzed in complete shock.

Mother, I'm that baby you're looking for. I'm Beloved. He told her almost in a shout. *Mother, look at me; take a good look at me. Don't you recognize me?*

But he could see it plain on her face that his words didn't register in her consciousness.

And before anyone could stop her, she got up and jumped at my father, both her hands clutching his neck, trying to choke him with all the enormous strength of an insane woman, choking him for stealing from her a baby more worthy than life itself.

Everyone, all her servants and even Lek rushed to pull her away from him, and yet she struggled fiercely with all her strength to set herself free from all the hands holding her. After her hands had been bound, she tried another attack by snapping him with her teeth. When her bite narrowly missed his neck, she howled and snarled in fury. Frail and feeble as she looked, her outburst of violence was so savage and frightening, her dull and vacant eyes now ablaze with all the hatred of the entire world toward him whom she accused as the one who had stolen her little darling Beloved.

And there she was. His sister Rumpai burst into the room an instant after she heard her mother's hysterical screams. Behind her was Nanny Sook, who suddenly and completely lost herself when she saw him and darted toward Beloved while bursting into wild sobbing. *Khun Tan, my little precious.* Beloved's hands began reaching out to his old nanny like being spellbound, his trembling lips whispering *Nanny, Nanny,* but Lady Rumpai had grabbed his nanny in time before she squeezed him into her arms.

Lady Rumpai stared hard at her brother for one long minute. When she began to speak, what she'd said seemed to shrink him.

Beloved, go away. Now, you see with your own eyes what you've already done to your mother. Do you come just to torture her more? Aren't you satisfied enough?

His sister stood guarding her mother, who, after the sudden erupt of her intense rage, collapsed in her daughter's arms and was hurriedly carried to her bed to recover. The poor lady now lay exhausted, grasping for a breath while her daughter stroked her and with her cajoling voice, whispered some words in her ears, some specific words that were able to calm her down like a miracle. Perhaps Rumpai used this tactic every time a hysterical outburst happened.

Mother, I have the good news. Someone has found Baby Beloved. He will return to you by tomorrow. I promise. Yes, I promise. But... her voice became more assertive as if talking to a stubborn and disobedient child. *If you don't rest and don't have a good sleep now, I won't let you see him. No, I won't.*

Instantly, his mother stopped whimpering. Her face suddenly lit up. Her whole body trembled from that miraculous good news. She completely forgot that her daughter had repeatedly used that old tactic to calm her down, but luckily, she couldn't remember even once.

So, she opened her smile through the streaks of tears before jerkily forcing her eyelids to close as if she were so afraid it was not fast enough and they wouldn't let her see her baby when tomorrow came. But, again, suddenly, her eyes opened wide anxiously.

Promise to wake me right away when he shows up tomorrow...

please

In her small voice, her hand clutched her daughter for that promise, and as soon as she saw vigorous nods of assurance, the old lady hurriedly and eagerly went back to her sleep.

Within minutes, sleep overtook her, and peace returned to that room. Rumpai tucked a soft satin throw for her mother before turning to confront her brother, her eyes glowing with rage.

Just go! Go, or I'm going to call some men-servants now!

My father went down on his knees, hanging his head and begging her, strangled sobs torn from his throat.

Rumpai, I'm so sorry, so-so sorry. I miss Mother. I really do. That's the only reason I came. Don't make me go away from her now, please...

Perhaps his agony moved her. His sister observed him quietly for a moment, and then she began to tell him in her more subdued voice.

No need to come back anymore, Beloved. Since you left, Mother has never recognized anyone, neither our father nor any of her children. And now it's heartbreaking to know she didn't even recognize you, the one who has taken up the entire room in her heart since you were born. The rest of her memory is now gone. What remained was only a speck of reminiscence. Of course, she still remembers you; nothing can deprive her of that memory. But it is only a fraction of the memory about you as a little baby back then. And the worst is, whereas most of her memories are gone, her passion, the whole array of her emotions, not only stays but also intensifies many times as it points to one sole direction and targets only that small fragment of her memory of you. Now, her only awareness in her life is that her baby Beloved is missing. Someone has kidnapped him. And she will move heaven and earth to find her little one.

Rumpai paused, struggling with her strangled sobs.

Now, we have to watch her night and day. A few months ago, one of the servants found her at the front gate, attempting to break it open. That happened in the dead of the night. Though she's insane, she's far from being stupid. She can fake her sleep to fool us, then sneak out of her room. After what had happened, Father had to lock her up in this room because otherwise, she would run out into the street to search for you whenever she had a chance.

Rumpai burst into tears and dashed to pull him in for a crushing hug.

Sister and brother then wept together for the life they found had gone terribly wrong while Nanny Sook, crouching nearby, wrapped her arms around his legs and was shaken with her wails at the top of her lungs.

And what Rumpai was lamenting almost broke Lek.

Oh, my baby brother, I blame myself for what happened to you. If only I had come back earlier from Grandpa's house that day and could have saved you before you wandered into the concubine quarters and came upon that evil woman. Oh, If only...

Late that night, after my father had left, leaving his nanny to almost shatter in pieces, his mother died peacefully, almost serenely, in her sleep. Lek was the one who brought that news to him the following day. But he never had a chance to be at her funeral because his father forbade him to attend. Someone, probably one of his half-siblings, out of his spiteful purpose, had told the old lord that his outcast son sneaked himself to see his mother that night. The lord outrageously condemned Beloved for causing his mother's emotional outburst, which he claimed led to her death.

And since his mother's death, his father ordered everyone to treat Beloved as if he were long dead from his family and never again to mention his name to the old lord. The lord was worn in black to his last day, mourning for his dead wife and mourning for his living son, whom he treated as dead from his life. Lek knew somehow, that Lady Rumpai tried in secret to get in touch with her brother and to help him with her own lump-sum money to get back on his feet, but it was also in vain. Her little brother never replied to her letters. He just disappeared from her life until she received the news of his death. Poor sister...

I clenched my jaws to force back my tears until it hurt me when the story was completed.

"When he was young, Beloved was very close to his sister. He always climbed onto her lap, and she would tirelessly read story books for him. He learned how to read from her even before he started school. I know how much he missed his sister. But he didn't want her to get into trouble caused by their father's rage."

Then Lek smiled at me.

"Your father refused her money. He'd rather live on his pride."

"The old lady's suffering breaks my heart," I blinked my tears away.

"Don't feel sorry for her, Pran. You overlook one crucial fact. She didn't die in suffering as she was at almost every moment when she had been alive. She died peacefully, holding fast to her blissful hope that when tomorrow came, she would hold her baby son once again in her arms," he sighed. "If I can choose how to die, I want to die embracing my hope, just like her."

"Probably you're right," I said feebly.

"I'm certain that if she hadn't suffered a breakdown that shattered her memory into pieces, she'd never have left her son to struggle with that fate. Never. She would have supported him one way or another with all the money of her own, even though it was against her husband's will. She wouldn't have cared, I'm sure. Her family is extremely wealthy; some said even wealthier than the lords... The vast land in the Old Capital, including the one where you once lived, is all her family's estate," his voice eventually became incoherent and more like a babble. I could tell by his outburst Lek still devoted every ounce of his being to my father.

"She would have never let the old lord's grudge ruin their son...as...as it turned out that way. What a miserable, old tyrant."

"No, Lek. Maybe we're wrong." My disagreement surprised both Lek and myself, so he let me continue.

"The old lord must love him as much as his wife did, or perhaps more. It's just because he was never prepared for the worst. Remember his heart stopped instantly after he'd looked close at my face? His frail heart couldn't take the pain when he realized Lin Jong had taken revenge on him by tricking his most beloved and prized son into her trap to ruin him. And my... plebeian blood that stamps on my face was...her last laugh over everyone."

At that particular moment, it was clear to me why poor Lady Rumpai could not give me her love and affection, not to mention Nanny Sook's cruel and sick treatment while I stayed under her roof. Maybe it wasn't all their fault. Born Lin Jong's flesh and blood, I understood now I deserved their ultimate hatred.

"But despite her suffering from her brother's doomed life that makes her shift all her hatred to you, I agree that Lady Rumpai is fair enough to take you into her care and support you with her own money for years and at least waited until you were able to be on your own and then let you go. I always thought she was so heartless to you, but I realize I might be wrong. If she has no heart as she seems, she must let you go hungry on the street, or send you to some orphanage house from the beginning and no one ever blames her for that."

My throat started to swell at Lek's new remark on Lady Rumpai: "I brought up Beloved's mother's death because I hope it can help us forgive everyone who played a part. To begin with, those grudges will never start if there isn't any cause to ignite them."

"Lek," something was crossing my mind that bothered me

for so many years. "I went to my neighborhood school when I was young. The woman teacher who owned that school was well off and respected in my neighborhood. Her name was Riam. Do you know anything about her?"

"Riam?" Lek frowned, then slowly nodded. "I believe she's Lady Pearl's distant cousin who helps oversee the lady's property in that Old Capital area. Why?"

His answer shed light on my long puzzle.

"She treated me very, very badly. Now I know why. My father might not initially know she was his mother's distant relative, and she must know about the lady's mental breakdown. Otherwise, he would never think of bringing me to her school."

"Now, you understand her motive."

In a quiet defeat, I put my hands to cover my face.

"Why! I come into Papa's life only to be his curse…"

"Remember your father's letter? He wrote to me that you are his deliverance for his sin of causing Baby Boy's death."

`"If I am truly his deliverance," I met his eyes, "Of all people who suffered because of me, why did he get the worst? Hadn't I been born, imagine how his life would have changed. But I popped up in his life only to destroy all his loved ones, particularly his fiancée. I even caused his father a heart attack when he came to his son's funeral and saw my face for the first time. His stare at me just before he died still haunts me to this day. Oh, he must know right away I am not his flesh and blood. Without me, Papa would have become someone of great success, not the one who died from snakebite in a small boat like a deplorable beggar. He is dead because of me also, Lek. Oh my, I'm a curse even to myself,"

This time, Lek was silent. It was a bare fact no one could deny. But finally, he replied,

"No, Pran, whatever made his life go wrong, you are not the cause."

He turned silent again. It took him a moment to continue.

"You are only the last consequence of the unspeakable act

my aunt Sook had done to your father in the first place. His mother was never aware that the nanny she gave her son into care for so long and in full trust had something twisted inside her mind. Her over possessiveness of Beloved since he was a small boy in her care pushed her capable of committing all the unthinkable to *own* him."

I knew. I knew this one would finally be brought to light. It was only a matter of time before Lek's guilt compelled him to open his mouth and discuss it. But I understood him; after all, Nanny Sook was his aunt who had raised him.

"She made him engrossed in sex since he was no more than fourteen. She'd kept feeding him with it in his bed for years. It opened the door for Lin Jong to come to exploit what his nanny had already planted in his groin since his adolescent years."

Hardly anything could surprise me anymore at this cesspool of libido that one naïve lad was driven head-on by hand after hand into its pitch-dark bottomless.

Lek went on but without glancing at me.

"Since he was a small child, Beloved was very close to his nanny. He needed only his nanny when he was scared. Everyone knew about their unusual attachment, though they never knew what'd led to it. Besides, everyone wanted to stay out of trouble rather than poking their nose into it."

He gulped. His voice started trailing off.

"When he was no more than fourteen, I once came to his bedroom to clean up. Usually, no one was there in the late morning. But when I carefully pushed the door ajar, I saw my aunt was mounting him on his bed in broad daylight while he was whimpering softly. So damn lucky she turned her back on the door where I stood in utter shock. They were into it with all the heated ardor that the breakfast on the tray she'd brought for him was left untouched and cold. That sight repulsed me as if watching a starving she-boa opening its large, drooling mouth while its beady eyes were hypnotizing the prey, a little puppy, to stay stiff and paralyzed before swallowing that puppy into its enormous body in whole. I fled right away, all shaken, and never cracked a word to anyone. And even though I did, no one, not even his mother, would believe what I had witnessed in that room. Poor Lady Pearl always believed it was good for her son to have his nanny stay with him at nighttime so she could always watch over him. The lady seemed unaware of her son's coming of age. Yes, in a mother's eyes, her child is still a little child forever."

Lek sighed heavily.

"Normally, no one could escape the lady's sharp and scrutinizing eyes. But she mostly used it to watch and find fault in her husband's other women and hence overlooked those she trusted. That's why what happened inside her son's bedroom went unnoticed for years. And…I felt too afraid to tell anyone, mostly to the lady herself."

"Your aunt would surely get you into big trouble if you let anyone know. But why did my father never tell his mother that his nanny had…sexually abused him? Sorry, I used that severe term to describe her act because it happened without his consent. But his silence encouraged her to dominate him even under his mother's nose. Why didn't he do something to defend himself?"

"I understand him, Pran. He was born with a bleeding heart. Remember that? Incapable of hurting even the one who harmed him. His feelings toward his nanny were mixed between affection and fear in equal intensity. To him, since he was so young, she had been his motherly figure, second only to his own mother. So, he only kept it quiet to save her ass. And she took his soft spot to her advantage…

" However, when he couldn't keep that shameful secret inside him anymore, he eventually let me know about his long, morbid relationship with his nanny that went on steadily even after he'd met Grace. He told me that marrying Grace would be his best chance to cut himself from his nanny. Yet, that intention to free himself was shaken whenever she hysterically threatened to harm herself if he didn't take her to live with him no matter where. She knew she was always on the upper hand because that threat disarmed him when she brought it up. So, when the wedding was planned, Lady Pearl, who trusted the nanny for her relentless devotion to her son, agreed to bring in his nanny to care for him after he'd married Grace....

"Of course, my aunt had never been more rejoiced for the chance to possess him for life. She knew it wasn't hard to keep Grace under her control as she already had her dominance over Beloved. Although Grace never understood why her fiancé cared for his nanny that much, that tender-hearted girl would comply with any of his requests. His nanny even demanded that although she would stay in her place as his nanny to keep their true relationship in disguise, once behind everyone's back, she would reclaim her place in his bed no less than Grace would have from him. However, while confronting that dilemma, Fate played the most ironic role in sending Lin Jong to be his salvage. She popped up into his life out of the blue to snatch him from my aunt and left her with a loss so severe she had never recovered from that bereavement."

"When I moved to stay under her roof," I said. "I was bewildered to see faces of my father at different ages everywhere in her house, from the infant to the young man," then I couldn't help shuddering. "Once, I even caught her tiptoeing into that living room. Her eyes began to linger on each of his pictures. Suddenly, she collapsed on the floor and burst into wild, loud sobbing. I'd never thought of finding her in that hysterical act, which really crept me out."

"Crept you out? Now, listen to this. I never slip a word to anyone. At that time, my aunt was no less than forty but robust for her age. So, I wondered why she often took some rare herb and sustained the bad abdominal pain that'd caused her to stay bedridden for days. I knew that because I had to look for that herb in medicine shops whenever she needed it. She threatened me not to tell anyone or otherwise. Can you guess what that thing is for?"

I chose to silence.

"I asked the shop owner what this medicine herb was for. He hesitated and asked me who wanted it, but I didn't tell him. However, he told me it was used for eliminating the unborn conceived in secret."

This time, I couldn't help uttering a cry with a long gasp.

"Had...had he ever known it?"

"I'm sure she would never let him know. She knew he couldn't take it, and he would stop their deviated relationship. No, she couldn't bear to lose him. I believe Beloved had never pictured his nanny as a woman; she was only a nanny to him on his mind, and that's why he was oblivious to the consequence after they had been in bed together several times..." Then, he sighed. "How twisting a life can be. He'd sacrificed everything to save a child who was not his, but he had never been aware that his own never had a chance to be born. I bought the herbs for her not only once. One time, she asked me to double the intake..."

"Oh my!"

"She let it stay too long... I guess she wanted to keep it until the time it was due but later feared the consequences she must face. I vowed I would never open my mouth to tell him about this. I could never hurt him more than I've already done."

"She's sick... How could someone sleep with the boy she nursed and raised as if her own?" I was shuddering, "it's almost as sick as an incest,"

"She is, of course," he nodded. "What she'd done to him was too sickening to take as normal."

Several years had passed since I left the nanny's house, but her image as a respected, intimidating matron had been etched into my mind. It was hard to erase that image and think otherwise of her.

"Nothing seems as it appears. And...no one is what he seems to be."

"Accept that. You, me...we all are parts of this heinous, dark thing. Yet, so sick as my aunt is, she can't match with Ling Jong. What she had done to Beloved was out of love, although that love went off the scale into sheer madness. But, in Lin Jong's case, she was incapable of loving any soul even him. So, all she had done to Beloved was contrary to love, driven by pure malice. That is the big difference between the two women who both ruined Beloved's life in almost equal measure."

There was another long silence between us before Lek said in his subdued voice.

"If you still believe you are a curse to your father, I must be part of this curse too…" he turned his face away, "…because I beget you."

Lek then slowly stood up,

"All right, Pran, curse or not, to be Beloved's son, this alone can outshine all."

End of part two

Part Three: The Stalker

Part 3: Chapter 1

Come & Go Lucky

*A*fter completing the whole journal, I destroyed it *immediately as if that thing had never existed. While watching the flames licking at all the pages into ashes, I made myself forgive every person mentioned in that journal, and in return, I wished them to forgive me for my being born, which I didn't deserve from the beginning.*

But there were the two I could not forgive and never could. The first was the woman who gave birth to me.

Never did she deem me as another human being, not to mention as a child she gave life to, but a mere object used for causing malevolence to all humans who crossed her path, which, in turn, made me a target of hatred from all those affected. I couldn't help but feel grateful to my father for putting her out of the face of the earth forever. She truly deserved to be dumped into her grave like a carcass and left to rot.

Yet apart from her, there was another one I loathed in the same extreme. And it was even worse because he lived within me and breathing my breath. As much as I couldn't forgive Ling Jong, I also couldn't forgive myself.

From that day forward, I sank deeper into alcohol's toxic spell, using it to cocoon myself in oblivion—escaping my past, present, and future—as my only way to prevent mental collapse from my overwhelming self-abhorrence. The liquor never failed me in these hours of need.

Usually, after drinking myself to sleep, my childhood nightmare would return: a female figure wrapped in white, banging on my door and screaming *Let me in, let me in, Pran! This time, you can't escape me!* It was so real that her screams still echoed even after I'd jerked open my eyes. I knew *who* she was now. That made the nightmare more nightmarish than when I was just a boy who had no clue about this walking bundle.

Also, I have always dreamed of a mysterious woman in a yellow skirt. In the dream, I found her coming towards me, an eight-year-old boy then who was waiting for her on the sidewalk with all his crushing hope. As instantly as I saw her stop in front of me in plain sight, I jumped on her, crying to myself I would never again let her leave me. She looked so happy to see me while pulling me into her arms. *Poor boy, have you been waiting for me right here all the time? Never mind, I came to bring you to stay with me forever...* Then she handed me a bag she brought with her and opened a smile, that unforgettable smile I'd been yearning for all those years. *I got you this. Oo-o, Look! look what's inside the bag.* She urged me excitedly. So, in one instant, I put my hand inside that bag with all my blissful joy. In a flash, I felt a sharp sting on my hand.

I howled with sudden pain, realizing in terror that that something wriggling and hissing in the bag had bitten me. While I was howling in pain, she drew me into her chest and whispered. *Do you want me to take you with me? If so, it's time to go now, my sweet boy. But because I have no life, I can't bring you with me alive.* Then her smile slowly dissolved into a smirk of a dark shadowed figure of a stranger, a man so unknown yet so familiar as if I always saw his face daily among the sea of people coming and going everywhere, only that I must walk past him and did not notice his presence that was just as close as my arm's length.

After the loss of my father, I still had some strength left to pull myself together and get through all of my ordeals, but this time, I couldn't even drag myself to face the sun outside, and therefore, I started to be absent from my school and my job. I found no meaning left for me to go on with whatever awaited me in the future.

How could any meaning be left to me after finding the man who meant the world to me was not my father and the mother whom I had searched for my entire life turned out to be a she-monster whose single mind centered only on ending my life in cold blood? She would have succeeded if the man who meant the world to me had not risked his life to save me, strangling her to death in time.

Now, the fragile link to sanity I had clung to for so long was snapped, sending me freefall into the bottomless void.

During the following years, my life went to pieces as a result of alcoholism. I was fired from my job and expelled from law school. Hadn't Lek come and dragged me back to his dingy place with meals to eat and shelter to sleep in, I could have ended up my life as a street bum and got killed by some gangsters and hooligans in that area. Lek could have never imagined my father's miseries would affect my life so profoundly that I let go of my entire future. He must have felt responsible for what I'd become as he was the one who first handed me that journal.

Losing my father once, Lek couldn't afford to lose me. He might believe at least it was better for the time being to indulge me in my drinking habit as my only means to escape than witnessing me commit the worst to flee this world. Though he hardly believed in praying, he began doing so every night after taking me in, hoping to bring back the person I used to be.

The place that became my refuge stood on the street corner near the alley where I lived. I came daily to 'celebrate life,' aloof and alone, at this shabby noodle shop, where everything you asked, from coffee to street foods to liquors, was served.

To attract more customers in the neighborhood, one small corner of this store was now converted into a partly convenient store where you could come in urgently through the night until the next morning and ask for items such as first-aid kits, cold medicines, cough drops, matches, soap, toothbrushes, and cigarettes, all stacked in order on the shelves against the wall. Even lottery tickets were available here so that you could flirt with your luck. Besides liquor, lotteries are the best-selling items.

Before entering that shop, you might look up and notice a big rectangle sign at the top of the door frame: *Ma Dee Pai Dee*. As they believed, the auspicious name literally meant *Come & Go Lucky*. It was also where most regulars—truck and tricycle riders and construction and labor workers—hung out and spent their meager and hard-earned wages on their drink.

The shop, worn and run-down as it seemed to passers-by, became their comfort, a momentary sanctuary. With some drops of the elixir of life pouring down their throat from a bottle of cheap rice whisky, they felt an instant and magical transformation. They felt love and joy, the rarest of all things they possess, radiating from their pores and wrapping them like a warm security blanket, and they snuggled in their own mother's arms. But they knew they could not cling to their "happy hours" forever. Soon, they had to get up, pay the money, totter out, and disappear into their own bleak reality waiting for them out there.

Now you finally understood why I'd become a drunk and suicidal man obsessed with hatred and bitterness, as if I were perpetually wearing an utterly dark pair of lenses that never let me tell day from night except stark grayness. Night after night, the regular customers in that shop always spotted me sitting alone, aloof, and quietly on the same table at the same corner, doing the very same thing—getting drunk and, in between, making some noise like babbling to myself.

On some of my worst days, when I was utterly lost, I would sit so still, my vacant eyes staring at the blank wall opposite me in silence. Whoever saw me must have wondered if anyone put a dummy in that corner. I would blink back my tears or accidentally knock over my glass and spill my drink on my table. Sometimes, I startled them a little when they, all of a sudden, saw me weep so bitterly, like a child crying his heart out for an unspeakable loss, lamenting over his own lifeless, lonely life. This led them to the opportunity on their day off from work to start a delicious gossip and then end up in a betting game.

This incident occurred a few weeks ago, and it shows how miserable I looked in the eyes of others. One group of four was drinking and clustering around a table opposite mine.

Hey, we're going to ask him downright what the hell is troubling him. But before that let's bet.

One of the groups stole a curious glance at me and whispered, which unfortunately came out loud enough to eavesdrop because he seemed on the brink of being drunk himself.

Whoever guesses closest will get the bottle of whisky we all chip in. Deal? Let's flip a coin and see who will be the first. If the head turns up it's your turn first, if the tail, mine.

These thrill-starving truck drivers, construction workers, factory men, and so forth could always look for anything within their sight and reach and turn any of those into a thing for gambling away the heavy boredom that always hung over their monotonous and struggling lives. They can gamble on any topic, sports, games, events, politics, and people: from boxing to cocks and fighting fish to the new prime minister and even to the color of the outfit the next woman walking past them was wearing and so on. (If their being drunk is at its peak, it can be changed easily to the color of her underwear in place of her outfit.) They would turn to one another if they ran out of ideas for things to bet on, which was very rare. One of them could figure it out and shouted excitedly, let's see who can withstand the drink and become the last one to get drunk. And now, they were turning their focus on the topic of what caused another human being his great suffering. It was a very creative and interesting bet.

A breakdown from a loss in his family, I bet—definitely a tragic and grisly death.

Number One started the game.

To get to the point, I believe it must be the death of his wife. He doesn't look old. Twenty-five? Twenty-six, maybe? So, he couldn't get over it. Bet a truck has just run over her, poor thing. May she rest in peace.

It was Number Two who helped add more vivid and gruesome details. He was nodding his head vigorously in full conviction.

Good guess. But don't you want to know who was driving that damn truck?

The voice of Number Three was booming. He showed his gleeful grin as if he were holding a secret waiting for the right moment to unfold.

I'm telling you now. It must be him. I can't find anyone else accountable for her death.

His smile broadened as he noticed his remark, making every pair of eyes widen.

You mean it's just a clumsy accident, don't you?

Number One narrowed his eyes suspiciously as if he were secretly expecting the opposite.

Stupid, don't you see at all it isn't an accident? No, no. Not an experienced truck driver like him.

Number Three lowered his voice, looking more serious, excited, and sordid. He obviously enjoyed being the center of all the attention from his group.

If so, why does he look so distraught? Look! He's just a piece of wretch—a walking bottle of whisky himself.

Number Two, the group's youngest and probably the most naïve one, still asked doubtfully.

Why not? He's not suffering at all, young man. That's from his overjoy because, finally, he could get rid of his bitchy wife. She always raised all kinds of hell on him. So, what he's doing at that table at this moment is celebrating his wife's death plus his own brand-new life.

Number Three guffawed at the end of the sentence before continuing happily.

Poor guy, he never realizes that he's over-celebrating it. He's drinking himself to his own death now. Ha! Ha! All the twists and turns behind such a story. Now, who wants to bet on this? An accident or a murder, anyone?

Having a great deal of fun and expecting more to come, they all laughed, roaring.

One of them, apparently the most drunk of all, even went further.

Let's forget about the bet. Now, I'm dying to know what's wrong with this man. Isn't he an eye soar whenever we step in, and there he is, again and again, drinking in front of us? It's as if he were practically living in this shop. Let's move over to join him at his table and squeeze the juicy truth from his mouth once and for all. All four against one.

Suddenly, Number Four, the oldest one, who seemed the soberest and rarely joined this conversation, hushed the rest with a warning and reproaching tone.

Why does no one think this man's just plain crazy? A cuckoo? Just look at his bloodshot eyes on his face closely, and you'll tell yourself you want to stay at least a hundred yards away from him.

He dropped his voice as if he were telling a hair-raising story, and now frightened looks were spreading all over everyone's faces.

Don't you think he might have a pistol in his pocket and give us a killing spree just in one instant and for no reason? Stop sticking out your neck into trouble. Do you listen to me? Just leave him alone.

I felt so thankful for Number Four, even grateful for the serious warning he gave to all of them. At least my alleged blood-thirsty craziness rescued me from those thrill-starving men visiting this place.

After a few weeks of this incident had passed, they still came to hang out at this place and, as normally, saw me drinking alone at the same corner. Fortunately, they no longer paid me any attention because they might believe I was beyond all help and hope. Imagine a dull and dusty piece of old furniture in the room that no one any longer noticed its color and shape, let alone its presence.

All I wanted, while drinking my life away with no one bothering me, was to brood over most parts of my life, the parts I desperately wanted to wipe out from the face of my own existence.

This rice and liquor shop stood plain and humble, yet it exuded a warm glow of hospitality at the corner of a run-down street by the riverfront. It entirely viewed a new, massive, modern bridge over the broad river beyond. On the other side of the river stood the Old Capital town, where the Temple of Dawn's lofty pagoda rose, towering over the sky by the river's bank. Whenever I saw it, the memory of that particular day flashed and choked my throat. It was the day my father and I crossed the ferry and watched the pagoda backdrop with the beautiful sunset sky, and that also was the day he died.

Nearby the footbridge, where the trams ran leisurely along their track on the street side, with a bell clanging, signaling their arrival to passengers, there was a dark and long dirty alley leading to an open market that started to be very busy and active at the crack of dawn as soon as the first pale pink and golden streaks appeared on the eastern sky.

There, one could find any edible animals one could ever imagine available early in the morning—some were still breathing and alive. Very few people wanted lifeless, dead meat, no matter how fresh they looked, for cooking their everyday meals. The shoppers would stroll along the market site looking to quench their cravings. The fish were gasping desperately for the air inside pails with too little volume of water to sustain their life; chickens and ducks still pecking insects which they could find on the ground inside bamboo coups; snakes coiling and writhing inside cages; frogs and toads jumping and leaping around in big plastic basins completely unaware of their impending doom; and a swarm of small worms wriggling and crawling up the tubs ready for being turned into the deep-fried delicacy.

Once an unlucky fowl was picked, with an approving nod from a buyer, it was swiftly grabbed onto a solid wooden board by the earnestly grinning butcher. In a lightning flash, before the poor thing had any chance to squeak and squawk, its throat would be slit—alive—with a huge sharp cleaver, its head chopped off, and its legs split apart. Its belly would be ripped open, and its red, soft, fleshy innards—a still throbbing heart, a bloody liver, a spleen, lungs, a stomach, a ribbon of intestine and colon—all would be pulled out and cleaned for delicious cooking. Their dripping fresh blood would be drained to the last drop and poured into the liquor mixed with some herbs as a local medicine if it was the snake's blood or hard-boiled if it was the blood of chicken and duck.

Sometimes, I felt as if I came to visit a slaughterhouse.

On some summer mornings before the monsoon carried in the first torrent of rain, if one was lucky enough, one could have a better chance to buy one of the rarest and most seasonal pricy delicacies considered caviars of the East— the red ants' larvae. A handful of them piled on a banana leaf would cost more than a big chunk of red and white meat.

A hunter had to painstakingly climb up to the treetop so dense with deep green foliage, risking his fall if the limb on which he was stepping snapped and facing the fierce attack from the army of thousands upon thousands of red ants. Their burning acid bites on a human's soft flesh could send any mortal man a loud howl of pain. Once a nest caught his eyes, the hunter started using a long-handle fruit picker, long enough to provide a safe distance, to yank out the ants' leafy ball of nest well hidden behind dense foliage until it dropped to the ground below. After drowning all the little creatures in a pail full of water, the precious translucent white maggot-like larvae, each the size of a mung bean, were carefully scooped up and ready for a good sale.

Along the row of small stalls, there were also varieties of snacks for nibbling: charcoal-grilled squids and beef balls dipped in sweet and hot sauce, sour pork sausages, and spicy papaya salad. The best sale always fell to crunchy and tasty golden deep-fried thumb-sized locusts—perhaps the by-product of farm plants' mass pesticide. Their taste was claimed by so many that shrimp would pale by comparison.

I couldn't agree more with hearsay that men's bellies were the biggest graveyard where all sorts of living things were buried; just named it.

All activities in this open market usually lasted a few hours and died out as soon as the sun passed its zenith. Until the following morning, the bustling area would be dead. All kaleidoscopic sight, smell, and lively sound were gone. What was left remained dirt and garbage. Then it was about time for beggars and homeless men to roam the area and fumble into all the trash cans for some still edible leftovers thrown inside.

Due to a busy market, at the dead end of the alley, there was a large empty lot locally known as a garbage dump site. Here, the foul smells from heaps of garbage permeated faithfully day and night, welcoming stray dogs, rats, and an army of cockroaches to share their ample feast—the bountiful treasures for their survival.

I could not ignore a group of beggars and homeless men taking up permanent residence around this area and sometimes sharing those treasures with their unwelcome guests—cockroaches, rats, and stray dogs.

I usually roamed along this winding alley with no other purpose than refreshing my mind and making myself sober after quite heavy booze at that Come & Go Lucky shop. But the true reason might lay in my desperation to find camaraderie among those fighting their own battle just like I was. I roamed the area of a dirt-poor neighborhood, walking past all signs of poverty—rows of shacks, shanties, and sheds. The shelters practically sat across a narrow sewage ditch running along the alley. One could peek through a crack in the shelter's floor and see the stagnant, black, filthy water underneath.

Why did those shelters sit precariously across the ditch and not on the solid ground? It had to be the only available space that was not private property. Sheets of rust-eaten and weathered zinc were used for the roof of most of these shacks, bamboo slits for the supporting structure, plank boards and mats made of jute for paving the floor, and cardboards and newspaper leaves with pieces of rags pasted and patched up together, in an unexpected collage art style, for the shelter walls. Rain droplets leaked through the small, numerous roof holes, and oven-like heat from the sun pierced through the cracks of those crumpled walls. If it rained dogs and cats, whoever was sleeping under that roof was soaked as if he were lying in the rain.

Despite all these hostilities, they insisted on using the term home for these structures. It might not be in terms of a snug and secured construction building against rain, heat, crimes, and all kinds of dangers as a home in general terms rather than of a few private square feet of their own that at least shielded them and the scene caused by their need for sexual acts from the eyes of the nosy world.

Poverty seeped into the fabric of everyday life of these people as rain and heat had done to them. To be poor became a natural part of their state of existence, and some of them felt nothing wrong anymore with such a life. At least, it could not prevent them from their coupling, which they could enjoy as lustily as any rich couple who were living in the tower made of ivory could.

The last scenario that became my last straw was when I had, by pure chance, encountered one girl at a dim street corner one night in this neighborhood.

After nightfall, it was a normal scene for any passers-by to run across a small group of girls roaming that area. Anyone could easily guess who those girls were and what they did at night in this seedy part of the street.

With a surprise of the world, I recognized that girl right away. She changed a lot. Yet her heavily makeup-painted face was as pretty as when I'd last seen her several years ago. She stood near a gas lamp post wearing a flashy-looking outfit with a cigarette between her pursed lips. She was with three other girls who looked no different from her.

I didn't think much about her now, as I often did earlier. Yet, occasionally, a sweet nostalgia for her came back and lingered. Her face, from time to time, floated across my mind as the only girl still in my wet dreams. No wonder that die-hard feeling was suddenly coming back and flaring up at the unexpected chance of meeting her again. Oh, that girl had once swept me off my feet so completely that I was blinded to its disastrous consequence, which had still damaged my life until now.

That sudden feeling of elation put me into a half trance. I staggered toward that girl until a smell of perfume from her sensual body hit my nostrils.

"Took-ta… You remember me?"

I didn't expect her to recognize me at once. I knew I had

changed drastically. After she'd heard her name, she turned to me and squinted at me; then, a recognition flashed in her eyes.

"Oh, that's *you*."

She stared at me in genuine surprise, but her expression quickly changed to feigned exaggerated astonishment as she cried out, "Good heavens, what really happened to you?"

I just gazed at her. I was sure she knew what had happened to me after that fateful day. She went on with a scoff.

"Oh my! If that old bitch had risen from her grave and had seen you now, she must have laughed her teeth off at how you look."

"Is she dead?" I held my breath.

"She stumbled down the stairs in her house and broke her neck. It happened a year ago. That's what I heard." she laughed mockingly and shrugged. "Oh, you should know this too. That crazy old bitch hired me to get you laid so she could accuse you of raping me and kick you out of her house. She paid me good money. So why not? Stupid you! I would never let her abuse me and then throw me out like you. She treated her dog much better than you; its food, its sleeping place, and everything. It serves her right to drop dead. Who would give a damn?"

Took-ta was right. That nanny deserved more for all the malice she did to me, not to mention the heinous things she'd done to my father. I couldn't help touching the ugly scars that her goddamn dog had left on my hands and arms. If I hadn't guarded my throat in time, I probably wouldn't have survived today.

It was obvious now that Took-ta disliked Nanny Sook, which meant that although the nanny hired her to ruin me, she only did it to make herself survive, all against her own will. My heart began to swell for what I assumed.

I always wondered where Took-ta had been for all those years, and oh, I couldn't help but wonder if she had ever thought of me as I did to her after all. So, I tried to linger on for a little longer talk with her. No matter what, she still made my heart swell despite what she had apparently become right now.

"It's been a while. Took-ta, I always wonder…how have you been?

She stared hard at me in response. "Oh, never be better."

"I often passed this area. Maybe I can see you again around here."

Suddenly, she blurted out, looking me up and down in cold staring.

"Hey, you're in my way. Just get the hell out of here now."

I was stunned. That was so plain and clear of what she actually felt about me. I just stood there, gazing at her like a dumbass as my response. That seemed to aggravate and annoy her. I saw her turn to the girls in her group and shout.

"Hey! Help me kick out this scum. He wants to fuck me for free."

That seemed enough to put the whole group inflamed. They rushed to me like a pack of she-wolves.

"Hey, if you want a free fuck, go home and fuck your wife. You hear me?"

This time, I withdrew from that spot as hastily as I could. But in such a hurry, I stumbled and fell onto the street. I heard their rowdy whoops and vulgar laughs, followed by a loud spit from one of them, showing me a downright contempt.

"Get the hell out to rot elsewhere out of my sight, you stinky bum! We don't do a charity. No money, no fuck. Don't you dare show up your face again!"

The shooting feeling of worthlessness was too painful to take. This was the day I was hit by the worst humiliation I'd ever faced. But who could be blamed? It was nobody else but me who had put myself into this lowest stratum of human beings, even in the eyes of these prostitutes who'd done no better than prowling the night street hunting for any male customers who walked past them.

And yet, Took-ta and these hooker girls acted as if they had justification for dehumanizing me with their humanless acts.

This was the very last straw that snapped and broke me.

After that encounter, I came staggering to this soulless place, this time not for a habit of feasting a sense of camaraderie from its misery-ridden inhabitants but to walk straight to my final destination at Great-Great-Grandpa Tree, the chosen spot where I was going to end my life.

It was uncannily cold tonight. I couldn't believe the fog from the river could creep out that far. Its clammy touch chilled me to the bone as much as this eerily quiet night crept me out. Bad news on the rising of the Japanese army's undefeatable power over Asia even helped add to the despairing atmosphere over the entire city. Like the creeping mass of fog, the presence of war was now at our doorstep. Well, who cared anymore? War or no war, people just died. Just like me, who would, in a short moment, I wouldn't be there anymore to acknowledge all the damn things on this earth. Today was my birthday. Life, however, was so rotten beyond fixing. The present for my birth wouldn't be better than my death.

But it was a noise interrupt that stopped my further movement.

In dead silence at the heart of the night, I was startled as I abruptly heard a loud noise, a clunking and clattering sound about twenty yards away, where all the garbage was piled up and sprawled all over the ground. I felt wide awake. My eyes caught a movement of something and then a glimpse of another figure in silhouette. I was fully alerted now. People always said this place was haunted. Yet, I believed it must be a human: no reason and no need for a ghost to perform that act of survival. I saw the figure climbing clumsily toward the top of one garbage heap piled up six or seven feet high from the ground.

As he pushed and forced himself, making his way up, he slipped a couple of times, causing loud noises in the middle of the dead night. With all his efforts, struggling, and sheer force of will, he eventually reached the top and precariously perched on it triumphantly. Now, I shifted all my attention to him.

The noises woke up a few stray dogs. They barked at him frantically, trying to defend their claimed territory from a human's intruding and plundering of their possessive treasure. I heard the man curse as he flung an empty can, targeting one of the canines. It can precisely hit that dog, making it yelp, whimper, and retreat reluctantly.

The man then began to delve feverishly into the pile with his spade, holding a small pail tightly in his other hand. The higher you climbed, the better your chances of finding untouched treasure.

Beggars, homeless men, and dirt-poor children in this neighborhood take the dump site as their hunting ground. From dawn to dusk, they dig, turning the trash upside-down in the hope of a hidden fortune. On some rare occasions, if luck is mercifully and surprisingly on their side, a few can make a big discovery; they might find a ring, a watch, and even crumpled bank notes.

There was a story that some kid, by accident, stepped on a gold chain as thick as his finger while tramping across the sprawl of garbage. The rumor spread, dramatizing and exaggerating the original story, making a discovery of one gold chain into two and three, and, at last, four gold chains as the most satisfying numbers, luring more desperate people to this site. However, if not a gold chain, finding anything made of metal—a discarded pot and pan or any broken and chipped utensil—is a good enough catch of the day. Depending on the weight and value of the piece of metal they have found—from copper to iron to tin and aluminum—they can trade them into some small money and, in turn, a decent meal.

But there are always too many occupants claiming and fighting over things worthless, such as empty cans or rusty nails, during the busy time of the day. The night, especially the middle of the night, becomes the most auspicious time for this man to seek things all alone. No one else—grown-ups or children likewise—will shamelessly come to bully him and snatch his treasure. Sometimes, the swarm of children came like a hungry wolf pack, ambushing and attacking him off guard. *You, scavenger. You, vultures in disguise.* He probably screamed at them after they had knocked him down, fleeing with his treasure in their hand.

As that figure conquered the summit, the street light above his head illuminated him clearly as if he were playing a reality show on stage under a spotlight. I stood some yards away from him to see him in full view while I was luckily out of sight. The spot where I hid myself was under the deep shadow of Great-Great-Grandpa.

With his face and body in full view, I felt even as startled as glimpsing an apparition. I was not able to tell his age at all with his gaunt, pock-marked face, broken teeth, scraggy body, and unkempt, matted long hair, which made him look more like a living dead. I strongly believed he could even scare all the dead on Great-Great-Grandpa to another death quite easily by his ghoul-like appearance. His bony chest was bare, and only his groin was covered with a piece of filthy rag cloth, wretch looking beyond description. There was no doubt to believe that he had been who he was now for so long and perhaps would stay that way for the remainder of his life—I would generously give him a maximum of four more years to keep himself above the ground and not under it. However, the grin on his face told me that whatever he was doing, he believed it must come out rewarding.

He dug and dug. Every movement was forceful and hopeful. A short moment later, I saw him eagerly taking something from the pile. I held my breath, feeling so anticipated as if I had become his comrade due to our mutual hope. I started to share his hope with him. I sensed hope—oh, that long-lost sweet feeling of hope suddenly coming back, pulsing and warming up a cold void of my being. I felt alive again.

My heart sank. Under the streetlight, I saw in plain sight that what he was picking up was a piece of chard from broken glass.

I wished I could have a magic wand to cast a spell on every piece of junk on the heap and turn all of them into pure gold, like King Midas in Greek mythology, making this Junkman the richest human the world had ever recognized. Instead, I heard a shriek, a long, painful cry uttered from him as he quickly jerked one of his hands from the pile. I saw some drops of blood dripping down his hand. He got a cut from something sharp hidden beneath him. I had no idea how deep the cut or the gash might be. I saw him put his knuckle into his mouth and started sucking his blood, swallowing it down hastily, one gulp after another.

The light reflected on some glittering pieces of sharp shards broken from empty whisky bottles. His knuckle got cut by one of these numerous pieces. They scattered across the dump site in almost every square foot, glistening and sparkling in the dark, over here, over there, and beyond, as though he was sitting in the middle of a dazzling diamond field. Let's do the math again. How many empty whisky bottles did those drunk and broken people discard each day? How about each week, each month, and each year? Perhaps there were millions upon millions of them.

That picture made me wince and shudder. What if the piece that pierced the Junkman's flesh had come from my own bottle? What a cruel joke! Probably one of the nights after I was on my way home from that noodle shop, my empty bottle was tossed carelessly into the trash can at the corner of the kitchen. Then, in the morning, it started a journey that finally ended up at this dump site, cracked, shattered into shards, smashed into pieces, turning one of its sharp edges up, waiting menacingly to hurt and harm.

I had to admit that naturally, I was far from being a bleeding heart, way different from my father. My life had been so wrapped up with my miseries—like living in a four-square-foot dungeon surrounded tightly by four massive walls. Those walls, though invisible, were so dense and suffocating that they barely let me slip out to touch and feel the misery of others.

Yet, haunted by the gash on his hand because somehow I might be the real culprit who caused it, I decided to step forward and out of the tree's deep shadow.

"Don't make a big fool of yourself. Get down. The things you found are just pieces of broken dreams of somebodies who had given up their hope. That's all, honestly."

My voice, which seemed to come out abruptly out of nowhere, startled him. He hastily craned his neck around and then to the direction of my voice and suddenly spotted me standing a few feet below him.

He looked perplexed at first as he peered down at me. Probably, the very fact that I had just told him did not make any sense to him. Why, his life had been drowned deeply into the graveyard of those buried dreams for so long that he was never aware of their hidden true identities surrounding him. Just like fish in water, they never realized that it was underwater where they were spending all their lives.

An instant later, he screamed at me.

"Get out of my face, asshole! I won't stop until I find something. Do you hear me? I must have *Something*."

I started to walk away. There was no point in arguing with him. Shame took over me after I'd realized I should leave him alone and stop tearing down his hope for finding his dream-come-true out of that garbage heap. Yes, he was right—never let go of hope in the face of hopelessness.

Strangely, that Junkman's adamant hope somehow began to rekindle my own. No one really wanted to die, even though they said they really wanted to. So, I began to toy with my fate and give myself a last chance. I would take the Junkman's hope to gamble on my own fate.

If he kept on carrying his hope, I would win the game and spare my own life as a reward, bringing me a new life chapter. But if he gave up digging for his treasure, I lost. And my life would be gone along with the loss of this game.

As I stepped away, farther from that spot, I still heard the persistent noises from his digging and cursing, digging and cursing, echoing behind me. Oh, those steady noises of hope now became as important to me as my own heartbeats.

Suddenly, all the noises stopped. The immediate silence that followed was so deafening that I jerked up. I swept my gaze around. My heart sank when I found no soul at the top of the garbage heap anymore.

Tears of despondence and anger filled up my eyes. Why! Wasn't he aware my life was hanging on his hope? His hope mattered to me in equal extreme. After hours of asserting his will against all odds on this life battlefield, why did my iron-heart hero suddenly let go of his hope and crumble it just like most people had done to their own, including me?

I lost this game. My last hope perished. Nothing was left for me to go on, even for another minute.

* * * * *

Part 3: Chapter 2

The Great-Great-Grandpa

I stumbled to the dead end of the alley, which greeted me with the stench of garbage mixed with the foul odor of a decade-old rotten pool of urine on top. A few yards in front of me, there was a long brick wall once blank and cleanly whitewashed but now tainted with all varieties of graffiti scrawled along the length of the wall.

Needing to empty my bladder, I should empty my bladder, having my body cleansed in order to honor my impending death.

Then, I had to stop short. On one section of the wall right in front of me, I stumbled on a big sign scrawled boldly in red paint. It was quite dark, but faint streetlight allowed me to glimpse the sign.

The message screamed—*this spot is reserved for dogs to piss only. Men are not allowed.*

I hurriedly zipped up my pants without sharing that spot, which was sarcastically reserved as the dog's privy. I sheepishly retreated to stand under the deep shadow of a long, huge branch sticking out from an enormous banyan tree trunk that dominantly stood five to six stories high in front of the wall perimeter.

No one in this neighborhood knew the actual age of this timeless towering tree. You had to tilt your head upward to see its canopy soaring toward the sky.

The Tree.

It looked three centuries old or more, with numerous aerial roots growing down the soil decades after decades and forming additional trunks that spread around the original one. Local people claimed their great-grandfather told them the tree had already stood there, strong and stout, when he himself had just been a wee boy. Even people from old times had already called that supermassive tree *Great-Great-Grandpa.*

Then, I caught a glimpse of the glittering roof of the Buddhist monastery beyond the wall. The soft wind was sweeping the rustled leaves again as I heard the sweet and serene sounds of the temple wind chimes jingling in the wind from a distance. Like a sweet lullaby, lulling venerable monks into a calm and peaceful meditation. This ten-foot-high, thick brick wall with two parallel rows of barbed wires running on top along its length guarded and protected—or, more precisely, blindfolded—this sacred monastery from such an ugly and grim reality of the world. Ironically, the wall itself, though as towering, invincible, and formidable as it appeared, was so vulnerable and powerless from the abuse left by some itchy hands. They used the wall face to practice, with black charcoal and white chalks, their porno graffiti, and obscene words.

People rarely passed by this spot at night; not only was it close to a dump site, but they also believed that Great-Great-Grandpa was haunted.

Some people in that neighborhood swore they always saw a man disappear and emerge from Great-Great-Grandpa's enormous trunk at night. They believed he must be an evil spirit dwelling in that tree responsible for several deaths that had occurred on the tree.

Hopeless men, one after another, had hung themselves there

in the past two decades as if suicide were a highly contagious epidemic spreading around this hopeless neighborhood. People there, as usual, clung to their superstitious belief an unrest and vengeful demon dwelling inside the tree was waiting at that spot and beckoning anyone passing by to come over and end his life by hanging himself. By finding a replacement, the man's spirit was believed to free itself from its earthbound state.

No wonder why I usually saw a few strips of bright red, green, and yellow faux silk bands wrapped around that ancient trunk with bunches of small jasmine garlands hanging on the lowest branch and a handful of burning incense stuck in front of the tree. These were a few things meant to bestow on the dead as offerings or, more precisely, as bribes not to haunt and harass us, the living.

Barely a week before, a young man hung himself on that tree. Rumor had it that he climbed up the tree and reached that lowest branch, which I believed was right above my head, where I stood. He tied one end of his rope around it. In contrast, the other end was fastened firmly around his neck, ready and even grateful for the unknown journey he was about to take in another instant. This journey would carry him away from the living hell he endured.

As he settled on the branch, he drew a long, hearty breath and then another, playfully mocking the life itself since he no longer cared for an existence called life. He merely realized that his own life was just nothing but his ruthless master with such an unrelenting demand that, day in and day out, he had to wait on hand and foot. If his life was hungry, lusty, or just plain bored, and if it demanded him to add more zest and thrills, he had to enslave himself to lie, to cheat, to harm, to steal, to rob, to rape, and even to kill to serve those whims.

But as he looked at this moment, he was turning the table on his own life. He could tell that all parts of his body were sensing their impending doom and alert in unison against his betrayal. They all were begging him to be merciful, not to crush them. All his five senses were working in perfect synchrony. He felt his heartbeats frantically kicking his rib cages in wild protest, his mind screaming loudly through his ears pleading with him to stop-stop-stop and please stop at once, his eyes sending desperate scalding hot tears down his face to melt his unyielding adamancy, and finally his brain, the mastermind of all tricks and deceptions, suddenly flashing and flashing right before his eyes what he yearned for the most; the long lost childhood memories he had shared with his loved one who had long, long departed.

Suddenly, his nostrils perceived the soft scent of baby talcum that seemed to float from far, far away and slowly come to linger softly in the air surrounding him and arousing his happiest and most nostalgic memory of all—the memory of one midsummer night, when his mother had patted the soft talcum powder all over his body to cool his skin. It was such a long time, almost like a ribbon of dreams. She cooed and held him up so high in the air he squealed and giggled with joy and delight. He blinked back his tears, trying to stop his quivering lips and swallowing his sobs.

All these are beckoning him to come back to life...

Just before his weakness could win him to surrender to those callings, as it had done to him for all his entire life and had never failed to take him back, he triumphantly jumped off the tree immediately with his last laugh.

How glorious and wonderful to taste, for the first time in his life, his utmost freedom—his own power and master over his life. He would never regret his death in exchange for this ultimate glory...

I was envious and awe-struck by his utter courage in taking the dare. It was so hard to live, and yet it was even harder to die, especially with your own hand. I knew it took mountains of courage to take your own life.

Why did I know?

That's because I myself had attempted it a couple of times, but somehow, the voice of someone deep-seated within me always emerged at that crisis moment. That voice reasoned with me, coaxed me, and even forced me, as if I were still a little boy, to put down a rope at the very last minute before the knot was tied around my own neck.

Listen to me. You don't have to love everybody, Pran. But don't harbor hate for anyone, yourself in particular. Remember? You promise me to find out the origin of hatred and suffering.

You promise to unfold these mysteries, you promise.

My father's voice.

That young man's dangling body, swaying back and forth cold and lifeless under that fateful branch, was found at the crack of dawn, when all the roosters in that area called and echoed each other's crows as the sun was rising, radiating its golden glory and signifying a new bright day. It was one saffron-robed monk who had found the young man's body on his way to his routine trip, asking for his morning alms.

The news spread around the neighborhood as people rushed to the suicide scene to identify the body. Someone recognized him as a penniless criminal, a fugitive at bay who the police had hunted down for months for some homicide case. Upon taking down his body, his shirt and trousers pockets were hastily searched, and a few coins with crumbled banknotes still left inside one of the pockets were fished out by an anonymous hand. At least the owner of that mysterious hand had some decency—and mercy—enough to leave his trousers and shirt intact. Before this incident, another dead body had been found naked like a newborn. He was stripped off every piece of clothes he had worn.

I lifted my head and peered yearningly up at that fateful branch a few feet above. As a gentle breeze rattled through Great-Great-Grandpa's dense foliage, making soft, rustling, mournful sounds, I felt a call, barely audible, whispering in my ears. That voice was urging me to start climbing up that particular branch.

Suddenly, at one corner of my eyes, as the icy cold started running down my spine, I caught a glimpse of a silhouette figure under the deep dark shadow—but clear enough for a figure of a young man—perching on that branch with two legs dangling from it. One of his hands had grabbed the nook tying around his neck. That figure was beckoning to me with another of his hands to come and join him up there and taste the same sweet freedom he had already had. This time, he promised in his whisper over and over into my ears that no one would ever stop me this time.

Come. Come. Come to me. Come to me. He moaned. *If you have no rope with you, the leg of your trousers will be as good. Come up now.*

Now, one of my hands slowly groped in my pocket, ready to take out a small coil of rope I had prepared and brought.

My life has repeatedly failed me. It deserved punishment by my own hand.

I made a mental confession to the figure perching on the branch, who was now slowly revealing his pale, almost translucent face that seemed eerily glowing against all ambient darkness.

No, you are wrong. Dead wrong. To die is not a punishment. On the contrary, it is a reward for a soul whose life failed him but whose death will celebrate him. I am opening the gate for you to enter my realm, where you will be safe from life because life cannot abuse you any longer. Hurry up and come over me. Do it now. Do it.

It was so irresistible not to follow the convincingly soft, luring, soothing voice that suddenly turned fierce and demanding. My feet started awkwardly to put one step forward toward that persistent voice as if I were in a half trance.

Do it. Do it. Do it. Do it. I said do-o-o-o it. NOW!

That voice became close to a snarl. A snarl with a smile as

I started trying to move myself up to meet him.

Your promise, Pran. Remember your promise...

Only one blinking of my eyes and suddenly, that branch stayed as empty and desolate as it had been seconds before; only soft, mournful sounds from rustled foliage remained. The above apparition, either real or merely from the trick of my brain caused by my heavy drink to cloud my sense of reality, vanished entirely, leaving me alone, safe and sound below the tree, yet shaken and deeply ashamed.

Remember your promise to find that answer for me...

Again, the voice of my most loved one was saving me in the nick of time from whatever appeared on the tree—whether it was a spirit or my own delusion.

I flung that coil of rope into the ground as far as I could and walked off.

I couldn't die now as long as I hadn't finished that mission.

Some sense came into my mind before I reached the main street some thirty yards ahead. I had a nagging funny feeling that a pair of eyes was watching me silently behind a clump of trees along the dim and desolate alley. It just crossed my mind that someone or something was stalking me. I tried to dismiss the feeling, but it persisted, creeping into my spine. I told myself no need to be scared. If I was indeed being stalked, it must have been by that old crazy beggar, not the other one grinning at me from the tree branch. The Junkman was probably attempting to frighten me out of his grudge. But when I managed to collect myself and decided to turn around, getting it over with once and for all, I strained every nerve not to jump.

There was indeed someone behind me. For better or worse, it wasn't the beggar, nor the dead man on the branch.

Instead, I saw a tall figure in silhouette, an outline of a man standing in the dark shadow under a tree. There was no other sound except the rustle of the tree foliage against the soft breeze. When he saw me gazing at him, he startled me by stepping out of the dark. However, it was still quite dark, and I could see only the outline of his face.

"You're drunk," he said quietly. "You need help."

I managed to turn my back on him and kept on walking ahead, and yet I still heard his calm voice following me.

"He's still waiting for you."

Something in his voice urged me to look back again. I slowly turned around and faced that man, half curious and half unnerved. Then, I saw his finger pointing to the direction at the end of the alley beyond from where I had earlier runoff.

"Do I know you? Who is waiting for me? Who?" I shouted at him, trying to use my anger to drown my fear.

"How easily you forget that young man up there on the Great-Great-Grandpa Tree."

His reply had taken me aback. I froze on that spot, too flabbergasted and appalled to respond.

"What…" my voice came out now so close to the whisper. I could tell he was grinning because suddenly, I saw his white teeth flashing in the dark.

"You're looking for the escape, aren't you? I'll bring you back over there if you want. Trust me, there's no way out for you. Only this."

His left hand disappeared deep inside his pants pocket. When he took it out again, a rope coil was somehow clutched in his hand.

"Only this," he repeated, then grinned at me. Why? You dropped this rope under that tree. Oh, sorry. You didn't drop it. You *threw* it," his smile was more insidious, almost a smirk now. Now, take it back and try again."

"Try what?" the words almost choked in my throat.

"I believe you perfectly understand what I mean," while he was engaging me in conversation, he had never taken his eyes off me, and oh, his grin… "Why! To join him. Remember that young man on the branch?"

My blood ran cold when I felt the coil of rope slapped

against my palm.

"Don't forget your purpose for coming to that tree with this rope. Come on, have some guts."

Without even thinking, I brushed off the rope and let it drop to the ground again. In the dark, the coiling rope resembled a crawling snake. My most terrifying childhood memory suddenly flashed. I resisted with all my effort not to scream my head off from that horrible memory…

The image of a cobra snake.

Under the dim streetlight, it was not the rope anymore; I swore because a coil of rope could never be writhing and wriggling while crawling toward me as if it had life.

I used that moment to run off. That man scared the shit out of me. I was too frightened to look back for fear that no matter how fast I sprinted up, trying to be farthest from there, I still found him behind me.

But what if he had instead, at this very moment, lay in wait ahead of me on my way before I hit the main street? Any impossibility seemed just possible after all those bizarre things I had faced a short while ago.

After a few minutes of sprinting like a lost soul and panting from exhaustion, I once again found myself stumbling at the Come & Go Lucky noodle shop's door—my old sanctuary.

I ordered a cheap bottle of rice whisky and, with my trembling hand, poured myself a boost, slugging it down my dry throat as if there had been an empty desert deep down my guts that needed a heavy soak of torrent. I was desperate to reassure and comfort myself that the occurrence in that dark alley sprang from the state of drunkenness.

Whatever I saw, it couldn't be real.

Yet, real or mere illusion, it still scared the daylight out of me. What if that man had known where I was? I quickly looked around and then sighed with relief. I found only the presence of a few customers in the warm light.

The first gulp made me feel relaxed and more of it carried

me farther away—back, back into the same place in the past where Papa always stood at the heart in the realm of my true joy.

That memory was like a white speck of happiness the size of a tiny pinhead against the immense black wall called Life...

It was someone's hand that was shaking me, waking me from a long slip so far away into the staggering depths of my past. I opened my eyes, blinked, and looked at a small pendulum clock on the opposite wall. It was almost four o'clock in the morning. I must drift into a doze for hours.

"What...." I croaked.

The person who broke that spell was the owner of Go Lucky himself. The shop extended to open 24 hours on the weekend and tonight was Sunday night. He worked the late-night shift until morning before his brother came to take turns. He was standing beside me, holding a glass of drink. He grinned and put that glass right in front of me.

"A glass of Scotch whisky from the gentleman sitting over there. He said it's complimentary for you," announced he proudly.

No sooner had I craned my neck in that direction than I saw a man stride across the floor toward me, a pricy imported bottle of Scotch whisky in one of his hands. The next instant, he dropped himself on a stool at my table and made himself at ease.

"May I join?" His voice was pleasant and friendly, and he had a broad smile on his face.

"Leave me alone, please," I scowled and blurted out. "I'm fine. I don't need company."

"But I believe you do," his words were earnest, yet his tone was amused. Apparently, he ignored my refusal, only continuing his easygoing tone of voice.

"I've been watching you brooding in this dark corner for hours. I can tell you are free-falling to the bottom of your misery. Are you all right, my friend?"

Maybe it's time for me to leave. He sounded cheerful and

good-natured enough, yet I disliked someone prying into the affairs of others. I steadied myself with one of my hands against the table but lost the balance. I stumbled back to the seat.

"Just go away," I repeated stonily. "Leave me alone."

"No," he grinned widely as he firmly shook his head. "Obviously, you need some help. Look! You are too drunk even to stand upright."

I tried to open my eyelids and squinted, studying him at my best through my blurred vision. I was confident that he wasn't one of the regular patrons of this shop; most faces were all the locals and looked familiar to me. This man was a total stranger. If judged by the western dark-blue suit he's dressing together in a silk bow tie and the poise he's bearing, he shouldn't belong to this rundown neighborhood. It's more possible if he had just waltzed out of some grand reception ball party and then went straight to this place.

How old was this man? I tried to figure it out. At first glance, I believe he must be in his fifties with his salt and pepper hair and a thick mustache. And yet he had an astonishing complexion of youth: so ruddy and radiant that his strong and quite handsome face seemed to glow under the light bulb on the ceiling. I wondered why it was so difficult to tell his exact age. So, the light and shadow that was taking turns to play some trick on his face every time he slightly moved probably created that strange effect.

However, his imposing presence vaguely reminded me of my father's aristocratic old man, Lord Phuvanathnurak, whom I had encountered a long time ago at my father's funeral. Yet, his image had been stuck in my mind ever since, especially his wide-open eyes that still glared at me even after his breath stopped. However, the compelling eyes I found in this stranger seemed more powerful. His thin lips were fixed with a pleasant and easy-going smile that made him look like he had stayed in a separate boundary where all the miseries from this world could not edge near. And yet, that smile greatly contrasted a pair of his world-piercing eyes set deeply below bushy, thick eyebrows. Just like two deep black holes that pulled everything down into their bottoms but never allowed a single thing to return, so powerful those eyes could bisect me in half as his gaze was fixing on my face.

Yet, although I wanted to, I knew I couldn't deny this man's peculiar charisma that was shining around him.

And he was right. I was so drunk I couldn't even lift a finger to brush him off when he bent himself to touch my arm, which made me feel so electrified I flinched at that touch. Therefore, I helplessly watched him sit beside me and resume his drink.

"No one can escape misery with bottle after bottle of alcohol. I hope you know that," he began to engage me in a conversation. "No one. So be it."

I responded with sulky silence, hoping that ignoring him would make him go away. But it didn't work. He broke the awkward silence with another subject.

"Look like I'm annoying you to death. Well, I bet this must get you hooked on. Want to hear?"

"Hey, just go. I'm warning you for the last time."

"*You* warning *me*?" he let out a belly laugh, not paying attention to my hostility. "Listen, don't you know I stalked you all the way to this rat-hole shop."

This time, I tilted up my head and stared hard at him.

"You dropped this. So, I decided I should bring it back to you. It belongs to you." He smiled and looked into my eyes. "Um… Let me guess. You came over there to take your own life on one of the Great-Great-Grandpa branches, and tsk… tsk…"

He made me stare harder at him.

"Let me have another guess—just a guess, so it could be wrong. You want to dump your life because you can't take the guilt that has been haunting you both in your sleep and waking hours, the guilt that you were born merely to make the lives of all your loved ones flip upside-down. Tell me, am I right or wrong?"

His eyes seemed so powerful that if his gaze had fixed on me a little longer, they could have cut me in half.

"What—" I was speechless this time. Of course, I'd never cracked a word about myself to any soul on earth.

His amused smile was at the corner of his lips as he playfully pulled a coil of rope out of the thin air right in front of me. I swore I did see him doing that before my eyes like a magician performing his trick. He lifted it up and let it dangle in front of my face.

"We'd just met at that Great-Great-Grandpa dark alley a couple of hours ago before you fled me like I am a ghost. No, don't take me wrong. I'm not a ghost. Never be any of them."

he sneered at the word 'ghost' and went on.

"But I tell you, I am worse. Much worse. Why? Ghosts can haunt you as long as you feed them your fear. Their existences rely heavily on that crap because fear is a core energy to help animate and empower them. Without fear from the living like you to energize them, the dead starve and fade into a mere shadow. So, to handle your wicked mother, you ignore her, and she will be too feeble to trail behind your every move. But no, what can work on ghosts can't work on me," his grin wider. "I am an exception. I've stood above all rules."

Help me, please. Can someone help me?

I tried to raise my voice, hoping desperately that the shop owner could hear and come to my rescue. But only a long gasp came out from my throat. There seemed to be no place to hide from this mysterious man. No matter where or how it appeared, he would find you.

Something was terribly wrong; I wished it was from my own unstable mind rather than from this man whose presence began to spook me more and more.

"Why…" my voice slurred, "Why…are you stalking me?"

"Stalking you? Oh my!" He scoffed at my question, which

was probably so blunt that it sounded too crazy. "Now, just relax. Wrap your hand around my shoulder. Good, good." he was coaxing me like a small child. "And now let's get out of here."

"No... Please... Don't hurt me..."

"Hey! I'm just going to bring you with me—no harm from me whatsoever," his soothing whispering voice was close to my ears. "Why! I'm sure I need not lift my finger to put that rope around your neck. You will do it yourself very soon," he chuckled, "because after I let you go, I'm sure as hell you're going to believe there's no point in living anymore."

I struggled to get loose of him, but no strength was left. I knew I could flop down on the floor like a rocking doll if he let go of me. The store's owner came to assist that stranger holding me. The poor man seemed unaware of the bizarre and unearthly thing between that stranger and me.

"Help me... He's going to...hang me on that haunted tree..." My voice was so incoherent the owner probably didn't understand or didn't bother to.

"This young guy always comes here alone and has suicidal drinking. They said he used to be a straight-headed guy. So sad to see he's killing himself this way," the owner shook his head and sighed. "I don't know what has disturbed him inside his head, but it must be huge."

"Aren't you going to close your shop now for cleaning? It'll be daybreak soon. But you can't throw him on the sidewalk and let him sleep there. So, I will help bring him to his home."

He had assured the relieving owner before walking out, dragging me along with him.

During that walk, my consciousness flickered and was almost gone. I felt like I was being thrown and spun within the vortex of rolling tidal waves. Everything was reverberating in that wall of whirlpool. I became so weightless I felt my feet didn't touch the ground level while being dragged in half, floating to the end of that alley, the spot where he had told me I had encountered him a couple of hours ago.

He kept walking steadily while dragging me along with him toward that Great-Great-Grandpa. As suddenly as I saw that tree in plain sight, I could guess what he would do next.

"Don't hang me... Please," I started to whimper.

But no, he didn't. He ignored my words. Instead, I saw him stretch out one of his hands to stroke the tree's enormous trunk.

Right before my eyes, he'd taken one step forward and begun to press himself against that primordial tree, which was as impenetrable as a gigantic pillar wall made of massive granite rock.

Still gripping my arm, he started to penetrate into that tree, dragging me along with him.

"Let me go..."

It was my last croak. Before a blackout took me, I glanced up at the sky, seeing the first sign of dawn on the horizon.

* * * * *

Part 3: Chapter 3

The Slaughterhouse

A sudden swirl all around me made me jerk back to the state of consciousness. As my eyes flicked open, my vision became distorted and blurred as though I was now suspended beneath the water's surface; its underwater current created ring after ring of ripples sweeping across every direction from where I was floating up and down the void.

As those ripples expanded, everything they reached crumbled into numerous fragments and scattered in slow motion as if they had lost their cohesive strength and could no longer hold their own weight. Those particles floated around me in distorted millions of shapes while increasing pressure from above and below kept endlessly reshaping those forms. That tremendous pressure was more than I could stand. I could only shut my eyes and cover my ears with barely controlled hands.

As soon as the tumult let up and my eardrums stopped ringing, I tried to open my eyes again, only to find myself in the middle of the last place I could have thought of.

Right in front of me was that old small shack where I once stayed during those nightmarish years under the care of Nanny Sook. I stood frozen with the old terror facing the closed door of that shack. At least, I heard no sign of life inside. It was the very last place I had ever wished to come back to revive the worst episode of my life that had still been traumatizing my soul up to this present day.

The surroundings of that shack were quiet. The main house seen at some distance where that nanny had lived lay in the sinister dim shadow. I looked at the night sky above and found the bright, full moon shining up there. The moon cast an eerie, silvery light on where I stood in a daze. The familiar sound of a dog barking came from the main house while the sweet smell of the night jasmine vines along the fences beyond lingered in the night air. The fragrance suddenly brought back a bittersweet memory of that girl Took-ta coming to water those blooming night jasmines while I hid behind the bushes, passionately watching her every movement. Yet, the more familiar the atmosphere and the surroundings were to me, the harder it was to believe this was really, really real.

From that moment, I told myself I must rely only on my intuition alone, rather than my deceptive senses.

No matter what, it was impossible to re-enter this old dwelling. My reminiscence told me this spooky, mysterious man had dragged me straight into the Great-Great-Grandpa's trunk and made himself and me disappear inside it. That act occurred just one instant before I found myself reappearing in this place.

"Welcome home, young man!"

A sudden voice from behind startled me. I turned around and found a male figure appear behind me, the same man who brought me to this place but whose abrupt presence scared me out of my wit. It wasn't only he had known every detail about me, perhaps more than I had known myself, but the creepiest about him was when he had earlier introduced himself to me as someone much worse than a ghost.

"Where…am I?"

I blurted out. Although there were thousands more questions to ask, this was the one I could think of for now.

"Um… You are somewhere that can't be found anywhere. Clear enough?"

His riddle-like reply couldn't bring light to me at all.

"It will make more sense to you only if you were not what you are."

"It's not funny. Stop playing a puzzle game on me."

"No offense. It's too bad you are blinded and have never realized you are. So, you've never known there's a sun even though you are looking right at it. This is why you are blind to me."

What on earth was going on?

"But why this shack house? Why do you bring me here?"

"I called this place *my domain*. So, you can't see it as it truly is. Why! You will never see things as a whole in my place with your far inferior optics. Your eyes enable you to see only swirls of fragments of things that break into millions of pieces and float around you without fixed shapes and forms. Of course, it doesn't make sense to you, right? To help you feel at ease, I have to rearrange things to accommodate your limited sense of vision."

His words mystified me even more.

"So, I delved into all your memories that were restored in your brain and brought the one that has most traumatized you out into existence. I checked it up, and it happened to be this particular one—your old memory of this old shack that gave you one of the most terrorizing and dehumanizing experiences. Can you feel the old atmosphere that's carrying you back to the nightmare of the past?"

Suddenly, he lowered his voice and turned his head around cautiously.

"Now, listen to that fierce barking. I'm sure you never

forgot that dog. It could have killed you if you hadn't raised your hands right in time to cover your fragile neck. Am I right again?"

After a stretch of silence, I mumbled something that sounded so stupid even to myself.

"Why… Why do you make me go over this terror?"

I watched him open a sly grin.

"I will tell you later why. No time to talk now. Listen! Are you hearing *it*?"

I turned around in alarm but did not hear any sound.

Suddenly, he cried out.

"Oh, that awful dog is now smelling you out. It's rushing from that house to greet its old foe."

Even though this crazy man had already hinted this was only a sensory trick he was playing on me—how he was able to, I had no idea—I began to feel the immediate terror of that particular day that suddenly creeping back into reality. Those ugly big scars from the sharp fangs of that black dog were still left on both sides of my arms, so deep they couldn't fade away even though the fresh wounds had long gone.

"Oh my! Watch out! That psycho nanny in that main house just unloosed her monster dog. Damn it! It is sprinting toward us," he cried out again, this time in urgency.

Now, I heard the dog's barking in the distance. Within only seconds, that barking became more distinct. It mixed with fierce growls and snarls as the menacing noises approached me.

I became so panic-stricken I was not able to move. There was nowhere to hide from the dog's attack, which I believed was about to happen any instant.

"Hurry up! Open the shack's door quickly and slip inside!" He started to yell at me.

The surge of uncontrolled fear was escalating until I felt my bowel being churned upside down. I tried to yank and kick that door open, but it was deadlocked.

"Hurry up! Watch behind your back! Watch out!"

His warning came too late. The beast, Nanny Sook's black watchdog, which I'd never forgotten, jumped on me from behind with all its furious force. My throat was its sole target. The last time, it missed my throat. But this time, its saw-like sharp teeth, with the support of its solid and crushing jaws, were sinking into the nape of my neck as if it were a chunk of boneless meat for its dinner. I saw the spurt of blood gushing out in a sudden stream from two deep holes pierced by the dog's enormous fangs.

As I screamed my head off in shock and horror, the presence of things around me abruptly turned into a complete blur. All began to collapse as if a sudden massive earthquake shook the whole surrounding. It started with that devil black dog in the middle of tearing up my throat. I breathlessly watched its body soundlessly crumble into a cloud of dust. Then, the whole shack house was following suit. Then, the long row of trees and shrubs, along with all the ambient landscape in my vicinity.

I swept my eyes up the sky only to find the luminous lunar orb from afar began to explode like a burst of firework all over the sky. When I turned back to that man standing beside me, I also found every portion of his body, from his head to his torso and limbs, begin to dissolve into shapeless, amorphous forms right before my eyes.

All pieces of torn-apart elements, including that man's shredded body, were now being knotted together. Those tangles were turning into one enormous pulsating mass. Each piece struggled to free itself from the whole mass that each was caught in but to no avail. That huge mass still floated in slowly swirling movement around me like an unknown living thing in a nightmare.

"Oh no! Look what you've done. Stop screaming like an idiot immediately."

I heard a yelling above my head. It was coming from that man's floating head. One of his hands started drifting out of that huge mass and hovering around me. At least his head and one of his hands could get loose from these tangles. But the rest of his organs must still be lost somewhere inside the chaotic swirling mass.

"Your high-pitched scream is causing ripples of waves. It's knocking over and messing up everything I had organized for you so that you'll be able to see things in sequences and harmony. You understand now?"

"I am...so sorry," I said, still dumbfounded. I had to say something that resonated with all the damages I was blamed for causing. "...Are you all right? Can you...reassemble your body?"

"Hey, don't freak out. I'm fine," his cheerful voice returned as he winked at me. "This is only a playground for getting some fun. I love fun. Come and get inside that shack. I have a more extravagant show to make you squeal with delight."

Suddenly, that single hand gripped my neck in a tight hold as his stark head grinned down at me. Somehow, a stare from that face chilled me to the bone. And when that face opened a widest smile, it was so gruesome I had to suppress myself from opening my mouth for another good scream. But it was in vain. I let out a shriek at the top of my mouth, knowing I was descending into madness.

"Good! Good! Let out all your fear. Let it all out !"

Instead of stopping me from screaming, this time, he began to yell at me excitedly to do otherwise.

"You asked me why that shack and that damn dog popped up. Here is the answer. I want your fear."

"What?"

"I conjured up those illusion tricks to make you reexperience and revive your worst fear."

"For what?"

"I want to taste your fear at its peak. No, this isn't a figure of speech. I literally want to taste your fear."

As he said, I heard him clicking his tongue while widening his mouth gleefully.

"Umm…It tastes pretty good to my taste buds. Not bad, pal."

I had no clue what he really meant. However, it sounded spooky enough to stop me promptly from asking more.

Yet, whatever I had faced—before that gross hand lifted me from the ground and carried me straight inside the shack—seemed to pale by comparison with the new encounter I was facing at this instant.

The place he had brought me into was supposed to be the inside of the shack. But once I entered it, I swore I was not the inside of the most familiar place where I had once stayed for more than a decade. No, not in the least.

It became a place elsewhere beyond the wildest scope of my imagination.

Whatever was surrounding me now, I was at a loss for words. As I swept my eyes in utmost amazement across the entire interior of that place, my whole life experience seemed inadequate to interpret what I was eyeing.

All over this panoramic spherical wall appeared millions upon millions of pinpoints of blinking light. These countless star-like specks emit their light in various colors and degrees of luminance; half were glowing in extraordinary brilliance, whereas the other half were dimmer, and some almost vanished from view.

The longer my gaze fell on that immense curved wall, the more I felt I was gazing at an ocean of infinite stars in the midnight sky. Trying to comprehend the incomprehensible, I found those starlike specks of light were constantly moving, pulsing here and there at their own pace across this vast, gigantic vault.

I was wondering if I was inside a planetarium dome somewhere. But it couldn't be. There was no planetarium in Bangkok at that period. Most of all, you were not likely to float up in any planetarium as if you weighed less than a feather, except that this couldn't be real.

There must be a few rational explanations for this most bizarre phenomenon.

It was possible that I was now in my lucid dream and would jerk my eyes open at any instance to find myself still hanging in that liquor shop. If not, this man could be a wizard seeking applause to feed his ego for his magical performance. So, he must be using magic to cast a spell on me to control my mind. But I had already long outgrown believing in magic, witchcraft, and all sorts of such childish stuff.

Or he was a purely imaginary figure created from my disoriented mind that I had been developing from chronic heavy drinking. However, I didn't care which one he could be: a wizard who survived time, an unreal man in my dream, or a figure manifesting out of my mental hallucination, as long as he wasn't someone 'worse than a ghost' he playfully introduced himself when I'd met him at that noodle shop.

This mysterious man suddenly reminded me of some insane scientist I'd read in the foreign comic books in my school library. When I was younger, I enjoyed reading those kinds of stuff to forget forlornness so much that the comic characters often crept into my fantasy-like dreams at night. My favorite comic stories were more or less about a super-evil figure who invented an unprecedented, deadly apparatus to destroy the world. But before the world was zapped into oblivion, one superhero was always appearing to save the world and its entire world population. That brave hero, whom I'd always taken that role in my dream, would fight that villain to the last breath until he gained a proud victory over that evil at the end…

"Who are you? Are you…a human like me?" I asked him outright.

"That's a tough question. It depends on how you define a human. If you define a human as one who can think, memorize, and be aware of oneself and one's surroundings, I would be glad to find myself fit into that category."

"Fit into a human category? It means you are not human," I stared hard at him. "You couldn't be. Humans can never do such things like you can, not in a million years."

"Like what?"

"Like to enter a tree and emerge out to this other side…" I looked around, unable to find the right term to name this place. "So, you *can't* be human. Absolutely not."

His voice began to edge with impatience. "Stop bombarding me with that silly question. You already know the answer. Come on, you don't want to miss out on the chance of your lifetime to unearth the mystery you have been moving heaven and earth to find for your dear father."

My jaw dropped. I could have expected the whole sky to fall on me, but never had I expected this. There must be only one explanation: He had the power of mind reading.

"How do you know? How…?"

As I kept asking him, my teeth began to chatter. That reaction came from a fear of facing the greatest mystery I believed was too far to reach. But out of the blue, there came a flicker of possibility for access to that mystery—the mystery too mind-shattering for me to be ready to leave my comfort zone and throw open its darkest door, for fear that the unpredictable impact of disclosing it must have shaken me and my present world upside down.

He didn't answer me but nudged me to draw nearer the spherical wall until I was afloat in front of it at arm's length.

"Look! Now, you are within a hair's breadth of that wall. Tell me, what do you see?"

"I…see only blinking specks, millions of millions of them, or I'd rather say billions of billions…" I honestly told him.

"Look closer!" he said. "Closer!"

I looked, gazed, stared, and squinted at those million specks of blinking light as he had urged me. All I could see were still the same twinkling specks of light that were still glowing in different hues of spectrum color—red, orange, yellow, green, blue, or purple—except their sizes grew larger as the wall was close enough almost to touch it. I noticed that each blinking speck did not remain only in one color. Each of those million specks constantly switched into different colors and variant shades and tints almost non-stop, from fiery to faded red, from vibrant to faint orange, from brightest to pale yellow, or from most brilliant blue and indigo to the palest tint hardly seen with ordinary eyes.

Yet, the majority of color I saw was stark red. Red was the color the light specks switched to most of the time. Besides, when one of those blinking specks began to switch from its previous color into the red hue, their light became brightest, so blazing and burning bright I had to narrow my eyes and squint while gazing out in utter mesmerism. All blinking specks of distinct colors and their variant shades constantly moved at different speeds. They moved and clustered, then dispersed into different directions, as I had seen all over the vast panoramic wall.

While I completely lost myself in that mouth-gaping manifestation of the rainbow display on the wall, that man kept observing my response in silence. Suddenly, he chuckled.

"Want to know what those specks of light are?"

"Are they something significant? Or do they have any meaning?"

"Oh, yes! What you've seen on the wall screen will give you *all* the answers you have been searching for. Are you satisfied now?"

"I…don't understand. How come they have anything to do with me?"

"What if I tell you—"

He stopped short and, instead, spread out his hands like a magician beginning to put on a magnificent show after a curtain was pulled open.

"Listen to this! Every one of you, yes, I mean each one of you, is one of those innumerable lights you have seen on that globed wall."

`I stared at him but with a blank expression. It took me more than one minute to register his words. To squeeze some sense out of them seemed impossible.

So, I shook my head and laughed weakly in protest.

"That's *too* ridiculous. I don't want to listen more. Just let me get out and go home."

"I know, I know. It sounds like I'm telling you nonsense downright," Then he looked at me with his deeply poignant expression, which I knew he faked. "But sorry, it's a truth. Nothing but the whole truth that very, very few have known. And look! You are honored to be one of that handful."

"I don't believe these craps. Enough of it... No..." my voice began to falter.

"To deny things you're too scared to believe cannot make those things disappear. No matter how many times you close and open your eyes, I and this place will be right before you..." he then said solemnly. "That's because I am real. Got it now? I'm not an illusion as you are desperate to believe."

"You are real... How could it be? If you are real, you can't crumble into bits of dust and become whole again. In the presence of reality, everything has to be happening under one unchangeable, rational rule. You find things happening outside that rule only in your dream."

"Hey, don't claim it's just you that are real. Me too. I am as real as you believe you are," he assured me mockingly. "We just live in different levels of reality. The only difference is that you and I don't follow the same rule that makes you are you, and me, me. This is the core reason why you aren't able to *do* what I am."

"Are you...a supernatural being or something of that sort?" I said almost in a whisper. "Are you a spirit?"

"No," his voice sharpened. "Don't put me into the supernatural being category. Especially a weird form, like some ghoulish creature that crawls from a grave at night to suck your blood and scare people shitless. But most of you have created me into such a baloney image," he guffawed, "You can't imagine how embarrassed I *feel* when people come to the Great-Great-Grandpa tree, praying to me to make them win the lottery."

"So…who—" I paused. "what are you?"

"The truth is, I belong to a realm above and beyond anything you could understand. Let's say I am in a boundary that some of you've called *Ajintai*. Does that word ring a bell to you?"

I didn't answer. But, yes, it was the term my father referred to when he couldn't find an answer to a certain question I kept bombarding him with."

"All you said means you have existed on 'the other side,' which is totally unknown to the one I stay…"

"Can't be more correct," he beamed at me. "And yet, while I can cross that dividing line and enter your reality as if it were my own domain, what you try to squeeze out of me is the same as the puny flies trying to understand humans. Some vague idea the flies could have about you is only that you are towering, mystifying beings that could smash them into pulps in one instant. By the comparison, I can peel off layer by layer of you to learn from inside out, but you will never have any slightest idea about me if I won't open myself to you."

While I was still at a loss for words, that mysterious man, or whatever he could possibly be, began to laugh again.

"Now, look again at your own speck of light. Do you notice any change?"

"Its color is fading, I guess," I said warily.

"Yes, it is," he nodded. "Absolutely. But why?"

"Why? Why the hell is it fading?" I blurted out. He was quite excellent at drawing my attention to it.

"If you get the right answer, it means you find a key to unlock the main gate to proceed to its heart," he implied. "Listen! That's because, at this moment, your white-hot anger is cooler, almost normal. Tell me honestly. Is what I say right or wrong?"

I inhaled sharply. Yes, this man was right again.

"But...what the whole thing is all about? What are you attempting to tell me?"

"Why are those distinct colors on the light specks so important? By now, I believe you can figure it out yourself."

"Are you telling me any of my moods can be caught in the form of a certain color? Really?"

"Exactly. Your light speck can run the entire gamut of your emotions."

"But why?" I cried out. "Why is it so extremely important that you put all your efforts to drag me to this place of yours only to tell me you know every mood of mine from a color display on this wall? All this for what?"

"If you want that answer, I must bring out this one. Remember, after you had decided to end your life at Great-Great-Grandpa a while back, I'd heard your suicidal thoughts echo like a loud outburst of a thunderclap through the deep silence in the middle of the night. At that particular moment, your suffering reached the peak that you couldn't bear it anymore. I saw your light speck radiating the deepest purple, indicating you were on the verge of going to take your own life. Whoa, I swear you almost made me tear up for you."

I was too stunned to speak.

"Remember? When you broke down the twenty-five years you've stayed in this world into days, they came out as ninety-one hundred and twenty-five days. And when you combined all moments of happiness out of your long ninety-one hundred and twenty-five days, you'd found it barely added to a single day. Your life left room for you to feel joy and happiness less than one percent. In comparison, ninety-nine percent of your life had been wasted on...let's say...pain, grief, despair, distress, loss, agony, shame, and, of course, your incurable self-hatred, with no more room left to fulfill any dream or accomplish any goal that made your life more meaningful. And if so, what was the purpose of your existence? With that fact in hand, you couldn't anymore endure those miseries you had never made sense of. That led you to believe eliminating your life was the best solution to uproot those miseries."

"But I didn't kill myself," finally, I collected myself and protested him. "I realized I have a purpose to live. I have to live for my father. I still have an unfinished task I promised him to complete."

"Let me guess again. That unfinished task is to find out why no one can live with true happiness. Why do terrible things happen to all men, whether they are good or evil, rich or poor? Do all I said is right again?"

I didn't feel surprised anymore at his uncanny clairvoyance.

"Be patient, my friend. You're about to know it in this instant."

I was shaken now by a surge of emotion, torn between wanting and not wanting to know. But the former overwhelmed the latter.

"Let's start with this to enable you to perceive a more wide-angle view. I always watch you strolling an open marketplace near the area where my Great-Great-Grandpa has been towering over for ages. Remember?"

"You… Are you stalking me at every step? Really?" I asked him in disbelief.

"Why not? You often walk into that place to feel its vivid atmosphere of…" With a cynical smile on his face, he went on, "…of a slaughterhouse."

"Please get down to the point. You're driving me insane with your bizarre game."

"Throwing a tantrum on me never works. Be a good, patient boy, all right, or I'll send you back, and you will never know things you're dying to know."

I hardly believed I had already fallen headlong into his trap. I was dying to know them, and nothing could stop me. So, as he had warned, I tried to put myself together.

"In that open market, people come to choose any living things on their whim to suit their taste buds. From live animals dragged down from trees to the ones shot down from the sky where only winged creatures could reach, and to the ones netted out of the deep ocean where humans have never imagined there could be any lives down that bowel. Most of such animals, still alive and kicking, were brought to have their heads chopped out and be slaughtered at any buyer's choice. The sky is the limit for men regarding their food varieties. And best of all, you could gobble all living things with a great comfort that you will never be eaten. It is because you were born into this world as a human—and stay on top of the world as an alpha predator."

"And so…" at this point, I became more baffled at things he was bringing up.

"And so…"

He turned to me and stared into my eyes.

"The immense spherical wall in front of us is, in a sense, not much different from that slaughterhouse place you enjoyed visiting. That entire screen wall represents a diagram mapped for observing and selecting a prey at will out of millions of you."

He sighed heavily in a mimicry of someone remorseful of what he had to say the next moment.

"My apology for announcing that…inevitably, you are one of them on the map of my hunting ground."

I tried to resist the impulse to scream at his face. This was way too much to take. I was now shaken from anger at this insane game he played with his one-way fun.

"Oh, no, no, no. Please stop your anger. Just stop at once," he feigned his alarm. "I'm showing you why you must stop."

For the first time, I noticed that he was holding a square black box in one of his hands, a mystifying device no bigger than his palm. His finger was now pressing one of the buttons on the dial of that small, mysterious device.

"Look at that screen wall. Now! Look at that particular one," he said in fierce triumph.

As my eyes fell upon that wall again, suddenly, one particular speck of light among the countless on the wall was beginning to grow from its original speckle size. I watched until it enlarged at least ten to twentyfold and turned into a blazing orange orb, so bright and burning as if it had been set alight into a ball of fiery flames to outshine all the rest on the wall.

"It's *you*, that fiery speck of orange," his eyes were blazing with excitement. "Your light speck is now under my magnifying device. I'm warning you it's not wise to send out your outburst of anger as you're doing now. Look! how easily it catches my eye. You're making yourself an easy target in this hunting game."

"No…" This was all that slipped out in my reaction to his weirdest explanation. "No…"

"Yes," his voice squealing in delight. "It's the center core of your mind that helps me trace your existence. Your mind enables me to hunt you to the world's edge and beyond. The entire gamut of your human primal instincts—and all negative thoughts—will generate the energy wave signals and emit off your head, ready to be detected and captured by my detector device. Those waves from each of you will then be transformed into a speck of bright light projecting and blinking nonstop on this immense map screen. The more intense your passions, the brighter they will show on the screen, and the easier for me to trace."

He then eyed me critically.

"Each person has his own unique wavelength, existing within the visible spectrum range that helps me identify anyone with perfect accuracy. Your light speck can shift its color depending on your state of emotion occurring at that instant moment. I can distinguish every aspect of emotions that spontaneously controls your mind from each specific color of your light speck on the screen. Let's say a glowing red speck reflects lust; orange dignifies hatred, grudge, and anger; yellow depicts greed and all possessive desires; green renders envy and jealousy; blue represents fear and cowardice, and purple represents grief and despondency. Now, guess what type of emotion in humans is the easiest to detect?"

"It must be...lust," I gulped and somehow tried to avoid his eye contact. "Because it shows on the screen in blazing red light."

"Red is the hardest to elude my detector," he nodded approvingly. "It's the most noticeable wavelength in the visible spectrum, so it signals the backbone nature of humankind: lust. "

"I don't understand the scientific terms you are using. Can you simplify them?"

"That's fine," he was chuckling. "As long as you understand that each human's wave frequency from his brain is similar to an individual fingerprint, it enables me to identify each wavelength among billions accurately. So far, I have never mistaken one person for another due to his unique brain wavelength. And this is my secret why I can..." he paused to smile widely, "stalk you from the cradle to the grave and beyond... Got it now?"

I would be damn if I believed him. But I knew if I didn't, I could as well be damn.

"But, of course, you cannot see your own wave. The human vision and the rest of your physical senses are far too limited to allow you. It means all visible to your eyes is merely a tiny fraction of all existences surrounding you. In other words, you can see only 0.0035 percent out of the total electromagnetic spectrum range—"

"Use simple language, will you?" I reminded him again, but with no patience left.

"Oh, sorry. You know how hard it is not to show off your vanity."

This time, he made his smile look genuinely apologetic.

"So, let's simplify things to make a dummy like you see a

clearer picture of the whole scenario. Now, imagine yourself locked up in a small cell somewhere. Its door is permanently locked; you cannot see the full view outside. All you can do is squeeze your eyes and peek through a tiny keyhole of that door. But whatever you can glimpse outside that cell is no more than the periphery of the tiny keyhole can allow you. That means your eyes are deprived of seeing more than ninety-nine percent of the world outside that door. And as long as you are locked up in that perpetual dark cell. The whole world remains nearly zero-known to you."

His smile widened.

"But I am the one who's watching you from outside. More than that, I hold the key to open that door and grab you anytime. In another sense, I bet you never see our role as a jailor and a prisoner in a clearer view than at this moment."

I closed my eyes and turned my face away from that wall screen. I felt that if I glanced at one light speck on the wall that he had claimed as mine, I would no doubt see its hue turning into a glow of purple, the color of a void of hope.

"Come on, don't look so beaten up. I hate losers. I've already seen millions of losers and quite upset to find you becoming one of them. Of course, I am invincible, but probably not *that* invincible."

He then lowered his voice to an exaggerated whisper.

"I'm going to tell you how to win me. How's that? If only you could find and fix your Achilles heel."

When he noticed the expression on my face, he sneered and taunted me.

"Oh my! You don't know Achilles, you dummy. According to Greek myth, Achilles was a mortal man. Yet, he would never die because his mother dipped him into the sacred river Styx, so every part of his body became invulnerable except for one small part on his heel, where she held him while dipping him underwater. That was the weak spot Apollo found out and, therefore, was shot dead by an arrow from his divine enemy in the Trojan War. Now you see, I've studied human thoughts and mindset and their pseudo-beliefs since ancient times."

"But...why do you dare to unfold your secret for my advantage? Why?"

My voice must be overwhelmed with suspicion. Whatever reason, I'd never believed he did that out of his bountiful heart."

"Oh, sorry. You aren't the dimwit I believed at first. Indeed, you are not easy to be fooled. Yes, though the way to defeat me seems so simple as counting one to ten, it's ironically nearly impossible for you or anyone else to succeed. Because when I talked about Achilles heel, I meant your most vulnerable spot that holds you from escaping me...

"And now listen and listen well. Less than a quarter of humanity have color signals that are weaker than the rest. This small group is somewhat able to restrain themselves from their inborn impulses. The less passion, the weaker the signal they send onto my screen, causing more strenuous work for me to detect them. As you know, my screen loses the capacity to capture the body of the wavelength if it becomes weaker. Therefore, extremely weak wavelengths are able to elude my detector like a grain of sand passing through a sieve and leave no evidence for me to trace further. Now, you can figure out how to dodge my detector device. Just stop your response to all stimuli, and the connection between us will be completely cut off, and you will set yourself free from my stalking for good. But do you really believe it's as easy as child's play?"

I knew better than to give him any answer.

"No, it's not that easy. The chance is less than one percent. In fact, it's proved to be the toughest effort for humans to shut down the wavelength inside their minds and cut themselves off for good. In every moment of your awakening hours, your mind must react to whatever stirring your senses of sight, smell, sound, taste, and touch. How do you stop your terror if you see your father dying in your arms? Or how to knock down your lust if that ravishing girl...what's her name...yes, Took-ta, strips off her clothes right in front of you…"

He looked at me, feigning a regretful sigh.

"Well, if you had succeeded in resisting that doll-face's seduction, and so had your father in resisting his Ling Jong's, the whole course of his future and yours would have turned one hundred eighty degrees," he smiled. " But, see? Both he and you failed head-on. Why?"

His 'why' made me blush, so I didn't reply.

"Even in your sleep, your light speck doesn't disappear from my screen. It turns brighter because your mind works more actively in response to freakier things manifest in your dream than when in your normal waking hours."

"But remember? You coaxed me to kill myself. You must lose me if I do."

"Your death?"

His gaze fell on me in half pity and half satisfaction. Suddenly, he handed me a new device that looked close to an ordinary pair of spectacles, only larger and as dark as pitch black.

"Wear this on your eyes. It will help expand and deepen your human vision scope. Your eyes now can detect the wavelength of 'bodiless entities' that exist by the immediate edge of spectrum range."

After I'd taken that pair of spectacles from him and put them on as if hypnotized, then blinked repeatedly for adjustment, he began pointing to one part of the wall screen, where a white span of shimmering clouds appeared to my eyes. The mass of clouds was similar to the immense Milky Way plane I always saw spanning the curve of the dark sky on a moonless night.

"You are watching a cluster of human energies in the form of so-called souls. Though they are dead in your sense, their minds are still alive, even more so than the living, since they no longer have to share most of their pure energy with their physical body. In fact, your soul never changes no matter how many times it returns, whereas your body can be altered into different bodies, like clothes and garments. Hey, now look again!"

After he had pressed his finger on his detector, I saw part of the clouds begin to enlarge until countless pulsing colorless light specks stood out from the clouds. Suddenly, one tiny speck of the entire cluster started growing larger than the rest, as I had seen a moment ago on the one that claimed to be my own.

"Now, watch that particular one closely."

I watched that enlarged, colorless speck as its dim light began to glow in a brighter and brighter sphere.

"I sent that soul back into its new body. This way, I can use him repeatedly, or in better terms, that soul will be recycled endlessly. Do you understand now your death means nothing to me? Now, look one more time!"

A large, iridescent ray similar to a belt of rainbow suddenly manifested on the screen. It began to engulf that light speck, turning it into a sphere of brazing light.

"What's happening?" My increasing curiosity forced me to ask him.

"I bestow on him what all humans are dreaming for—wealth, fame, and power—to feed and fatten his ego."

Then, that iridescent beam began to recede. And all that was left was a red fireball as red as infernal fire.

"Something's happening?"

"He is losing what he believes will forever belong to him Now, look how his unexpected loss can ignite his rage in full blaze.

"You control...our fate?" I stared at him with utter wonder and awe. "Don't...don't tell me you are God."

"God? Um... No, thanks. That name sounds out-of-date. Who wants to be in the image of some ancient, grumpy old man acting like a spoiled brat who throws a fit at whoever disobeys him? So, better praise me with the term the Immortal One if you want. Why? I can be reborn every instant a child is born into this world. I can live for eternity as long as you humans have fed me for a hundred millenniums with twists and toxins in your mind. Isn't it more fun than becoming the outdated God?"

He gave me a peculiar smile, making his face suddenly younger than it had been one second ago. It couldn't be my illusion to see him at this very instant somehow look like a youth of eighteen or so before my eyes.

"To tell you in a nutshell, you *are* my food."

"You…eat me?" My blunt question sounded so ridiculous, but I couldn't think of anything else.

"Yes, only that I don't eat you as you eat your food in your primitive process. I consume and digest your negative thoughts, or more accurately, I am living on humans' miseries. And now you begin to understand humans' miseries do happen for a reason."

"Good Heavens!" I let out a gasp.

"But a handful of you are just like a few bites. I need the whole mass in each meal to sustain my existence."

He found me speechless, so he went on as merrily as he could be.

"Allow me to explain in simple terms. But first, take a guess: what is the main diet that keeps me *alive*?"

My expression was still as blank as ever.

"*Lust*," his eyes were piercing me. "I need *that*. The fiery lust from all of you is the primary source of my life force."

"Lust? Why…?"

"It is vital to me as the protein is to you," he nodded. "I am so fortunate that lust is the most abundant food source. Why? Anywhere on this planet, if you find two humans, there you find lust."

His voice was growing more insidious.

"Too bad that lust alone can't entirely sustain my well-being. I need more of various stuff to keep my nutrients in balance."

Little by little, I began to see the whole picture, which had once been scattered pieces of a jigsaw puzzle to me..

"I need your *hatred* and *wrath,* as you need carbohydrates stuff to generate my energy,

"So do our *greed, fear*, and *despondence...*" I said warily.

"You got it," he looked pleased. "Those act as minerals and vitamins to boost all my functional systems that enable me to stay immune and invulnerable by all odds."

"Is that what we are for, to you? Your food?" I asked incredulously.

"Yes, nothing more, nothing less."

This was too much for me to respond. So, I only kept glaring at him as he continued.

"The Earth you live in is no better than a cage full of captive creatures, princes, and paupers likewise. Once born in that cage, they will be fattened with miseries in their own way until they are fat and succulent enough to become my luscious meals. The best tool to stimulate miseries in all of you that I've found is to cause you suffering by depriving your life of any sensible reasons. And that will ignite your rage as you brood over why bad things often come so senselessly, despite nothing you have done. And now you're beginning to find that miseries do happen for a reason."

His face now hardened.

"And this will answer why, year after year, your time in this world yields less happiness than a single day in comparison."

"But... I am lost. We have watched one particular soul on the screen since his rebirth until he became wealthy. Later, he loses all he has and suffers. How come the entire episode of the ups and downs in his life takes as swiftly as one minute while I watched it? Something is incongruous in the measure of time."

"No, you are not lost. You only need to learn more about the nature of time under different...um...time zones. If you study some ancient scriptures in Hinduism, you will see they mentioned what is called the Dimension of Time. This concept may seem inconceivable to you at first. It says a split second between inhaling and exhaling of Brahman, the Creator in

Hinduism, equals one million years on earth. It means that whatever action takes one second in that zone will take a million years on Earth. And remember, now you are under *my* Time Zone, which is, in your sense, inside Great-Great-Grandpa's trunk. That explains the time inside and outside the Great-Great-Grandpa are in different planes."

"Does it mean that if I spend a single minute here, years will pass outside? Then, when I step out again, will I become so, so old no one can recognize me anymore?"

"In fact, this place has *no* time. In other words, it means time stops to exist. It has not moved since the moment you stepped in. Not a second has passed. This place is a time capsule, free of the past, present, and future. I am out of the power of time. I stay outside its rule. That embodies my omnipresence. I can cross the forbidden border of space and time to appear anywhere and any period of time simultaneously."

Then he winked at me and laughed heartily.

"Although I hate to be called God, if God does exist, I admit I must be his match."

Now, I wanted so desperately to believe every word he had said because that meant he must be extraordinaire enough to let me take a glimpse of my father, who must be the one among those millions of light specks on the screen.

"Please, tell me, where is my father's light speck? I miss him so much."

He gazed at me with a strange look. After a pause, he started to shake his head.

"Why?" my genuine puzzle continued. "I still have the spectacles for my vision upgrade."

"No," he repeated. "Any spectacles can't help you. You hear? His wave signal frequency increased, causing his light to fade until it vanished from that screen and was beyond the observatory range."

"That means he has transcended," I whispered as goosebumps broke all over my body. "He must now exist somewhere beyond anyone's sight," I held my breath, "including yours."

My remark didn't anger him. He ignored it.

"In rare cases, some individuals are born with an unusual faint signal impulse. Rarely can hatred, greed, or fear affect their inner being. Your father is in that case, too. But no, that won't concern me a bit. I watch them escape all the traps because at the very end of their way out, lust, the humans' number one impulse, will await them and make them fall head-on and get stuck there. There is no escape when lust is at work. Your father is one of the best examples."

Then he began his obscene smile.

"He could overcome his other flaws with little effort. But just like every male, he fell victim to his lust if women came to arouse his hidden carnality. During his coitus with any of his women, I could see his impulse light signal turn ablaze in the equal extreme as if the screen were caught on the wildest fire." he chuckled. "Let's say lust is his Achilles heel."

"But he made it," I said slowly. "He disappeared from your map without a trace despite his Achilles heel. How could he?"

But he went on as if he had not heard my question.

"Anyone who ever crossed his path was destined to be his curse, one way or another. And you are his number one curse. You are meant to kindle his grudge and shove him to me."

"But…he never regrets having me in his life. If you are my stalker, you must know it."

"Yes, I admit I was disappointed to see him love you like his own son. I can't believe when he, who never wanted to kill even one single ant, strangled one female to death without a second thought to save a boy who was all the cause of his tragic life. I'm lucky that this case is rare among millions of humans. Otherwise…"

"How about Lin Jong? She must be the best source of nutrients for your life's sustenance."

"One of the vilest creatures she is I could find in humans—

my top specialty. But she's too valuable to be gorged down my throat in one bite. To find her match in dragging other humans down to the pit of their misery is not easy. For this reason, I'd rather save the extra-wicked human as my bait to lure others into their miseries."

"May I ask about one more person?"

"Of course, you can, son," he replied in his mockingly kind voice. "I'm opening a rare chance for you to question anything your limited capability as a mere human allows you," he paused, "before you start to pay me back. Deal!"

"My father's fiancée, Grace... Where is she now? A pristine soul like her must be able to escape you as my father did."

A cunning smile flickered on his face before he answered.

"Believe it or not, she failed, terribly failed."

That utterly surprised me. Oh, sweet girl. I always remembered Grace's unique smile in that photograph, which became my keepsake, although the flame of fire had already licked every page of my father's journal into ashes. No matter what, I would save Grace's image deep in my heart as the mother I wanted, wished for, and died for.

"She was born into this world with an unsurpassed start: heart, brain, and mind. Those qualities she possessed made her no less than perfect. But what defiled all her good and so dragged her down to my grip was her blinded and crushing love for your father. It was her Achilles heel that made her unable to accept the cruel fact of losing him, so she took her own life and died in utter agony. Her self-pity made her a coward compared to your father, who was determined to endure his far worse agony with far more courage and dignity."

The man's words were moving me to tears.

My father turned his back on his best future to live his worst life with a heart of steel. All that he had done was for an unwanted orphan infant to have a chance to live and have a father. The ordeal from that ultimate sacrifice must have chastened and cleansed his soul so completely that he had transcended his old suffering self, like a caterpillar, once trapped inside its dark cocoon, finally metamorphosing and emerging as a free butterfly. That must be why that devil's radar device could not detect the pure, selfless soul he has become.

* * * * *

Part 3: Chapter 4

The One

*S*uddenly, something was flashing in my mind.

"I know another mortal man born into this world was said to find a passage to escape you. It happened a long, long time, several thousand years ago. Is this true? "

The flickering smile appeared on his lips. He knew in one instant the one I was mentioning, yet he said nothing.

"Can you reveal that to me? I want to know the whole truth from you, not just from other sources in some ancient scrolls passed on for thousands of years and perhaps have already lost their authenticity over time."

"Nothing is free. Wait and see what you have to pay me back."

"No, it should be the other way around," I said, shaking my head in protest. "Is it you who owes us all the miseries of humanity? My request is so small compared to *what* you have taken from us."

The man burst out his guffaw. He seemed pleased at my

response.

"I'm so impressed, Mr. Pran. I bet one day you can become the best attorney of law for your clients to win all your cases," he sighed regretfully. "But first, you must help yourself escape from this place. It's as hard as to escape death?"

But then his bearing abruptly changed.

"If the one you mention is that Gautama prince named *Siddhartha*, I admit he is my formidable match in fighting. We fought tooth and nail to win one another. Yes, we did. That's why, of all humanity on earth, he must be the last one I could ever forget…"

While he spoke, he was turning to face me.

"Look now! I'm going to project that particular part of my memory on you."

At that moment, it was as if he were hypnotizing me to stare deep into his eyes. I couldn't turn away from those abyssal eyes that were not the eyes any longer but portals into the infinity. The deeper I gazed, the more I felt I was looking across the vast expanse of an immense transparent mirror reflecting something flickering and moving at the center. I tried to focus as the foggy, shadowy image of a dark figure gradually appeared. Until it became clear enough that it was the figure of a man.

It must be him, the Stalker's formidable match.

At first glance, I felt disappointed. He did not possess the celestial appearance of a divine being. I had always pictured him as one of the holiest, most sacred figures on earth. His height, look, and demeanor were not different from those of an average, ordinary man of twenty-nine years of age I found everywhere—no greatest splendor of divinity, no aura of the glowing halo around his shaved head as I had often seen in his grand illustration painting in my present-day.

In his moving image, which seemed to project forward from the man's eyes and suddenly fully appear before me as if the ancient past was coming alive again, I saw *him* wandering barefoot amid the cloud of dust in the air. It must be in the middle of a dry season. The vast land was parched, the trees scraggy, and the field grasses dried everywhere.

He was heading toward some remote village where a group of cowherds was tending their cattle nearby. A small dry gourd was hanging loosely from his shoulder, with a worn, dirty robe wrapped around his thin, exhausted body. Beads of sweat from the sun's heat at noon dripped from his gaunt face with every step he took. He had walked for two days with nothing to fill his stomach. His gourd for containing water was empty. But with his calm composure, no one knew that he was struggling against his growing thirst, hunger, and fatigue at every step he attempted to head toward that small village.

He walked into these cowherds who were idling under the cool shade of a tree while their cattle were grazing around them in the fierce sun's heat.

Phrata, I am a pilgrim traveling from the north. May you spare me some water from the well yonder?

They looked at him suspiciously. They must have mistaken him for a penniless beggar coming to beg for food.

Our well is only for the Brahmin clan. No one else is allowed to use or touch it. Otherwise, the water will be contaminated by the impure hands of the lower castes. Let me know the clan you belong to.

He then bowed his head humbly.

I already abandoned whatever once belonged to me and whoever I once was. With no possessions to taint my soul, should I be pure enough to touch that water?

But he was astonished when they shouted at him in alarm.

Stop where you are! If you belong to none of the castes, you are a Chandal, an Untouchable. Don't come too close to me. Your impurity will defile my pure soul if your feet step on my shadow.

However, the young ascetic attempted to reason with them.

Brothers, between the one whose perception is clouded by ignorance and the one clear from it, who should be the purer?

If you want to ensure I am telling the truth, think the opposite of what your Guru has taught you.

Our Guru teaches us God's words. How dare you challenge our Trimurti Lord?

The young pilgrim replied in his modest manner.

First, you must put aside God from your mind if you want to see the truth that has been hidden behind all the beliefs you are being taught.

Get out of our village, you sinful. Get out, worthless beggar!

His reply made them scream in anger and chase him out by throwing stones at him.

Brothers, I come in peace to seek the truth of what causes all of us to suffer. You cannot beg God to help you because He can't. It is beyond God's power to make these sufferings disappear from men. But if I succeed, I will return to free all of you from all sufferings. Please remember I shall return.

The outcast ascetic had told them in his determined but tranquil voice while the drops of blood from the stones kept trickling down his face. Before he was gone from their sight, those outraged cowherds threw more stones at him.

Don't you dare come back, beggar? Or you will be stoned to death by our god-fearing villagers for your blasphemy.

Before his image disappeared entirely, he turned to face me. For the first time, I saw his face in close-up and looked into his eyes. Oh, those eyes.

It was the moment the world stood still, and I ceased to exist until I blinked and eventually returned to be myself once again. In the instant of that moment, I knew this must be Him, the man who would become the Buddha, the Awakened One.

"Isn't it *him*?" My voice was barely a whisper. "Isn't it the one who defeated you?

I heard the stalker man scoff.

"He looked too beaten to lift his finger to fight anyone, not to mention defeating *me*. What a poor, pathetic beggar. Well, that's what he asked for. All you just witnessed in that hologram—"

Then he stopped and laughed.

"Hologram! Pardon me again for using that fancy term you've never heard of, and you will accuse me of showing off. All I want to say is I didn't conjure up those images you've seen. You've just visualized the genuine event that happened and has been stored in my memories being projected out as a short motion picture for you to view. That particular event you just watched happened right after Siddhartha left his palace paradise in secret and ventured into the world outside. He must have been shocked when he was chased out with stones for merely asking for water to quench his thirst. And so, he began to learn his lesson on how this unfamiliar new world he was about to enter could be so ruthless to him without his overprotective father and his regal status. It should dishearten and stop him from going forward. And you know what?"

I braced myself every time his sly smile appeared on his face.

"I *was* one of the cowherds who started throwing the stone at him and urging the others to follow. I know he must suffer from the wound because my stone hit him right on his temple. Don't look startled. Didn't I tell you I can be anyone and present anywhere?"

"But he never gave up. Before he defeated you and had countless followers, he must have undergone all kinds of humiliation and harassment countless times much worse than that one he received from these cowherds, I believe."

"If you want me to tell you about him, you better shut your mouth from interrupting me and listen well. I watched his speck of light on this very screen like I've watched everyone else. I kept stalking him, therefore no one on earth had known him inside out more than me. All right?"

"But *his* light signal? Did it have colors…" I couldn't help wondering when he mentioned that light signal, "…just like the rest of us?"

"Of course," he chuckled. "A flicker of his anger flashed on my screen when stones hit him. He is a mere human. Especially in his early life, excess pleasures perpetually surrounded him. Besides his gorgeous wife, you must know he also had many concubines to beguile him all day and all night from all kinds of aesthetic entertainment, wine, dance, poetry, and, of course, erotic pleasure from them. While I kept stalking him, I must see to it that his light signal must be constantly alighted by these mundane pleasures to distract him from his awareness of all human miseries in this world."

"Can you tell me more about his life as it actually is? Not from his grandiose legend full of inflated miracles, but in flesh and flaws from what you had observed him."

"Of course, there won't be anyone who knows about him better. Listen…" he said proudly.

Then, the whole story that he assured me was true and authentic began to stream out.

"I'd kept watching Siddhartha since he was a little prince of the Gautama noble clan. As you already know, he arrived into this world on the full moon day in the springtime of May in the Himalayan region nearly three thousand years ago…

"Although his mother, Queen Maha Maya, died after giving birth to him, I witnessed him living the fairytale lifestyle that his father, King Suddhodana, had set up to pamper him and shield his young son from the harsh reality of the outside world and all kinds of sufferings known to men. The sun and the moon were the only things his father could not climb up and take down to him if Siddhartha wished for these celestial things. He was protected to the extreme to ensure that aging, sickness, and death were entirely unknown and unheard of. His father had forbidden anyone in his royal court from letting his son know of those horrid facts of life. Any gravely sick and dying persons would be promptly brought out of the court to die somewhere else out of the prince's sight…

"The reason behind that extremity had stemmed from his father's ultimate hope for Siddhartha. The prince was expected to be crowned as the greatest ruler according to the prophecy given to him since his birth. But I'd kept watching his unusual, feeble signal among the detectable millions on my screen since he was born. I sensed he would one day become my top archenemy, so it must be necessary to stop him since his early life. I started a plan by visiting his father in a subconscious state in his dream, disguised as a great oracle, and stirring his fear by warning him that I had foreseen the future of his rebellious son, who was born with a benevolent heart beyond measurement, that he would reject all material success his father paved for him and choose to pursue a spiritual path. The only way to prevent it was to confine his son to wealth and power. Never allowed him to know the reality outside. My prophecy frightened him to death. Poor king, I borrowed the father's hand to prevent his son from escaping me. And it worked more than I could ever expect. After that, Siddhartha had become no more than a captured bird in his gold cage…

"The old king was never aware that amid this unsurpassed splendor that he had showered his son, the prince always vaguely felt his life was missing some meaning more worth living for. The older he became each year, the more he loved to be alone, looking out the window and watching birds flying in freedom inside his lush and beautiful garden. He constantly pondered; he had heaven and earth in hand, whereas the birds only had wings. But why did those birds seem happier? What true meaning could it be to fill the void his life had become…

"As the future king, once in a while, his father sent Siddhartha to visit the outside of the palace in a horse-drawn gold chariot, surrounded by protecting guards. Every time, he found the townspeople all young and cheerful with their happy faces, welcoming him with garlands of marigold flowers and music. The greeting *Jai Jai Rajkumar, glory to the crown prince* from the crowd as they relentlessly chanted to their prince was drowning all other unpleasant sounds while his chariot gracefully passed them along the main street. He saw everyone sing and dance in exuberance as if all they had ever known was joy. *This is our great state, and you will reign one day, my son. Haven't you witnessed how felicitous all our people are? They need you as their great ruler to keep our state in such glory forever.* The king never forgot to remind his son every time Siddhartha returned to his palace with the pile of gifts he had received from his people...

"But one day, out of curiosity, he found a chance to sneak out of his palace, disguised as a commoner with only his charioteer Janna tagging along. That day had turned his previous world upside down, and it forever changed his view of life. Merely a few steps he made out of the palace gate, a strange, heinous creature he'd never seen rushed to him and collapsed at his feet. *Young man, spare me some coins. I am dying from hunger.* The prince gasped and cried in alarm. *What is that creature, Janna? If it is a human, why does it look so grotesque? Yet, if it is an animal, why is it able to speak?* His loyal chariot finally gave his naïve prince an honest answer. *Yuvaraj, he is a human. He is nothing different from us. Only he is old and sick; his sparse hair is turning all white, and his face and skin are all wrinkled like dried dates. Oh, none is left on his wrecked body except his own skeleton...*

"Suddenly, that old man began to convulse, blood spurting down his mouth, prompting Siddhartha to cry in terror. *What happens to him? What, Janna?* And so, Janna reluctantly replied. *That pauper is suffering from hunger and prolonged sickness. He is dying, your Highness. Dying, Janna?* He asked again, his eyes turning blank. *The poor man just stopped breathing, sir. He is dead now. Dead? What is that?* The prince was still puzzled. *It means he no longer exists in this world, your Highness.* Finally, Siddhartha began to grasp the concept of death. He shuddered and murmured, *Does this death thing happen only to this man or to everyone, to you and me also? Yes, your Highness, death occurs to anyone at any moment and often in the least expected way. All of us will face this inevitability of death with no exception. That's why His Majesty wants to hide this most appellant truth from you. Your Highness, we cannot leave the dead over here. The body is going to deteriorate as soon as its owner dies. It needs to be cremated before rats and maggots feast on his flesh...*

"As Siddhartha listened, he felt something he had never known until the sudden sight of the pathetic dead man awakened that long-dormant feeling. Its powerful impact caused tears down his face and sent him a pang of pain that crushed his heart. *Oh, poor, poor thing. May you take this pouch of gold coins and give it to any passerby in exchange for helping cremate his corpse.* But his charioteer replied. *This man must be an outcast, an Untouchable. No one wants to touch him, but it will work, my young prince, with your gold...*

"After that, he and Janna blended among the townspeople in the marketplace. He was determined to delve deeper into the cruel reality his father had hidden from him since his birth. Siddhartha began to realize that all the glorious things in town he had seen earlier were staged to fool him. But today, he was encountering a reality of life full of struggle and suffering. He passed a one-legged cripple staggering on his cane and begging around. He found children in rags, perhaps also the Untouchable, searching for food scraps in the garbage piles. Channa begged him to return since he had ventured too far, but Siddhartha kept wandering further into the dark alley full of filth and foul smell from cow dung until they heard the clamors among a small crowd at one corner. They were fiercely yelling and beating a lad who was crouching painfully on the ground. *Please stop. Please don't hurt him.* Siddhartha rushed to the beaten lad and helped him to his feet...

"But his act infuriated that crowd. *It's none of your business, young man. He is a thief who sneaks here daily and snatches money from the pockets of the passers-by. He deserves a beating to his death.* Siddhartha, now understanding the meaning of death so well, held that lad closer to him and said, *Before punishing him, you should find what truly caused this lad to become a thief and help make it right.* But they spat at him and continued their zealous beating with the clubs. Siddhartha eventually became part of being bludgeoned as he attempted to protect that young thief. But those acts instantly stopped when Janna raised his hand and showed them the crown prince's emblem badge, which he had concealed inside his bag for the prince. That place immediately fell into silence, and everyone crouched on the ground, trembling with fear and shock. They had known death was the sole punishment for any common man who dared to touch the crown prince, let alone harm him. That man would be burnt alive, along with the rest of his entire family. Although that vicious crowd had left a few bruises on some parts of his body, Siddhartha only asked Channa to bring him out of that place without creating a scene. But when Channa noticed those bruises on the prince's arm, he was aghast and cried. *Your Highness, please forgive your loyal servant. I know you want to remain anonymous in public. But that frenzied crowd could have torn you to pieces if I hadn't let them know who you are. So, please allow me to remind you that as their future king, you possess great power over all your subjects under this kingdom. As your father always says, power enables you to rule the world and put every life under your feet, including all those puny market people whose lives are also at your mercy. Please, you must recognize the face of the one who bruised your arm; he must pay one hundredfold for his act.* But the young prince shook his head firmly in refusal. *No, this is not what I want. If I have such power, I want it to help free my people, not oppress them."*

That man paused once again to show me another sinister smile. What I unmistakably read from that smile was: *You guess right. It's me again who bruised the prince's arm. Oh, just to help him change his mind and so turn back to his palace, where all the dangers would never penetrate those golden walls to harm him again."*

Yes, I knew. There must be no one else but this ubiquitous

stalker.

"And then, one night, his pregnant wife, Princess Yasodhara, gave birth to a son. Never before had Siddhartha witnessed how greatly a woman could suffer from childbirth. Amidst her utmost agony from labor pain, his newborn child arrived into the world with a loud, piercing wail to render the suffering and pain as his mother did. In great distress, he saw his infant child struggling to grasp his first breath as his frail, tiny body was still soaked with blood. Another soul was born into this world to meet a prelude to more miseries waiting to come into life. Oh, his poor child was far too innocent to realize it. That vision made Siddhartha's heart burst with great sorrow not only for his newborn son but also for all humanity who were ever born only to become aged, sickened, and then dead. Yet, in between, they knew only the never-ending sufferings that mostly caused others to also suffer as if all were linked together to form an endless cycle that trapped everyone within. The occurrence in that marketplace suddenly flashed in his mind, showing how cruel and heartless people could treat one another out of their own struggle for survival. Although breaking that cycle was still a mystery to Siddhartha, he was now dead set on breaking it, even at the cost of his own life.

"I knew that his time was coming. His wife, in her profound repose due to the prolonged exhaustion from childbirth, was not conscious of the moment of her husband's departure. Otherwise, she would try all possible ways to deter him from leaving her. Attempting my last chance to stop him, I stirred his sleeping child in a crib awakened, and so started his loud wailing, beckoning Siddhartha to come and keep him in his arms. As he watched his wife in her tranquil sleep, he bent to kiss her farewell and forced back his tears. All the cherished moments they shared together were flashing in his mind. But finally, he suppressed it and silently walked out from his endearing wife and son. When he stepped out of their bed chamber, their attachment as man and wife was permanently cut. Yet before he left everything behind in search of a higher meaning in life, he would keep her as the best part of his memory during his temporal life. Without him, at least his wife and son could still have a comfortable life under his father's good care, which helped comfort him from his guilt of leaving his loved ones behind. He intended to return to her only when he became the Buddha and free her from suffering with the truth he found."

"That means the truth about your existence," I said grimly.

He nodded. "Yes, he found my existence, which was as old as time. He himself saw with his eyes that I am not a personified figure but, as real as he is, only far superior. Why? I could be present simultaneously everywhere in disguise of everything on earth. That's why I could stalk every move he made and approach him in whatever befitting forms to obstruct or distract his steadfastness to achieve enlightenment."

"Now I know you are *Mara*, the Great Demon," I acclaimed excitedly. "You are recorded and mentioned through millenniums as Lord Buddha's greatest nemesis in ancient Buddhist doctrines, especially in his enlightenment-day episode."

"Thank you. It is an honor to acknowledge my never-fading celebrity," he chuckled. "You are right. Most Buddhists, and you too, have known me as Mara, the Lord of Desire. That part is correct because human desire is fundamental to my existence. It's my food…"

"If you are Mara, you are the one who turns good men bad and bad men evil with all possible tricks."

"That is me in a nutshell."

After a moment of silence from me, he continued to pick up on that subject.

"After leaving the secular world, your prince led a secluded life of asceticism for six long years, sometimes staying by himself and sometimes joining different ascetic groups. He sought the correct deliverance method to tame and calm the dynamic of mind among many strict practices until he realized that his practice of severe self-torment only led to a waste. He decided not to follow those wrong paths and find his own despite the insult from other ascetics that giving up was an act of failure. So, I assumed this was good news, a sign he had finally given up his pursuit and returned to his secular life. It would ease my work. All I needed after that was only to check him at random."

His voice then began to falter.

"I became aware that I underestimated him. How foolish I was. Suddenly my watching alarm device went off to alert me. On my map screen, my eyes caught Siddhartha's flickering light signal becoming dimmer until it was barely visible. I knew something phenomenal, as never before, was about to happen. And I must stop it immediately...

"That night almost three thousand years ago, by the measure of human time, those memories are still so lucid as if it was happening at this instant. No, he didn't give up. I found him seated alone beneath a massive pipal tree by the white sandbank of the Nairanjana River. The full moon cast the luminous and serene light upon the ripples of the crystal-clear river, on the tree foliage, and on his moonlit-illuminated body, which was as still as a sculpture while entering his ultimate meditative state. What a beautiful human. Even though he was my bitterest foe, as I watched him, I couldn't help but admire him with even a touch of respect for his adamance in seeking what he believed would break the cycle of suffering for all beings...

"But on that well-known episode of the last battle that I'd played a significant role in that part, they portrayed me in that scene in an image of Mephistophelian Mara, the supervillain Lord of Demons, with my stretching one thousand hands, well-armed, riding on one immense elephant surrounded by an enormous, all-powerful, demon army. The dynamic movement of my monstrous army marching to defeat Siddhartha was so thundering that heaven and earth were quaking and almost rolled into one. It darkened the skies, swirled the ominous clouds, and crackled the air with almost supersonic thunderbolts. All for smashing him under my feet. All the angels earlier descending from heaven to witness that ultimate battle between him and I became so intimidated by my grandiose arrival that they eventually fled and left the prince to face me utterly alone under a lone pipal tree, where he was seated to meditate the whole night."

"You mean it was you and all your army against one mere human," I said incredulously.

"It's my last chance to crush him. There is only one rule when you are at war: might is right. To scare the living daylights out of my enemy, I had to conjure an atmosphere of violent tempest, raging winds, and deafening thunders as if the apocalyptic day were arriving."

"Did it work?"

"If it worked, his light signal on my wall screen must show a spark of blue and indigo from his fear and terror. But…no. That light still faded steadily from the screen, prompting me to use another strategy, the last and yet the best."

"What is that?"

"Turning his light signal as red as infernal fire. Remember what I told you? You might overcome your anger, greed, and fear. All except one."

I was aghast. I knew what he was implying to me.

"As depicted in the Buddhist doctrine, I sent my 'daughters,' all three of them, Tanha, Raga, and Arati, to appear and reveal their unearthed beauty before his eyes. They came to reinforce my impending victory. How beautiful were they? Ah, even the beauty of all goddesses descending from Heaven would pale by comparison when my daughters appeared side by side with them to transcend them all."

"Are they your real daughters, as it said?" My voice was full of doubts.

He laughed. "They are, in a sense. They are, in fact, the embodiment of me under different entities and genders. Once they appeared, they seduced him with the flowing grace of their sensual movement as they sang and danced under the night sky while the moon cast the moonlight on their faces, their cascade of shimmering dark hair, their soft curves of quivering breasts, and their sculpture-carved limbs twisting in fierce and fiery desire in Siddhartha's presence. Since the time they came into existence, no single male on earth could ever resist their feminine mysticism that radiated to pull man after man into their black-hole embrace where nothing in this universe was able to escape after it had been pulled and disappeared into. Their erotic power could break the mightiest male as if it broke a twig in one instance, not to mention the one like Siddhartha, who, since entering a secluded life, never had a chance to be even as close as an arm's length to such a beauty who could revive his manhood at his first touch on her."

"But they couldn't move him as nothing could move the rock mountain. Did you detect any flicker of red in his light signal?"

Finally, he slowly shook his head.

"At the crack of dawn, his light signal suddenly vanished entirely from the screen, leaving me utterly devastated and helpless. This was a phenomenon that a human could conquer me for the very first time. Due to this final battle, he made my detector device malfunction. The whole screen shut down. I couldn't catch any movement on the white blank screen. And while I exhausted myself to death trying to fix that device, he made some people aware of my existence and sneaked them behind my back to the way out..."

I felt the ripples of shiver running all over my skin. It was true. Whatever I had learned about Siddhartha the Buddha was so true. He was not some obscured figure, merely referred to in the ancient scrolls and doctrine textbooks, whom I knew had achieved Nirvana state of mind and then brought light to us with a truth that all humans' sufferings originate from their own desire and internal basic instincts inside their mind and not from the external occurrences. Right before my eyes, that mythical Buddha emerged as a real man, a man of flesh and blood who once walked the earth and struggled and suffered from his dark desires just like every mortal man on this planet, my father and I included. But what made him different from all the mortals was that he had found the secret to overcoming his instincts: the origin of all sufferings. How ironic that the evidence of the Buddha's existence was confirmed by this man—no, I meant this entity—who was standing tall and ominous in front of me.

"You are so omnipotent, so God-like, whereas Gautama Buddha is merely a human, a small fly to a mammoth like you. And yet he defeated you."

"Defeat me?" He scoffed, "For how long? Ah! you are as ignorant as most of his followers. Listen! Nearly three thousand years have passed since his death. Is this world more peaceful *now*? Do men suffer *less*? Think! And be brave enough to give me the honest answer."

I knew I wouldn't have gained any advantage if I had answered him with bleeding honesty. So, I let him have his triumphant laugh.

"It's me who has a last laugh. His victory lasted as briefly as a flash of lightning compared to your world's four billion years. Yes, in a wink, the flutter of his victory was out, and the darkness returned as dark as before. How many men was Gautama Buddha able to bring to freedom from my bondage? Very, very few indeed. If all humanity could be compared to all grains of beach sand on earth, the ones Gautama could salvage through his eighty years of age were only a handful he scooped up into his palm. And what did he do with the rest he left to be my food as ever?"

After a short moment of silence, I sighed and murmured.

"If only our world could have been without you…"

"You hurt my feelings," he smiled mockingly. "I know you hate me to the bone. But, well, thank you for that because I thrive on your hatred. However, would you mind learning more about me in order to hate me even more? Who am I? Why am I here?"

No need to try to hide my bursting enthusiasm. Of course, no one on earth could mesmerize me more than this man."

"So, please let me introduce myself," his smile was genuine when he noticed an unhidden eagerness sparking on my face. "First, I must take you back to the beginning of time... And now listen...Once upon a timeless time, in the silent void of space, somewhere in an infinite and barren cosmos..."

And his voice seemed to come from a distance afar.

"There, for the first time, a birth of consciousness had emerged from the depths of the mysterious, vast mass of dark matter."

"Dark matter? I've never heard of that."

"To make the complicated simpler, it is the counterpart of the visible matter that co-exists within this cosmos. But dark matter is invisible, therefore non-existent and perpetually unknown to its counterpart, which you men belong to."

"But to me, you do exist. I can see you," I wondered around.

"Yes, you can see me, but only through one of my numerous disguises as you perceive me right now in a male human form. So far, the singular human among billions who's able to see the real me is your Buddha. He was also the first to use the *Ajintai* term in classifying all the inexplicable to humans, including my existence."

"But how come your original form is nonexistent?"

"I try to be patient with your bombardment of nonsense questions," he sighed heavily. "All right, at least talking to a curious human never bores me. The answer is that I was born out of the womb of dark matter, the invisible and, hence, the most mysterious substance in this universe. Dark matter doesn't emit light, unlike the other form of matter that adheres to it. And because any non-existence does not contain mass and so it can't have weight. The way to prove the existence of dark matter is only through its gravity.

I understood only half of what he explained, yet, it was still so fascinating that I urged him to continue.

"Maybe you want to know how I was born. My earliest state of consciousness happened suddenly amid the infinite void. In one instant after its birth, that consciousness became aware of itself, which led to its awareness of other things in its surroundings. From that moment of its primordial birth, it multiplied from a single pinpoint into a whole network of lines, and with that came the length, breadth, depth, and level of dimension upon dimension complexity that led to an entire growing of consciousness, which finally hatched into me, me, me, a shifting darkness of living mass invisible to all but itself. Finally, I am alive and kicking. A lone, living dark matter in the universe. And yet, having one attribute of primal instincts all alive things have shared, I started an enormous hunger for food to keep myself alive…

"Amid the cosmic abyss, I scented the aroma of a food source for life sustenance permeating the void across the vast expanse of space—the aroma of some dark malevolence that would fuel my life force. So, with my fluid entity shrouded in ink-black dark that no light could penetrate such darkness, I started my desperate and longest journey searching for food…

"After being lost and drifting for a seeming eternity, with my ravenous hunger growing with each passing moment, I followed that aroma until I entered the other side of visible matters unknown to me. And finally, I came into a world where the source of that aroma was found. It was so bountiful, so lush with lives—living things that created all kinds of malice and chaos for one another, so perfect to be my food. So, I secretly settled down in this small paradise and grew stronger by hunting its inhabitants for eons," then he laughed heartily at his joke. "Luckily, I'm not a human. Because with such a rich diet, I must have a problem with my high cholesterol and excess blood sugar."

As a surprise, I couldn't help interrupting him.

"I thought it's you who has caused suffering in the first place. Human suffering had happened even before you arrived, hadn't it?"

"You become too smart. I don't like it, all right?" he snapped and then continued. "Humans are inborn with seeds of evil. It is inside you, and sorry, that has nothing to do with me because I came after the birth of humans from the other side of the cosmos. But after I'd arrived, I kept cultivating and fertilizing those seeds in humans until they boomed tenfold before reaping them for my food. That could explain why the series of mass destruction that has caused great miseries to erupt continuously, here and there, throughout human history. Now, choose one villain. Who is the world's most evil man in your eyes? Choose!"

"It should be Genghis Khan, the Mongol ruler who lived around one thousand years ago." I picked that name without a second thought and found him smiling.

"Well done. And a reason for that choice, please."

"That man mystifies me for the unparalleled horror he left the world to remember even after he had gone one millennium ago. No one could think of him as a human but a slaughtering machine. I read that the blood-spilling genocides from his countless wars across half of the world helped him create the largest empire ever to exist on earth, with half of the world population perishing during his act of massive bloodshed ever recorded in history.

"Now, let me tell you the role I played. Prior to that period, the world seemed too harmonious and peaceful, meaning my food was becoming scant. With urgent alarm, I must seek a maniac whose Achilles heel was an insatiable thirst for blood and power—someone born on the opposite pole to Siddhartha Gautama. Finally, I found the perfect one matching my criteria: Temujin, a young man from a remote tribe in the Steppe region who had undergone such a miserable childhood that nothing was left in his heart except the grudge he held against the entire world. To make a long story short, I, in disguise, paved my way to become one of his most trusted counselors after he rose to power as a leader of his tribe. I was the one who kept fueling him with an image of himself as the world conqueror. I whispered to him every single day that, as a mortal, his time on earth had a limit, so he must bring his power to find no boundary before his swift life was gone...

"I coaxed him to leave his footprint as an immortal legacy no mortal man had ever achieved, the legacy that would shake the whole world to turn to recognize him as the greatest warrior who ever walked the earth. And it worked as you have witnessed in history. It did. What he breathed in and out throughout his sixty-five years on earth was not the air but power, the power to kill and create suffering for humanity on the largest scale ever known to men. Now, choose one more world-notorious villain, and I will tell you how I helped galvanize the evil inside that one."

"No!" I almost screamed. "That's enough!"

"No?" he kept toying with me. "You will miss one of my masterpieces. Are you sure you want to skip this part?"

However, he opened his smile and continued.

"You could always find me at the heart of every major genocide. I bet you've heard of the ruination of the Aztec and Maya Empires, which caused their entire civilization wiped out about five centuries ago. It was the work of the Spanish conquistadors who defeated the two kingdoms and ruled them as colonies. Of course, you could find me in that conquistador group. I told the admiral of the group that waging open war against the two great empires alone would take years to conquer, and we might lose. So, I suggested a genius plan to befriend the indigenous by giving the clothing brought from our home country as amiable gifts. But they were not new clothes," he sniggered. "They were already used by sick and dead people who had smallpox…"

I stared at him, my throat as dry as dust.

"As a result, more than eighty percent of the Aztec and Mayan population died from the wide-spreading smallpox epidemic. That deadly disease, which was unknown to them, completely weakened their strength to resist our attack and plunder. Only ten percent survived and were enslaved. I wish you could see us loading tons of their gold into our fleet. And one ship sunk from the overload during the trip back." He was shaking his head. "How greedy! How greedy!"

Oh, what should I do with this monster? I remembered he'd earlier told me he didn't need to get rid of me. Only let me go, and I would realize how pointless to live anymore in this world.

"I was in this paradise *Sans-Souci* until this Gautama Buddha stood bold in my way and warned the world of my existence and my sustenance on human defilements and flaws. At first, I was so devastated. What if all the men had believed him and left me alone in a barren and empty world without food? But eventually, I could figure out the most brilliant plan, which I called 'the tactic of divergence.' Oh, I've taken that as paragon over all the works I have ever done…"

He knew he could spark my curiosity over again, the reason he paused and flashed the brightest smile.

"The most ingenious scheme to retaliate him was to 'idolize' him. Do you know what that means to idolize?"

I stared at him in wonder. How could I defeat someone so evil as much as so ingenious?

"Listen! After he had passed into nirvana at eighty, I began to launch an operation 'Buddha the God.' Century after century, I appeared in various disguises of high-rank monks and blended with many reverend groups. I kept advocating the 'upgrade' of their Lord Buddha into deity status, a subtle and brilliant plan to shift people into believing that their Buddha possessed a god's power to bestow on his devotees the material success, wealth, and longevity to their heart's content…

"You see, the last thing Siddhartha Gautama wanted was to see himself change into God. I've used him as the perfect bait to lure most of his followers to me. That's why in this present time, you've seen his sacred statues on the altars to be worshiped by his devotees everywhere, not different from a hundred other idols in other religions. Apart from that, all sorts of rituals and prayers have been added, which lead to the false hope that those rituals' performance alone can grant all wishes and ward off all misfortunes. I used Siddhartha's hand to cut off the path he paved to help his people escape me. Today, the truth about me that he disclosed has been ignored and nearly lost in time. It has turned into a mere legend or a tall tale no one has taken seriously. While other religions have fed rage and violence to their fanatic believers, Siddhartha's religion, as observed today, has turned into a nursery where seeds of greed and desire are cultivated and flourish. Oh, I feel thankful to the religious diversity in this world for creating varieties for my diet. "

"You must be Evil yourself," I whispered. "And if Evil exists, so does God and his wrath."

"Oh, no! You should know God is indeed a reflection in the mirror. But don't you know you can't expect a mere reflection to come out of the mirror either to bless you or to curse you? But if you need God, I can be him for you. Who else is all-powerful over the whole of mankind if not me? If this entire planet were my home, religion would be my underground chamber where I could act in disguise of God to trick men into being my food. And so far, no suspicion has passed through anyone's mind that they have faith in the wrong God—poor, poor creatures. Have you ever wondered why violence and bloodshed always erupted among religious zealots? If men use religion to get away from me, they never realize that their ego and grudges and greed ignited under the name of religious faith are dragging them to stumble onto my feet."

I couldn't figure out why this monster brought me here and revealed what he should have guarded as his ultimate secret. But, I was absolutely sure he had not done that out of his benevolence. However, he promptly clarified my doubts as if he could read whatever was popping up in my mind.

"That's because I have a monotonous life. Therefore, I need a little more thrill when I get bored with easy catches. This time, I invite you to join a catch-me-if-you-can game. To encourage you, I showed you the direction to escape me. I even let you know there has always been a chance of escaping because a handful of you had already made it. Not to mention the prior one, like Siddhartha, even one of the runaways was the closest to you. Isn't it all fun watching you fly off in glory and pride until the enormous weight of your weakness begins to drag you down?"

"But why? Out of the millions, why do you pick me into your game?

"You are the one who is drooling over the truth, aren't you?" his smirk grew wider as he answered. "You are so desperate to know why all humans always suffer even though some don't deserve those sufferings. Today, I throw some light on this mystery. Hence, you need to pay back in return for that acknowledgment."

"We've never done wrong to you. Why! We even have no idea at all about your existence. Please, stop exploiting our sufferings. Please leave us alone."

As I begged him, he slowly turned to face me. He looked at me with a surprising expression of deep contemplation—this was the first time I had seen him with that expression.

"Have you ever wondered if animals have never done wrong to humans, but why do you take their lives by eating them? Is it wrong to do so? No, you don't think so, right? Why? Because if you don't consume other lives, you will otherwise lose your own. As simple as that."

The tone in his voice suddenly softened. And I only stared at him as he went on.

"I don't know," he repeated. "I don't know the real culprit who creates this system for our cosmos that way. Whoever is should be the one to be blamed for, not me."

All of a sudden, his subdued expression was gone. A flash in his gleeful eyes and his grimace returned.

"It's the same reason I can't afford to let all of you run off, one by one, and leave me to starve to death."

"It's not fair," was all I could think of. " Never fair at all."

"Stop whining and accept this harsh reality. At least I know that every existence was born into this cosmos, not for its own but to make use of one another so that the complex network as a whole will keep moving forward by this dark, negative force. Do you think you were born for your own merit? Do you believe each of you was designated to be in this world to accomplish something for your individual mission? How humans are driven by their enormous ego despite their complete ignorance."

He was pointing at that wall screen.

"Now, take a look. Your signal is now growing as bright as the sun. It shows that your bitter anger is uncontrollably spiraling up. Stop it now, please, for my own sake. How do I have fun if I detect and catch you right away? Oh, come on. Calm down, will you? I want a prey-hunting game that enlivens me with challenge and thrill."

"A pervert! You are a pervert!" That was what I could think of.

"Ah, I can feel every pore on my being digesting your rage energy," he raised his head and sighed deeply, his nostrils flaring up, his tongue smacking his lips. "Ah, how luscious."

I watched his face turn younger, his cheeks rosier and healthier, and every pore on his skin aglow as if illuminated from within.

"Now, look at me!"

What a beautiful, young creature he was transforming into before my eyes, in a sublime image resembling the ideal figure of an angel. I knew my rage had boosted it. It was generating his power energy to glow as if an angel being were now descending in my presence.

Our eyes met.

Then I saw what was lodging deep inside that pair of glittering eyes. Perhaps since the dawn of humanity, all human's lust, hatred, greed, and fear had taken root and flourished at the fathomless pit of his deep sockets. I saw the faces of my loved ones, of the ones I despised, and of the countless unknowns among the sea of faces of humans were imprisoned down, down there.

Who was to be blamed for his existence? In the name of humanity, we all were responsible for the accelerating thriving of this carnivorous entity. Each individual's toxic nature contributed to empowering this Stalker Being.

I heard him now coaxing me.

"Come on. You'd better feel fortunate to be a human. At least you don't stay at the pit-bottom level of this food chain system. While millions of living things on Earth are all your prey, you have only me and…yes, also your own kind as your predators," he paused, his smile widening, "In fact, I believe I am more merciful if be compared to your kind. I declare you humans are the most atrocious and savaged beings I have ever known. It's so fortunate that I am far, far superior to you. Otherwise, I could have met the same gruesome fate as those animals in that marketplace."

I hardly listened to him now. My mind was drifting back to the very moment I watched my father dying on my lap. Under the fierce sweep of the oars, four neighbors were racing that boat with every ounce of strength and energy to bring him to the medical station in time. They put all their efforts to win Death as if it were their own lives they must save, not my father's. I'd never forgotten that worst moment…

Yes, out of that worst moment of my life, I realized it also allowed me to witness the best in us humans. That day, I also witnessed the boundless kindness that my fellow humans had poured into a dying man and his heart-breaking son.

I heard my voice almost in a whisper.

"But you also told me the cosmos is far too complex. Didn't you tell me no one, *even* you, has ever conceived where it begins and where it ends, not to mention what a mystery is lying out there in between? You told me you came from 'the other side,' which is nonexistent to my perception. So, it's possible there must be more that are yet nonexistent to your awareness. And if so, how can you believe you are standing atop as the lone supreme of this infinite cosmos?"

I paused. Goosebumps began running all over my body. I felt my father's warm presence so close to me. It seemed like he was whispering his deep insight into my mind.

"Oh, have you ever thought of your *own* predator watching and stalking you in this same manner? There must be one, the alpha predator, for you to keep the cosmos in balance, too. Time to hide yourself now."

As my words, or perhaps my father's, came out, I saw him turning to stare at me.

He didn't immediately react to the essence of what I'd said. His movement stopped, but his steady gaze continued until his mind began registering its meaning.

I knew that by hitting the bullseye, I was flying head-on into a face of extreme peril, but I couldn't resist the urge. Now came one rarest chance in my insignificant life to humiliate, intimidate, and infuriate this...oh, whatever he might be, it didn't matter now as far as he regarded himself as a top predator.

"Ah, now you begin to feel what a prey must feel—just like all of us. Welcome to our camaraderie club in your new role of prey."

Only an instant later, he startled me with a fireball of rage suddenly blazing out of his eyes. The intensity of his rage could have burnt me alive, but at least I found myself still unscathed. That gave me a sudden chance to get back at him with what he had used to taunt me a moment ago.

"Oh, no! You're losing your temper. Stop at once for your own sake. Or you will make yourself an easy target for that predator who is perhaps watching you. Can you detect its presence now? Look around!"

It took me by surprise to watch his body suddenly jerk and twist. He quickly turned his head from me. I was not sure what was happening. Was it possible that what I said to evoke his rage had a grain of truth?

"If you believe my life exists only to be your food, how about your own? Apparently, you were born to do nothing more than consume me as well. When coming to this point, our lives are no better than one another. What insignificant existence we are sharing in this infinite void. Why... Who creates us that way? Why has the entire system been driven by the malevolence our hunger has caused? "

My voice faltered, and I felt a heavy lump in my throat. My rage dissolved into a new emotion that immediately erupted with equal intensity. I began to recognize that the feeling I had now was very close to a deep pity—a pure, naked pity at the depths of my heart I felt toward myself and also toward this creature who denominated himself the Stalker. What a strangest, eerily sense of kinship I began to feel toward him.

But when I looked at him again, his solid body seemed to blur, shift, and twist. He started to shrink and then fade until he became semi-transparent, enabling my eyes to penetrate through his glass-like body to see some part of a curved screen background. However, the complete absence of a sense of reality in this place made it almost impossible to be sure whether all the manifestations my eyes were witnessing—especially this man's presence—were mere illusions or actual realities.

Only a second later, his whole substantial body returned. He became a man of real flesh again, but this time, his fury frighteningly escalated. It doubled and then tripled until I could feel his white-hot heat permeating the entire chamber.

"Shut your mouth now!" he roared in pure rage.

"Puny creatures, a swarm of grubs under my stomp. Just one more damn word from your fucking mouth and your fucking whole planet will be smashed to smithereens."

I tried to imagine what would have been if my father had encountered the same circumstances that were looming over me now. How should he have responded and interacted with this entity? How? I must follow his standpoint to rescue myself from this hellish peril.

Papa, help me, Papa.

I was a little boy again, running into my papa's arms and crying for help. Amid my mounting desperation, I felt him. I felt him calmly speaking to that stalker in my voice.

"There's a saying you are what you consume. Now I see where you get your sky-high ego from. Have you realized you've devoured countless stuff of poison from humans?"

He glared at me, but I was not cowered.

"Before you came to our place, I have no clue how you were, but you've been feasting on the bad stuff in humans for hundreds of thousands of years. They must shape the fundamentals of your being. That's why the image you've created for yourself and your mental state is not different from all of us, the puny creatures you scorn. And, of course, you've also consumed tons of fear from humans, which must be stored in your structured body system. But it had never been used until the existence of your predator, which I've just brought up, starts to generate fear. Now you understand how it feels when one is afraid. No wonder you want me to shut up. You don't want to hear about it."

My father, living within my mind, went on attacking him relentlessly.

"But let me desperately hope you have not consumed only toxic natures from us humans but also absorbed our worthiness—kindness, compassion, and the like. Perhaps these virtues have been ignored and left for ions in your bowel..."

I couldn't help but smile my most insidious smile while sending this crucial message.

"Dig out that worthiness and use it to escape your own predator. No need to mention the great Buddha; my father alone proved he could escape you by using these virtues. So, just learn from him how to save yourself from your predator. Oh, watch out! That alpha predator of yours could be stalking you right this instant. So, hurry up. Stop your wrath and—"

Before I could finish, the thundering eruption of his wrath

abruptly emitted a violent wave. I felt my body swirling from its force as if it were a thin straw in the whirlpool of the ferocious storm. An instant later, my body was slammed onto the wall. The sharp pain shot through all parts of my body, and tears from raw pain stung my eyes.

"How dare you!"

He roared in naked rage.

After his thunderous roar nearly shook the whole chamber, I saw him grab his detector device and frantically pressed his fingers on the row of buttons in one swift motion.

Wispy white smoke appeared only seconds later and covered the entire map screen. Its density soon increased, so my eyes could not penetrate and see the map screen behind it. I saw nothing now but only the gray mass of smoke that crept in, curled and twisted as if it were a primordial creature shaking in violent pain. Finally, the smoke expanded and engulfed every square foot of the entire space.

Then I heard his explosive laughter behind the dense, massive gray mass.

"What are you doing? What?" I tried to control my increasing panic.

"Oh! Just a good lesson to teach you," his usual and playful voice was back, "a lesson mankind must remember until the last day of this planet. Get out! I change my mind now. This time, I let you live to see the hell outside awaiting you to witness. And *that* is for insulting me. Go now! Go before I change my mind. Go!"

Since the smoke obscured my view, I had no idea where the stench came from. Before I realized it became so overwhelming, I began to gag and convulse. It was unmistakably the stench of bloated and rotten flesh from decayed bodies in mass.

Not hundreds or thousands of them, but countless upon countless bodies that you could come upon only in a mass grave after the massacre in some major battlefield. Or, maybe they were the bodies of countless humans who had been his victims since the dawn of humanity.

That stench seemed to crush me with its invisible yet powerful grip. I felt my lungs burning, and my nose started bleeding.

The heat was increasing and increasing. I felt as if I was trapped to be burnt alive inside a room engulfed by the infernal fire from every corner. I let out a frantic scream as I groped awkwardly to find my way toward the exit, which was now completely shrouded by ominous dense smoke. As I struggled to move across the vast bouncy space, I finally found the door and yanked it open. As I stepped out, my feet finally touched the solid ground. Then I began to run for my life. Run to where? So far, I had no idea. I knew only I had to run.

I ran screaming out of that shack while that same damn dog appeared out of nowhere and jumped on me in ambush. This time, I already learned that the vibration from my high-pitched screams could stop that beast from further materializing. As I opened more screams, I saw the dog bursting open into dust in mid-air, followed by the whole shack I had just fled from, along with all the rows of trees and shrubs and everything within my field of vision.

If I couldn't make it in time to the fence gate that opened to the outside world, I knew the fence that outlined the perimeter of this place would be molten and vanish like everything else I was witnessing, and I would be trapped forever in the middle of nowhere amidst that chaotic, explosive current.

So, I blindly banged open the gate, slipped outside as swiftly as an arrow, and immediately plunged into the infinite expanse of the dark, dark abyss.

* * * * *

Part 3: Chapter 5

Inferno

*H*elp, help. Someone help me now....

No sooner had I heard my own screaming voice than I felt I was jostling against someone so hard that I stumbled on the ground from that strong impact.

"Hey, watch out! Watch out! Who can help you? We are all on our own now. Damn it!"

When I opened my eyes again, I blinked in disbelief.

Like suddenly jerking up from a dream, I opened my eyes and found myself sprawling on the ground under the dark and enormous canopy of the Great-Great-Grandpa Tree.

I found a middle-aged male rolling by my side; maybe he was the one who had just bumped into me. No one else was in that area. The first sign of daybreak had sparked the far end of the eastern silver sky, changing its horizon into a pinkish glow to signify a new day.

I watched the sign of dawn in a complete stun. It had been already at dawn before I was dragged inside 'that place', And now, after I'd emerged, I saw the sky still at daybreak. How much time had actually passed during my stay inside that place? It seemed like zero seconds. Time completely stopped moving as I was told.

That stranger man was now scrambling into his feet. He seemed to pay no attention to what had happened to either of us.

As soon as he got on his feet, he began to pant heavily with harsh and labored breaths. He ran from somewhere without any halt. And when he was ready to open his mouth, his voice was so shaken as if he flew off from some nightmarish place similar to the one from where I had just fled as well.

"Damn it! The Japanese just got us. The Japanese!"

At first, I could not grasp what that man sputtered out. I still felt stupefied probably from last night's boosting. The sour smell of alcohol still lingered on my breath. So, he screeched into my ears.

"Hurry up! Get the hell out of here. The Jap soldiers are now all over the streets."

"The Japanese…." I repeated, still blinking.

"When they caught me snooping around, a group rushed to me. Oh, like the savages hankering for blood, the big samurai swords in their hands. The whole group chased after me, but I flew and zigzagged through an alley maze and thanked the heavens that that quick act really saved my life. I knew they lost sight of me. Holy Buddha! They are swarming Bangkok like an army of killer ants devouring every living thing in their path."

An instant later, I was thunderstruck. A wave of terror began to whirl in the pit of my stomach as I realized the essence of those words.

My mouth went as dry as dust, and my words were frozen. I helplessly watched him turning his back and running from me, frantically announcing the same message at the top of his voice. The wall along the alley echoed his shrill voice back to where I stood even after that man had completely disappeared from my sight.

Help! The Japanese just got us. Help! Help! Help!

I found *Come & Go Lucky* noodle shop only two blocks away from that alley. The shop always opened early for morning coffee and light breakfast, such as poached eggs and steamed buns. A moment later, I staggered inside that shop. All tables were empty now, except at the corner where a couple of customers were idly having their hot coffee while flipping through newspaper pages. They glanced up at me curiously, and then their eyes swiftly returned to their newspaper.

The atmosphere seemed quiet with a sense of usual boredom. A female strayed dog sneaked inside the shop while the owner was busy behind the counter. She frantically sniffed the floor, desperately looking for some food scraps, her raw-boned body quivering in fear of being caught and kicked out. A street dog searching for food was part of the ordinary daily scene, and one could glimpse and swiftly turn his eyes away as an eyesore. It was just another ordinary morning, not different from any other day.

I went straight to the table where I spent hours with that stranger last night. I dropped myself on the same seat, reaching out my trembling arm to finger the opposite seat on which that man had settled earlier. What's the hell going on? I kept asking myself. Was that man real, or my intoxicated brain had conjured him up?

If he was real it meant I found the answer why human's sufferings had never gone from this world.

"There you are!" The shop owner greeted me with a grin, half astonished, half curious. "Are you all right now? Didn't your friend bring you home? Tsk, tsk, your face is as white as a ghost. What's up?"

I didn't expect to see him still working in his shop. Probably he was now waiting for his brother to show up and take the morning shift. But at least he was the only witness of all the bizarre things happening hours ago while I was inside this place.

"So, you…saw *him* too. You did see that man dragging me out." I murmured.

He looked genuinely perplexed.

"Why? Before he dragged you out with him, he came to me and was generous enough to pay for all your drinks and even left me some good tip—"

I cut him off. "Did you have a chance to touch him?"

"Hey, hey, what do you mean? Me touching him? Oh, yeah," he paused as if trying to remember. "He patted me on my shoulder and thanked me. Such a civil and well-mannered gentleman!" Then he stopped short. "I thought he was going to bring you home. But what's wrong? You just left a moment ago. I swear. How come you can come back here again faster than a speeding bullet?

I did not answer. To be more accurate, I was unable to find any rational answer. After putting myself together, I ordered a strong hot coffee to clear my head and asked him to turn on the radio and find a news broadcast station.

"Why? It's just another pleasant Monday morning. I want to keep all troubles at my arm's length?"

He amusedly objected to my request, but after observing my desperate expression, he walked grudgingly to the radio box that was placed on a shelf up the wall behind his counter.

After the momentarily crackling noise, as he tried to tune in on the national broadcast station, we all heard the arousing music of the national anthem suddenly thundering from that radio. Everyone in the shop exchanged glances. A sense of ominous premonition, like invisible masses of smoke, permeated the peaceful atmosphere in this small shop.

When the anthem's blast stopped, a news reporter's crisp voice suddenly boomed from the radio set.

He was making an emergency warning, and what he would announce was one of the worst news of the century. It happened unexpectedly between midnight and early dawn of today, December 8, 1942. The Japanese Imperial Army had successfully made the amphibious invasion landing on the south of Bangkok to seize hold of the capital city and at various points along the south and west coast of the Gulf of Thailand. The Army demanded passage from the Thai government, which had earlier declared neutrality, for Japanese troops on their way to occupy Malaya and Burma, both now the British Dominions, the Allied Powers side. So far, the ceasefire in Bangkok was underway, but elsewhere, there was still some fierce resistance from the Thai Royal Army.

The broadcaster went on, with growing grimness in his voice, that up to this moment, not only Siam, which recently changed its name to the Kingdom of Thailand, but also the Philippines, Singapore, and Malaya had shared the same fate evoked by the Japanese lightning and fierce invasion force.

But the most horrendous incident that would absolutely inflame the act of war, as the broadcast continued, was the simultaneously atrocious and surprise attack from the Japanese Air Force commanded by General Hideki Tojo on the United States Pacific Fleet and Air Force base at Pearl Harbor in Hawaii that had just occurred within the same day as well. The attack cost the United States thousands of men casualties, including all eight major battleships and nearly two hundred aircraft. The broadcaster was now nearly at the top of his voice as he concluded that although it was yet too soon to measure the casualties of U.S soldiers as well as civilians, this Japanese undeclared and bold attack had already sent a profound shock to the Americans who had earlier declared neutrality on this conflict.

Therefore, what happened today was believed would inevitably lead the United States to join the Allied Powers and declare war on the Axis. In no time, we all would face another possible World War, which was predicted to be far more destructive than the prior one occurring two decades ago, thanks to more advanced weaponry from both sides. And no one was yet able to foretell the loss of human lives from all over the globe caused by this new annihilation.

The news broadcast ended in dead silence.

Before I realized it, a tidal wave of rage hit me so hard that it drowned me in its enormous boiling whirlpool.

What's that bastard doing? Ravaging the world at his fingertip over and over again on his global map screen. The smoke, I'd remembered the enraging mass of smoke before I fled.

Through my nostrils, I drew every particle of hatred into my lungs. Hatred was now ringing inside my eardrums in the form of laughter; the victorious and diabolic laughter rippled from the earth's bowels where every human being's signals were being watched on the immense global map screen. The air was vibrating with laughs. That laughter mocked me, implying that my very own light-wave signal on that screen was now throbbing, pulsating, growing uncontrollably, growing and growing with hatred and rage.

He must see it. That's why I believed I heard the echoes of his last laugh. Why was he willing, even zealous, to show me how to escape him? Because he knew I could never have succeeded, no matter how I attempted to. What hindered me was not him. It was my own hatred and rage that always dragged me back to his feet, over and over.

I collapsed face down on the table with utter despair. No one in the noodle shop paid attention to me because as soon as the broadcast ended, everyone, including the owner, rushed out and shouted in panic.

"Go quick to warn the women to lock themselves inside their house. Go! Go!" Someone screamed.

On the street in front of the shop, a growing crowd—men, women, and children alike—began running and scurrying in all directions as if the whole city was being engulfed by wildfire. Panic and shock were written on all faces: chaos from the unknown fate and impending terror expected to occur any minute.

In less than a minute, I was left utterly alone, too helpless to respond. The only companion in the world I had at that moment seemed to be that strayed dog crouching on the dirty floor and hiding under my table.

The instant her frightened eyes met mine, she started to retreat as far as she could, obviously for fear that I could righteously harm her on my whim. Her abrupt motion stirred the flies swarming around her raw and inflamed skin where her tufts of hair were missing from repeatedly fighting over bits of food among street dogs. She did not take her eyes off me as she trembled and made a soft whimper, showing her utter fear and hunger.

I picked my untouched breakfast, a stout pork bun, from my plate on the table and absent-mindedly placed it on the floor, watching as that dog instantly jumped to the bun. She didn't gobble up the bun as immediately as I expected. She just gripped it in her mouth, and in a flash, she was gone.

I noticed her swollen nipples drooping from her skeletal body. No doubt she must have her hungry litters waiting for her at some safe corner where she had hidden them.

No sooner had the poor creature gone from my sight than I realized I did not save her as truly as she had saved me. She did save me from sinking into the eternal black hole of monstrosity.

Goosebumps were running all over my skin.

If everything happened for a reason, as most believed, why did this canine appear inside this shop if not to stir a flicker of the human heart? I thought it had been lost forever by my own miseries. Yes, because of her presence, I found it still kicking at the depths of my soul. That canine immediately showed up right in time to rescue me from losing myself forever, as most of mankind had lost themselves, to that Stalker.

I started to wonder who had sent her to me. But life was a part of *Ajintai*, as my father used to say. It would never yield the answer we wanted, we needed, and we were dying to understand most.

Then I broke down, weeping in silence.

* * * * *

Part 3: Chapter 6

Heaven and Hell Found

Neither he who seeks Heaven
Across a span of seven seas
Will ever find Heaven
Nor he who flees Hell
To the edge of the world
Will ever escape Hell
Till he is brought to light
That Heaven and Hell are not elsewhere
But deep in one's own heart

Our small rowing boat meandered along the shady and winding canal late in the afternoon, Lek paddling at the bow while I helped tug at the stern.

As our boat glided through the silver ripples of water flickered by the afternoon sun, clusters of thatched huts along the lush green banks came into view. Their veranda, jutting out into the water, was lined up with clay pots of crimson and bright yellow roses while honeysuckle and magenta bougainvillea were creeping to cover some half-rusty zinc roofs. Beyond those huts, standing so tall and erected against the sky, thin betel palms formed the line as the far background. Sometimes, behind clumps of dense trees, we glimpsed some temple's roofs and tall pagodas. Their spires glittered in the fading sun, and their brass chimes jingled in the wind. I drew in the air filled with the smell of brown, muddy water to assure myself I was coming home.

Deep into this orchard area, life seemed to stay so still, just like the bygone time of yesteryear, an untouched still-life painting. The modern world outside couldn't penetrate its heart and soul. Yet no one seemed able to predict for how long this deep tranquility would last.

Now, the Japanese soldiers freely roaming Bangkok streets became a familiar yet intimidating sight. The country was inevitably set up to be the Japanese command center on the Southeast Asia front. After that fatal day, which resulted in the staggering casualties of two thousand lives, including the loss of all eight major battleships and nearly two hundred aircraft at Pearl Harbor, the United States immediately declared war on Japan in the Pacific and Germany in Europe. And Thailand, without choice but to sign the alliance with the Empire of Japan, had declared war on the United States and the United Kingdom; the horror of war began to overshadow Thai soil all at once.

Thailand became the overnight target for the bombing raids by the Allied forces in retaliation for the nation joining their bitter enemy. I witnessed the night sky, especially on the bright, full-moon nights, turning into the worst bloody nightmare I had ever eye-witnessed. I watched in terror as the American B-29 Superfortress heavy bomber appeared like a formidable monster from a high-altitude sky, too high and stealthy to get attacked by the Japanese ground defense. It dropped bomb after bomb from its bowel, like a series of explosive diarrhea over the area of Bangkok, and swiftly left as its mission was accomplished, leaving apocalyptic destruction down below.

Though the major targets of the bombers were Japanese military installations, ports, and railway systems, the civilian death tolls increased almost every day. Some evacuated to the safer countryside far from the capital city, where the bombing raids were the most intense. Yet, some chose to stay at the heart of Bangkok, hiding themselves and their family at best in homemade underground air raid shelters whenever they needed it. Yet, the wailing sound of a warning siren signals the aerial arrival of the formidable Allied bomber aircraft.

Lek and I couldn't afford to move elsewhere outside Bangkok. We stayed at the same place and faced possible death almost in nonchalance. It was not that I had a heart braver than most people. But my fear gave way to my outrage that erupted repeatedly as the disaster increased everywhere surrounding us.

We began to get accustomed to the gut-wrenching sight of men or women squatting on the street sidewalk, wailing and screaming among debris and rubbles of the ruins that once had been their roof and walls, their trembling hands caressing something hidden beneath a tattered blanket they were holding. Passersby always walked past and scarcely paid attention to that bundle until they noticed an infant's hand soaked with blood and gore sticking out and hanging lifelessly outside that blanket...

They were all victims of both sides of the war. Terror rained down in the shape of bombs from Allied planes to instantly wipe out lives *en masse*. Among the loss and tears in humans, stray dogs and swarms of flies gained ground. They feasted on torn pieces of bodies and entrails, scattering and bloating in hot and stinky air on the streets.

On rare merciful occasions, what the British or American pilots dropped from their planes were not bombs but showers of propaganda leaflets boasting their coming-soon victory over those Japanese midgets. Children who hankered for fun rollicked ran after those planes and shouted merrily. They fought among themselves over hundreds of fine-quality printed papers that had flown over the sky before scattering to the earth. Anyone on the ground had little chance to glimpse fine-quality papers as the war proceeded. As the battles escalated, anything paper, metal, or fabric cost like solid gold. Even the common and local products found in every household, like soap, sugar, matches, and nails, were almost non-existent in general stores at any marketplace.

The fertile country so abundant with greens and grains now began to experience staple food scantness and famine as never before.

But terrors did not only rain on over their heads. It also spread on the ground level from a slow torture by Japanese authorities carried on inside their own house if native people were suspected as informants or Allies sympathizers. Since oil fuel was treated as liquid gold, some faced their horrid fate by being coerced to drain into their stomach a gallon full of gasoline that they had risked their life to steal from the Japanese army's supply storages.

People were now breathing in fear and breathing out hatred. Fear and fury were eclipsing every corner of Bangkok like a pandemic plaque contaminating every soul.

Those damned feelings swept over me every time I heard the air-raid siren howling during the air strikes from the Allies, followed by the people's stampede, which I was also among them. The hatred on an immeasurable scale was attacking me now with full blast.

For my own sake, I knew I must suppress that damned hatred at once. I must if I wanted to win the game set up by that omnipotent, omnipresent, and omniscient entity whom I crowned the Stalker.

And I wondered. I wondered if I should be blamed for this calamity suddenly erupting in this Asia Pacific region where the

Japanese were occupying. After this happened, not a single nation in this world escaped this global-scale war that had first erupted from the heart of Europe, where the German Nazis and Italy seized most of the European continent and, in this present day, expanded over every part of this globe now under the new official name of the Second World War.

The terror of Adolf Hitler, the Nazi leader, became widespread across all the continents from his overnight rising to power and his unprecedented and insane attempt at the genocide of the Jews and other ethnic races considered inferior to his Aryan supreme race. Yes, whenever a genocide occurred on our earth, I could find my omnipresent Stalker there; that was what he'd told me. I had no doubt now who must be the mastermind behind this number one villain of this modern era.

The most bizarre event from that fateful night still haunted me to my core.

I remembered the devilish mass of smoke twirling and twisting until it completely shrouded the entire map screen as that mysterious monster, out of his infernal wrath, madly played with the apparatus he called the human detector. That madness happened after I had defied him, and whereas he believed himself to be the most invincible, he could also have met the same fate as us humans. He could possibly one day become prey to a higher-power supremo predator staying above him since all living existences—including him and me—were all part of the infinite network of the cosmic food chain.

It meant that this monstrous being was giving me a lesson to remember for the rest of my life for bruising his stratospheric ego. To demonstrate his power, which he believed nothing could be equal to, he turned our entire world into infernal hell at his fingertip, hence hurtling all humanities to be enraged and grieve tenfold so that the colossal scale of human suffering and pain would be more than enough to quench his insatiable, fathomless hunger. No matter what would come out, it was always a win-win situation for this ravenous monster.

Yet, I must try. I must, even though it was like a wee fly trying to look for a way to smash something the size no smaller than a mammoth.

My purpose for this trip was not to harbor hatred but to uproot it, which I know was the hardest. Yet, for the sake of my beloved father, I could not fail him on that after I'd terribly failed him by wrecking my future on alcohol. It was time to turn over a new leaf and start over on a law study after several years of such a waste of life that I had done to myself.

Hot tears of remorse stung my eyes. While I hastily blinked it away, Lek turned his face to me. He frowned.

"Something's upsetting you?"

"No, I'm all right," I lied to him to ease off his worry which in these days had already been written enough on his face. But he still observed me quietly.

"Lek…" I hesitated and blurted out. "When you hate someone's guts, how do you get rid of that hideous feeling?"

"Get rid? Come on. I will storm out and punch that son of a bitch right on his face to get over it. Then my mind will be as clear as the sunny sky," then he chuckled. "No, don't listen to me. Your papa always said if you want to expel hatred, it will never happen if you use hatred to force out another hatred.

Then he smiled sadly and looked around, "Oh, how I miss him…this place…"

As our boat glided along, once in a while, some peddler's boats approached and passed us in a slow-moving; their boats so heavy with heaps of green and yellow plantains, coconuts, mangoes, and sugar canes the water capriciously brimmed almost over the boat's side. To let them pass safely we had to turn away our boat until it nearly glazed the bank and inevitably frightened a flock of birds perching on the tree branches to swoop down and fly away. Their shrill cry echoed into the sky.

A flock of ducks swam past our boat, their ducklings trailing them faithfully. Lek smiled like a child.

"When you were small, you always begged your papa to mimic a duck quacking and then laughed your head off because his quack came out more like a hen's squawk. Remember that?"

How could I ever forget our best moments together?

Gray soft smoke curled slowly from some roofs as the prelude to the evening meal. Some men sat fishing idly on the edge of the plank bridge. They looked up and suspiciously watched us strangers. But as our boat glided past them, they quickly averted their eyes from us. In wartime, no one could afford to trust one another and risked being accused of being a war traitor. And so, our boat moved on, leaving them far behind.

As our boat went forward, the wind carried the sounds of dogs barking and chickens squawking from afar. In the water, I heard loud splashes. Naked children were jumping from the plank bridge, then diving, and emerging with a handful of mud, throwing it to one another. The ripples of their hearty laughter echoed, and a pang of nostalgia hit me. Weren't those sights, sounds, and scents so familiar once?

At first, Lek was hesitant, but I insisted on coming home to see her, who had given birth to me. There was another reason besides uprooting my hatred. We were coming to prove my father's narrative in his journal and give myself peace of mind because my lifetime quest for 'a mother' would finally end after this trip.

But the most essential of all was to forgive and be forgiven.

Because of my stubbornness, Lek finally caved in. But he insisted on accompanying me to my childhood place. He firmly said my father wouldn't be happy if he knew I went out there alone. He even suggested sneaking to that place at near dusk to avoid being noticed by people in the neighborhood. He wanted to ensure that no one would ever know what we planned to do for my father's sake.

We must keep his lifelong secret buried forever. His journal book was long burnt to ashes. After my death, there would be no evidence of Lin Jong's death and its cause left in this world.

I began to understand why Lek had lied to his aunt from the beginning, which led to my confusion. This confusion eventually made me believe Lin Jong was not dead but had run away with one of her lovers.

To protect my father, he would do everything he could, almost at any cost, to atone for what he had not been able to protect him from his aunt's pervert acts that he had long witnessed.

I patted Lek's arm fondly as his eyes rested on me in explicit concern. I could sense the growing affection in his eyes whenever he stole a glance at me. He hid it, and perhaps now there was no need to. Today, there had been an unspoken bond between us that deepened our ambiguous relationship. Yet I still called Beloved my father because I couldn't imagine anyone else in the whole world would replace him. Even Lek himself still respectfully mentioned him to me as *your father* every time we fondly talked about him. We have a mutual understanding that Beloved was, had been, and would ever be the only father I had.

"Promise me you will quit drinking for good. Will you?"

In the middle of the trip, he suddenly blurted out.

"I've never asked you for anything except this. Can you do that for both your fathers, for *us*?" His request must be deadly serious. Because it was the first and the only time he officially mentioned himself as my father to me. After that day, I'd never heard him say that again to me or to any soul. I nodded absentmindedly and then murmured.

"How does she look? Tell me."

"She?"

He seemed perplexed at my abrupt and irrelevant question. Yet only an instant later, he understood whom I was mentioning. He swallowed a lump, then closed his eyes and muttered.

"She was the most bewitching she-devil. All her feminine mystics pulsed from every pore of her sensual flesh. I believe she is the nocturnal nymph of darkness no other female on earth can replace," then he cried in defeat. "How do I find words to help you envision her?"

"She must be very pretty," my eyes looked abstractedly into the distance.

"No, she's not the prettiest. Beloved's mother probably is. Even when I saw her when she wasn't young anymore, her beauty still radiated. Simply put, if born without beauty, most women cannot believe they exist. But Lin Jong's unearthly, outlandish, almost supernatural dark charm made her stand out independent of what we define as beauty. That peculiar charm can twice draw males to fall headlong for her. Yeah, her, um... fierce sensuality once swept all three men of different ages and statuses off their feet: your father, his father, and me. And who knows how many more?"

That was a perfect description of Lin Jong, but Lek needed more. He suddenly added, laughing.

"If Lord Mara's daughters are real, Lin Jong must be the reincarnate of one of them. She must be Raga, who has all heaven and hell power for seducing men to plunge headlong into lust and be drowned there. I believe you read about it in some Buddhist books."

"I know Raga is real, Lek. She's not just a personification."

"You silly boy," he laughed.

I nodded. "Yes, she is."

That was why Lin Jong's image grew so vivid that I could sense her silent presence close to me in this boat. Now, I felt her warm breaths on the nape of my neck. I saw her smiling her whimsical dark smile and heard her laughing her mischievous, soft, silky laugh while gloatingly accompanying us to her own grave.

After a moment of silence, Lek suddenly said,

"She's one of the smartest, too."

"Even smarter than Grace?"

Lek grudgingly nodded. "Not one single word could she

read or write. But Lin Jong could find a hit-the-bullseye reason to outdo a Mr. Know-All like your father. Once, they argued over what provided a true value for humans: to take or to give. I read about their argument in your father's journal."

"I remember that too," I muttered. "Yeah, she took a taker's side and found her unique reason to win him." Then I sighed. "Overall, she seems to have no equal. Only she needs a heart…"

"Of all the men coming into her life, I believe your father is the only one who can crack open her heart for a glimpse of love."

"If you do love someone, you just can't destroy the one you love," I forced a laugh. "I swear that's not love."

"If you were females, just take Grace and even my aunt Sook as the best examples; you couldn't resist loving a nonpareil like Beloved. And Lin Jong was no exception. Too bad that her love for him was so fragile and wispy it couldn't last. When she felt bruised and pained because she realized she couldn't win over his fiancée, her passionate, fiery love swiftly dissolved into hatred in equal extremes," he said sadly. "This happens when love is not planted in an ordinary woman's heart but in a she-devil whose heart had a different, toxic soil that could grow only hatred and malice.

Suddenly, Lek cried out.

"Now I can notice some parts of her in you, Pran. Her nose…her cheekbone," he then smiled. "But, how fortunate you inherited only her brain, not her heart."

"In my father's journal, he wrote that as I grow up, I just look more like…you."

"Unfortunately, poor, poor boy," he shook his head as if pitifully while beaming at me.

"And he told me I'm left-handed like you, too," I added.

We stopped the boat and tied it at the squeaky old plank bridge where my father and I used to take our daily bath and carefully climbed up onto the ground above. All childhood memories flashed and then choked my throat.

The sweet and sad reminiscence about my beloved father lingered everywhere. I forced down the surge of melancholy which suddenly swept over me. Then we trudged past the knee-deep dense growth of weeds and brambles toward that bungalow. Lek and I wore long pants, long-sleeved shirts, and shoes instead of sandals to protect ourselves in case we encountered snakes that still swarmed this overgrown area.

It was a heartbreaking sight, nearly in ruins. Some part of the roof collapsed, and the veranda fell to the ground. The front yard was choked with overgrown weeds and creepers. The pond in the backyard, my father's favorite spot, was still there, but the lovely pink and white water- lilies blooms were all gone. It was now taken over by slimy green duckweeds and dense float-ing masses of water hyacinths with their scraggly purple clusters and thick, glossy round leaves that spread to carpet most of the stagnant surface. In contrast, unkempt tall grasses and reeds and sedges tightly covered the soggy ground around the edge of that bleak pond, fighting over any possible space to outgrow one another for their own survival.

The incessant noise of swarming insects were everywhere, so loud it deafened me. Yet the place turned into utter silence the instant the millions of tiny creatures sensed humans' approaching footsteps.

This ruin was still the property of my father. So, as his legitimate heir, I had a right to claim this property. But I had never wanted it. I'd instead left it to the real flesh and blood of his family. Yet one thing that I would never change was my last name *Bhuvanarthnurak,* which my father had given me to verify the legal status of his son.

However, no one dared come near that abandoned area anymore, especially at nightfall. A tall tale spread in the neighborhood that this place was haunted.

The rumors went as some said they always found mud blots, which looked like footprints encircling the house every time they walked by. Some spiced up a spookier story; they even found more traces of those footprint-like blots not only stamped on the clapboard outer walls but also climbed up on the roof. It seemed like the footprint's owner untiringly and ceaselessly went on stalking whoever was living inside that house, hunting and searching blindly at every corner of that place for a particular one who had been taken from her, even though there wasn't even a single inhabitant any longer nowadays.

What was left in that sad ruin was only a giant void of life.

I remembered now. I remembered the night after coming back from my father's cremation a long time ago. I remembered Lek looking dreadfully at the trail of mud blots on the veranda floorboard. And I remembered him staying up all night long, looking out the bedroom window, alert and watchful. I knew now that he had been in the act of guarding me—after reading my father's journal—from the very same she-being that my father assumed would come to harm me if he allowed that to happen.

"Do you believe she came in one stormy night to take you with her even after her death?" He whispered.

"Maybe…" I hesitated. A childhood nightmare never stopped flashing: a shadowy figure bundled in a blanket thudding on the veranda and calling me to open the door for her.

"Oh, I always think you never believe in such stuff," he said in mild surprise. "Are you believing now?"

"My childhood nightmares have come back. Now, I always dream she knocks on the door and screams to let her in. That's why I need to be over here. I think she wants me to come to see her face-to-face in her grave. That's why she keeps coming."

Lek became silent. Then he slowly said.

"Remember that night after your father's funeral? During our walk home, you were freaking out and telling me you saw someone wrapped in a white bundle under that tamarind tree. I said I didn't see it. But I did… I did." he was nodding slowly. "She'd stood right there under that tree, watching us… But she slowly faded into dark shadows when she knew I'd seen her."

Now, everything we considered impossible could become otherwise. That most bizarre phenomenon I had encountered the night before the Japanese army's invasion had turned my previous belief upside down. Yet I merely told him.

"Remember what my father's American teacher told him?"

And it was the same uncanny remark that that malevolent monster had also told me.

"Men can perceive only one percent, just a small fraction, out of the entire reality. Ninety-nine percent are still total mysteries since they exist out of the reach of our limited senses. And that means there are millions upon millions unknown everywhere, even inside our hearts. Remember that in Buddhism, such an unknown domain is called *Ajintai*?"

"Oh, you are your father's son as always," Lek rolled his eyes in defeat, "when it comes to sophisticated matters." He stressed the word 'sophisticated'.

I followed him in silence to that lonely spot, hearing only the thud of my footsteps and the rustle of dry leaves under my feet. Something was flashing in my mind. What if I were hearing was not my own but the footsteps of the one who kept watching me and never seemed tired of stalking me to wherever, whenever, and in disguise of whoever befitting the scenario?

And if so, the fifteen-minute appearance into my life of that lady in the yellow skirt, whose maternal kindness had integrated into my heart since that day, now I was realizing, must be no more than a hoax he had played with fun to befool and mislead me deeper, deeper into a false hope.

Oh, I should have been acutely aware of it way, way earlier if my famishment for motherly love had not blinded me that much.

As we moved forward, our feet sank into knee-high grasses growing everywhere. Creepers and vines entwined trunks and tree limbs like green draperies hanging over our heads.

Lek clutched my arm, pulling me to stop abruptly before

my foot tramped on a grayish brown, scaly length of something stealthily crawling across my path.

"Watch out!" he shouted at me in alarm.

I gasped and froze while watching that insidious reptile swiftly disappear under dense bushes. I closed my eyes and imagined if Lek hadn't been fast enough to pull and stop me in the nick of time…

Lek chuckled. But there was no humor in his tone.

"A big cobra, did you see? What a warm and hearty greeting you received just a few minutes after you set foot in this creepy place!

"Lek, if she couldn't kill me when I was only a defenseless infant, how can she now?" I whispered to him.

The air was once again vibrant with a sense of raging hatred. A sudden gust of wind hissed and whispered, shaking and rustling small branches and leaves surrounding us. Yet, worst of all, I felt that raging hatred was tearing its way into the innermost of my heart, throbbing and tumultuous as if suddenly alive.

I was nearly in tears of despair. Please, I was too tired to struggle in this labyrinth of hatred without finding an exit. So many times, I'd tried and seemed to head in the right direction to the way out. But sooner, I found myself only walking in a circle, still seeing no way to let go of that deep-rooted hatred. Perhaps the only thing that could bring me out of that pitch-black labyrinth was a miracle.

We began to dig up the loosened, soft earth under the deeper shade of the old tamarind tree. The last glow of twilight of pink and copper shimmered through the tree's scraggy branches. Yet, in only a few minutes, it would be gone, allowing the pitch dark of the night to creep into that area. No words passed between us, only Lek's raspy, laborious panting as our shovel blade was thrust deeper into more hardened ground. The unpleasant smell of dank earth floated to our nostrils.

When it reached almost three feet deep, the tip of my shovel hit something, which sent a hard and hollow sound. I hold my breath. We exchanged glances, but no words escaped. The shadow deepened as daylight was fading and the dusk gathered. Lek began to light the lantern that he had carried with him, adding an even more eerie atmosphere to that place—the tiny circle of bright light surrounded by infinite darkness and the silent presence of something immense, malevolent, and yet incognito lurking behind two puny mortal humans who were huddling together inside the small circle of light.

How was a speck of light able to save us from such darkness that was shrouding impenetrable mysteries of timelessness and harboring that malevolent entity that embodied the darkness itself? I wondered. But, as my father had told me, the only way to win out was to face that unknown you feared.

Our work went on arduously as the bone-white substance emerged bit by bit from the deep ground. Then Lek signaled me to stop.

Lek raised the lantern above the assumed grave as I leaned forward and peered into the furrow we had excavated. I felt a cold chill of vague fear as much as exuberance and anticipation. All the childhood yearning I once had for the Lady in Yellow Skirt now flooded me so suddenly and overwhelmingly that it choked me with suppressed sobs. I felt myself turning into a lonely eight-year-old boy, sitting unwearied day by day on a street sidewalk, clinging to his impossible yet singular hope that one day he would find his mother among the sea of faces walking past him. But now, that once foolish boy had come to know better.

At the bottom of the pit, partially exposed in the dark soil, a human skull grinning up at me. It stared at us with one of its eye sockets, a hollow dark hole, as another of the pair was lodged with clumps of dirt. I swept my eyes over the length of the molder skeleton and caught something that looked like the remnants of torn clothing, probably the blanket that my father used for bundling her body before burying her.

At that instantaneous moment, the void of emotion, the dull numbness overtook me. I didn't know how to feel and respond to the stark reality that was revealed before my eyes. My gaze fell on the human remains in plain wonder.

It was too surreal to acknowledge the naked fact that that moth-eaten, bare skeleton at the bottom of the pit had brought me into this world.

"There she is…for all those years," Lek lowered the lantern closer to the grave. He murmured. "Well, mother and son meet, at last."

I added flatly. "You should say all three of us are together at last. The first and last union of our family."

He didn't say more but looked at me with his saddened, painful eyes.

"Yes, all three of us… All three of us who help destroy Beloved's life. If only I hadn't slipped a word about your father's law school to her that day. If only…" he began to weep bitterly. "Beloved never brought up the truth about your obscure birth to me, not a word…until I found out myself in his journal after his death. He bravely took all agony and pain alone, keeping them to only himself to save others. The braver he is in my eye, the worse I feel about myself. What a coward I have been all along."

"No, don't blame yourself. I believe my birth was not simply an accident as she told my father. I think it's just another lie conjured up by a born liar who took distorted pleasure in tormenting every human being with her lies and her manipulation. We both were her victims to be used to carry out her vengeance. She picked you, my father's most trusted soul, to impregnate her in hopes that my father's hatred of me would be tenfold, enough to burn him alive. But when she found his affection for me had never faltered, it tremendously infuriated her because this was far beyond her scope of understanding the self-transcendence nature of a man like him. So, she intended to kill me as an alternative way to torment him. It took her nine months or so to complete her plan. Then I believe she would plan to go back to the whore house that she felt was her real home. A whore house for a whore."

I hunched myself, trying to stop the sudden attack of hatred accompanied by a shudder. The image of Daughter of Mara flashed in my mind again.

"It's so cryptic. How could one human, just a mere speck of one human among the whole ocean of humankind, spin something so massive, destructive, and macabre beyond measure to affect so many? We all fall into her prey, every single one of us..."

"She thought you belonged to her. She set her mind to take you back. I believe she wanted to see you, not your father, dead by that snake. She wanted her last laugh, to finish her unfinished work, which is to watch your father alive in the form of a living dead because of your death. It's too bad her attempt failed. That's why, after your father's death, I had to bring you out of this place before she would strike again." He then muttered, "I never trust her, alive or dead."

"My father has triumphed, whereas Lin Jong has failed. She has failed terribly," I went on, the heart-wrenching emotion still gripped me..."because he died in his selfless soul whereas she died eaten whole by her own savaged hatred."

She died eaten whole by her own savaged hatred...

Those words were echoing in my head.

It enabled me to feel her raging hatred as if I were carving my way to sit inside her heart and touch how it felt to hate and hate infinitely. How to be churned and simmered in a cauldron of hatred and stay in that in utter agony not only for all the waking hours of her life but also follow her in her grave for eternity.

I closed my eyes and tried to imagine. That was not different from burning alive in hell forever.

A shudder was suddenly running through my body. How

come I'd never thought of her from that view; how come I'd never thought how *much* she had suffered?

Oh, a mountainous weight of agony that crushed inside her must be beyond any of us could ever imagine. Even a degree of my suffering and of my father's, which were almost too heavy for us to bear, seemed probably pale in comparison to hers alone.

One thought suddenly struck me as never before; yes, Lin Jong was merely another prey, being exploited repeatedly by our same predator... He had fed on her infinite hatred as he had fed on lust and fear and greed and all kinds of weakness and evils from millions of others.

But Lek went on with finality. "A stalker, yes, she must be. Never stop going on a prowl for her prey as long as she could breathe," his voice grew increasingly grim. "Or...even after that, as she has intruded into your dreams."

I was silent, then slowly shaking my head.

"No, Lek. I just realized she's not."

Lek raised his eyebrows.

"She's only another prey, just like all of us. I found out there is a real stalker creature out there..." my voice trailed off. "That one has been living off our miseries caused by greed and grudge but, most of all...lust. At her core, she has everything in the extreme I'm mentioning. So, He has used the extraordinary type like Lin Jong to lure other humans to feed him on and on. That stalker creature has been thriving on our shortcomings since the beginning of the existence of life itself. You must believe me, please. You must. This is an answer I finally discovered for my father. Our human miseries are His food."

Lek glanced at me in mild perplexity. He knew my father's final request so well and even urged me to do it for him. But perhaps this one just sounded too absurd and senseless for him.

It seemed useless to tell him in more detail how I stumbled on that answer for my father: why we humans had to suffer. Or at least I wholeheartedly believed I'd finally found that answer.

No, Lek wouldn't think I was telling him a downright lie.

He would simply think the bizarre tale about a mysterious predator stalking and devouring humans' miseries for its food sprang out from my delusion during my chronic state of alcoholism. I never forgot that Lek always had deep concern on his mind about my prolonged drinking habit.

He did not ask me more but tried to divert me from that subject.

"It's dark already. I heard the Japanese are having night patrols on boats. Soon, they will set up a curfew around this area. And no one knows what those savages could have done to us natives. Hurry up and bury her quickly."

"Wait…"

I edged nearer the open grave and stooped over; my hand reached down until my fingers grazed what had partially been hidden by the dark shadow at the bottom. It was cold and lifeless to the touch. Yet, as my fingers gently caressed a particular part of her skull, a part that had once been her warm, soft cheek, somehow a sense of calmness and tenderness strangely began to permeate all over me, possibly the most sublime feeling known to us, which humans ever gave to one another.

I felt goosebumps running all over me. *That* feeling I was giving her. Yes, it must be *that* feeling.

Like a flash of miracles on me, I was coming to glimpse what seemed hopeless and impossible. While I went on searching for it everywhere throughout my life, I couldn't believe it had always been awaiting me, just as close as beneath my bosom, in my heart.

I was coming across our best weapon for battling against that Stalker.

That same feeling I'd just given to Lin Jong.

There were no other weapons to destroy that mysterious stalker except that singular feeling of forgiveness.

That point brought me back to one particular moment I had never forgotten and now suddenly flashed up. That was when I looked at that mysterious stalker and found him twisting, fading, and shrinking just after a deep, soulful pity I felt for him arose.

I had seen him shrinking during our encounter inside his operating chamber, yet I had no clue about the cause. But in this instant, a thought was sparking in my mind. It must be a sudden pang of sympathy I felt for him that caused his shrinking, which meant all our goodwill sent to him could affect his invincibility as poison could harm a human.

We could weaken this monster. The good in the human heart could shrink and shrink him...

That spark of realization made my heart swell with sky-high exults.

Even though his shrinking had lasted only in a blink before he swiftly resumed his substantial appearance and stayed again in all-powerful glory, at least I knew he was not *that* invincible.

At least, he shrank. At least I found his Achilles heel.

So, came the time to utter a word to someone I had searched for all my life and found in that grave. I collected myself and uttered the holiest word in all human languages.

"Mother...be at rest. I forgive you. I forgive you everything."

At last, this moment of genuine forgiveness was coming. I'd never dreamed it could ever happen. My long and endless agony from the smoldering hatred I had for her and all humans but most of all for myself seemed to be lifted the instant my tears erupted at the word *Mother*.

I blinked and blinked in amazing wonder. What had been eating me alive for so long that I saw no hope for a cure was gradually gone.

As I kept stroking her cheekbone with tenderness, I began to imagine something immense—maybe the size of the universe itself—was being shrunken somewhere, somehow, shrunken by the power of love and forgiveness we mankind had given to one another as our true weapon to fight—until that Entity, once emerged from the depths of the cosmos darkness and was empowered by the darkness itself, ceased to exist and perished into a void of nothingness.

That hope in this present moment was perhaps still close to impossible, I knew, and yet I believed, among the vast ocean of humankind, there must remain that steadfast hope in the hearts of a few bravest ones who identified with my father in this fight and would at last prevail when the dawn of tomorrow arrived.

I laid on a part that was once her bosom, a small, beautiful wreath of white jasmine, a token of motherhood that I had brought with me. As the serene and sweet scent of jasmine lingered, a growing sense of peace and euphoria glowed all over me.

Rest in peace, Mother.

The moon began to rise, casting silver and tranquil light on the earth, turning the world below into a spellbound, dreamlike landscape.

"All right, let's bury her now," I said softly.

"Let's do it," Lek smiled at me.

Oh, I couldn't wait for His presence at this instant moment

Let that almighty Stalker witness the prelude of one small human gaining the biggest victory over himself, which all in good time would lead to the victory of mankind over Him.

Come and see it now. Come, you Stalker.

The End

www.ingramcontent.com/pod-product-compliance
Lightning Source LLC
Chambersburg PA
CBHW030538020726
47494CB00005B/1425